POWER &
BEAUTY

POWER &

a love story of life on the streets

BEAUTY

Tip "T.I." Harris with David Ritz

wm

WILLIAM MORROW

An Imprint of HarperCollins*Publishers*

POWER & BEAUTY. Copyright © 2011 by Tip "T.I." Harris with David Ritz. All rights reserved. Printed in the United States of America. No part of this book may be used or reproduced in any manner whatsoever without written permission except in the case of brief quotations embodied in critical articles and reviews. For information address HarperCollins Publishers, 10 East 53rd Street, New York, NY 10022.

HarperCollins books may be purchased for educational, business, or sales promotional use. For information please write: Special Markets Department, HarperCollins Publishers, 10 East 53rd Street, New York, NY 10022.

FIRST EDITION

Designed by Lisa Stokes

Library of Congress Cataloging-in-Publication Data has been applied for.

ISBN 978-0-06-206765-4

11 12 13 14 15 OV/RRD 10 9 8 7 6 5 4 3 2 1

Acknowledgments

I'd like to thank God above all. Without his grace, patience, and abundant blessings, I would be nothing and nothing I've done would've been possible. I'd like to thank David Ritz for bringing organization to all the creative chaos that fills this "brilliant literary mind" he so generously says I have, and Craig for introducing this unique opportunity, yet again flossin' his visionary-thinking capabilities.

Thank you to all who were involved in the process of completing this project: our editor and publisher; my management team, Jason Geter, Gee Roberson, and Brian Sher; my lawyer, Jonathan Leonard; my lovely wife, Tameka Harris; my mom, Violeta Morgan; and my beautiful children, Zonnique, Messiah, Domani, Deyjah, King, and Major. To the rest of my family, friends, fans, and supporters, I can't thank you enough for all you've done for me. You'll never know how much your loyalty means to me.

To the special people in my life who watch over me from above: my father, Clifford "Buddy" Harris; my daughter Leiah Harris; my grandmother Mrs. Willie Bell "Mother" Morgan; my aunt Beverly Dobbins; my friend and brother forever Philant "Big Phil" Johnson;

my cousin A. Tramell "Toot" Morgan; and my patnas J-ru and Bank-head. We miss you all.

Lastly, to all the people in prison and in the projects who have ever lived or still live lives similar to any of the characters in this piece; I hope y'all enjoy it. We did it for you. Just know there is a way out, even if it doesn't seem like it. Keep praying and keep pushing. God is real and blessings are coming to all who believe. I'm living proof. If I can make it, so can you. REAL TALK!

—TIP

David Ritz would like to thank:

Tip, a great writer and brilliant literary mind

Craig Kallman, for making the connection and being a friend

Our editor, Esi Sogah

Our publisher, Lynn Grady

Jason Geter, Jonathan Leonard, David Vigliano, David Peak, Ruth Ondarza, and Matthew Benjamin

My wonderful wife, Roberta; daughters Alison and Jessica; Pops Ritz; Esther and Elizabeth; sons-in-love Henry and Jim; precious grandkids Charlotte Pearl, Nins, James, and Isaac; all my great-nieces and -nephews; and friends Alan Eisenstock, Harry Weinger, Richard Freed, Richard Cohen, Herb Powell, and soul scholar Aaron Cohen.

Special gratitude to the Tuesday-morning God Squad.

Thank you, Jesus.

POWER &
BEAUTY

Turn the fear into energy
'Cause the toot and the smoke
Won't fulfill the need

—MARVIN GAYE

HIM

The Nightmare, the Dream

It was a Saturday in June, nine o'clock in the morning, when the explosion hit. It rocked our little apartment in Conway Court; rocked our whole neighborhood; rocked my world and flipped the script on our lives.

After that morning, just two months before my sister and I turned sixteen, nothing was ever the same.

At first I thought it was a terrorist attack. But why the hell would terrorists be launching attacks on niggas on the west side of the ATL?

"It's Charlie's Disco!" my sister started screaming. "I can see it from here!"

Charlie's Disco sat right across the street from where we stayed. Charlie's Disco was run by Moms's friend, Charles "Slim" Simmons. Moms helped Slim with his bookkeeping. Sometimes when she was working in his office above the club she'd let me sit downstairs at the bar and drink lemonade. I liked that. I liked being inside the smoky club with the black leather booths and plush ruby-red carpet. I studied the disco ball that hung over the dance floor and imagined what it was like when the place was packed with the flashy pimps, hustlers, and hos—Slim's best customers.

But Moms would never allow me in there when the place was packed. Moms knew better. After all, she started out as a waitress at Slim's. She said Slim was always good to her, but Moms wanted to do better. Moms went to night school to learn bookkeeping so she could buy me and my sister, Beauty, nicer clothes. Moms put money away in our college fund. Moms always said she was raising me to be a polite Southern gentleman. People said Moms was the only woman Slim respected. Everyone respected Moms.

"Where's Mom?" I yelled, jumping out of bed when the explosion hit.

"I don't know, Power," Beauty said, her voice shaking. "She mentioned something about going over to see Slim."

My heart started racing. My brain started panicking.

Moms couldn't be at Slim's.

Moms had to be okay.

Just last night Moms had made us dinner. Just last night Moms had helped us with our math homework and read out loud from the Bible.

Moms was a young woman, healthy and strong. Moms hadn't gone over to Charlie's this morning. She probably just went shopping. Moms was fine.

I threw on some sweats and, together with Beauty, ran across the street.

Holy shit!

Charlie's was ablaze. Biggest fire I'd ever seen up close. The heat was incredible. Fire trucks, firemen, cops, folks milling around, everyone trying to figure out what the fuck had happened.

"Anyone inside?" someone asked.

"They pulled out one body. The woman was dead."

The woman was dead.

Beauty and I heard the words at the same time.

"Can't be Moms," I said to my sister. "Moms went shopping."

Beauty didn't speak, but I knew what she was thinking.

"Moms is probably already home by now," I said.

Beauty ran over to the firemen and started asking questions. The fireman directed her to a cop. The cop said something that made Beauty's eyes go wide. She put her hand over her mouth. She started screaming. I ran over there.

"What'd he say?" I asked.

"He's gonna take us to the hospital. We gotta get to the hospital."

After that, my brain went blurry. Riding in the cop car. Sirens screaming. Arriving at the ER. Running through the hospital. Looking for doctors. Talking to nurses. Going up and down hallways until we finally found the one doctor who asked the question that I didn't wanna hear.

"Are you related to Charlotte Clay?"

"She's our mother," said Beauty.

"I'm afraid she's gone."

"Gone where?" I asked. "Gone to Macon? Gone back to where she was born in Alabama? Gone *where*, motherfucker?" I was losing it.

"She's dead," the doctor said.

"Can't be dead!" I started hollering. *"Must be another woman. My mother went shopping. She didn't go to no Slim's. Not that time of morning. She'd have nothing to do with Slim that time of morning. It's all a big mistake!"*

The doctor put his arm around me. I pushed him away and screamed even louder. *"Fuckin' hospitals get shit mixed up all the time! Fuckin' hospitals can't keep nothing straight! That woman who died ain't my mother!"*

"Would you like to identify her?" the doctor asked.

I couldn't.

Beauty could.

Beauty went into the room.

I stayed behind.

Beauty came out, shaking and weeping, running to me, falling in my arms.

"She's gone." Beauty was crying.

My heart was hammering so hard it felt like it was coming out my chest.

"She's gone," Beauty said again. She looked up at me and asked, "How we gonna live without her? How are we going to make it, Power?"

Relatives and friends called. Relatives and friends came by. The crib was packed when we got back home. But we made it clear that we really couldn't be with anyone. Seeing other folks weeping and sobbing was too much. We told them that we appreciated their concern, but we needed to be alone.

No mother. Just sister and brother.

That night, the first night without Moms, Beauty slipped into my bed. She was crying so hard her body was shaking. Her shaking didn't stop until I held her.

She wasn't my blood. Beauty had African-American/Asian blood. She had Asian eyes, Asian skin. Mom had adopted her five years ago when we were both eleven. But she was still my sister. Didn't matter that she was beautiful; didn't matter that she had a killer body that every boy in school was looking to tap. I knew that I couldn't see her that way. Moms always said, "You gotta watch her back, boy, not her backside. She's family. And never forget it." But at times I did forget it. I took me more than a few peeks in the keyhole when she undressed at night. And I caught her taking more than a few peeks at me coming out of the shower.

Sometimes—well, more than sometimes—*most* times when I jerked off, I saw Beauty in my mind. In my mind, I did everything to Beauty to make her scream out my name. But that was fantasy. When it came to reality, I did what Moms told me to do.

But tonight Moms's body was at the funeral home, and Beauty's body was next to mine. She had come to my bed. She needed to be held. I needed to be held. We needed to do something to make this new and horrible fear go away. The fear was all over us.

The midnight hour came down on us.

We were alone in the crib without our mother.

We were alone in bed.

Beauty brought her mouth to my mouth.

I had never tasted her mouth before. It was soft, sweet. I pressed my lips against hers. I felt her tongue touching mine. I felt her opening her heart, her mind, her soul.

I knew it was wrong.

She knew it was wrong.

We were crying out to each other.

Moms was gone, Moms was dead, we were alive, we were holding each other, feeling each other in a way we'd always wanted to but never had.

We couldn't.

We shouldn't.

But the horror and the confusion of losing the most important person in our universe had turned our universe upside down. The person who made sense of the world, the person who kept us safe, the person who gave us the rules was no longer there. The rules were no longer there.

We could do what we wanted.

In our confusion, our pain, our fucked-up fear, we faced each other that night in bed. We did what we had longed to do.

It was not the first time for Beauty, and it was not the first time for me. But it might as well have been.

Once we started, we couldn't stop. It was crazy. My mind couldn't stop saying *crazy crazy crazy crazy* but my body wasn't listening, my body didn't care, my body fought off my mind.

For five years we had fought for Moms's attention. We had teased and taunted each other to the point of tears. For five years we were rivals.

Now we were lovers, loving so deep and with such crazy don't-stop don't-ever-stop passion that I wasn't even sure it was really happening.

I had fallen into a dream. I was loving Beauty in a dream. In a dream, we were doing everything we had long dreamed of.

But when I woke up, the dream was there next to me.

I was naked.

She was naked.

The dream was not a dream.

The dream was real. The nightmare of Moms's death was real. Our reaction to her death now seemed like a nightmare.

"Power," Beauty said to me, "we can never tell anyone. We can never do this again."

"I'll never say a word."

"Never," she said. *"Never ever!"*

Slim

I'll take care of everything."

Those were the first words of the first person who showed up at our doorstep the day after the night everything changed.

"Don't you worry," said Charles "Slim" Simmons. "I'll take care of everything. Your mama was my best friend. I treasured her like a precious jewel. She was my heart and her kids ain't gonna want for nothing—not now, not ever."

We were in the front room of our small apartment. Beauty was sitting in front of the television, staring at a blank screen. She wasn't even looking at Slim. It was a hot day, and she was dressed in cutoff jeans and a T-shirt. She wasn't even looking at me.

I was looking at Slim.

He was about my height—this year I'd shot up to five eleven—and where I was thin and wiry, he was big-boned and thirty pounds too heavy. He had a belly on him. I guess he'd been slim when he was young. At forty-five, he looked his age. He had good hair that he styled in silky waves. I got kinky hair that I cut short to my scalp. His skin was light tan; mine is dark like Moms's. His eyes were green; mine are brown. He wore an open-collar blue silk shirt, black alligator low-top boots, a fancy Monte Carlo Panama fedora, and a sleek slice of dazzling ice on each wrist. Matching diamond wristbands were his trademarks.

Slim wasn't a smiling man. He had a serious vibe, a take-care-of-business vibe, and before this day, he had never given me a second's worth of attention.

"Just got back from Cutler Jefferson's funeral home," he said. "Cutler's my friend from grade school. I said, 'Cutler, give this great lady the send-off she deserves. Lay her out in satin and ermine. Make her even more beautiful in glory than she was in life. Set out your best coffin, the one made in hand-polished mahogany where the hardware is fourteen-karat gold. You dealing with a queen, Cutler. You dealing with royalty. Spare no expense.' This here tragedy happened in my place. This here accident, where the gas heater blew up and caused this terrible explosion, this thing was something so unbelievable that only God knows why. She didn't deserve this. You kids know that. You know it better than anyone. Your mama was a sure-enough angel of the Lord. She's gone, but I'm here, and I'm here to set things right for y'all."

I didn't know what to say or do.

Beauty kept looking down. She never did face Slim.

Slim saw Beauty. All men saw Beauty. She was just an inch or two shorter than me, and her long black lustrous hair fell halfway to her waist. Her almond-shaped eyes gave you a dreamy feeling; when she did look at you, it felt like she was writing a poem about you. She was small-waisted and slender like a model. Lots of models have small breasts, though. Beauty's breasts weren't small. They were perfectly proportioned to her body. They jutted out. They stayed up and out. She never wore a bra because she didn't need a bra. She had amazing breasts. Her lips were thin and her mouth wide. Her cheekbones turned up to the sky.

Her mama, Isabel Long, had worked alongside my mother in the bookkeeping department at Fine's Department Store for years. They lived in an apartment right next to ours. Beauty's daddy was some Japanese dude who knocked up Isabel and wanted nothing more to do with the whole affair. When Isabel died, my mother felt like she had no choice but to adopt the girl, whose name was Tanya. Even as a baby, Tanya was so gorgeous everyone called her Beauty. She and I grew up together. She was just like a sister.

At about the same time eleven-year-old Tanya came to live with us, my daddy, Paul, fell down at his job at the plant. He was just a young man, but a stroke did him in. He was in the hospital for only a week before he died. He was the one who called me Power. I'm Paul Jr., but when I fell in love with the Power Rangers at age three, Daddy renamed me after my favorite toys.

"Power," said Slim, "I'm taking you and your sister outta here. I'm taking you to my crib. You gonna live with me."

For the first time, Beauty looked up. She stared straight at Slim. Her eyes looked at him like he was some kind of devil. She didn't say anything. She didn't have to.

"I got six bedrooms and I only use one," Slim said. "You'll have your own bedroom and your own bathroom. One of the bedrooms has a canopy bed and a little room right next to it with a vanity table, the kind where women put on their makeup and do all that womanly shit. That'll be your room, Beauty. You gonna love it. Power, I'm putting you in the room above the garage. It's like a private apartment, with its own entrance and everything. You'll come and go as you please. If you wanna bring your bitches up in there, I got no problem. Youngbloods gonna do what they gonna do."

I didn't know what to say, so I didn't say anything.

"I gotta slide outta here," said Slim. "I'll be back later with all the details on the funeral. The funeral will be something no one will ever forget. My man Cutler is going to turn this funeral *out*. So start packing up your things. I'll have one of my boys come by with a pickup and take your suitcases over to my place whenever you're ready. God bless you both. God bless your beautiful mother. I loved that lady, and nothing in this world can stop me from making sure that her kids get every last goddamn thing they need."

Wanda Washington

After Slim left, time hung heavy on our heads.

What could we say?

The shock of Moms's death had caught us up in a terrible grief. The grief was choking us. The fact that we had slept together fucked with our minds. The guilt was choking us. Grief and guilt were all over us; we couldn't even look at each other.

I was sitting on the couch. Beauty was sitting on a kitchen chair, her back to me. The morning was hot. The TV was off. The windows were open. A neighbor across the way was screaming at his wife so loud we could hear every last word.

"Bitch!" he yelled. "Why do you care if I get home at four A.M.? You ain't giving up no good pussy anyway!"

"That's 'cause that sad old dick of yours can't stay up long enough to please no normal woman. You out there foolin' with them freaks."

I got up and closed the windows, muffling the fight.

Finally Beauty spoke, although she still wouldn't look at me. "I'm not going to live with him."

"Why not?"

"He's a grease ball."

"Moms liked him."

"Moms liked everyone. She had a generous heart. But she saw through him. That's why she never married him."

"He's a powerful dude," I said. "He owns half the barbershops in the city. Plus all those car washes and hot-wing joints."

"He's a gangsta."

"Moms was looking to help him. Now he's looking to help us. That's all there is to it. What else we gonna do?"

"Stay here."

"Just the two of us? And live like a couple?"

"Don't put it like that, Power. Don't ever say that. That's never going to happen again. *Ever.*"

"I understand, but I'm saying it's going to look funny."

"I couldn't care less how it looks. I know what I want to do and where I want to live—and it's not with Slim Simmons. I'm not going anywhere near that man."

Beauty got up, went to her bedroom, and closed the door behind her.

A half hour later, the doorbell rang.

I looked out the window and saw Wanda Washington standing there carrying great platters of food. I opened the door.

"Hey, Power," she said, "I brought y'all some eats. Should last you a few days. Got all sorts of treats here."

Wanda walked in the house like she owned it. She went right to the kitchen, opened the refrigerator, and started putting the food away.

"Where's Beauty, baby?" she asked.

"In her bedroom."

She sat down on the couch and motioned for me to sit down next to her. Miss Washington was a heavyset woman. Her cheeks were chubby and her friendly eyes sparkled. Her mouth was fixed into a permanent smile. She was incapable of *not* smiling. She wore a heavy perfume and a fancy wig that flipped up on the side. She owned

Wanda's Wigs, and she always claimed that she was her own best advertisement. She wore a different wig every day.

"Get Beauty in here," she said. "I want her sitting with us."

"Beauty!" I cried. "Miss Washington is here."

When Beauty walked in, Wanda got up and hugged her.

"Now you sit down here next to me, baby. We gonna pray. We gonna say, Father God, we here to praise you, we here to give you the glory, we here to thank you for this new day that you made, we here to say that we love you with all our hearts, even though our hearts are broken and souls messed up. These children don't got no mama, Lord, and they hurting. Oh, they hurting real bad. Their hearts are crying, Father God, their hearts are crying worse than they ever cried before. We live in this mean ol' world, Father, and things happen that we don't understand. We don't understand why this wonderful woman, their mama and my friend, Charlotte Clay, gotta be gone so soon. We don't know why you took her, Lord, and we don't know why you left her children to fend for themselves. But we trust you, Father God, yes we do. We know you got our backs. We know you got the master plan. We know that everything happens for a reason, even if we can't understand that reason. And we don't understand. We're filled with hurt. Oh, the hurt goes deep. The hurt is all over us. We crying real tears, Father—"

At this point we were all crying. Beauty and I broke down. Wanda spoke through sobs.

"We crying and we trying, Lord. We trying to pick ourselves up and look life right in the eye. Life without these children's mama. Life without my friend Charlotte. We doing our best, Lord. We know we can't lose our minds. We can't hide from life. Life goes on, yes it do. We got things to do, Father God. This boy Power, Lord, he's a brilliant student. He plays basketball on the school team and he's a star. Keep him strong. Keep him righteous. And sister Beauty, she's a special child, a special young woman. She can sew, Lord. She can sew like a woman who's been sewing her whole life. She makes her own designs and she sews them herself. You gave her talent, Father, so let that talent blossom. Let these children prosper. Let them find the strength to go on. They got to go on. Got to keep bringing it. Your will is for us to spread your love. To love each other like you love us. Psalms says, 'Weeping may endure for the night, but joy will come in the morning.' Bring us that joy. Even in the midst of pain, let us feel your joy. You are our joy, our bright morning star, our shining prince of peace, our all in all. Bring us peace, Father God. In the name of your precious son, Jesus, bring us what we need to run this race. Amen."

"Amen," I echoed.

"Amen," Beauty whispered.

"Now let's eat," said Wanda, getting up from the couch and heading for the kitchen. "I'm heating up a lasagna that's gonna hurt your mouth. You ain't never tasted nothing like it."

Moms loved Wanda, and of course, we couldn't help but love her too. Moms was a humble woman of few words. She dressed tastefully. Wanda's taste was different. She wore too-tight pantsuits, like the green-and-purple getup she wore today that didn't hide any of her fat. She didn't care. Moms loved that Wanda didn't care. She liked women like Wanda who, unlike herself, weren't at all conservative and quiet. She got a kick out of Wanda. Moms always said that Wanda, like Beauty's blood mother, Isabel, was a friend she could count on.

"Count on me to get y'all through this," said Wanda while serving us big portions of her meaty lasagna. "And count on Slim."

"He was here this morning," I said.

"I know he was. He told me that he was coming. I told him it was too soon, but you can't tell Slim nothing."

"He wants us to move into his house," I said.

"Well, I think that's mighty generous of him. That's like when he bought me my wig store."

"I didn't know that it was Slim who bought it," said Beauty.

"He owns it. I work for him. But I make him a pretty penny, so he leaves me alone to run it as I please. He's a rough man, Slim is, but he's not a bad man. He's got good in him, and I know damn well he wants to take good care of y'all."

"I'm not going," Beauty flatly declared.

"I can sure enough understand how you feel, sweetheart. Leaving this place is not going to be easy."

"It's not going to happen," Beauty reiterated.

"Charlotte always said, 'That Beauty's got a mind of her own. That child has her own ideas about things.' She respected that about you, Beauty. You a strong young woman. You got that streak of fire running through you. I got that same streak of fire running through me. And I tell you, girl, that ain't no bad thing. We need that streak of fire."

Beauty didn't respond.

"But in this day and age, we also need help. You gonna need a lot of help. Now Slim, he got him this house up in Cascade Heights. It's a big beautiful house, yes it is. With lots of room and lots of privacy. He can go about doing his business, and y'all can go about doing yours."

"I don't trust him," said Beauty.

"You don't got to, baby. I got my eye on that man at all times. I know him well. Hell, I talk to him practically every day. I see how he do. I know he's an operator. He can operate for good, and he can operate for bad. Right now, when it comes to y'all, he's operating for good. Besides, Beauty, I ain't letting you out of my sight. I want you with me at Wanda's Wigs. Summer's just begun and I'm gonna have you working down there every day. I wanna teach you the wig business, baby. You're a natural."

With that, Wanda went over and gave Beauty a great big hug. Beauty tried to fight back a smile, but she couldn't. No one could resist Wanda.

Cascade Heights

The funeral was massive, one of the biggest our neighborhood had ever seen. The church was overflowing, and Slim brought in an extra choir from another church. Moms's casket was covered with dozens of lilies and roses, her favorites. Never seen so many flowers in my life. Beauty and I sat next to Wanda in the first pew. Slim came over to sit in the empty seat next to Beauty, but Beauty said she was saving the seat for her best friend, Tanisha. Slim started sitting there anyway until Beauty got in his face and said, "You are not sitting here. My friend is. Find another seat." Naturally that embarrassed Slim in front of the whole church. Beauty didn't care. She couldn't stand being near the man.

I hate funerals, and I hated my mother's funeral worse than any I'd ever been to. I had friends who'd died on the streets. Their funerals were awful. But this was worse. Moms always thought Reverend Nolan Everett was a jackleg preacher. He was a salesman who made a fortune selling Jesus. He wore sharkskin suits and drove a Bentley. He lived in Cascade Heights down the street from Slim. He was Slim's preacher. And because Everett's church was big and rich, Slim wanted Moms remembered there. Our church, Mt. Calvary, was small and poor. Slim allowed Reverend Atkins from Mt. Calvary to give the eulogy, but after Atkins spoke, Everett spoke even longer. He spoke in fancy ways about a woman he didn't even know. Meanwhile, I was hurting so rough inside that I hardly heard the words anyone was saying. The music helped. Gospel music always helped. A couple of those ladies in the choir could really blow. For a second, the music got my mind off Moms. For a second, the music had me happy. But happy didn't last.

The plan was to drive to the cemetery in a stretch limo—me, Wanda, and Beauty. When Slim got in the car, Beauty turned her head to avoid his eyes. Beauty whispered to me, "He's acting like he's the husband. Your mother wouldn't have married him if her life depended on it."

"Let's just get through this thing," I whispered back.

Both preachers, Everett and Atkins, were at the grave site. Atkins spoke first, and he spoke from the heart, but then Everett had to be longer and fancier.

It was a horrible day.

Afterward, family and friends were invited out to Slim's house, where he had catered a fancy dinner. Beauty didn't want to go, but Wanda convinced her. "You don't want to dishonor the beautiful lady who took you in. You gotta make an appearance."

This was the first time I had seen Slim's crib.

Two great gates, painted in gold, guarded the entrance. When the gates automatically opened, I couldn't see the house. We kept driving down a twisty lane until finally, after a sharp left turn, the two-story structure rose up like something out of MTV's *Cribs*. It didn't look like it belonged in the ATL. Looked like it belonged in Miami. It was sleek white and edgy modern. Big windows, flat roofs, painted sculptures of jungle animals all over the lawn, tall palm trees planted everywhere. When I walked inside, the front room felt as big as a barn. In the middle was a sculpture of a life-sized mermaid swimming over a waterfall. The water was real. The mermaid looked real. On the walls were huge paintings of Atlanta superstars—Hank Aaron, Evander Holyfield, Dominique Wilkins. The walls were ice white and the floors white marble. The furniture was gleaming steel and metal. From every room you could see the palm trees and painted peacocks. In one section of the garden sat a cage.

"Is that a black leopard in there?" I asked Wanda.

"Yes, indeed, Power. Only Slim's crazy enough to keep a black leopard."

Beyond the garden was a regulation-sized basketball court. Next to the court was a swimming pool formed in the exact shape of the state of Georgia.

Slim was at the front door directing traffic. He was dressed in a black satin suit. He wore his diamond wristbands and flashy fat diamond earrings. The women serving food on silver platters wore long black dresses. They were middle-aged and not at all flashy. "I told him he couldn't let none of his young bitches up in here," said Wanda. "He had to do it with dignity. Had to show your mama some respect."

Beauty found a seat in the dining room, where the chairs, like the oblong table, were all glass. It was a see-through house. But no one could see through my sister's eyes. My sister's eyes were faraway. She was acting like she wasn't there.

Hundreds of people came through. Hundreds came up to me to pay their respects. Mr. and Mrs. Yamamoto, the Japanese couple who had bought Fine's Department Store that employed Moms, said to me, in broken English, "We are so sorry for your loss. We are so loving of your mother. She was good woman, good worker, fine lady." Their teenage son, Kato, also paid his respects. After bowing before me, the Yamamotos sought out Beauty and offered her condolences as well.

The afternoon dragged on. Sunlight flooded Slim's house in a way that gave everyone a golden glow. It was like we were baked in gold, flooded with money. "Let me give you a quick tour," said Wanda when the crowd was thinning out.

She took us straight to the room Slim had picked out for Beauty. "I decorated it," said Wanda. "Did it all in the last two days."

The room was big and light. Windows everywhere. The wallpaper was made up of the covers of old issues of *Vogue,* Beauty's favorite magazine. There was a brand-new super-fancy sewing machine in the corner. "Picked it out myself," Wanda told Beauty. "Most expensive Singer on the market. You'll love it, baby." There were photographs of all the models that Beauty had followed, like Iman and Naomi Campbell. Beauty was stunned. She didn't know what to say. For all her attitude about Slim, she couldn't deny that this was her dream bedroom.

"Wait till you see yours," said Wanda to me.

We followed her down the stairs out the back. Above the four-car garage, where Slim kept a Benz, a Rolls, a Corvette, and a Lamborghini, there was a private apartment.

"He used to call this his secret getaway," said Wanda. "He's giving it to you."

It was a bachelor pad straight outta *Hustler* magazine, a two-room suite. The first room had a wall of built-in stereo equipment and a gold leather couch. The second room had a round bed and a mirrored ceiling.

"It's creepy," said Beauty.

"I like it," I said. And I did. What teenage boy wouldn't?

"You ready to move in?" asked Wanda.

"Don't see why not," I said.

Beauty didn't answer. Beauty was holding out. But I knew Beauty; I could hear the wheels turning. She was thinking about that super-fancy Singer sewing machine.

Just Got Paid

That summer I played in the summer league. Because I'd shot up in height, I'd moved from point guard to center. It took some adjustment, but I liked the change, and before long, my game was tight. Our team was on a winning streak. My teammates would pick me up at Slim's and drive me over to the gym where we practiced. They couldn't believe I had an apartment of my own. I had friends before, but when I moved into Slim's, I became Mr. Popularity. All the older cats with cars wanted to give me rides.

During the last minute of a game when we were behind by a point, I looked over at the wooden stands and saw Slim. He was wearing a bright blue derby and gave me a wave and thumbs-up sign. Coach called a time-out. When play resumed, I got the ball, shot a hook, and won the game.

Slim came out on the floor and shook my hand.

"Time to celebrate," he said. "Meet me in the parking lot after you get changed."

Fifteen minutes later I climbed into his Corvette.

"This is my favorite jam," he said, cranking up the box.

The lyrics were "Check the mirror, lookin' fly." The song was "Just Got Paid."

"Ain't that the truth?" asked Slim. "Ain't nothing sweeter than getting paid. You hungry, boy?"

"Starved."

"Good. Got me a spot where they know how to cook beef."

"You gotta be dressed up?"

"Everyone else does, but you're with me."

The spot was called the Regal Eagle, and it sat atop the tallest sky-scraper in downtown Atlanta. It was a members-only private club. Dark wood paneling, jazz trio in the corner, and wraparound windows that gave you a spectacular view of the city. We had two young waitresses serving us, one black, one white, one prettier and bustier than the other.

"I'm Rita," said the black chick.

"I'm Joanie," said the white one.

"Y'all blend together real pretty," said Slim. "Now bring us our drinks."

I'm not much of a drinker, but that night I had champagne. It went right to my head. Looking around the room, I saw people I knew from TV—Ted Turner, Andrew Young, Walt Frazier. Slim greeted them all. Slim knew them all.

"Thing is," said Slim, sipping on his champagne, "you seem like you doing fine up at the house. You staying busy this summer playing ball. But Beauty don't seem happy at all."

"Beauty's different," I said. "Always has been."

"She gets back at night, goes up to her room, and locks her door. I'm hoping that at least she's calling over to your room. She needs someone to talk to."

The truth was that she wasn't. Beauty had disconnected from everyone except Wanda.

"She likes Wanda," I said. "Wanda's keeping her busy down at the wig shop."

"Wanda tells me that Beauty's doing more than selling wigs. She's designing them. Wanda thinks she's a genius."

"Beauty's really talented."

"But what about boys? She don't got no boyfriends?"

"She's had a couple," I said, not feeling too comfortable with this line of questioning. "But she's got real high standards. She's independent. You can't tell her what to do."

"I see that. Kinda like your mom."

"Moms said Beauty was going places—that she'd have her own fashion magazine, her own line of clothes."

"Don't she understand that I can help her do that?"

"After she lost her real mom, she got real close to my mom. So this has been super-rough on her. She's still dealing with Moms being gone."

"We all are."

The mention of Moms killed the mood. When the steaks arrived, we ate in silence. Rita and Joanie, the super-sexy waitresses, brought us chocolate cake for dessert without even asking. Slim wolfed down his. I didn't touch mine.

"Mind driving home?" Slim asked me when the valet brought around the Corvette.

"Don't have my license yet."

"But you know how, don't you?"

"I can drive. I learned on a pickup truck."

"Good," said Slim. "This motherfucker is stick."

I got behind the wheel and, after some nervousness, settled in. It shifted easy and I couldn't help but get excited. The thing was a rocket.

Slim directed me where to go.

"Gotta make a few stops."

The first was at one of his wing joints. As we pulled up, a guy came running out and handed Slim an envelope stuffed with cash. The next stop was a pizza place, where the routine was repeated. After four more transactions, Slim had so much cash he had to get another briefcase out of the trunk just to hold the bills.

By the time we reached the crib in Cascade Heights, he had collected more cash than I'd ever seen.

"Put the car in the garage," he said. "You can give me the keys tomorrow."

It felt great to be trusted.

I let Slim off at the front door and parked the Corvette. I looked at the main house and saw that Beauty's lights were off. She was already asleep. I walked up the stairs to my apartment above the garage. My mind was spinning from the evening.

I got undressed and was wearing nothing but my pajama bottoms when I heard a knock on my door. I figured Slim had come back for his keys. But it wasn't Slim. It was Rita and Joanie, the waitresses. They were wearing halter tops and short shorts.

"Slim said you won a big game tonight and deserve a big prize," said Rita.

"We're the big prize," said Joanie. "Mind if we come in?"

I didn't mind. Didn't mind at all.

September

In August both Beauty and I turned sixteen—her birthday is the tenth, mine's the twentieth. Slim wanted to give her a lavish sweet sixteen party in a fancy hotel, but my sister refused. Beauty wanted nothing to do with Slim.

"She uses my house like a goddamn hotel," he said. "Wanda picks her up, takes her to work, brings her back, she goes to sleep, and they start all over again. She never even eats here. The little bitch won't even look at me. I'm offering to give her the party of her life, and all she does is snub me. What's wrong with your sister?"

"It's hard to lose a mother. She's lost two."

"Hey, man," said Slim. "You can keep telling your fuckin' sob story for only so long. My mother had seven kids by four different men. She got wasted by a drunk bus driver when I was eleven. My daddy sent us to live with an aunt whose old man was pimping bitches outta the corner barroom. That's just life. You moan for a hot minute, and then you move on. I see you moving on, Power, so why can't she?"

I didn't have an answer. As much as Slim might have been thinking about Beauty, I was thinking about her a lot more. The night after

Moms was killed never left my mind. I relived it a million times. The night that Slim sent Rita and Joanie to fuck me was exciting. Shit, it was goddamn thrilling. But for all the moves they put on me, for all the freaky things they did to each other, when I was actually making love to them, I couldn't come until I fantasized about Beauty. In a silent voice, I even called out Beauty's name.

I was ashamed of that—ashamed of what I'd done with Beauty and ashamed of having to put the picture of her naked body inside my head while I was loving on other women. After it happened with Rita and Joanie, I was sure it wouldn't happen again.

Because word got around that I had this dope apartment above Slim's garage, other older women got interested in me. Slim gave me my own private line—just as he gave Beauty hers—and I started getting calls. As a young dude at the height of horniness, I wasn't about to turn down pussy. That's against the religion of the hood. But no matter how good the pussy, no matter how beautiful the chick or how hot the fuck, I still had the same problem: I couldn't bust a nut until I imagined that I wasn't balling the girl I was balling; I had to imagine Beauty.

I kept this secret to myself.

I also knew that Beauty kept it to herself. She couldn't look at me any more than she could look at Slim. Every time she saw me, she had to be remembering what had happened between us. And she also had to be remembering how much she loved it. For all the wild times I was having with these willing women—and, man, they were some wild-ass willing women—nothing even compared to the nuclear explosion I'd felt with Beauty.

June, July, and August had been all about going with Slim on his collection runs, playing ball, and partying. The culmination was my sixteenth birthday party. Slim opened up the main house for me; brought in Bonafide, the hottest rapper in the city; and told me to invite whoever the hell I wanted. I invited everyone, more than a hundred people, and we kicked it till sunrise. Beauty never showed up. The night of the party she stayed at Wanda's.

Two weeks before school started in September, I started getting in serious shape for sports. Slim vacated one of the garages beneath my apartment and turned it into a gym. We went down to the sporting goods store, where he peeled off five one-thousand-dollar bills to pay for the latest in high-tech cardiovascular and weight-training equipment.

I liked the way Slim operated. When he wanted something, he got it. When he saw I wanted something, he got it for me. Sometimes when we drove around, he'd start talking.

"You know the reason I never had kids?" he asked.

"No, sir."

"'Cause I couldn't. My sperm don't swim. Doctor says the little motherfuckers don't got no tails. When I heard the news, man, I was one happy nigga. That meant I could prove that any woman claiming to have my baby was a lying bitch. And believe me, Power, over the years I've done just that. I got four different copies of those medical papers saying I can't father no children. My lawyer's got a copy and my doctor too. You best believe those papers have saved me a fortune. You should see the faces of those greedy hos who come at me with their fancy lawyers. I just kick back, wave my papers, and laugh my ass off. But then what I thought was a blessing started feeling like a burden. Man gets to a point where he feels like he wants to share some of the shit he learned along the way. Also the goodies. The goodies are there to be shared. All that workout gear, for instance, is good for you in a way that it ain't good for me. When I was your age, I didn't have your discipline. I like that about you. I liked sports, but I wouldn't work out. I knew I had a good mind, but you couldn't get me to read. I see you reading all the time. That's good. Keep the mind sharp. Keep the body lean. That's what makes a warrior, and I see you got what it takes to wage wars and win wars. I'm always in a war.

Fuck, life's a war. I built me up an army—you've seen some of my lieutenants—but none of them, even those twice your age, got your brains. They depend on me to make all the decisions. They scared of me. Well, that's good, 'cause on one hand, they need to be scared of me. But on the other hand that ain't good 'cause they don't got the balls to challenge me. They ain't thinking of better ways to expand our businesses. Businesses either expand or die. I gotta think of every-thing. I gotta figure out the odds and place the bets. I gotta breed the horses. Gotta feed the horses. I gotta run this motherfucking race all by myself. Now ain't that a bitch?"

"It doesn't sound easy."

"It ain't. You ever play chess, Power?"

"No, sir."

"Well, I play. Not with my lieutenants. They too dumb for chess. So I got a couple of guys from the university who come up to the house and play. You'll meet them. One guy teaches French. The other teaches history. Both PhDs. Case you don't know, that means doctors of philosophy. Well, neither of those doctors of philosophy have ever beat this nigga at chess, not even once. And you know why?"

"Why?" I asked, eager for the answer.

"'Cause I didn't learn how to play out of a book or in some uni-versity, but at Georgia State Prison in Reidsville, Georgia."

"I didn't know you were in prison."

"There's a whole lot about me you don't know. It was in Reidsville that I met my master. Cat called Sylvester Brooks Sanders. We called him Mr. S. He was a white man who worked for the biggest bank in the state. Finance guy. He'd figured out some scheme to skim mil-lions, and he would have gotten away with it except that pussy tripped him up."

"Pussy?"

"Pussy will make a smart man dumb. See, Mr. S was married for twenty years. He was pretty loyal to Mrs. S except for the strip joints.

Couldn't stay outta the strip joints. One stripper in particular caught his eye and turned him out. Mrs. S found out and went crazy. Mrs. S did him in. She guessed he'd been scamming the bank, and going through his safe, she found the evidence. She wanted to put him away—and she did. So Mr. S winds up my cell mate. That's where he started talking this philosophy about how life is a chess game. He thinks if you can win at chess, you can win at anything. He studied the game his whole life. Won tournaments and shit. Says there ain't no one who will ever beat him, short of a few cats in Russia. I say, 'Teach me, Mr. S, and I'll whip your sorry ass in a year.' A year is all I was in for."

"For doing what?"

"That's another story. This story is how after a month or two, I was playing quality chess. I took to it like a duck to water. It all made sense to me, especially the part that said you gotta think six steps ahead. I saw that if I had thought six steps ahead, I would have never wound up in jail. I took the game seriously, Power. Studied it with a mighty concentration. Mr. S had to admit I was a natural."

"You beat him?"

"That's the funny part, son. It was a month before my release and I still hadn't beaten him. We'd played at least twenty thousand games. I'd come close—real goddamn close—but this dude was sharp. If I was two steps ahead, he was three. If I was four, he was five. And then one afternoon, the sun came out. It had been raining for days. Lightnin'-and-thunder rain. But on this day the little window above our beds was flooded with light. Sunlight just pouring through. Sunlight lighting up the chessboard where me and Mr. S were head-to-head in a ferocious match. The light was what I needed. It lit up my brain. For the first time, I saw his master plan. I knew what to do. I saw how to corner him. I was on the verge of declaring checkmate and claiming victory. I saw him straining. Saw him sweating and twisting. Oh, man, I was excited, I was ready to pounce on him, when just like that, the motherfucker keeled over and died. Massive heart attack. Dead two days before his fortieth birthday. What do you think of that?"

"He wanted to die undefeated."

"That's how I saw it. He wanted to go out the champ. You interested in being a champ? You interested in learning chess?"

"I don't see why not."

Heart to Heart

First day of a school was a Monday. That Sunday Beauty called up to my room. It was seven A.M. and I was fast asleep.

"Power," she said. "We gotta talk."

"You wanna come up here?" I asked instinctively. The thought of Beauty coming to my room excited me.

"No," she was quick to say. "Let's just take a walk."

"We can take a ride on my moped."

"I don't want to ride on your moped. I just want to talk."

Slim had given me a super-slick touring-style moped scooter to ride to school. It was jet-black with red pinstripes, a customized wind-shield, thirteen-inch wheels, a chrome muffler, and a rear trunk for my books. He even threw in a helmet with a black-and-red color scheme that matched the bike perfectly. I was in love with the thing. He said it was a gift for my having read more books on chess in a week than he'd read in a lifetime. I learned the rules quickly and threw myself into it. I wasn't at all intimidated. I had a feel for the strategy and immediately understood why Slim loved the game.

"Meet me outside the gate," said Beauty. "I'll be there in ten minutes."

I washed my face, brushed my teeth, and threw on a pair of Hawks basketball shorts and a Braves tank top. When I got to the gate, Beauty was already there. She was wearing narrow-legged jeans that fit her like a glove. Her black-and-white-striped T-shirt was loose, but I knew what was underneath. I'd never forget what was underneath. Sometimes she wore her hair in a ponytail; sometimes she wore it loose. This morning she wore it loose so that it fell below her shoulders. She smelled of flowers and fresh soap. The morning smelled of fresh dew. The air was chillier than I had expected.

"Where we walking to?" I asked.

"Doesn't matter. We need to talk. And we can't talk in the house."

"Why not?"

"He's got it wired."

"Oh, come on," I said. "You're paranoid."

"Am I? I found the wires in my closet. He's also got hidden cameras in my room. They're even in my bathroom. I know where they are. I found them the first day, and I busted the lenses. A week later I saw that the lenses were fixed, so I just covered them with towels. He's crazy."

"He's different—that's all."

"He's dangerous."

"I don't think so," I said.

"Holy shit, Power! How can you say that?"

"I've been around him more than you."

"That's the problem," said Beauty. "You're blinded by all the shiny new toys he's given you. And he wants to keep you blind."

"For what purpose? I don't have anything he needs."

"He needs to rid himself of the guilt he feels for killing Moms."

"*What?* That's fuckin' whack, and you know it. It was an accident. He loved Moms. He had no reason in the world to harm her."

"You don't know that."

I stopped Beauty in her tracks.

I took her hand, looked her in the eye, and said, "What happened to Moms has fucked us all up—you, me, Slim, everyone. But it's making you crazier than anyone, Beauty, it really is. You don't do anything but hide out in your room. You've cut off your friends. You've barely said a word to me in three months."

"You know why."

"I know what happened between us, and we promised it wouldn't happen again. We promised that no one will know—and no one will. But that doesn't mean we can't even look each other in the eye."

Beauty looked away. We started walking again. The morning was starting to warm. A little kid rode by on a bike. He was throwing copies of the *Atlanta Journal-Constitution* on the driveways of the mansions that lined the street. The suburb was silent except for the birds chirping in the trees.

"He's the devil," said Beauty. "He's the creepiest man I've ever met."

"I think he sincerely wants to help us."

"I think he sincerely wants to jump my bones and is just waiting for the chance."

"He'd never do that. He had too much respect for Moms to hurt her kids."

"Then how do you explain the cameras?"

"I can't. But why don't you just ask him?"

"I'm not about to have a conversation with him. I can see how he seduces people. He buys them. I love Wanda, but he's bought her, just like he's buying you."

At the end of the street was a little park. In the center was a white lattice gazebo that was empty except for a circular bench.

"Let's just sit down for a while," I said. "Let's just look at this thing objectively."

I sat on one side of the bench; Beauty sat on the other. She wasn't about to sit next to me.

I started in calmly. "Okay, let's look at this guy. We know he's not all bad or else Moms would have never tried to help him with his books."

"Bullshit. Moms thought everyone had a good heart. That was her problem. That's what got her killed, Power."

"You keep saying that, but you don't have a single piece of evidence."

"I have my instincts."

"And your instincts are fucked up because of everything that's happened to us. Your instincts are feeding your imagination, and your imagination is making you nuts."

Beauty swept her hair away from her face, leaned forward, and looked me straight in the eye. I couldn't help but think that she was the most beautiful woman in the world. Her features were perfect— the shape of her eyes, the sheen of her skin, the slight flare of her nose, the delicacy of her hands, the way sunlight bounced off her long lustrous black hair. I tried to forget what it was like when she was caught up in that fire of passion, urging me on, crying out my name. I tried to block the memory, but as she sat there, I undressed her in my mind. I saw her naked.

"Look, Power," she said. "We can go back and forth like this for hours, but there's really no point. I just called you to say that I'm leaving."

"When?"

"Today."

"Just like that?"

"Just like that."

"What about school?"

"I'll be going to school in New York. I found an arts high school there that has courses in fashion design."

"How are you going to pay for it? Where are you going to live?"

"Moms left us some savings."

"That's hardly anything."

"Wanda has a friend in New York. I'll be staying with her for a while. But Slim can't know that Wanda's helping me. Wanda's scared that he'll be pissed. I'm not even telling Wanda that I'm telling you."

"Then why *are* you telling me?"

"Because I think you should get out too."

"And go where?"

"Anywhere. Just out of Atlanta."

I moved over to sit next to Beauty. When I took her hand, she let me. "I know you have big problems with Slim," I said, "but I swear this man will help you. He'll help you get whatever you want. I've been with him. I know him. By leaving, you'll just be making an enemy out of a friend. You'll be leaving the most comfortable situation imaginable to go to a place where you don't know a soul. Why in hell would you do that, Beauty?"

"To save my life. I'm telling you all this, I'm trying to reach you"— and with those words she squeezed my hand—"because I want to save your life too."

"You've actually gotten yourself to believe that my life is in danger?"

"I feel it so deeply that I wake up at night crying."

I started to say something, but the words didn't come. I put my arm around Beauty and kissed her forehead. Before I knew it, she was kissing my lips, and we were in each other's arms. We stayed there for a long, long time.

At the same time, we said the same words.

"I love you."

Her cheeks were wet with tears. We slowly got up and walked back home in silence.

By noon that day, she was gone.

That evening, after Slim saw she had moved out, he asked what had happened. I lied and said I didn't know. I saw him pick up the phone and call Wanda.

"Wanda doesn't know either," he said. "But fuck her. She'll be back. When a bitch runs out of money, she always comes back."

Dreams

I wanted to stop my dreams. Short of that, I needed to change them. I even went on the Internet and started studying ways some people were controlling their dreams. They were writing out what they wanted to dream about before they went to bed. I did that. I wrote out dreams where I got signed by the Atlanta Hawks and tore up the NBA, dreams where I climbed Mount Everest and won the Indianapolis 500. In another dream I projected that I became the chairman of the board of a giant corporation with ten thousand people working for me.

I kept a pen and pad by the side of my bed and described these dreams in detail. I tried not to think of sex. Everyone said keep your mind clear of the images that you don't want in your dreams. Sex images always went back to Beauty, and Beauty had been in practically every dream of mine since she had gone to New York. Those were the dreams I wanted to stop. In those dreams I kept seeing her incredible body, kept hearing her moan in the act of making crazy love. I'd wake up in a sweat; sometimes I'd wake up covered in my cum. It even got to the point where I took a shot of whiskey before I went to bed, even though I hated the taste and could barely get it down. I thought that would knock me out and keep me from dreaming, but it didn't. Beauty starred in every one of my dreams, night after night.

When I woke up, I wanted to call her in New York to see how she was doing, but I didn't. I figured that would only make it worse. I also figured that living in New York she would meet guys. They would fall in love with her. She would fall in love with them. Some would take her to bed. I hated all these thoughts—and even hated the fact that I hated them. Why should I even care? Why should I be feeling all these feelings about someone who wasn't even my sister? Why should I be bothered by hot sex dreams when I was living a real dream life and could have all the real hot sex I could handle?

Except for these dreams, my junior year in high school was cool. I played varsity basketball, and though we didn't have a great season, we had fun. Slim came out to every game and cheered me on. If he brought anyone, it was usually Andre Gee, called Dre by his friends. I think he brought Dre because he was a well-dressed dude who made a good impression. Slim didn't want to embarrass me by showing up with any of his shady-looking henchmen. Dre was Slim's number-two man, a barrel-chested brotha who liked to talk about how he'd been recruited by the Falcons at fullback and was set to start until an ankle injury did him in. He had a lisp and a bad stutter, and when he got stuck on a word he'd squeeze his eyes closed. Dre never went out in anything but cool custom-tailored suits that fit him like a glove. He liked wearing oversized orange horn-rimmed glasses that gave him a bookish look that clashed with his razor-sharp suits. He had a big clean-shaven head and dark happy eyes. Dre had a happy disposition. He had a white wife named Gloria who was a top saleswoman at Wanda's Wigs. They didn't have kids but treated their four cats and five dogs, all strays, like their children. Dre liked to laugh more than he liked to talk. He didn't like his lisp and stutter, so he kept his words to a minimum. He liked me a lot—and so did Gloria, who knew my mom. After Moms died, they took a special interest in me and usually had me over to dinner at least once a week. "Look at us like f-f-f-family," said Dre, who kept an elaborate electric toy train setup down in his basement, complete with bridges and tunnels. He loved going down there, putting on his gray-and-black-striped cap and playing engineer.

Dre had begun as Slim's driver and rose up the ranks. I wasn't exactly sure of his tasks, but I saw how Slim trusted him. Slim also humiliated him. One of his favorite stunts was to ask Dre to make a phone call for him and laugh when his stutter wouldn't let him get the words out. He especially liked doing this when other people were around. Everyone would get a good laugh at Dre's expense.

Late in my junior year Slim decided to give a party for a local politician who was running for the city council. It was a fancy catered affair with waiters in white coats carrying around champagne and caviar. I didn't even want to attend, but Slim insisted. He said important people would be there. One politician's name was Edward Kingston, a black man in his thirties who'd gone to my high school, where, like me, he'd played basketball.

"I know who this young man is," he told Slim as he shook my hand. "I've seen his moves on the court. He has spirit."

"He also has a head on his shoulders for business," said Slim. "I'm teaching him, I'm bringing him along."

"That's beautiful," said Kingston, who, at six feet eight, towered over everyone at the party. He was a blue-eyed light-skinned brother who kept circulating the room and shaking hands.

Slim kept introducing me to his colleagues, mainly bankers and accountants, real estate brokers and car dealers. One guy owned over a dozen McDonald's franchises in Atlanta alone. There were women as well, mainly the wives of the businessmen. Everyone had dressed conservatively except for Wanda Washington. She was wearing a leopard-skin cape over a black blouse and leggings. I was glad to see her and to get a chance to ask about Beauty.

"You speak to my sister?" I asked.

"She's doing fine, Power." Wanda spoke in a whisper. "Slim don't need to know nothing about her 'cause he's still pissed on how she left and all. But she's in school and she's doing fine. She's living with Anita."

"Who's Anita?"

"My homegirl Anita Ward. She's a buyer at Bloom's department store. She's in the thick of that New York fashion world. She's taking good care of Beauty."

I wanted to hear more, but Slim started hitting his glass with his fork, signaling to everyone that he wanted to say something. It took a while for the party buzz to quiet down. When it did, Slim raised his voice. His diamond wristbands were blinging strong. On this occasion he also wore matching square-cut diamond earrings.

"Welcome to my humble abode," he said. "Welcome one and all. I want to thank y'all for coming to meet and greet one of the fine men in this community, my friend and yours, Mr. Edward Kingston. Ed's a guy who understands business and business understands Ed. He understands our community and is gonna give it all he's got to make sure honest hardworking folk like you and me are represented on that city council. Ed needs your support. I want Ed to say a few words to you, but before he does, I'd like to ask the executive vice president of my operations, Mr. Andre Gee, to make an announcement about our personal contribution to Ed's campaign."

Dre looked surprised, even shocked. He hadn't expected this and did the best impression I'd ever seen of a black man turning white.

"Go ahead," said Slim, urging him on. "Tell everyone how much we're donating to Ed's campaign."

Dre swallowed hard and tried to speak. "T-t-t-t-t-t-t- . . ."

Slim filled in the word for him. "Ten," said Slim. "But ten *what*, Andre? Tell our friends ten *what*."

"T-t-t-t-t-en thou-thou-thou-thou-thou-thou . . ."

By this time, Slim was laughing out loud, letting us, his assembled guests, know that it was okay to laugh. The more Dre choked up on the word "thousand," the louder the roar. Finally Slim just said it: "What my man is trying to say is that we're kicking off this party with a ten-thousand-dollar contribution."

Edward Kingston's speech followed a round of loud applause. In the middle of it, I spotted Dre sitting out on the patio all alone. I went out there to see how he was doing.

"Sorry about that, Dre," I said.

"N-n-n-n-no need, li'l bro."

"He shouldn't have done that."

"Slim? Oh, man, he just having his f-f-f-f-fun."

"It doesn't make you feel bad?"

"I'm used t-t-t-t-to it."

"Still not right."

"That's just S-S-S-S-Slim. He don't mean no h-h-h-h-harm."

"You're a forgiving soul."

"He's the b-b-b-b-b-boss. You gotta forgive the b-b-b-b-b-boss. Plus, he pay me g-g-g-g-g-good. Slim's a good m-m-m-m-man. Slim's all right."

In my world, everyone was familiar with Slim's reputation. That included the kids in school. They knew the story of how Slim had taken me in and how I was living in the apartment above the garage. The dudes envied me and the chicks flocked around me. Being Slim's boy gave me status.

At the end of our junior year, with the summer coming on, it was time for the election for senior class officers. I was nominated for president. I thought I was a shoo-in. I had the support of the jocks and the cheerleaders and most of the class leaders. My grades weren't great, but they were good enough. I was easy to get along with; I gave the best parties; I was good at sports; I liked to dance, dated the coolest girls, and even loaned out my moped when friends wanted to take a spin. When I was nominated for class president, I was pumped. I liked the recognition. I liked the status. And, of course, Slim, who never made it through grade school, was pumped too. He made sure that the POWER FOR PRES signs were professionally done, with bright red letters against a black background.

My opponent was Barry Tanner. He didn't have a chance. Even though he was smart—maybe the smartest student in our class—he wasn't part of the inner circle. I knew him because he was president of the chess club, and since Slim had been teaching me chess, I had challenged those guys a couple of times. Barry was a helluva chess player. I couldn't come close to beating him, but the brotha was a geek. The cool kids didn't care that he was a three-time science fair winner. The cool kids looked at his nomination as a joke. Didn't matter that he had straight A's. Matter of fact, his straight A's made kids jealous. Barry could be arrogant with his intelligence. He wasn't easygoing and he had nothing going on with the girls. This was a popularity contest, and popularity-wise, the boy couldn't come close to me.

Going on seventeen, I was looking like the guy who had it all. And whatever crazy dreams I might have been having, whatever deep feelings were running through me about missing Moms and desiring Beauty, my status kept me sane. My status said that I had everything everyone else wanted. They saw me as their ideal. That's why they wanted me as their class president.

The morning of the election I was rocking a pair of black felt Akoo jeans, a black Akoo medallion T-shirt, and fresh green-and-black Nikes that I'd ordered from Japan over the Internet. My homies were acting like I had already won. "It's all about you," everyone was saying. I was feeling it.

Barry Tanner had put up a few weak little posters here and there, but his campaign didn't have the look of mine. My posters were everywhere, and that simple POWER FOR PRES really caught on. Slim had a thousand buttons made that my friends were wearing. The girls especially liked wearing them. It was only a question of waiting for the end-of-school assembly when the results would be announced and my victory made official.

We gathered in the school auditorium. My boys were elbowing each other to get a seat next to me. Man, everyone was my friend. The principal took the stage with a notebook in his hand. He calmly announced the winners: School treasurer was Cynthia Weiss. No one cared about the school treasurer. Secretary was Judy Hathaway. Judy was a cheerleader. Everyone knew she'd win. Vice president was John Springer, who beat out Leonard Baskin. John was captain of the basketball team and wanted to run for president, but I was thought to be the stronger candidate. Leonard Baskin was Barry Tanner's boy, another geek who didn't have a prayer. It was a bad day for the geeks. Then it was time for the announcement we were all waiting for.

"And the senior class president next year will be . . ."

I began to get up . . .

"Barry Tanner."

I sat back down. I couldn't believe it. There had to be some mistake. My throat went dry and my breath got short. Maybe it was a joke, a cruel joke on Barry the way Slim joked on Dre. This couldn't be right. But there was Barry, walking up to the stage, and not only that, there was the entire student body, on their feet and applauding and hollering like crazy. They were loving it—loving the fact that I had lost a race I knew I had won, loving how humiliated I felt!

I had to get out of there. I just walked around the hallways in a daze. I felt like someone had punched me in the gut. Not since Moms had died in the fire had I felt so bad. I don't know why, but I even felt scared. I didn't know if I could cope with this. I felt under attack. When the assembly was over and the kids started filing out of the auditorium, I went outside to the parking lot. I didn't want anyone to see me so humiliated. I got on my moped and started to drive. I drove around aimlessly, my head reeling with confusion and anger, disappointment and all kinds of other feelings I couldn't even name. I couldn't believe what had happened. Didn't want to believe it. In fact, the more I rode around, the more I was sure it really *was* a mistake, some kind of miscount. I circled back to school.

By this time, the school was empty except for some of the teachers. I went to the principal's office and saw Miss Croft, a stout black lady, gathering up her things.

"Oh, Paul," she said. "Sorry about the results." She was a stern disciplinarian, but she had always liked me. She knew I made my grades and stayed out of trouble.

"Miss Croft," I said, "I know this sounds a little crazy, but I've been thinking about this and, well, I know the students here and I got a pretty good feeling for the support behind me. Nothing against Barry. Barry's a smart guy and a great chess player, but there's no way in the world he could have beat me. So I'm wondering if somehow the ballots got mixed up or counted wrong. These things happen."

"Yes, they do, Paul," said Miss Croft, "and, believe me, son, I was as surprised as you. That's why I personally went back over the count that was done by my secretary. I looked at the ballots myself and I saw with my own eyes what I would never have believed. I don't tell you this to hurt your feelings, Paul, but since you came here to ask, I think you should know. Not only did Barry win, but he won by the biggest landslide in this school's history. It was overwhelming."

"But . . ." I started to say, trying to recover from still another punch to my gut.

"You have to look at it this way, son. It's an honor to be nominated."

Bullshit, I wanted to scream but said nothing. With my head down, I walked out.

Back on my moped, I rode out to Slim's house. I was glad he wasn't home 'cause the first thing he'd ask was whether I'd won. Slim looked at my accomplishments like they were his. He'd hate this, and after all he had given me, I didn't want to tell him what happened. I had no explanations.

I was walking over to my garage apartment when Dre happened to pull up in his Lexus.

"What's g-g-g-g-good, baby?" he said.

"All good, Dre."

"You don't l-l-l-l-look all g-g-g-g-good."

"Just one of those days."

Getting out of his car and walking toward me, he asked, "W-w-w-what happened?"

Dre was one of those cats you could talk to. He was never looking to pass judgment or criticize. I started talking. I told him the whole story, how I was 100 percent certain to win, how Barry Tanner was basically a nerd that no one cared about, and how he had creamed me in the election.

Dre stood there listening. When I was through, he came over and put his arm around my shoulder. I could see in his eyes that he was feeling the pain that I was feeling.

"M-m-m-m-m-man," he said, "that's some rough sh-sh-sh-sh-sh-shit there, bro. But I understand it."

"You do?"

"Oh, yeah, Power. I d-d-d-d-do."

"Tell me."

"You just now l-l-l-l-learning 'bout haters. You got you some s-s-s-s-serious haters, brother."

"Hating me for what?"

"Who you are. What you got. Who's t-t-t-taking care of you."

"Slim?"

"I saw it when I f-f-f-f-first start working with the man. He got him some h-h-h-h-haters. Folk be envious. Hateful. They don't l-l-l-l-like seeing you having it easy as y-y-y-y-you have it."

"I don't get it."

"You will. See, when you m-m-m-m-made up your mind to come on over here and a-a-a-a-accept being Slim's b-b-b-b-boy, you done made a choice."

"A choice about what?"

"A choice of g-g-g-g-g-going into the l-l-l-l-l . . ." Dre couldn't get out this last word. Sometimes when that happened, I would complete the word for him. But in this case, I didn't know what word he was struggling to say. So I asked him again.

"What did I choose to go into, Dre?"

Dre blinked his eyes. Sometimes this helped him get the word out. He took a deep breath and, with a big effort, said, "You done chose this l-l-l-l-l-l-l-l-l-l-l-l-l-l-l-l-l-life." He took a deep breath and repeated the words. "You done chose this l-l-l-l-l-l-l-life, bro. And I'm afraid that it d-d-d-d-d-don't come ch-ch-ch-ch-ch-cheap."

If my moms had been alive, this was something I could have talked to her about. She'd have understood. Or Beauty—Beauty would also have understood; I wanted to talk to Beauty, I wanted to talk to my sister. It had been nine months since she had left Atlanta. The last time we spoke was in December. It was the first Christmas without my mother and I was missing Beauty; I was thinking of her all the time. I just had to hear her voice. I wanted to wish her merry Christmas, but Wanda wouldn't give me Anita's number. I had to beg to get it. I called, and Beauty answered on the first ring.

"It's Power."

"You don't think I know your voice?"

"I've been missing yours," I said.

I could hear her struggling to figure out what to say or what not to say. I could hear her struggling with her feelings.

"I didn't mean to catch you by surprise," I said.

"You okay?" she finally asked.

"I'm good."

"You still staying at Slim's?"

"Yes."

"Then you're not good."

"I didn't call to get into that. I just called to wish you merry Christmas."

"Merry Christmas, Power."

"And that's it?" I asked.

"That's all I can say, it really is."

"Then I'll leave you alone."

But now, all these months later, I didn't want to leave her alone. I was hurting, and I wanted to talk to her. I wanted to explain my confusion to her. I wanted her to help me get through this. So I called the number Wanda had given me. The answering machine picked up. The voice of an older woman said, "This is Anita Ward kindly requesting that you leave your name at the beep." Instead of leaving my name, I hung up.

The election was on a Thursday. I was relieved when Slim didn't show up that night. Dre said he'd gone to Birmingham on business. Next morning I considered skipping school. I didn't want to face it. But I knew that eventually I'd have to, so I forced myself to get dressed, climb on the moped, and ride in.

The students acted differently toward me—I could feel that immediately. Most of them looked the other way when they saw me. As much as I didn't want to face them, they didn't want to face me either. I couldn't remember ever feeling more alone in my life. The only dude who stopped me in the hallway was Barry Tanner. He was wearing this big goony smile on his face.

"Hey, Power," he said, "you ran a good race and I just wanted to tell you I'd like to put you on one of the committees that's looking to get more money for the chess team to travel out of town for tournaments. What do you say?"

I didn't know what to say. Didn't know what to feel.

"Whatever" was the only word that came out of my mouth.

My stomach was hurting. I felt queasy. I went to the bathroom and was in a stall with the door closed when two guys came in. I recognized their voices; it was Anthony and T-Shot, my teammates from basketball.

"He been acting like he's all that for months now," said Anthony.

"Living large off a gangsta's money. He's got attitude that tries a nigga's patience. Serves him right to get his ass whipped like that. Who the fuck does he think he is?"

"Far as I'm concerned, he ain't nobody."

"His fancy ride, all them parties up in his crib, all that pussy he been getting. Well, he wouldn't be getting nothing if he wasn't the golden boy of Charles 'Slim' Simmons. Slim Simmons thinks he can buy his boy anything, even make him president of his class."

"That nigga thinks he owns Atlanta."

"Fuck him."

"And fuck Power. Without that old-school thug behind him, Power don't got no power. Power don't got shit. Power *ain't* shit."

"And now he knows it."

I just sat there until they left the bathroom. And when they did, I pulled up my pants, washed my hands, dried them, walked out of school, and never went back.

New Education

When Slim got back from Birmingham, first thing he wanted to know about was the election. He wanted to congratulate me for being class president. My first reaction was fear. I was scared to tell him that I'd gotten swamped by a nerdy chess player. I knew that Slim was living through me. 'Cause he had done lousy in school, he loved how great I was doing in school. I didn't want to disappoint him, but there wasn't any way out of it. I told him outright. I even told him what I had overheard in the bathroom. I guess I told him because I knew it would piss him off and make him understand what I was going through. I wanted Slim as pissed off as I was. I wanted him to see how he and I were joined up in this humiliation—that, in a way, it was as much his fault as mine. He took the bait. He flew into a rage—not at me but at them.

"Fuck them motherfuckers," he said. "You don't want them, you don't need them, and they don't fuckin' deserve you. Just fuck 'em. Haters, man. Haters come poppin' out the woodwork soon as a man goes and does something good. For every one dude who shows he's got game, a hundred dudes get to hating on him. It's that jealous demon, boy. That jealous demon wants to fuck up whatever's good and turn it bad. That's the way of the world. That's why I done created my own world, Power. I keep telling you that, son, I keep showing you that the world regular folk think is fair and square is full of shit and twice as nasty as what those fuckin' squares call the bad life. See, they call it the bad life because it ain't run by their rules. Their rules are fucked. Their rules say, do something good and we'll undercut your ass. Achieve something nice, and we'll start talking about you like a dog. Their rules say, you win, and then we'll make you lose. Fuck their rules, Power, forget their rules, forget that motherfuckin' school. I didn't need no school and neither do you. What you got to learn, boy, no school can teach you. Fact is, school can hurt you the way it hurt me. Made me feel like I wasn't smart as everyone else. Well, truth is, I was smarter. And so are you.

"Besides, those assholes ain't giving up no love no how. You too smart for their namby-pamby asses. You too slick. You got too much going on. They don't like that 'cause they don't got that. You feel me, son? They out to destroy you just like they was out to destroy me. But I busted a move back then—oh, yes, I did. And you busting a move too. You don't need those motherfuckers. You want an education? You want teachers? You want to learn what's happening on the real? Well, I got the real, baby. I got the education and I got the teachers to set your young ass straight. I don't ever want you going back to that school, not for another goddamn minute, not after what they done to you. One day—and it ain't gonna be long—we gonna buy the land where that school sits and burn the motherfucker down. That's what we gonna do. But before that, you *will* go to school, but not to no regular school. I'm talkin' 'bout a school no one ever seen before. I'm gonna make up this school for you, and I'm gonna pick every one of your teachers, and they gonna teach you shit no one ever learns, they gonna teach you the real deal, baby, and when you graduate you ain't just gonna be bad, you gonna be the baddest motherfucker this city ever seen. You won't be bad as me—that ain't ever gonna happen—but you'll come awfully goddamn close."

. . . .

Slim said just what I wanted to hear. He understood. Most dads would have either ignored my humiliation or told me to go back and face the music. I loved Slim 'cause Slim said fuck the music. Slim said fuck school. He knew that I didn't belong there. He cosigned my get-out-of-jail-free card. 'Cause that's what going back would have been. Prison. Once I learned what everyone really thought of me, once I knew that they'd been using me for the parties I'd been throwing and nothing else, I suddenly knew what I thought of them. I hated them. If they were going to shame me and judge me because I was living large and they weren't, I was going to judge them for being narrow-minded fools.

With Slim's enthusiastic support, I was glad to leave high school at the end of my junior year. And even though I could hear Moms saying, "Paul, you got to complete your schooling. We're counting on you to go to college, even to law school, son," Slim's voice was louder. Slim made it clear I was doing the right thing.

"If you wanna be a man," said Slim, "I'll show you how to be a man. Forget those punk-ass instructors in school. I'll get you some real-life teachers."

Irv Wasserman

My first teacher lived in Chicago, which is where I moved that summer. Never in my life had I met anyone like him.

"Gruff on the outside," said Slim, "cream puff on the inside. That's Irv Wasserman. He'll teach you about survival, son. See, survival's the first lesson. Reason you looking at a rich man when you look at me, boy, is that I learned that survival shit. Irv is the cat with nine hundred lives. They ain't caught up with that motherfucker yet, and they never will."

I flew to Chicago first-class and stayed at the Hilton hotel on the lake. Slim, who made the arrangements, was always cool that way.

"You go first-class," he said, "and you feel first-class. You hang with first-class people doing first-class shit. It's a beautiful way to live."

I was booked into the Hilton because the night I arrived Irv Wasserman was being honored at a banquet in the grand ballroom. When I checked in I saw his picture on a poster advertising the event. The Center for the Underprivileged had named him man of the year. He had a low forehead, thick curly hair, and a strong nose. In his photo, he didn't seem happy; his dark eyes looked right at you. When I picked up my key, I saw that he'd left a ticket to the banquet for me. I went upstairs, unpacked, showered, put on a dark suit, and went down to the ballroom. The festivities were just getting under way. There was a cocktail party before the dinner where I didn't know a soul. I just observed. The crowd was about half white and half black. It was an older group, with most of the men in their fifties or sixties. The women looked a little younger, but there was no one my age. I felt out of place. There was a political atmosphere to the party, and I figured that many of the guys worked for the city or the state. Out of the corner of my eye I caught a glance at Wasserman, who was working the room. At six three or four, he towered above everyone. I began to make my way over to introduce myself to him, but just as I got close he reached out to shake the hand of the man standing in front of me and said, "Mr. Mayor, I'm honored you came!" I backed off and gave them space to talk.

The banquet began promptly at eight. I was seated at a table with three couples and a black woman. The woman, probably in her late forties, sat next to me. She had midnight-black skin, a wide sensuous mouth, and a hip, short-cropped wig that gave her the air of a model. Her clothes were fashionable too. Her dress looked like it was made out of thin gray metal. She was tall and leggy and her eyes were on fire. It was almost like she could burn you with her eyes.

She introduced herself as Evelyn Meadows. She wanted to know my connection to Wasserman.

"He's a friend of my uncle," I said before asking about her connection.

"Irv managed my late husband, Johnnie Meadows. You've heard of him?"

"Sure."

Johnnie Meadows was an R&B singer who'd died the previous year of a heart attack onstage. He had a big following all over the country.

"I didn't know Mr. Wasserman managed singers."

"Oh, Mr. Wasserman does everything," she said. "Mr. Wasserman is a genius."

Evelyn Meadows spent the rest of the dinner drinking. She downed two martinis before starting on the wine. Meanwhile, speakers were praising Irv Wasserman to the sky, talking about his generous contributions to every charity you can imagine. A priest spoke, then a rabbi, then a minister, and then, much to my surprise, Bonafide, the same rapper whom Slim had hired to entertain at my sixteenth birthday party. Since then Bonafide had blown up and gone on to national fame. Bonafide seemed completely out of place in this ballroom—what with his baseball cap cocked to the side and his oversized jeans hanging off him—but there he was, talking about how Wasserman's record label, Complex Music, had taken him to the top and given a whole generation of young people a chance to be heard by the public.

"This here man is a legend," said Bonafide, "and is about the only cat I know who goes from old school to new school to all schools while graduating first in every class. Yes, sir, he has paid the dues to tell the news, and, baby, this is your night, Irv."

The mayor, who talked about his long association with Wasserman through good times and bad, presented the award, a sculpture in the form of helping hands. "Irv might look like a giant," he said, "but he's for the little man. He's for the downtrodden. He cares."

Everyone stood to applaud except for Evelyn Meadows. She was on her third glass of wine. After I sat down, I felt a shoe rubbing up and down the back of my leg. I looked over and caught a wink from Miss Meadows. I didn't want to respond. After all, I had just gotten to Chicago. I had Wasserman's telephone number and would call him tomorrow. He had promised he would find a place for me in his organization, and I was eager to learn what that would be. I didn't need any complications right now. Miss Meadows was a beautiful sexy full-grown woman, but good sense told me to leave her alone.

Wasserman's acceptance speech was short and not too sweet. He spoke with a gruff tone and never did smile. He sounded sour. His words were correct—"This is a big honor and I wanna thank everyone for putting on this great evening for me"—but he didn't seem all that pleased to be up there.

When the ceremonies were over, Evelyn Meadows leaned over and, with her tongue seductively brushing my ear, whispered, "Have you met the man yet?"

"Mr. Wasserman? Not yet."

"Well, let me be the first to introduce you, baby. Let's hurry before it's too late."

We got up from the table and walked across the ballroom. Wasserman was surrounded by all kinds of people wishing him well and wanting to shake his hand. He put up with it, but he looked like he was in a hurry to get out. A couple of beefy guys stood next to him, surveying the room. Evelyn and I stood in the back of a long line to greet him. We waited five, ten, then fifteen minutes. I practiced what I was going to say to him—"I'm Power, Slim's nephew, and I'm really happy to be here, sir"—but as I got closer, I wondered whether I should use my real name, Paul. Meanwhile, I saw one of his guys go off to get him a drink while the other turned around at the sound of a tray of dishes that a waiter had dropped. At that moment, Evelyn Meadows approached him. Seeing her all decked out in her cool outfit, Irv managed a small smile and opened his arms to hug her. I just happened to look down and saw that, rather than respond to his outstretched arms, she opened her little silver bejeweled purse, grabbed a small pistol that was hidden inside, aimed it at his heart, and fired. Out of instinct, I grabbed her arm and brought it down so that, instead of shooting his chest, the bullet shattered his lower leg. Eyes wide open, Wasserman fell. So did Evelyn's pistol. As I restrained her with a tight bear hug, she screamed at the fallen man, "You fuckin' son of a bitch! You killed my husband! You killed him because he was about to blow off the lid! You'd kill anyone who was gonna tell the truth!" By then the bodyguards, not knowing what had happened, had both me and Evelyn in headlocks. She kept screaming, I mean screaming so loud that everyone in the hotel could hear, *"This man is a fuckin' hypocrite! This man is a murderer! This man stole money from his own mother and murdered his own brother! This man is a no-good rotten filthy piece of shit!"*

This was my introduction to Irv Wasserman.

Two days later I was seated on a bench in the hallway of a hospital. Irv had sent for me.

Because his eyes had been wide open, Irv had seen exactly what had happened. He never lost consciousness. The police took Evelyn away. On Irv's orders, his bodyguards released me, but not before getting my name. In no time, an ambulance rushed him to the emergency room. Next morning, his picture was plastered all over the newspapers. A photographer had actually caught me in the act of diverting Evelyn's arm. I was simply identified as an "unknown man."

When I called to tell Slim the news, he had already heard.

"Beautiful," he said. "Couldn't have gone better if you had sent up a motherfuckin' prayer. God is on our side, son. God's looking out for us on this one. Now there's nothing to do but wait for the call. It'll come."

It came at eight in the morning. A man gave me the name of a hospital, a room, and said to be there at four sharp. When I got off the elevator on the fifth floor, I was greeted by the beefy bodyguard who had turned his back just before the shooting. He wanted to know my name and see my ID. Then he walked down the hallway and pointed to a bench. "Don't move till we call you," he said.

An hour passed. I hadn't brought anything to read. I kept checking and rechecking my iPhone for e-mails. I wondered if there were other patients on this floor, because I heard no noise and saw no other visitors. It was weird. Finally, a door opened and a man came out. It was the other bodyguard I'd seen at the hotel. He pointed at me, indicating I should follow him into the room.

It wasn't a room. It was a suite. I didn't know hospitals had suites. I walked into a living room that had polished dark wood floors and fancy overstuffed chairs and a long couch. Irv Wasserman sat in one of the chairs, his long right leg propped up on a small table. The leg was in a cast. In the other chair was a red-haired girl maybe a year or two older than me. She was wearing a black turtleneck top that hugged her chest tight. Her breasts were super-sized and pointing right at me. She had on black slacks but because she was sitting I couldn't tell anything about her backside. In a rough kind of way, she was pretty in the face. She wore a lot of makeup, especially around her eyes. She had Irv's eyes. She had to be his daughter.

Irv sat in the other chair. He was in a gold silk robe. I saw his initials, IW, sewn in white over the breast pocket. He wasn't smiling. He was just looking at me. He was scrutinizing me. I could hear him thinking.

"This here is my Judy," he finally said. "She doesn't want to go to college. She says she doesn't like school. You been to college, kid?"

"No, sir."

"What about high school?"

"I quit after my junior year."

"How come?"

"I want to learn business, Mr. Wasserman. I want to learn about the real world."

"You hear that, Judy?" said Wasserman. "He ain't in school, but he's got plans. He knows what the fuck he wants. Do you know what you want?"

"You said when I graduated high school I could decide what I wanted. Well, I graduated, didn't I?"

"Barely," said Irv.

"And I want to open a beauty salon."

"With whose money?" asked the father.

"It would only be a loan," said the daughter.

"Parents don't loan money to their kids. They give them money."

"Okay, then give me the money."

"And what do I get back?"

"You'll own the beauty salon."

"And what makes you think you know shit about running a beauty shop?"

"I got people to help me. Older women I know."

"Do I know them?" asked Irv.

"I don't think so. I can introduce you."

"I don't like the idea of my daughter introducing women to me."

"It's a business thing, Dad."

"Your mother wouldn't like that."

"You divorced her five years ago."

"That's beside the point. We'll ask the kid what he thinks." Wasserman turned to me and said, "Do I give my daughter money to open some fancy-shmancy beauty shop?"

"I wouldn't know, Mr. Wasserman. I couldn't say . . ."

"Why not? You scared of your own opinion? You scared of saying something I don't want to hear? You one of these kids with a confidence problem?"

"Well, if you put it that way, I'd say, if you can afford it—"

"Shit," Wasserman interrupted, "you know goddamn well I can afford it."

"Then I would say if you open up in the right location, it might be a good idea. Women are always worrying about their hair."

"My daughter, Judy, she wants to open in a black neighborhood. What do you think of that?"

"Black women pay a lot of attention to their hair," I said.

"My Judy is like me. She likes the blacks. Her mother doesn't. Her mother always said, 'Stay away from the blacks. You can't trust them.' I trust them. I always have. Take your uncle. I trust him with my life.

And then he sends you to me, and then you save my goddamn life. What do you make of that, kid?"

"I really can't say, Mr. Wasserman . . ."

"What if I say I want you to help me with my Judy? What if I say I want you to help her with her beauty shop?"

"I'd say, well, I want to help you in any way I can. But I gotta be honest, I don't know much about—"

"You don't gotta know much, kid, you just gotta watch the money. You know how to watch money, don't you?"

"I can watch money," I said.

"Like a hawk—that's how you watch money. You don't need a college education to watch money. My brother, Louis. The great Louis Samuel Wasserman. My parents gave him a middle name—that's how sure they were he'd make good. Me, I got no middle name. By the time Louis was born, fifteen years after me, they'd given up on me. I was in the streets and out of school. But Louis Samuel Wasserman, he was going to school. He was going to college. Then he was going to law school. He was setting the world on fire. Not any college, but Yale University. Not any law school, but Harvard Law School. You ever hear of Louis Samuel Wasserman, kid?"

"Afraid not."

"If you go back a few years and read the papers you'll read all about him. You see, after law school he didn't want to be no lawyer. He wanted to be bigger than that. He wanted to make big money. And naturally he wanted nothing to do with me so he moves to New York City and gets in with some famous financiers, the so-called legit moneymen who buy and sell bonds and commodities and raid corporations for cheap and then sell 'em for high. He wants to play in the major leagues, and he thinks I'm bush-league. That's what Louis Samuel Wasserman thinks.

"That's your uncle, Judy. The uncle you never even met 'cause he never wanted nothing to do with me or my family. That's your uncle who went to jail and died there. His famous financiers were crooked as an old bitch's back. His famous financiers were frauds. And Louis Samuel Wasserman, with all his education and all his degrees, couldn't see it coming. He didn't know chicken salad from chicken shit. He got taken for the ride of his life. When he said he didn't know about the behind-the-scenes schemes I half believed him because he was too stupid to see it.

"And you know what this did to Judy's grandfather and grandmother? It killed them. A week after the story broke, my father—may he rest in peace—died of a heart attack. A month later his wife of fifty-five years, Muriel Wasserman, had a terrible stroke. Six months later, we buried my mother. Two funerals in six months, and do you think my brother looked me in the eye? Do you think the great Louis Samuel Wasserman said a single word to his only living sibling in the whole world? Not a word, not a single fuckin' word. Then his first month in the pen he runs into some crazy man who cuts his throat with a butcher knife."

"Don't get yourself excited, Daddy," said Judy. "You're in the hospital."

"That's the best place to get excited. If I have a heart attack here, I press a button and they come running."

"You're not having a heart attack," Judy told him.

"I will if that goddamn beauty shop of yours tanks and costs me a fortune."

"So I can do it?" asked Judy, bouncing off the chair, going over to her dad, and kissing him on the cheek. When she bent over to kiss him, I saw that her booty was screaming as loud as her titties. Her body was incredible.

"Now you take this kid outta here," Irv told his daughter. "What's your name—Peter? Paul? But they call you something else, don't they?"

"My real name is Paul, but they call me Power."

"Where does the Power come from?"

I told them how I liked the Power Rangers when I was a little boy.

"Cute story. Okay, Judy, take the Power Ranger over to that old building we own by the lake, the one we turned into lofts. All the young people, they like living in lofts. Don't ask me why. There's a little loft over there that's empty. Show him where it is. You can drive him over there. I'm taking a nap. This leg is killing me. Where's that goddamn nurse when I need her?"

Hair Is Where It's At

Judy Wasserman knew what she wanted and how to get it. The "how" was her daddy. She wanted the okay to skip college, and her daddy gave her that. She wanted her own beauty shop, and Daddy provided the money. And when she wanted a nice-looking brotha, her father introduced her to me. Remembering how Irv said that Judy's mother had a thing against blacks, I wondered if I was his way to shaft his former wife. I wondered a lot of things about Irv Wasserman.

When Judy drove me over to the loft and showed me around, I was impressed. The room was large and clean. A huge floor-to-ceiling window overlooked Lake Michigan. The furniture was black leather. The walls were painted mint green and the island kitchen had marble countertops colored cobalt blue.

Judy had brought a bottle of tequila and right away started doing shots. I wasn't in the mood. She also had grass and a little coke. I told her that I wasn't into drugs. "Great," she said, "that means more for me."

Within thirty or forty minutes, she got blasted and made a move on me. I was hesitant. "Hold on, girl," I said. "I can't afford to get crossways with your daddy. I want to work for the man."

"Daddy wants us all working together, Power. Can't you see that he loves you for what you did for him? I'm the reward. I'm here to say thank you. I'm here with his full approval. You saw that with your own eyes. Now there's something else I want you to see with your own eyes."

With that, she brought that tight black top over her head, unhooked her brassiere, and slightly—very slightly—arched her back. I was gone.

When I woke up in the morning, Judy was gone. There was a note on the kitchen counter that said, "Call me when you're ready . . ." She wrote down her cell number and that was it. I stretched and yawned and remembered how long it had taken me to cum. Judy had loved that; she said she'd never seen anyone go so long, but what she didn't know is that I was fighting my imagination. I didn't want to imagine Beauty. For everything that was amazing about Judy's body—and believe me, amazing is an understatement—I still couldn't bust a nut with my eyes open, no matter how hard I tried. Finally, though, when she started digging her nails into my back and screaming that it was time, I shut my eyes, saw my sister, and exploded.

Turned out that Judy, like her dad, was a talker. After we fucked, she started telling me how she hated the private school her mother had made her attend. Her mother had remarried a guy named Harvey, who owned a car dealership. Harvey never said a bad word about Judy's father, but Judy's mother did. Six years ago she discovered that Irv was keeping a former Miss Venezuela in an apartment on Chicago's Gold Coast. When Judy told me the story, she laughed. She sounded glad that her dad was cheating on her mom. She had wanted to live with her dad, but her mother wouldn't hear of it. That got Judy even angrier. But, as far as I could tell, Judy liked being angry. The angrier she became, the more she talked.

She told me that the only blacks in her private school were two gay guys and three girls. The girls were her best friends. According to Judy, they were the smartest girls in school. One of the girls had a father who manufactured hair products for black women. That's how Judy got the idea of opening a hair salon in a South Side Chicago neighborhood recently gone upscale.

"Black people treat hair like art," she said.

I rubbed my head, just to remind myself I did nothing with my hair except keep it short.

"Not you," said Judy. "The women. Black women have the coolest sense of hair style. Haven't you noticed?"

"I guess I have," I said.

"They just don't do what everyone else does," she said. "They invent. They're not afraid of stepping out there. They're daring. I've been going around hiring stylists. It's like I'm forming a band, only it's a band of hairstylists. Do you understand what I'm saying?"

"Sure."

"And with these stylists and location and this interior designer I found to trick out the space, I can't miss. This designer just did a veggie restaurant in Greektown. It's amazing. You want to ride over and take a look?"

After our sex marathon, I just wanted to sleep.

"I'm a little tired," I said, my eyes half-closed.

She kept talking as my eyes kept closing. The next thing I remembered was waking up and seeing her note.

I walked around the apartment aimlessly. Staring out the big window at the lake and gray sky, I felt like I was still dreaming. I went to the refrigerator, but aside from a bottle of water, it was empty. After everything that had happened, I felt a little empty.

After getting beat for class president, I had felt angry and down. My spirits lifted when Slim got even angrier than me and sent me to Chicago. I was leaving one world and entering another one. That was great. But what was this new world? Seeing Irv get shot by the crazy woman made me a little nuts. Reading all the stories about it in the paper the next day was exciting but confusing. I was the "unidentified man" who pushed down Evelyn's arm. In one photograph you could see the back of my head. The articles were all about Wasserman's shady past and the fact that, despite his notoriety, the mayor was honoring him. It talked about his half-dozen brushes with the law and, in every instance, how he managed to avoid conviction. It talked about his so-called underground empire. All this had me curious.

Then when I met the man I didn't know what to think. He didn't talk like your average guy. He jumped from one subject to the other, and they didn't always seem to connect. Then there was Judy, looking me over like I was a piece of meat. And then Irv pushing me in Judy's business. And then Judy pushing me in her pussy. And here I was, the morning after, looking out over a lonely lake while I sipped on a plastic bottle of water. What was I supposed to think? Where was this Chicago thing going to take me? I could call Slim, but I already knew what he'd say. "Sit down. Be cool. Irv knows what he's doing." So I turned on the TV. The Cubs were playing the Braves. The Braves were killing them. I was glad.

I guess I dozed off because the postgame show was on when my cell blew up.

It was Judy. "You gotta get a car," she said. "You can't stay in Chicago without a car."

"I figured as much."

"Go to Hertz and get a car with a GPS. I'll text you Daddy's account number and the address of the salon. I'm at the salon now. Be here by four. Bye."

Judy didn't waste no time. I didn't either. By four, I was in a Chevy Impala, pulling up to a storefront on one of those streets on the south side of the city transforming from hood to hip. There was a coffee shop called Spilling the Beans, a shoe shop selling fresh sneakers from Japan, a clothing boutique named Past Future Passions, and, at the address Judy had given me, an empty store with a sign above it: HAIR IS WHERE IT'S AT. I looked inside. The lights were off and no one was there. I saw a White Castle a couple of blocks away. I walked over and ordered a cheeseburger and fries. I was famished. I wolfed down my food and went back to the store. Still no one. I stood there in front, just checking out the neighborhood, a strange mix of old and new. Some of the older black women looked like they had lived there forever. They carried shopping bags and watched their children to make sure they didn't run into the street. There were also black businessmen and businesswomen in tailored suits hurrying to the subway station. Next to a bookstore specializing in African-American literature called Black Words was a run-down Laundromat.

Finally, a Porsche pulled up. Judy got out the passenger side with a plastic glass of wine in her hand. Today she was dressed in white— tight white jeans, tight white top. A hulky white guy got out from behind the wheel. He was a little taller than me. He had blue eyes, wide shoulders, big biceps, and a crew cut. To me, it looked like his blond hair was dyed. He wore a gold chain around his neck and an oversized watch on his right hand. I couldn't tell whether it was a real Rolex or a fake.

"Power," said Judy, "meet my boyfriend, Dwayne."

I tried not to show surprise. I offered Dwayne my hand. When he shook it, I nearly winced in pain.

"Dwayne owns a gym just a couple of blocks away," she said. "Dwayne's the one who told me about this neighborhood."

"Any time you wanna work out," said Dwayne, who sounded a little like Rocky, "the first workout's on me."

He handed me a card that read, "Mad Muscles, Dwayne 'Ace' Foster, Owner and Chairman of the Board. Mr. Muscle Himself."

"Actually," said Dwayne, "I ain't the real owner. Judy's dad is the real owner. You know Mr. Wasserman?"

"I've met him."

Judy turned to Dwayne and said, "Daddy hired Power as the security guy for the salon. Until we open he's helping the crew put up drywall and stuff like that. He's from Atlanta."

"I never been to Alabama," said Dwayne.

I started to correct him but didn't see the point. I kept quiet as Judy unlocked the door. The space was unfinished, a complete mess.

"The crew's off on another job," she said. "They come back tomorrow. They usually get here at seven in the morning. Be here then. Me and Dwayne got a party to go to. We gotta run. Bye."

The first day was hell—absolute fuckin' hell. I had never done that kind of work before and hated it from the first minute. The contractor looked at me like I was dirt. All day long I was breathing in crap. Putting up drywall is a disgusting job, and I was no good at it. When the contractor saw that, he had me hammering. When I was through hammering, he had me sweeping, then mopping, then running to McDonald's to get the crew's lunch. In the afternoon, I was carrying in lumber that weighed a ton. By the end of the day, I was dead tired and irritable. I didn't like the contractor, I didn't like the crew; I hated everything about the job and wasn't going back. I didn't care if Judy Wasserman did have an incredible body and threw the best fuck in Chicago. Judy Wasserman was a complete bitch.

When I got back to the loft, I barely had the strength to get into the shower. I was drying myself off when the phone rang. It was Slim.

"I was just getting ready to call you," I said.

"I talked to Irv. He couldn't be happier with you. Says he's putting you in a key position."

"Irv's a fuckin' liar and his daughter is a fuckin' nymphomaniac."

"Slow down, boy," said Slim. "Slow the hell down."

"I'm not going back."

"Going back where?"

I explained what had happened—how Irv had turned me over to Judy, how Judy had screwed my brains out and then got me mopping floors.

Slim laughed.

"How can you be laughing?"

"'Cause it's funny, motherfucker."

"Laugh all you want, but I'm coming home."

"For what?"

"I don't know. That's for you to figure out, Slim."

"I already done figured it. That's why you're in Chicago."

"To do shit work?"

"To do whatever Irv tells you to do."

"Irv's a space cadet. He talks shit for hours. He goes in one direction, then he's off in another. I don't think he's playing with a full deck."

"You don't need to think, boy. You just need to go along with the program."

"What program? Fucking his daughter behind her boyfriend's back? Breaking my back hauling wood? I don't think so."

"Believe me, after you saved Irv's ass like that, he's not letting you out of his sight. He's gonna take care of you."

"When?"

"That's Irv's call, not mine. Look at it like this, Power. When you start a chess game you can't plan a strategy in advance. You move according to however someone's moving on you. You act and react according to what's happening in real time. You in real time."

"I'm in real pain."

"Pain passes. Now ain't that the fuckin' truth?"

"So what you're saying, Slim, is that if I come back—"

"You ain't coming back. Not now. You got shit to learn and it seems to me you're learning it. Now shut up, and stop whinin' about all that good pussy you getting."

Slim broke out with another big laugh and then hung up. One thing about Slim—he was always smooth and knew how to calm me down. I watched some stupid reality show about knuckleheads living on the Jersey Shore and fell asleep on the couch. When I woke up, it was midnight and Irv Wasserman was sitting on a stool at the marble countertop in the kitchen area. He was sipping tea out of a huge glass mug.

"I just bought the mug at Starbucks," he said. "I didn't know they still made mugs out of glass. Tea tastes better when you drink out of glass. I bought you six mugs. Use them in good health."

"Thank you. I didn't hear you come in."

"Tea is better for you than coffee. Coffee winds you up and gets you thinking too fast. The thing about thinking is that you can overthink. Overthinking is no good. For years, kid, I was an overthinker. I can feel that you're overthinking right now."

"I . . . I just woke up—"

"You're thinking, *What the fuck is old man Irv doing here?*"

"To tell you the truth, Mr. Wasserman, I was thinking that I just talked to Slim, who told me not to think."

Irv allowed himself one of those rare smiles.

"That Slim's a thinker, ain't he?"

"He's been good to me."

"And I been good to my daughter. You know that, don't you, Peter?"

"Paul."

"Sorry, Peter used to be my broker. Peter didn't see people, he saw numbers. But you're Paul. They call you Powerhouse, right?"

"Power."

"Right, you're the power man. Power is good. Except what the fuck is it? We got the power to have kids by sticking our dick in a woman and squirting the seed. That's a powerful thing. The kid is born, and we think that we're God 'cause our seed caused all that. The kid is our seed. We watch the kid grow up. If it's a boy, we hope he'll get strong and plant his seed somewhere good so we can have grandkids. Grandkids are beautiful. I don't have any. I had one daughter late in life. I waited because I cared. I waited because I wanted to find the right woman. It's easy to find the wrong woman. My dick led me to many a dumb broad. I got in, I got out, and then I thought, *This is getting me nowhere. This is no one I can talk to. This is no one who understands me. This is no one with a heart and head for Irv Wasserman.* So I waited. Patience is my strong suit, kid. You'll find that out. You'll see. You're looking at a patient man.

"I was, what? Forty-seven, forty-eight years old when I met Ginny Calzolari. Many men that age look for girls in their early twenties. I can understand that. There are advantages. But I looked at the drawbacks. I didn't want young. I wanted mature. I wanted Ginny because, even though we came from different backgrounds and had different faiths, I could see she was quality. I knew her father from business. He owned restaurants all over Chicago. Ginny was the hostess at his best restaurant, Le Beef. If I took you there tonight, you'd pay eighty dollars for a steak and you wouldn't complain because the steak is that good. Ginny's father is famous for how he ages beef. He's a good man. I could see that his daughter, a real beauty, was a good woman. I could see by how she treated the customers. She had class. Class is important to me. Ginny Calzolari spoke very well. She had gone to college for a year. She had studied business. Her father told me he had plans to make her manager of the restaurant where she was hosting. That's a big job, kid, because that particular restaurant has served the president of the United States of America. This is a top-grossing restaurant. I went there six, seven times, just observing her. Then I decided to ask her out. She knew who I was, of course, and she saw I was ten years older, but ten years' difference these days between couples is like ten days. She accepted my invitation to go to the opera. Personally, I hate the opera, but her father said she liked it. Her father was on my side. I sat through all that screaming singing. I asked her about sports and she said she liked soccer. I like boxing, but I took her to soccer. Box seats

to see the Chicago Fire, a cute name for a soccer team but a dull sport.
I sat through it. I saw she liked shopping. All women like shopping.
We shopped at the Water Tower Place. It's a mall on Michigan Avenue. You'll see it soon enough. I bought her things she liked. She
liked how I listened to her when she talked about running a restaurant. She wanted to know if I thought women could run things. I said
yes. I'm a modern man. I know women fly jumbo jets. I've seen
Muhammad Ali's daughter Laila, a beautiful woman, fight in the
ring. She fights like a tiger. These are things I don't deny.

"Long story short, we marry. A rabbi and a priest take my money
and do a joint ceremony. Three hundred people. A month later, she
says she's pregnant. I'm thrilled. Six months later, her father dies.
There's a fight in the family. Her older brother gets greedy and wants
all five restaurants, including the one that Ginny manages. I say that's
not fair. Ginny says she's no longer interested in working. She just
wants this baby. I watch nine, ten million dollars walk out the door.
Fine. Let's have this baby. Let's call her Judy. Let's get a house in Evan-
ston with a pool and a tennis court. Let's be happy and forget the ten
million dollars. It might have been eleven or twelve million. Who
knows? It doesn't matter. We have one baby, a girl. I want to have
another baby. I ask God to give me a son. But we don't have a son.
The fuckin' truth is that we don't have sex. At first I'm patient. You
have to be patient. After all, she just had a baby. But then how long do
you wait for the sex to start? Four months? Five? A year. After a year,
it's too much. You have to discuss it. You have to know why. I was
told there is no why. She didn't feel like it. Well, she felt like it before.
She liked it after the opera or the soccer game or the goddamn fuckin'
shopping at that Water Tower Place. 'Something happened, Irv,' is all
she said. 'I don't have the desire.' 'Well, I see you don't have the desire
to rightfully claim the restaurant that your father wanted you to have.
So what *do* you have the desire to do?' She wouldn't say, but I saw. She
had the desire to spend money. That was her job. Buy a new car. Fix

up the house. Get one of those landscape geniuses and give him a hundred thousand dollars to plant a few bushes. *That* she had the desire to do. And so do you know what I did, kid? I let her. I sat back and fuckin' let her. For the sake of our little baby, I wasn't going nowhere. I wanted to be Daddy. So I stayed. I said, 'Live and let live.'

"I lived. I found a way to satisfy the needs that God put in my body. I didn't argue with my wife. I moved on with my business. The someone who satisfied my needs was discreet. A lovely girl. We had an arrangement like millions of people before us. Such arrangements are commonplace. I never bothered my wife. I let her write her checks. She had her side of the bed, I had mine. She had no complaints. As a father, I was there for my daughter. There was nothing I missed—not a holiday, not a birthday, not a soccer game or a graduation ceremony. I took her to prizefights and she learned to love the sport. I took her to Wrigley Field and she loved the Cubs. Always box seats. Always the best. Maybe I did too much. Maybe I went overboard. Maybe I held on to resentment about her mother. Any fool knew that her mother married me for two reasons—for money and to have a child. Once the child came, the sex stopped. When the sex stopped, the love stopped. But all this anger I kept inside me because the 'someone' I had found gave me comfort. Every man needs comfort. Life went on until Ginny discovered the 'someone.' I had no apologies. I did what I did and I admitted it. Ginny flew into a rage. She hired a Rottweiler lawyer to go after me and my money. I hired my own Rottweiler, bigger and meaner than hers. I mauled the bitch. Financially, I had her where I wanted her. The prenup was ironclad and I could have left her penniless. But I didn't. For my daughter's sake, I could not throw her mother into the street. Judy wanted to live with me, but I knew her mother needed her more than me. I was generous, kid. I was more generous than I needed to be. Generosity is my downfall.

"See, my generosity has hurt Judy. Out of guilt, I gave too much. I spoiled her something awful. I saw it coming, but I couldn't help myself. Ginny was poisoning Judy's mind against me. I had to prove to my daughter that I wasn't poison. So I bought and bought and bought. I bought for Judy like I had bought for Ginny. Jewelry and clothes and cars and any little thing her heart desired. I couldn't deny her. And look what happened . . ."

Irv paused. He took a long sip of tea, closed his eyes, and sighed. When he opened his eyes, he got off the stool and walked across the room to look out the window. There was nothing to see. The cloudy sky blocked the moon. There was nothing but darkness. He looked into the darkness for a long while before turning his back to the window. When he looked at me, his eyes were softer.

"Judy is trouble, kid," he said. "I think you know that. You see how she is. I thought a girl would be easier than a boy, but I was wrong. Judy was never easy, not as a little girl, not now. She isn't even twenty and she drinks like a fish. Drugs—I don't want to know about the drugs. But I do know, and that breaks my heart. This is my little girl we're talking about, Peter—"

"Paul."

"Sorry, Paul, but Judy is my seed. You understand. You also understand that I have talked to Slim about you. I don't want to open wounds, but he has told me how you lost your mother. He has told me how you were treated at school. He has told me that you are a young man of tremendous integrity. He used the word 'integrity.' Slim is a hard man, and for him to care for you the way he cares for you, for Slim to speak of your character and of your future, well, that is a beautiful thing. And then you come here and meet this crazy woman Evelyn Meadows. Evelyn Meadows is crazy out of her goddamn fuckin' mind. You getting in the way of this crazy woman killing me is almost more than I can comprehend. I can only come to one conclusion. You were sent here to help me. And because I can't help Judy by myself, you were sent here to help her too. This boyfriend of hers, the one with the run-down gym I bought, he is no good. He sells drugs out of the gym. He takes drugs himself. I'd shut down this meathead and his whole operation in the blink of an eye—if I knew it wouldn't enrage Judy. So I have to be careful. I have to work in a way that promotes her welfare. You aren't a drinker, Paul. Power Paul, that's who you are. Power Paul is not a drug taker. Power Paul is a good influence. I knew my Judy would like you. I knew she'd see what was good in you. It is not an easy job I've given you. I'm asking you to be a man when you're still a teenage boy. I'm asking you to watch over a woman who's still a teenage girl. All this is a little crazy. I know it is. But sometimes crazy isn't as crazy as it seems."

Irv stopped talking. He walked over to where I was sitting, bent down, and put his right hand on my shoulder. He patted my shoulder two times, then turned away and walked out of the loft.

Winter

Chicago in February is no joke. The howling wind comes off that lake and body slams you against the side of a building. The snow hits so hard and thick that you can't see where you're going. The deep frost has you shaking and shivering like a stray dog. You gotta wear hats and sweaters and boots until you can barely walk down the frozen streets. And no matter how careful you are, at some point the ice will put you on your ass. I'd slipped more than once. As I carefully walked along the slippery streets looking for the restaurant, I reminded myself how much had happened since I arrived here during the summer. Fall had flown by and now it was winter. The city had turned white.

I made it to Le Beef, where Judy had asked to meet me. This was the restaurant Judy's mother used to own, the same place now run by Judy's uncle Marsh. It took up the entire ground floor of one of those old office buildings from the twenties. The décor was super-plush old-school, chandeliers and heavy leather booths.

I had on a nice suit underneath my coat and scarf. Judy was already seated at a table by the window. She was wearing a deep blue turtleneck cashmere sweater. Her tits always looked sensational. But her eyes were sad. I knew she'd been crying.

"I think my father killed him," she said.

"How can you think that?" I asked. "Irv would never do anything to make you unhappy. The man lives to make you happy."

"He didn't like him. He never liked him."

"Judy, he bought him a gym, didn't he?"

"Daddy didn't buy Dwayne the gym. He just let him run it. But he didn't do that for Dwayne, he did it for me."

"That's just my point."

"I don't believe it was just a deal gone bad. Dwayne was too smart for that."

"Any deal can go bad. Especially when you're selling high-priced steroids out of the gym to high-profile trainers and jocks."

"I don't believe Dwayne was doing that," said Judy.

"I saw it with my own eyes. It was obvious."

"Why didn't you say anything to me?"

"I did. You weren't listening, Judy."

"It didn't seem all that important. Don't all the athletes take steroids? What's the fuckin' big deal about steroids?"

"They're illegal. And they cost a lot of money."

"But no one's gonna kill someone over steroids," said Judy, getting all emotional. The tears started to fall. "No one's gonna break into your apartment in the middle of the night and shoot you in the head over some goddamn steroids."

"I think he was dealing more than steroids, Judy. And I think you think that too."

"He used to. But then he stopped. How long has it been since I got out of Betty Ford?"

"About a month."

"Well, even before I went in, he stopped dealing. He cut off all those connections. He swore off grass and blow when I swore 'em off. He did it to help me."

I didn't say anything. I just sat there.

"You don't believe me, do you?" asked Judy.

"If you want the truth," I said, "here's the truth—Dwayne never stopped getting high. The whole time you were in rehab, he was blasted."

"You're saying that because my father told you to say that."

"Bullshit! I'm saying it because it's true."

Judy broke down crying. I got up and put my arm around her. For all her craziness, I had come to like her. Back in the summer, when I told her I flat-out refused to be her boy toy and have sex with her, our relationship got good. She saw that I was willing to do whatever it took to help out in the salon. I worked like a dog. I did all the grub work asked of me. And when the place was finally built, I flew Wanda Washington up from Atlanta. She stayed for a week. Wanda's Wigs was one of the best-run stores anywhere, and I knew Wanda would make sure Judy was putting a good system in place. They got along like mother and daughter. Wanda saw that some of the older women advising Judy were not making sense. With Wanda's help, Judy put her staff together and hired three great hairstylists.

Wanda was a blessing, but when I asked her questions about Beauty, Wanda said she hadn't heard a thing. I didn't believe her, but I didn't want to press her. She had come to Chicago for Judy, not me. Once we got the shop opened, I was installed as the cashier. I felt funny at first. In a beauty salon, that job is usually given to some middle-aged overweight lady. But everyone thought it would be a good addition to have a young man behind the counter collecting the money. They thought the customers would appreciate it—and they did. Even Irv came by to see the place and was pleased to see me handling the cash and credit cards.

"Collection is everything," he said without the hint of a smile. "If you don't collect, you starve."

I didn't mind. I liked the electronic sounds of the high-tech register. I liked sliding the credit cards and waiting for approval. I liked lording over the money. I liked being trusted.

I also liked being around all those women. A few of the young customers slipped me their numbers. A few of the older ones too. Once I made it clear to Judy that I couldn't be screwing her, I got next to a few of the young ones. I was still looking to find that one woman who would remove Beauty's image from my imagination. But even the finest one, the one who showed the most passion, couldn't do it. In the end, in my mind, I was always loving on Beauty.

When summer turned to fall and fall became winter, it was clear that Judy was spinning out of control. Benita, the store manager whom Wanda had hired, was running the operation. If Judy showed up, it wasn't until late afternoon. She and Dwayne were deep in their drugs. Finally, in December, she fell out. She was on the phone in the back room of Hair Is Where It's At when we heard a loud thump. I ran back and saw Judy passed out on the floor. I called an ambulance. When we got to the ER, Irv was already there. Two days later, the doctor talked about the drugs they found in her system. That's when she promised her father that she'd go to Betty Ford.

Now, some four weeks after her release, I was trying to comfort her at Le Beef. I told her it was okay to cry. Crying was good for you. Ever since she got out of Betty Ford, Judy had been crying like crazy. She talked a kind of psychobabble that was hard to follow. She said she was in touch with feelings she never knew she had, but when she described those feelings they all came out like anger.

"Why the fuck should my father have stuck me with my mother?" she asked. "Why couldn't he have taken care of me? He knew she was a bitch. He knew that it was hell living in that house. He could have gotten me out of there. And so what happens—he dumps me and she takes all her goddamn bitchiness out on me. I'm just a nuisance to him."

"Didn't he come to Betty Ford during family day?"

"Yeah."

"And didn't your mom refuse?"

"She wouldn't walk across the street to help me."

"Well, doesn't his flying out to Arizona count for anything?"

"He didn't say much."

"But he was there. Look, Judy, I've gotten to know this man. I know he cares. I know he loves you."

"And killing Dwayne is his way of proving it."

"He didn't kill him."

"You don't know that."

Before I could say anything, a man with a curly gray wig came to our table. It looked to me like he had on eye shadow. He was wearing a purple silk shirt.

"Uncle Marsh," said Judy.

"How are you, my dear?"

"This is Power," she said. "He works for Dad."

"Power looks very powerful," Marsh said, looking me over. "I trust you're enjoying your dinner."

"Better than the food at Betty Ford," said Judy. "You do know that I was at Betty Ford last month?"

"Dear God, no," said Marsh. "I hadn't the slightest. How distressing."

"It was actually good. I'm in touch with my feelings."

"Well, I suppose that's good."

"Actually, I'm not sure, because right now I'm feeling you fucked my mother out of this restaurant. And when you fucked my mother, you fucked me."

Marsh flushed. "I'm afraid that your sense of history is distorted, my dear. Your mother had no interest in this restaurant."

"She used to run it," said Judy. "Then you pushed her out. I should be running it."

"Actually," said Marsh, "I should be running along. Nice to meet you, Mr. Power. Enjoy your evening."

When he was gone, Judy said, "Fuckin' fruitcake. He came running out of the closet the minute after their dad died. He's one of those evil fags."

"He seems polite."

"Because he thinks you're cute. If my father cared two shits about me, he'd get back this restaurant for me."

"You already have a beauty salon."

"It's running without me. I'm bored with the beauty salon. I like restaurants and by all rights this one should be mine. I'm gonna work on my father. For what he did to Dwayne, he owes me. Daddy owes me big-time. If he won't do this for me, I'll never forgive him."

"Judy, you gotta stop manipulating your father."

"My father's the biggest manipulator there is. You know that. You're manipulating him yourself."

"What are you talking about?"

"You got him to take you out of the beauty parlor and put you in the office so you can get closer to him. Everyone wants to get closer to him."

"That was his idea, not mine."

"You're saying that you didn't want out of Hair Is Where It's At?"

"I'm saying that I do what I'm told."

"Don't give me that Southern gentleman act. I don't buy that for a minute. You were told by my father never to fuck me again, weren't you? That's why you won't have sex with me, isn't it?"

"Me and your father never talked about that."

"Please, Power. Spare me the bullshit. You and my father talk about everything. You're the son he never had. You're the fuckin' golden boy. That's why he's got you sitting up in his office watching his every move. He's never let anyone do that. You're the only one he trusts. Well, trust me: If I don't get this restaurant to run, my father's got hell to pay. You tell him that."

"You tell him yourself."

"Fine. I'm also telling him that you can't keep your hands off me. That not only are you begging me to fuck you, you want to watch me and one of your girlfriends from the beauty parlor. You want to turn me into a freak."

"Tell him what you want, Judy."

"I want to order a drink."

"Don't."

"Don't tell me what to do."

"You drink and I'm out of here."

"Drinking was never my problem. It was the drugs. Drinking never did anything for me."

"So why order a drink?"

"Because I want to. Because this was my mother's restaurant and it should have been my restaurant and I can do any goddamn thing I want to do."

"Fine," I said, conceding.

Judy waved over the waiter. "Bring me a double martini."

"That's not going to help anything," I said.

"You gonna join me or make me drink alone?"

"Drink alone and eat alone. Later."

I got up and left. By the time I put on my scarf, hat, and overcoat and walked out the door, the temperature had dropped another ten degrees. The snow was still howling and the wind whipped around the corner and hit me in the face like God was angry, like God was telling me to get the hell out of Chicago.

"My dad came to Chicago in the dead of winter," said Irv Wasserman. "He came from Ukraine in Eastern Europe, where it was not safe for him and his family to live. Hatred was everywhere. My family was hunted like animals. My older sister was born in the old country and died a year after she arrived here. She could have been saved, but my parents didn't have money for the right doctor. I was born three years later. My father said I was a mistake."

It was early March and the weather had turned even colder. Irv and I were in the suite of Wasserman Enterprises on the seventy-first floor of the Hancock Building. Irv's corner office had a commanding view of a city blanketed in snow. He had given me a desk and chair, a smaller office that I shared with John Mackey. Mackey didn't seem to mind. He was a combination lawyer-accountant-secretary-manager-consigliere, a man of few words. He was pale, short, and addicted to skinny little cigars. He smoked them constantly. Irv told me that Mackey never stopped thinking.

"My mother said not to pay attention to my father," Wasserman continued, telling me stories that by now he'd told me at least two other times. I didn't mind, though. I liked listening to Irv. He talked in a singsong, hypnotic style.

"My mother said that I really wasn't a mistake, but I knew I was. My father never lied. He was a lousy businessman. He tried scrap metal but failed. From scrap metal he went into shellac. He and a partner started manufacturing shellac records. This partner, a man named Bender whose parents came from Poland, was shrewd. He wanted to do more than make the records. He knew that if he found and controlled the artists to sing on the records, more money would be made. The big record labels were ignoring the blues singers who had come to Chicago from the South. Bender saw that black people working the mills and the slaughterhouses went to nightclubs to hear these singers. Bender also loved the music. He knew the music. He went to those clubs, gave the singers a few dollars to sing in a studio, made the records, and sold them from the back of his 1943 Packard. Bender was the front man. My father was the worker. By the early fifties, serious money was being made but my father saw that Bender was hiding most of it in a secret account. They had words. Bender was a big burly man and intimidated my father. My mother scolded my father for being intimidated. A week later, he suffered what they called a nervous breakdown. He was never the same. When he recovered, he was a frightened man who Bender put in charge of taking inventory in the warehouse. Bender made millions while we barely survived. This happened when I was a small boy. I watched it."

"Didn't you wind up buying Bender Records?" I asked, pretending like I didn't know.

"There was nothing to buy. A year after my father passed—may he rest in peace—the warehouse burned down along with the manufacturing plant. Old man Bender had nothing but a roster of artists who hated him and were eager to record for someone willing to pay more. That someone was me."

"How old were you when you started Wasserman Records?"

"A little older than you, Power. Eighteen, maybe nineteen."

"Where'd you get the money?"

"I found partners. Enemies of Bender. Men he had been cheating."

"And they trusted someone so young?"

"I knew how to sell. I knew how to put on a suit and make a nice presentation. I was sincere. I told my investors I'd be working for them and my motivation was to double their money in a year. I accomplished that. I accomplished it by trusting the black man. A black man went to the clubs and told me which singers were the best. That's something I could never do for myself. Another black man wrote songs for these artists. And a very talented black man ran the recording studio. They were all well paid. To this day they will swear by me. They own their own homes. They have pension plans. They take their grandchildren on the Disney cruises. They go first-class."

"And the nightclubs came after the record company?"

"The nightclubs I wasn't all that personally involved in. They were investments. Good investments. You're too young to remember the disco era, but discos made money. Johnnie Meadows came out of disco. He sang in one of my discos. Then he had all those hits on my label. Big moneymaker. But he could never leave the broads alone. Broads were his downfall. That's why his goddamn wife was so angry—may she rot in jail."

"And rap and hip-hop—how did all that start?" I asked.

"Wasserman Records was not a good name for the new music. It was Judy who told me to call it Complex Music. She said the kids would relate. They did. It was the son of my studio engineer Aaron Kendle—Aaron Jr.—who was our first rapper. Little Aaron they called him. I didn't know what the fuck he was rapping about, but who cares when you get sales like Little Aaron got? Little Aaron also found the ChiBoyz. They had a run of hits when boy bands were big. Soon Little Aaron stopped rapping and became a full-time talent scout and producer. He discovered Hancock, the kid who named himself after this building, and last year he discovered Candy Girl. Candy Girl is the hottest thing going. I introduced you to Candy Girl, didn't I?"

"You did."

"She's a clever girl."

"Very."

"Sensational show-business talent."

"She's selling out the big arenas," I said.

"Next year the ballparks. I'm booking her into Yankee Stadium."

"Wow."

"Some guy is writing a book about her. Imagine writing a biography of a girl who's barely twenty-one. I don't want him writing it, though."

"How come?"

"Because Candy Girl is all about the mystery behind the crazy image. I don't want her unwrapped. The more mystery, the bigger the sales."

"Isn't she just a white girl from the burbs?"

"A fuckin' clever white girl who's got more ambition than Napoleon. That's why I love her. Before Judy went to Betty Ford, I was gonna have Judy work with her. But Judy was in no shape to work with anyone. Now when I mention it to Judy, Judy calls her a cheap whore. I think Judy's jealous of her. Have you seen Judy recently?"

"We ate at Le Beef."

"Why the hell did she pick that restaurant?"

"She wants you to buy it for her so she can run it."

"My crazy goddamn daughter. It wasn't enough to have a crazy wife. But to have a daughter who got all her mother's craziness—it's too much. I'm not doing it. I'm drawing the line."

"She thinks—"

"I know what she thinks. She thinks it's because of me that her meathead boyfriend got killed."

Irv stopped talking. I waited for him to deny it. Until now, I was pretty sure, given what I had seen at the gym, that one of those shady steroid cats had murdered Dwayne. Now I wasn't so sure. At the same time, I wasn't about to ask. The silence hung over us. Irv took several sighs before he started talking again.

"Look, Power, your uncle—or whatever he is to you—sent you here to learn. You've been a good kid. I like you. You been good to me and you been good to my daughter. You listen and you know when to shut up. So I'm going to tell you everything I know. It ain't that much. It couldn't fill a book. It couldn't even fill a chapter in a book. Here's what it comes down to: They say family comes first, but family fucks you. I was a mistake to my family. My father didn't want me, and I knew that every day of my life. My father fucked me up. Then, careful as I was before marrying, my wife fucked me up. Now you see my daughter is fucking me up. Families are supposed to be for comfort, but families are horror shows. Don't marry, Power. Don't ever get married. Don't get involved with family. You stay clear of family and your mind stays clear. You need a clear mind if you're going into Slim's business. Slim has stores and car washes and other thriving businesses. Slim is local. I met Slim when I needed an Atlanta connection for some of my thriving businesses. Slim helped me, so I'm helping him by helping you. I'm telling you to stay local. I'm in Chicago, I'm in Cleveland, I'm in Detroit. With this hip-hop business, I'm all over the map. It's too much. I have too many people I have to trust. You understand what I'm saying?"

"Stay local and keep it simple."

"You put it beautifully. Local can be lucrative. Local can be more lucrative than national because national can drain you. I worry all the time because I got so much shit to worry about. Especially my daughter. I've tried to make her happy. You've seen that. No father has tried harder. But if you ask me, Power, how to get ahead in this business, I'm telling you find one, maybe two people you can trust and stop there. If you need more than two, your business is too big. Right now my business is too big. And what do I got to show for it? Fancy houses, fancy office, fancy car. But a crazy ex-wife and a crazy daughter. And aggravation."

I wanted to say something to make Irv feel better, but I didn't know what to say. The man always talked about aggravation. There was no talking him out of it. And I knew what he meant about his business. I saw all the different operations that spread in different directions. He had let me sit in on certain meetings where he faced the guys who ran his nightclubs, his management firm, his hip-hop label, and his booking agency. He kept me out of meetings where he talked about his "other" operations. I never asked him what they were.

I saw how Irv questioned all his lieutenants closely. I saw how he wrestled with the business of trust. He didn't want to trust anyone, but he had no choice. Take the hip-hop label. He told me that he didn't really trust the label president, a man he had personally hired, so he put in another guy under the president. The second guy was there as Irv's watchdog, but after a couple of weeks, Irv began having doubts about the watchdog. What if the watchdog had been bought off by the president? What if the two of them were devising schemes to skim off the top? Of course John Mackey was there to oversee everything. Irv trusted John Mackey with his life. Mackey's loyalty couldn't be questioned. After all, Irv had made Mackey a millionaire many times over. When it came to numbers, Irv said that Mackey was a genius. Mackey was ten steps ahead of everyone.

But even Mackey made mistakes. Irv told me about how it was him, not Mackey, who figured out how their outside public relations firm had been billing them at twice their normal rates. Mackey didn't know anything about public relations, but Irv did. Irv realized his profile in that city had to be positive—and that would take work. But he also knew that was no reason for a PR firm to jack up their rates. He found this out by comparing bills with his friend Cooper Newberry, president of Great Lakes Bank. Newberry, who had once been indicted by the Feds, used the same PR firm. When the charges didn't stick, Newberry needed help to restore his image. "I wouldn't give two shits about image," Irv told me, "if a bad image didn't hurt business."

During these different business meetings with his underbosses, Irv didn't talk much. He listened closely. He kept a yellow pad on his desk and took notes with a fancy Montblanc fountain pen. The notes were mainly questions. When the underboss was done reporting, the questions came quickly.

"How did you get that figure?"

"How does this year's gross compare to last year's?"

"Why did you raise that rate?"

"Why did you lower that one?"

"What are the projected earnings?"

"What are the projected losses?"

"Where's the fuckin' backup data?"

"Why don't you know how the competition's numbers stack up against us?"

I watched as the men sitting across from Irv's desk squirmed. The cross-examination was rough, and if the answers didn't come in a timely fashion, or if the answers didn't come at all, that underboss would be replaced within a few days. The revolving door never stopped revolving.

Spring

It was April of the following year when I thought I saw Beauty walking into an upscale mall on Michigan Avenue. She was walking through a revolving door. I was a half block away, and as soon as I saw her, I started to sprint. Even before I saw her, the day felt good. Winter was turning to spring and the sun was finally out in force. I was full of energy. As the weather got warmer, Irv got crazier—and so did Judy. But the more they talked about their problems and the louder they became, the more I learned to tune them out. Or at least separate myself from the drama.

In mid-March, for example, when Judy's uncle Marsh was run over by a speeding pickup truck as he was walking across Rush Street, his restaurant business went into disarray and, at a rock-bottom price, Irv was able to buy the Le Beef location that Judy wanted. The driver and the pickup truck that killed her uncle were never found. Irv gave Le Beef to Judy but only on the condition that she enroll in a management school at a business college in downtown Chicago. She agreed. She hated the school and called it a waste of time until she a met a teacher, a California surfer-type guy in his thirties, and coaxed him into bed.

Meanwhile, during meetings with his underbosses Irv seemed on edge. He was more suspicious than usual. Once or twice, he lost his temper when the answers to his questions didn't come quickly enough. Irv had always told me how important it was to contain your temper. A couple of times he called me at night just to retell all the stories about his mother, father, and former wife that he had told me before. When he took me to opening day at Wrigley Field, he hardly watched the game. That was unusual because Irv loved his Cubbies. He spent the whole time on his cell phone talking to John Mackey. When the food didn't arrive at his private box behind home plate, he started yelling. I started wondering what was happening. I also wondered if at some point Irv would turn on me. After all, I didn't do much real work. I sat in the office with Mackey and got a pretty good idea of how the operation worked but had no real duties. "That's how it should be," Irv said. "Your job is watch and learn. Not do."

There was change in the air, and I couldn't tell which way the wind was blowing. Then, out of nowhere, I spotted Beauty. At least I thought it was her. When I saw her walk into the big store on Michigan Avenue, I felt my heart hammering. I'd dreamed of her just the night before. In the dream she was looking for me on some lonely beach. Well, here in real life she had found me. I ran into the mall and by the time I went through the revolving door, she was out of sight. The mall was crawling with people. There was a giant atrium and four floors of stores and restaurants. I looked in every direction but she wasn't there. I started on the ground floor and raced in and out of every dress shop and shoe salon in sight. Then I went to the next level. I looked in the jewelry stores, the stationery stores, everywhere. I ran through Macy's like a track star, and when I had covered the entire department store, I retraced my steps and started all over again. She had to be there. I had to find her. She was looking for me just like she had been looking for me in last night's dream.

After a while, I knew I had to pace myself or I'd use up all my energy. I stopped running and started walking. But I was looking just as hard. From behind, every tall, dark-haired, fashionably dressed female was Beauty. When I caught up and saw her face, though, my heart sank. The disappointment only made me more determined. I stalked the mall like a madman. Finally, after two hours, I had to admit defeat. I had to tell myself that maybe it wasn't Beauty after all. In chasing after her, I'd convinced myself that she was in Chicago because she knew I was there. She was looking for me. But that was more like one of my dreams than real life. I had to call Wanda for a reality check.

"Wanda," I said on the phone, "am I dreaming or did I see Beauty here in Chicago walking through a mall today? Is she in Chicago?"

"Honey," said Wanda, "that child is living her own life. I have no idea where she is and where she isn't. How's Hair Is Where It's At? They making money?"

"All reports are good."

"And when you coming home, Power? Slim's missing you like crazy."

"Oh, come on . . ."

"For real."

"Your friend Anita Ward must say something to you about Beauty," I said.

"She says she's doing just fine. She's in school."

"Which school? What's it called?"

"I got no details, baby. I got nothing for you but love, Power. You're one story, and Beauty's another. I wouldn't wait for her to come back."

"Come back where? To Atlanta? To Chicago?"

"I don't know if she's in Chicago, sugar. I told you that."

"But I saw her, Wanda. I saw the girl with my own eyes."

"How's the white girl with the cute figure? Judy—isn't that her name? She was a doll, and, from what I saw, she had her eye on you."

"She's crazy."

"What woman isn't? But at least this one is crazy rich."

"If Beauty calls looking for me, please give her this number."

"Of course, baby."

Just before my nineteenth birthday in August, I was worried enough about Irv to call Slim.

"He's forgetting stuff," I told Slim. "Yesterday he forgot my name."

"Old age does that to motherfuckers," said Slim. "I can see my own memory starting to slip."

"I'm used to him telling me the same stories three or four times, but now he's telling those stories four times in the same hour. I think it's time to get out of here. I think he's losing it."

"I'll call him. If you can't be useful to him anymore, you right. Time to get out of Dodge."

Next day Slim called back.

"Irv says he needs you more than ever," said Slim.

"Needs me for what?" I asked.

"You comfort him. Irv's a nigga lover and you his nigga."

"There's not much for me to do."

"Whatever it is, do it. If he needs you to hold his dick when he takes a piss, you hold it. I owe him. He'll let you know when he doesn't need you anymore."

I usually got to the office of Wasserman Enterprises at around nine. Irv normally showed up at ten. But on the first Monday of October, it was eleven A.M. and the boss wasn't there. John Mackey and I were sitting in Mackey's little office. I was reading about the World Series on my MacBook Pro. Mackey was looking over spreadsheets on his desktop Dell.

"You hear from Irv?" I asked.

"He's not feeling well," said Mackey, staying focused on the numbers dancing across his computer screen.

"Anything serious?"

"With Irv everything is serious."

I wasn't sure what that meant. But because John Mackey was not a man who invited conversation—or even a single simple question—it didn't feel right to ask him anything else. So I went back to reading about baseball. Once in a while I'd look up and sneak a peek at Mackey. I didn't know anything about him except that Irv said he was a genius. I didn't know if he was Jewish or Irish. He had an Irish name but a Jewish nose. His nose was too wide for his thin face. He wore a coat and tie every day. I saw that he picked out his outfits carefully. If he wore a brown sports coat and slacks, he'd have on brown shoes. His ties always contrasted nicely with his shirts. His clothes weren't cheap. Because of his slight frame, his clothes looked too big on him, but they had a nice drape. He picked out expensive fabrics. His only piece of jewelry was a thin Cartier watch from back in the day. It had to be an antique and was probably worth a fortune. His rimless eyeglass frames were slightly tinted so I couldn't tell the color of his eyes. After a half hour or so he said to me, "It's getting on noon. I better call him again."

He picked up his phone, dialed, and waited a long while.

"He's not picking up," he said. "That's not good."

"Have you noticed how he's repeating things?" I asked.

"He's been doing that for some time," he said.

"But lately it's gotten worse."

"I've noticed," Mackey agreed. "He's under a lot of pressure. This business with Le Beef and his daughter is madness."

"But isn't there always pressure?" I asked.

"There's pressure and there's *pressure*," said Mackey. "At his age the pressure is harder to take."

"Do you think he has some disease?"

"What kind of disease?"

"Alzheimer's."

"My older brother has Alzheimer's."

"Is he acting like Irv?" I asked.

"You have to understand, no one acts like Irv. Irv is not your normal man and he does not have normal sicknesses. Sometimes he acts sick to put you off guard. While you think he's not looking, he's looking closer than ever. Don't take anything for granted with Irv. Don't fool yourself into thinking that you know him."

For the all the time I had been coming to the office, this was the most serious thing that Mackey had ever said to me. I wasn't sure why he had started talking this way. Maybe he was really worried about his boss and the worry got him to jabbering.

"Do you know how I met Irv?" he asked.

"No."

"I went to law school. You knew I was a lawyer, didn't you?"

"I guessed you were."

"You guessed right. I was editor of the law review at Yale. After graduation, I was recruited by the most prestigious firm in Chicago. My father was also a lawyer but unsuccessful. He was a brilliant man who died a pauper."

"How did that happen?"

"Gambling. My father was a degenerate gambler. He couldn't leave the casino until he was completely wiped out. He brought shame to our family. When he was forty, he shot himself. My mother raised five sons alone."

I didn't say anything. I just waited for Mackey to continue. I could see he was just getting warmed up.

"My dad wanted me to take it further than he had—but I set my sights even higher. I was going to be a lawyer's lawyer. I saw myself on the Supreme Court. Corporate law was merely the jumping-off point.

From there I'd win a political appointment, I'd advance my way through the system, I'd become a judge, I'd climb to the top of Mount Everest. But early on I ran into some problems at the firm. One of the partners disliked me. To this day I don't know why. I suspect he was a closeted homosexual who desired me, but I can't say that for sure."

I couldn't see John Mackey being the object of anyone's desire. But naturally I didn't say a word.

"In any event, the man had it out for me. He resented my intelligence and conspired to make me look bad. This went on for years. I pleaded my case with the other partners, but they were loyal to my nemesis, who was also the controlling partner. There was little I could do. Wasserman Enterprises happened to be one of our clients and, in a junior capacity, I was asked to do some work for Irv. At a time in my professional life when I was being maligned, Irv saw my potential. He kept saying, 'Mackey, you're the smartest fuckin' lawyer over there. You should be running that place.' After a year of watching me, he proposed that I leave the firm and work for him. Wasserman Enterprises was growing by leaps and bounds. He needed an in-house lawyer. I became that lawyer. And given his spreading operation, I soon became much more. I worked fourteen, sixteen hours a day. There was nothing I would not do for this man whose business savvy was exceeded only by his generosity."

"When did you go to work for him?"

"Twenty-five years ago."

"That's a long time."

"A very long time."

"And you know him better than anyone in the world."

"I know him very well indeed."

"So do you think he's really sick or what?" I asked.

"I'm worried. He's missing appointments. He's making careless mistakes with associates. He's telling me to write checks to people who shouldn't be getting checks."

"What are you going to do?" I asked.

"What can I do? I'll do all I can to protect him. I owe the man my professional life. I owe him everything."

"Do you think he knows that he isn't right?"

"Irv never discusses his health. At least he never has. He keeps his personal life personal. He doesn't even talk about his daughter with me the way he does with you."

I didn't know what to say, so I said nothing.

"His daughter is poison," said Mackey. "She's the reason he's struggling right now. She has him tied around her little finger. I suspect you've seen that for yourself."

I still kept quiet.

Mackey went on. "He needs to be rid of her. He needs to give her one last big check and tell her to get lost."

"Do you have kids of your own?" I asked.

"No wife, no kids. When I started working here the first advice Irv gave me was not to have a family. He said that a family would be the bane of my existence. He said this even before he got married, before Judy was born. Then he met that woman and he went against his own wisdom. He has obviously paid a terrible price."

Mackey's face turned slightly red. He had really worked himself up into a state.

"I'm going over to his place," he said. "You may want to come with me."

The black woman who worked for Irv was named Dottie. She had been there for years and liked to boss him around. He didn't mind. She was a big lady who didn't take shit from anyone. She scolded him when he was late for dinner and when he didn't eat his vegetables. She cooked his meals, laundered his clothes, and cleaned his house. She was older than him but had the energy of someone twenty years younger. Dottie was a tornado.

When we got to Irv's Lake Shore Drive apartment, Dottie was crying. Her chubby cheeks were wet with tears.

"Something's wrong, Mr. Mackey, something's real wrong. When I went in this morning to wake him up, he didn't know who I was."

"Dear God," said Mackey.

"Then he asked when his mother was coming from the cemetery. How was I supposed to answer that, Mr. Mackey? What was I supposed to say?"

"There's nothing to say, Dottie. You're doing the best you can."

"You two go on in there," she said. "I pray he snaps out of it. I pray that Mr. Wasserman knows who you are."

The apartment was huge. Long hallways and lots of bedrooms. Wood walls and heavy carpets. Old furniture. Paintings of flowers and fruits on the wall. His bedroom was at the end of the longest hallway. Mackey knocked.

"You don't have to knock!" Irv shouted behind closed doors. "Come on in!"

Mackey opened the door. He went in first.

"Did you bring me the meat?" Irv asked. Wearing a pair of black silk pajamas, he was sitting up in bed.

"What meat?" Mackey asked.

"The butcher doesn't know what meat? What good is the butcher if he can't bring the best cut of meat?"

Mackey's eyes were shot through with concern. I could feel him suffering. This shit was so sad.

"Is this your son?" he said, looking at me. "Is this the butcher's son I've heard so much about? I can't tell you what I've heard, but I know it wasn't good. He's supposed to be a good boy, but he's not. You can't trust this boy—not for a fuckin' minute. Come over, kid. Come right over here."

I went to stand by Irv's side.

"Lean your head this way," he said.

He took my head in his hands and whispered in my ear. "Go home. Get the fuck out of here and go home. It's time for you to go home."

I kept quiet. So did Mackey. A few seconds later, Irv closed his eyes and began to snore. We waited awhile before quietly walking out of the room. When we got to the foyer, Dottie was waiting for us.

"Judy's mother just called," she said. "Judy went out again. She went out on the wild. She's back in the hospital. Her mama doesn't know what to do. I told her that Mr. Wasserman wasn't no good to hear any of this. She said I had to tell him. But how can I tell him?"

"You can't," said Mackey. "Just leave it all to me."

"How do you lose your mind?" asked Dottie. "How do you have your mind one day and lose it the next?"

Mackey mentioned his brother. He told Dottie that he had seen this happen before. He told Dottie that, no matter what, she would be taken care of. Everyone would be taken care of.

"And what do you think I should do?" I asked.

"What did he tell you when he was whispering in your ear?" asked Mackey.

"He said to go home."

"Then go home. That's probably the last sensible thing he'll ever say."

"Premature Ejaculation"

I saw the words written on a medical report that Slim had put in the garbage. I was looking for a receipt that I thought I had thrown away by mistake when I noticed "premature ejaculation" on a piece of paper. Don't ask me why, but it jumped out at me. The report was from a Dr. Tavis Harrison. I googled "premature ejaculation" and it didn't take long to learn that's what they call it when a dude cums too soon. "For some men," I read, "the very sight of a naked woman can excite them to the point of orgasm." Another posting said, "There are serious psychological consequences for men whose inability to sustain sexual intercourse results in a perpetual inability to satisfy their partners. The result is often frustration, shame, and even violent rage."

I went back to the report and saw that Slim's real name—Charles Simmons—was typed out as the patient. And underneath was all this stuff about premature ejaculation—how "the patient has complained of this disorder," how "this disorder has apparently plagued the patient for much of his life," how "repeated psychopharmacological medicines had yielded no positive results," and how "the patient has refused clinical psychiatric remedies."

After reading it four or five times, I tore up the report in tiny pieces and took it out to the trash. I felt like it was something I shouldn't have read, something I shouldn't know. I did read it and now I knew. Slim couldn't fuck right. It was like Slim couldn't fuck at all. I didn't want to, but I had to think about my mother. I'd done a good job all this time since her death of not thinking about her at all, but this was different. I knew she had been Slim's girlfriend. Or at least I figured she had. Why else would he be treating me like I was his son? Maybe sex wasn't important to my mother. Maybe sex wasn't important to Slim. But if it wasn't important, he sure did act like it was. Ever since I got back from Chicago, it seemed like Slim was showing off his women. Every night he had a different one at the house. He liked them big and busty. He liked them ten or fifteen or twenty years younger than him. He liked them all made up with lots of blue eye shadow and long eyelashes and ruby-red lipstick. He liked dark black women and pale white women and sometimes women from Mexico. There was a Chinese woman he brought home who couldn't speak English.

The morning after, if he saw me in the kitchen eating a bowl of Cheerios for breakfast or a cheese sandwich for lunch, he liked to say, "See that bitch who ran through here last night?"

"I saw her."

"What'd you think?"

"She was pretty," I'd always say.

"Man, that heifer couldn't get enough. It's one thing to bone a bitch twice in a night. I'm used to that. But three or four times, I mean, give a brotha a break. I ain't complaining, though, boy. You do what you gotta do. Besides, fucking overtime keeps me young. No, sir, ain't complaining at all. Matter of fact, got another one coming over tonight who's fine enough to make you wanna slap your mama."

When Slim talked this way, I never paid much attention. In a smooth way, Slim liked to brag about lots of stuff—his money, all the people who worked for him, all the smart moves he made. Hard as I tried, he still beat me at chess on a regular basis and loved to brag about that. I let him. I saw it made him feel good and that was fine with me. But now I had to wonder about his women.

The night after I tore up the report he was giving a party. Mo Turner, a dude Slim had known his whole life, was turning fifty. Mo owned a fleet of taxis—I think Slim might have bankrolled him—and Mo liked to party. He was a short squat cat, no taller than five feet three, with a full head of hair glistening with gel and a Bluetooth stuck in his left ear. The Bluetooth was studded with diamonds. Mo also loved cigars, the longer the better. A cigar was always sticking out of his mouth. He was a happy-go-lucky man who'd been married six or seven times. Slim would always say, "Some ho throws a hot fuck on Mo and Mo thinks it's forever. Mo thinks good pussy equals true love. Mo's a fuckin' fool when it comes to the bitches, but Mo's my man. You wanna have a good time, you wanna have a good laugh, you call Mo."

Usually I skipped these parties. The guests were the older crowd and I felt out of place. To Slim's credit, though, he always let me know I was welcome. "Boy," he'd say, "this is your house as much as mine. You part of everything I do, the good and the bad. And tonight, we gonna be bad." I'd drop in to say hi to Slim's guests. I'd make a quick appearance so as not to offend Slim. But then, when the old-school jams started and everyone started dancing like old-school fools, I'd skip out.

This time, though, I paid a little more attention to the guests. There were some friends and even married couples from back in the day, but there were more single women than usual. It looked to me like Slim had hired some professionals as birthday gifts to Mo. What made them seem like pros was that they didn't act like pros. They dressed cool and spoke well and acted like they could be managers at the local bank. I knew, though, by the way they made a beeline for Mo that Slim had arranged this special birthday treat. It was funny to see these gorgeous ladies, some of them nearly six feet tall, tower over Mo. "Mo likes to mountain-climb up those long-legged bitches," Slim whispered to me. "Look at the smile on that motherfucker's face."

I was just about to go out to the garage apartment when Wanda arrived along with Dre and his wife, Gloria.

"Br–br–br–br–brother Power," said Dre. "Haven't s–s–s–seen you since you g–g–g–g–got back from Chicago. Everything cool?"

"Everything's cool."

"How's my m–m–m–m–man I–I–I–I–I–Irv?"

"Having some health problems."

"Hate to h–h–h–h–h–hear that. H–h–h–h–h–he's beautiful people, ain't he?"

"Beautiful," I agreed. "And talking about beautiful, here's your beautiful wife and the beautiful Wanda."

"Boy," said Wanda, "last time I saw you in Chicago you were working in a beauty salon. I didn't know you were running a charm school as well."

I smiled and gave Wanda a hug. She had on a blond wig with black bangs where the sides flipped out in opposite directions like the wings of a bird. In her green satin dress, Wanda looked like she was about to fly. Not to be outdone, Dre was done up in a mustard-colored sharkskin suit and matching gator shoes.

"Are those d–d–d–d–d–diamonds Mo has in his Bluetooth?" asked Dre.

"You best believe his ice is cold," said Slim, who came over to greet the guests.

Wanda took me aside. "You on your way out?" she asked.

"Figured I better get some rest."

"Everything turn out okay in Chicago?"

"The old man isn't exactly seeing things right."

"Old age will do that to you. Besides, men are funny," she said.

There was something about Wanda that always made me feel good. I knew I could trust her. Her spirit was warm and loving. And even when she didn't tell me things—like how Beauty was doing up in New York—I got the sense she wanted to. She genuinely cared.

"Can we walk outside for a second?" I asked her.

"Sure thing."

We strolled over to a little patio area to the right of the big house. The night air was warm and the half-moon looked close enough to touch.

"I wanna ask you something that I know you'll keep to yourself," I said.

"Naturally, sugar. Everyone knows Wanda can be trusted. Wanda knows how to keep a secret."

"Well, this isn't exactly a secret. It's a question. Do you think Slim's a normal man?"

Wanda laughed. "Baby doll, ain't no man who's normal."

"I mean, normal in the physical way. In the sexual way."

"Do you mean is he a sissy? Oh, no, Power, Slim ain't no sissy."

"I know he's not gay. I wasn't wondering about that. I was just wondering whether he had some problems in doing it with women."

"What makes you think something like that?" Wanda asked.

"I saw a medical report."

"What you doing pokin' in Slim's private papers?"

"I found it in the garbage."

"Then leave it in the garbage. Ain't none of your concern."

"It just made me curious and I was wondering—"

"Look, Power, there's a lot about Slim that makes folks wonder. But I know the man. Been knowing him a good part of my life. Been working for him a good part of my life. Been praying for him a good part of my life. There's a lot to him. He got lots of sides, lots of angles, lots of good points and some points that ain't so good. You know what I'm talkin' 'bout. So my advice is to do what you been doing. Let the Lord lead you. The Lord put this man in your life, and the Lord is protecting you. Slim's protecting you. That's a beautiful thing, so keep it beautiful, child, but stay out of his garbage. And I do mean garbage. You feel me?"

"Yes, ma'am."

Next thing we heard was Slim calling everyone into the dining room to sing Mo "Happy Birthday." A huge cake, covered with five diamonds carved of frosting, was carried out of the kitchen and placed on the table.

"Before we start singing," said Slim, "I want to ask Dre, one of Mo's closest friends, to say a few words on his behalf. Dre . . ."

I could see Dre's body react nervously.

"I-I-I-I-I j-j-j-j-just w-w-w-w-w-w—"

"Spit it out, boy!" Slim cried.

By now everyone, even those who tried to stop themselves, was laughing at Dre. Naturally the one laughing hardest was Slim.

That night I didn't sleep well. The noise from the party was loud enough to keep me up. I kept falling in and out of a dream about Beauty. The dream kept changing. In one dream, she was living in a high-rise in Chicago. In the next dream, she was sitting in the back of a taxi and I was following her on a Harley. I never could catch her. In the last dream, she was water-skiing on a lake surrounded by snow-capped mountains. She was wearing a black bikini and her hair was blowing in the breeze. A big storm came up. Lightning was everywhere. She got washed away, and the last thing I remembered before waking up was frantically swimming in the middle of the sea, looking everywhere for Beauty and not being able to find her.

I was still looking for her when a loud knock snapped my dream.

"Hey, boy, you alone in there?"

It was Slim. "I'm alone," I said. "Come on in."

He walked in and sat in a chair across from my bed. Even early in the morning, he was clean. He was rocking a yellow Gucci tracksuit and fresh white Prada sneakers. His matching diamond wristbands caught the rays of the sun streaming in the window. His cologne was so strong I almost choked.

"Sleeping in, boy?" he asked.

"Bad dreams."

"I don't ever dream," said Slim. "Don't need to. I'm living my dream. And last night was like a wet dream come true. You see that tall bitch with them crazy cornrows?"

"Not sure I noticed."

"You had to notice. She was the one with the wiggle and walk that had every head turning. I'm telling you, last night she was the finest thing in the state of Georgia. Last night she was Georgia on my mind and Georgia in my bed. I nearly broke that bad girl in half, that's what I did. Power, I should be slowing down. Man my age shouldn't be rocking it hard as I'm rocking it. But what can I do? If it's in you, it's got to come out."

"I guess so," I said.

"Where's your board?" Slim asked, meaning the chessboard.

"In the closet," I said. "You wanna play?"

"Only if you wanna lose."

Slim had a habit of waking me up early to play chess. He knew I wasn't a morning person. Just after waking, my head's foggy and my mind's not too sharp.

"Can't wait till this afternoon?" I asked.

"You'll be gone this afternoon."

"I will be?"

"You got a plane to catch."

"Where am I going?"

"I'll tell you after I whip your ass."

Slim did whip my ass. It took him a little longer than he wanted it to, but he cornered me. He outthought me. Try as I might, I couldn't shake the cobwebs from my sleepy eyes.

"Don't wanna hear no excuses from you," he said. "Good chess player is ready to get it on, morning, noon, and night. And, boy, you got a ways to go."

"You gonna tell me where I'm going today?"

Slim walked over to my kitchenette and opened the refrigerator.

"You don't got shit to eat in here, boy."

"Try to stay lean and mean," I said.

Slim patted his stomach. He was vain about getting fat. "Never had this problem before," he said. "But I'm gonna cut out that sweet stuff and be back in shape in no time. Just a question of will. Never had no problems with willpower before and don't see no reason why I should have any problems now. If I can satisfy the bitches, that should be enough. I get me all the sweet pussy I need. I don't need to be eating like a youngblood. I can push back the bread and the potatoes. You watch, Power. When you get back, I'm gonna be leaner and meaner than you."

"Where am I going?"

"Like I keep telling you, youngbloods need schooling. I've told you that before, haven't I, boy?"

"You have."

"Irv was a righteous teacher, wasn't he?"

"He was," I said.

"Well, time for the next lesson. You ready?"

"I am."

"Had enough of that ass-freezing Chicago weather?"

"Yes, sir."

"Then how does Miami Beach sound to you?"

"Real good, Slim. Sounds real good."

Slim didn't say another word. In his ultra-cool way, he just smiled, reached deep into his pocket, fished out a boarding pass, and handed it to me.

"Your plane leaves at eight tonight. You're gonna love Sugar. And Sugar's gonna love you, especially when Sugar sees what you got for him."

Sugar

It was short plane ride, but the envelope that Slim gave me to give to Sugar was burning a hole in my pocket. It was thin, so I knew it wasn't cash. I figured it was a check, but it was sealed so I couldn't open it. When Slim had handed it to me, I'd asked him what was inside.

"Want you to be surprised," he said. "Want Sugar surprised too. All I can say is that when he opens it, you'll see a motherfucker smiling."

"What's Sugar like?" I asked. "Is he an old-timer like Irv?"

"You'll see him at the airport."

"He's coming to pick me up?"

"He's coming to pick up the envelope," said Slim. "You just happen to be the cat carrying it."

All during the flight, I kept fingering the envelope, holding it to the light, trying to see what I could see. I couldn't see anything.

When I landed in Miami and walked down to baggage claim, I spotted a Hispanic man in his sixties or seventies wearing a straw hat and looking like he was waiting for an arriving passenger. He had an unlit cigar in his mouth and a bored look on his face. His loud print shirt had flowers and palm trees all over it, and I got the idea he wanted to hurry up and find whoever he was waiting for so he could go outside and light his cigar. His pinky ring held a small diamond that had me believing he was my man.

"Sugar?" I asked him. "Are you Sugar Ruiz?"

He looked at me like I was crazy before saying, *"No habla ingles."*

I figured that, like Irv, he probably liked to play it low-key. Just as I was about to approach him again, I felt a tap on my shoulder before hearing the words "I'm Sugar Ruiz."

I turned around and looked in the face of a man in his twenties with a big broad smile and crazy green eyes—I mean deep green, fluorescent green, green so blazing that it was hard to look right at him. I felt almost blinded by the blaze. He had a big gap between his front teeth and shiny slick black hair carefully combed back. He was of average weight and average height but dressed extra dope: baby-blue Akoo driftwood shorts with cargo pockets running up and down the legs; an orange, blue, and green Akoo polo shirt that gave him a preppy edge; and butter-soft leather Ferragamo penny loafers worn without socks. Where you usually slip in pennies, Sugar had slipped in flashy green stones that looked like emeralds. I wondered if they were real.

"Hey, man, you must be Power," he said. "You gotta be Slim's boy."

"Right."

"Well, *bienvenido a* Miami, my brother. Let's roll."

"I got luggage."

"Give me the claim check and I'll make sure it's sent to the place."

"What place?"

"Sugar's Shack."

"Is that where I'm staying?"

"Hombre," he said, "that's where you be living."

Five minutes later I was sitting next to him in a black Lamborghini with thin red pinstripes running around the sides and up and down the trunk. The top was down and the night air was sweet. On that evening of my arrival, there wasn't anything in Miami that didn't look sweet. Women were waving at us. Women were everywhere. Palm trees were swaying, music bumping, music coming out of the cars on the causeway. The city seemed to be dancing to a beat that couldn't or wouldn't stop. Sugar lit a joint, passed it to me. I refused.

"You kidding?" he asked. "This is primo like you never known primo before."

"Makes me tired," I explained. "Makes me paranoid."

"Makes me happy," he said. "Energy. Creativity. Filters out the bad and makes the good even better. One hit is all you need. This is a special occasion, bro, so let's mark the occasion. You're about to see shit you never seen before. Open up your eyes. Open up your taste buds. Open up your heart. Life down here is a whole lot different than conservative old-school Georgia. Get ready, baby. Take a hit."

I figured, *What the fuck*. I took a hit. A very little hit, and suddenly the night got even brighter. The hum of the Lamborghini was like a sexy song by Sade. The twinkling stars in the sky looked like diamonds I could touch. The moon over Miami was fluorescent white. A week before Thanksgiving, and the weather was like summer. I felt like we were on a jet stream, no turbulence, just smooth sailing ahead, boats and yachts bobbling in the marinas, high-rises hugging the beach, fancy old hotels and hip new hotels lining up Collins Avenue, South Beach a colony of soft-skinned tan women in tiny skirts and too-tight shorts, little halter tops and skimpy blouses blowing in the breeze, women looking like superstar models, actresses, athletic women in perfect shape, women with perfect form, women walking like they owned the world, women giving off fragrances that had my head spinning, women coming up to the car at every stop sign and red light. Looked like Sugar knew every woman in town.

Sugar's Shack was a nightclub/hotel/condo high-rise situated at the southern tip of South Beach on Ocean Drive. I later learned that Sugar had hired a guy named Ortega Bouza, a world-famous Barcelona architect well-known for his super-funky style. The Shack was a thin building some twenty-five stories high designed out of pieces of rock and colored stones and sheet metal. The windows were all uneven and various shapes—circles and triangles and crazy oblongs. In between the rocks, stones, and metals were tubes of neon in candy colors like red, orange, and lime green. Maybe it was because I was blasted on grass, but the building looked like something a schoolkid might have drawn in his art class—but a cool kid.

"This is it," said Sugar. "This is the Shack."

"No sign in front?" I asked.

"No need. It's invitation-only."

On the ground floor the doors were wide open but a line of security guards protected them. The security guards were gorgeous women well over six feet, the kind who win volleyball championships. They were wearing khaki army shorts that showed off their long muscular legs. The minute they spotted Sugar, they stood at attention and gave him a smart salute. I watched as he went up and kissed each luscious chick on both cheeks.

I followed him through the first-floor club that had the same look as the outside of the building—cut-off pieces of blazing neon; walls made of metal, rocks, and brightly colored stones; tables of rough granite and chunks of slate; chairs of orange-Popsicle plastic; a dance floor made of burnt cork; and so many dazzling women with flashing smiles that I got dizzy and had to sit down when we reached Sugar's office in the back.

I had never seen an office with black leather walls before. The carpet was some kind of black suede. Sugar's desk was a shiny black Steinway grand piano. The keyboard had been ripped out and replaced by a flat plane where Sugar put his phone and computer. He said the massive chandelier hanging over the piano had been taken from the Hotel Nacional in Cuba just after Castro came to power. I later learned that Sugar's people came from Cuba.

We were alone in his office when he leaned back in the red leather judge's chair behind his desk and said, "Want another hit?"

"No, man," I said. "I'm already wasted."

"Did I say primo or did I say primo?"

"You said primo."

"Slim said he gave you an envelope."

"I got it."

"Before you give it to me, let's mark the occasion with a special treat."

"We already marked the occasion with a special treat."

"This is a better treat," said Sugar, opening a drawer and pulling out a small jewel box. He dumped the contents of the jewel box on a small mirror that sat atop his piano-desk.

"It's among the world's finest," he said, referring to the small quantity of cocaine spread over the mirror. "You need very little. The truth, man, is that I do very little of this stuff. I keep my distance. I know how to handle it. I'm an expert at this product. I should be. I've been selling it since I was a kid. There's nothing about this product I don't know. I know that you can't fuck with it much. The first hit is always heaven, but you gotta be smart enough to know you'll never get back to heaven. You land in heaven, you look the fuck around, you get out. That's it. One hit. Not one night or one week or one month or one year or one lifetime looking to get back to heaven. That's why cokeheads end up broke or dead. They think they can live in heaven. You can't. All you can do, hombre, is make a quick visit. So tonight, to celebrate meeting my new brother-man Power and his special delivery from Mr. Slim Simmons, we gonna take a quick trip to heaven. You ready?"

I wasn't sure how the blow, on top of the grass, would work on me. But given my already fogged-over state, I didn't have the energy to argue.

We went down on the coke and came up smiling. I came up clear.

My dizziness was gone and, at least in my mind, I felt like I understood absolutely everything in the world. Everything was in order. All the dust was blown out of my brain. My brain was working overtime. I suddenly saw that this guy, Sugar Ruiz, was absolutely brilliant. He knew how to use drugs. One hit and you stop.

"Nice, huh?" he asked me as he snorted up a few flakes.

I had to agree. "Very nice."

"Clean and pure. The product is here. The product is high-octane super-quality grade A-plus. The product has put me in the mood, bro. The product has put me on the cloud. The cloud is where I wanna be sitting when you give me that envelope. Sitting on the cloud and looking down on the sweet earth below. Am I reaching you, Power?"

"The cloud's soft," I said.

"And the envelope's thin, ain't it?"

"Real thin."

"That's 'cause it's only holding one slip of paper. You wanna slip it to me, bro?"

I reached in my pocket and handed Sugar the envelope. His green eyes were beaming.

"Let me just look at it first before I open it," he said. "It's kinda like when shorty is up in your bed flashing you that sweet pussy. You wanna take a minute and just look at it. You wanna cherish that motherfucking moment before you go in and actually taste it. So I'm fingering this here envelope. I'm getting it wet, baby. Then I'm going in."

Sugar held the envelope up to the broken shafts of light coming off the fancy chandeliers. He just looked at it.

"I know what you're thinking, Power. You're thinking if just a little bit of blow made us feel that good, a little bit more will make us feel better."

Sugar was right. That's exactly what I was thinking.

"But you gotta outthink the blow. See, the blow's designed to get you thinking that way. But this is the time to say no to the blow or else the blow will blow off the top of our heads. We don't want that. We wanna be cool. This is the perfect time to stop the blow and instead get a hit off this envelope. Compared to what's in this envelope, the blow ain't no stronger than Sweet'N Low."

Slowly, slowly, Sugar tore open the envelope. I was fixated by how much time he took to do it. It was all happening in slow motion. When the last eighth of an inch of the flap was torn and he reached inside, all I could see was a thin piece of paper with lots of typing on it and some kind of seal.

"What is it?" I asked.

"Key to the future. Key to expanding the empire."

"Are they ownership papers?"

"You got that right. Ownership papers to *the* business that I've been looking to buy for two years. This fool woman thought she had it tied up forever, but Slim outslicked her. When it comes to slick moves, Slim's king. I did Slim a serious solid some years back. He was grateful and said he'd take care of me when it mattered. Well, bro, this mattered big-time. With this," said Sugar, holding up the paper, "my man has come through like a motherfucker."

"What's the business?"

"The Holly Windsor Agency. Biggest modeling agency in Miami. Biggest in the South. She got a roster of the hottest models going. Models from all over the world come to Miami to get signed by Holly. But with this beautiful little piece of paper, we can wave Holly Windsor good-bye. She's out. I'm in."

"How'd you do it?"

"She got overextended in real estate. This building of mine was designed, constructed, and leased out before the market fell. But Holly, she bought a fancy hotel and high-rise up on Collins at exactly the wrong time. Ate up her cash and left her near bankrupt. She needed cash to keep the modeling agency open. Slim got her the cash, but with the proviso that if she needed more, she'd have to give him, at least on paper, ownership. She agreed. Two months later, the well was dry and she had to go back to Slim. She never thought he'd make her stick to the agreement and take over her business—or let someone like me take over. Well, I am taking over and the first order of business, my friend, is to kick her flat white ass out of town. What do you think of that?"

"Cool" was all I could think to say.

"You don't sound very excited," said Sugar. "You came to town with a piece of paper that's gonna change my life. You better get excited about it."

"I'm excited—excited to be here."

"You thinking that with a little more blow, you'd be even more excited, but that ain't happening. What's happening is this new agency. What's happening is that I finally got my chance to put up a slate of models like this world ain't ever seen before. I was born for this job. No one knows beautiful women like me. You can't argue with that. You can't argue with the truth, hombre. It's something you gonna see with your own eyes. So we ain't getting any more fucked up than we already are. We ain't turning into no freakin' cokeheads. Slim would have my scalp. Couldn't do that to my man Slim. Couldn't do that to his boy. He sent you down with a piece of paper that I'm holding high in my hand. Beautiful piece of paper, ain't it, bro? He sent you down here 'cause he knows you're interested in beauty. If you with Slim, you already seen beautiful women. Slim likes to talk about his beautiful women, but listen here, partner, this is Miami Beach, where beauty takes on a whole 'nother dimension. We going into that dimension on a personal and professional basis. You ready to follow me into that dimension?"

I could feel the effects of the coke fading. I wanted more. I wanted to go back up, not down, but I also knew that when it came to drugs Sugar knew what he was doing. I figured that Sugar's Shack was built on drugs. He was the expert and I was the amateur. Drugs had never sat well with me before. I understood that just because his grass didn't make me paranoid and his coke seemed to clear my mind didn't mean that more of the same wouldn't fuck up the works. I was better off chillin'. Slim had sent me to Irv, who, before he got sick and lost his mind, taught me not to trust no one. Slim was sending me to Sugar, another cat he admired, to learn whatever Sugar had to teach. Sugar was teaching me that one hit is enough.

"We going to VIP so you can see what this thing's all about," he said. "You ready?"

"Ready," I said.

"You cool?"

"Cool," I assured him.

"You like champagne?"

"I'll have me a little sip."

"My man! That's what I like to hear. You getting the idea, Power. A little sip. All we need is a little sip."

To get to VIP we followed the curvy lines of the club to a back door guarded by another one of Sugar's super-tall female security guards. She was a sista with a short-cropped Afro and the longest arms I'd ever seen on a female. The minute she saw Sugar, she stepped aside. He stopped to kiss her on both cheeks. She looked at me approvingly. I was still wishing I had had another hit of that top-shelf blow.

VIP was one medium-sized room with a dance floor and lots of smaller rooms with couches and easy chairs and TVs. There were no doors on the smaller rooms, just sheer curtains made of a see-through fabric. Like everything else at Sugar's Shack, the furniture was odd shaped, like it was designed by someone high on coke. The women dancing with each other—it was almost all females in there—were not odd shaped, just perfectly shaped. They all looked like models, tall, reed-thin, gorgeous in the face, edgy in their clothes—knee-high black boots and silver silk short shorts, flowing capes that flapped open to show their naked chests. I got the idea they had taken Ecstasy.

They had that X look in their eyes. They were floating to a smooth groove—a Latin groove with a techno flava—and a couple of them were making a little show by touching and kissing each other while they danced.

It was like a United Nations of beautiful women. Lots of Hispanic ladies, but man, there were chicks from all over. German chicks, Swedish chicks, French chicks, Italian chicks, Russian chicks, here a chick, there a chick, everywhere a chick chick. My eyes were popping out of my head. I heard all these different languages being spoken at once. I was knocked out by all these different skin types, different eye colors, different dancing styles. As Sugar took me through the rooms, he stopped to introduce me: here's Gretchen, here's Smeralda, here's Ingrid, here's Brigitte, here's Natasha, here's Olga, here's Liu, here's Mi. Mi stopped me cold.

Mi was Japanese. She was tall, just about Beauty's height—five ten or eleven, just a little shorter than me. Unlike Beauty, though, she had dyed her hair the color of red wine. Falling to her shoulders in a loose and breezy style, her hair had a purplish sheen. She had thin lips and a large sexy mouth. Her outfit looked like an art project—pleated pantsuit in stripes of purple and white made out of some kind of crinkly polyester.

"Mi just arrived from Tokyo," said Sugar. "Holly Windsor wouldn't sign her. According to Holly, she's too far-out. According to me, Holly's full of shit. And now that Holly's out, Mi is in. Isn't that right, Mi?"

Mi just smiled. She didn't know English, so another Japanese model named Yuko, who'd been living in Miami for a while, came over to translate. Yuko, though, didn't understand the word "far-out." She asked Sugar to explain.

"'Far-out' means 'different,'" he said. "'Far-out' means 'not afraid to do her own thing.' Far-out is good."

Yuko was several inches shorter than Mi. Her wide face and big eyes gave her the look of a baby doll. Her skin almost looked plastic. Mi's skin looked like silk.

"Mi was a model for Issey Miyake," said Yuko.

I hadn't heard of Issey Miyake, but Sugar said he was one of the most famous designers in the world. "Everything he does," said Sugar, "is far-out."

I was feeling far-out myself. The high from the grass and coke had gradually faded. The little sips of champagne had me a little tipsy. I was feeling strange. I was feeling like I wanted to talk to Mi more. I was feeling like I wanted to take Mi to bed.

"You want her?" asked Sugar, reading me right.

"If you think it's cool."

"No, bro, I really don't. Not right away anyway. See, she just got here and I don't want to overwhelm her. Don't want to confuse her. I'm guessing she's about your age—eighteen or nineteen—and I'm not sure it's good for her to start fucking the boss's assistant right off the bat."

The boss's assistant? So that's how Sugar saw me. Well, why not? The only thing that bothered me, though, was his tone. It was almost like he was saying, *the boss's water boy.*

"No problem," I said. "You're calling the shots."

"I'm calling someone who can show you to your apartment upstairs. Not the best in the building, but hell, at least you are in the building."

A few minutes later—with me, Mi, and Yuko sitting on the couch and listening to Sugar talking about his modeling agency plans—the security sista who'd been guarding the VIP entrance arrived.

"Yolanda," said Sugar, "take Power up to his apartment. Make sure he's comfortable."

"No problem," said Yolanda.

We had to go back through the club, exit, and reenter through a door for the residential part of the building. As I followed Yolanda, I found myself ranking her high bubble booty among the top ten I had ever seen. My eyes were all over it.

But by the time we rode the elevator up to the ninth floor and walked down the slate-and-metal hallway and into the apartment where I would be staying, my eyes were half-closed. The apartment was tiny, barely big enough for a double bed and a dresser. There was no kitchen, not even a kitchenette. The apartment looked like it was really a closet. My suitcases had been placed on the bed. Yolanda asked me if she could unpack for me. I said yes, and as she opened the suitcases and started putting my clothes away, I stretched out on the bed. I forgot about her booty. I forgot about everything. I was so dead tired from the trip and the drugs and the sips of champagne that my eyes closed completely. I couldn't open them. I fell deep into the sleep of the dead. And when I woke up the next day it was past noon and I was all alone.

The Renato Ruiz Agency

For you to understand what this dude has done," Slim told me over the phone the first week I was in Miami, "you got to know a little about his history. His old man was a kingpin in Cuba kicked out by Castro. He comes to Miami, sets up shop to sell his wares, and the first week he's in business the competition takes him out. Blows off the top of his head. Sugar, his sisters, and his mom have to scuffle 'cause they're left with nothing. The mom gets sick and dies a year later—cancer or a stroke, I can't remember. The sisters go back to Cuba to live with an aunt. But this Sugar, this young cat's got balls the size of cannons. He works the streets. He learns the city. He learns the trade. By the time he's your age he's got his own setup. He comes to Atlanta looking for opportunities. I met him when he started looking for real estate opportunities in our neighborhood. A young Hispanic kid looking to buy real estate in the black ghetto. That impressed me. His cash impressed me. We went in on some stuff together and everything he touched turned gold. We made money. Like me, Power, this kid had an eye for prime pussy. He was a magnet for beautiful ladies. The ladies love green eyes on a brother. Doesn't have to be a black brother. Long as he's tan. Anyway, next thing I know he's building his own building and buying up restaurants in South Beach. So after living that life with Irv in Chicago, I knew the last thing you needed was another old Jew. Sugar has something to teach you that even Irv doesn't know."

"What?" I asked.

"It ain't for me to say, Power," said Slim suavely. "It's for you to find out."

In the first days I didn't find out much except that my willpower to resist willing women was next to nothing. Sugar lived in a world of willing women. In his club, willing women were all over him, and when he announced that I was his boy—"his assistant"—they were all over me. I was tested. Sometimes I was tested twice in the same night. I proudly passed the tests with flying colors. When it came to sex, I was flying higher than I had ever flown. Yet even in these sky-high flights, even with world-class models whose bodies were most men's wet dreams, even if she happened to be a fair-skinned Norwegian or a Greek glamour girl with an olive complexion, when it came time to bust my nut, I'd have to give her Beauty's face.

This was something, of course, that no one knew. I wanted to unburden myself, but who was I going to tell? Slim? Hell no. Wanda. Of course not. Sugar? I was just getting to know the guy. I could see that he liked me and wanted to be my friend. He wanted to get me laid and was doing a great job of giving me the cream of the crop. He'd also seen that I had my eye on Mi. My idea was that of all the beautiful women passing through Sugar's Shack, Mi was the one who could break Beauty's spell. Mi did something to me that the others, no matter how gorgeous, did not.

All this was on my mind when, on a Monday morning following a crazy weekend devoted to an insatiable lady from Milan who was six feet four and once on the cover of Italian *Vogue,* I rode up on the elevator to the penthouse of Sugar's Shack. Once he had taken over ownership of the Holly Windsor Agency, he had shut down her office and moved it to his building. He had also renamed it the Renato Ruiz Agency. Renato was his real name. "Sugar is a good name for the club and the building," he said, "but the agency needs a Tiffany-type brand. Sugar's Agency doesn't sound right, bro. Renato Ruiz Agency reeks of class, doesn't it?"

I agreed, and I also agreed to work there every day and try to learn the business from a white woman named Pat Vine, the lady who had run the day-to-day operation for Holly Windsor and agreed to stay on and work with Sugar. Mrs. Vine was in her fifties. She was overweight, she wasn't pretty, but she was smart with computers and knew the game. She was no-nonsense. She was the one who told me that after the transition of ownership, most of the models signed by Holly Windsor were happy to stay on with Sugar. Holly was seen as pushy and bossy. Apparently she had a bad temper. The models liked the idea of working for a rich, green-eyed, playboy Miami Beach rock-star-style businessman.

"We have a good roster of models," Mrs. Vine told me, "but rosters are always being raided by the competitors. The key is not only to keep the girls we have but to be on the lookout for fresh talent. That means going to the fashion shows and seeing what models the designers are using. The idea is that Mr. Ruiz will be flying off to New York, Paris, and Milan, and that you and I are in the office making sure that the business is run like a business, not a hobby. Are you good with computers?"

"Pretty good," I said. "My mom was a bookkeeper and into them early on. She had me and my sister fooling with computers since we were real small. I'm comfortable with all the basic programs."

"Great. Then you'll be a quick learner. I'll show you how we inventory the models, the magazines, the art directors, the casting directors for videos—the whole gamut of buyers."

"Great."

"But I must warn you—the women can be a problem."

"I can imagine," I said.

"Here's our first problem coming through the door right now."

It was Mi. She came on a day that Sugar was away in New York. She was dressed in another one of those pleated pantsuits, this one with a pattern of purple sunbursts that matched the purple tint of her hair. She was stunning. With the exception of Beauty, she was the most fashionable woman I had ever seen. Her vibe seemed sad. I felt something was wrong. Her friend Yuko hurried into the office a few seconds later. She was holding two Starbucks coffees, one for herself and one for Mi. The two women faced Mrs. Vine and myself. There was a wall of windows behind us. Outside the sky was cloudy and across the street the Atlantic Ocean looked gray and angry. The waves were rough.

"I think that Mi . . ." said Yuko in faltering English. "I think she wants home."

"You mean she wants to go home?" asked Mrs. Vine.

"She not happy here," said Yuko.

Mi caught me staring at her. She smiled and looked away.

"We have a photo shoot set for her tomorrow," Mrs. Vine explained. "It's a cover shoot for *Luxury Living*. It's an important magazine."

"Yes, we know," said Yuko as Mi gazed out the window. She seemed to be studying the mysterious sea. "But this is not her . . . not her comfortable."

"You mean she's not comfortable in Miami Beach?" asked Mrs. Vine.

"Not comfortable here, no. She wants home," Yuko repeated.

"But we paid her fare from Tokyo. The fare wasn't cheap. And we have a contract."

"Contract no good in Japan," Yuko explained. "America no good for Mi."

"She's only been here a few days," said Mrs. Vine. "She needs to give it a chance. We have a considerable investment in her. And *Lux-*

ury Living's art director has already chosen her. Besides that, we have three other shoots set up. She can't go home."

Yuko quickly translated Mrs. Vine's words for Mi, who sat there and said nothing. For an uncomfortably long time we all sat there in silence. Then tears started streaming down Mi's face. Mrs. Vine handed her a tissue. I surprised myself by speaking up.

"Maybe we should give her a little time," I said to Yuko. "I know she's scared. Miami Beach is kind of a scary place. But maybe today isn't a good day for making a decision. Maybe tomorrow will be better."

Yuko translated my words while Mi looked at me with curiosity. Why was I saying those things? Why should I care? Then she said something to Yuko, who in turn said to me, "She is thanking you for your niceness. She is saying that she likes the ocean. The ocean is comfortable."

"Does she want to take a walk along the ocean?" I asked.

Yuko asked Mi, who nodded yes.

"Make yourself useful," said Mrs. Vine to me. "Take her for a walk and convince her to meet her obligations."

"I have appointment too soon," said Yuko. "I cannot go for walk."

"Let these two go for a walk," Mrs. Vine said. "Let this gentleman from Georgia introduce her to the healing properties of the Atlantic Ocean."

Mi and I left together. We walked out in silence and remained in silence. It was strange. I'd never been with a woman who didn't know my language. At first it was awkward and then it became something else. I'm not sure what to call it, but we were speaking without words, communicating without sound. It made me wonder—what the hell were we doing? I found myself remembering the connection between two characters in one of my favorite Sister Souljah books. When I had read the scene, I thought, *This is bullshit; no two people could bond so tight without a common language.* Yet that very thing was happening with me and this woman.

Mi led the way across the street to the ocean. She rolled up the bottom of her crinkly pants. I rolled up the bottom of my jeans. We took off our shoes and socks, left them on a bench, and stepped out on the cool sand. It felt great. It felt sexy. I looked down her at toes and saw that her toenails were polished the same purple tint of her hair and pantsuit. She saw me noticing and smiled. I followed her across the sand to the water's edge. The wash of the waves came up under our feet. She giggled and leaped a little in the air. Her mood was completely different from before; now she seemed actually carefree. She started skipping along the beach like a little girl. I skipped along with her. I felt silly, but I also felt good. She began running and I ran beside her. We ran at a slow, easy pace. We ran at the same rhythm. The cool breeze in my face and the fresh smell of the salty ocean kept my energy high. After the run, we walked far up the beach. We walked for miles, still not saying a word. How could we? She couldn't understand me and I couldn't understand her and yet we did understand. We knew what was going on.

We turned around and walked back as a few small rays of sun were busting through the clouds. The weather was warming. I wanted to reach over and hold her hand, but I didn't. I figured it'd be better for her to reach over first. She didn't. She just kept on walking, but every once in a while she looked in my direction with a beautiful smile covering her face. I couldn't say she was prettier than Beauty—to me Beauty was the perfect combination of black and Asian—but Mi was definitely gorgeous, and while she had me thinking of Beauty, I could see her in her own light.

When we finally arrived at the point where we'd started this long walk, we went to the bench to get our shoes. They were gone. Someone had stolen them. I was pissed but Mi just laughed and pointed to a shoe shop across the street called Flying Feet. They mainly sold sneakers, but I found a pair of sandals and Mi bought a pair of funky flip-flops in a purplish pink.

"Are you hungry?" I asked in slowed-down English. I pointed to my stomach.

"Yes, yes," she said.

We went to Prime One Twelve, a hip restaurant on Ocean Drive just down the street from Sugar's Shack. Sade was playing over the speakers. Mi looked at the menu and shrugged. I ordered a salmon salad for her and a sirloin steak sandwich for me. Sitting there, waiting for the food, I started asking her real simple questions, like "Do you have sisters and brothers?" and "Have you lived in Tokyo your whole life?" but I wasn't getting across. When she asked me questions in her slowed-down Japanese, I didn't do any better. We wound up just laughing at each other.

She liked her salad as well as the mango sherbet I ordered for dessert. I paid the check and she thanked me in English. We got up to leave, but where were we going? She just started walking and I followed. We walked to a park and then over to Washington Avenue, where we saw a bunch of interesting old-time architecture from way back in the day. There was a yellow building called the Jewish Museum of Florida that caught my eye. It had colored windows and fancy doors. For a second I was startled: An old man walking up the stairs looked like Irv Wasserman. I could have sworn it was Irv, but by the time I got closer for a better look he'd gone inside. I thought about going in there to see if it was really him but changed my mind. A lot of old guys in Miami Beach looked like Irv. Besides, why would Irv be in Florida going to some museum? I stuck by Mi's side. We kept walking; we walked for hours, stopping to look in the windows of the trendy boutiques, going into Starbucks for a coffee—Mi had green tea—pausing at a newsstand, where she bought a Japanese magazine.

By five o'clock, I was exhausted. Mi had to be tired as well. We'd been on the move for hours. She had canvassed South Beach from top to bottom. We must have walked fifteen miles. Where to now?

We found ourselves back at Sugar's Shack.

"Is this where you are staying?" I asked her, knowing she couldn't understand me. I presumed she was. Sugar kept rooms for many of the out-of-town models.

Mi smiled and attempted her first words to me in English. "You . . . you nice man."

"You," I said, "are a beautiful woman. A very beautiful woman."

I wanted to go to her room. I wanted her. I'd been wanting her since I first saw her. She was the one woman who could chase Beauty from my mind—or maybe bring Beauty to my mind. It didn't matter. I just wanted her.

She pushed the button for the elevator. We waited for it to arrive. It took a while. We got on. She pressed the button for the eighth floor. My room was on the ninth. I didn't press 9. When the doors opened, she stepped off the elevator, turned to me, and said, "*Domo arigato*. Thanks to you."

By the way she quickly separated herself from me, I got the message. I was about to say, "Can I call you later?" or "Can we have dinner tonight?" But there was no time. The door closed. Mi was gone.

I went to my room feeling frustrated. My room was tiny and the only window overlooked the back alley. I wanted to see the ocean, I wanted to walk along the ocean with Mi. Mi was only a floor below me. I could go down there and knock on the door, but I knew that would make her uncomfortable. If she wanted me in her room, she wouldn't have stepped off the elevator so suddenly. She liked me—I knew she liked me—but she wasn't ready. All these other chicks floating around Sugar's Shack had shown me they were ready. Some of them were ready before I was. But Mi, the one I wanted, wanted to wait. Maybe that's why I wanted her; maybe it wasn't just because she reminded me of Beauty, maybe it was because she had this special thing about her. She wasn't easy. Wasn't eager. She was soft and mysterious, and oh, man, the thought of what she looked like as she slipped off her clothes, as she stepped out of the shower, as she stretched in bed . . . those thoughts were driving me up the wall when my cell phone blew up. It was Mrs. Vine.

"Well, you obviously did a wonderful selling job," she said.

"What do you mean?"

"Yuko just called to say that Mi has decided to stay. You made her comfortable. Or maybe you just made her."

"I didn't. We just walked."

"Whatever you did, it worked. I called Sugar and let him know. He's delighted. His flight from New York lands at eight and he wants you, Mi, and Yuko to meet him for dinner at Tropical Deco at ten. Do you know where it is?"

"I can find it. Should I pick up the girls and take them with me?"

"Yuko said that she and Mi had something to do beforehand. They'll just meet you there."

I was buzzed. I was buzzed out of my fuckin' mind! Mi was staying. I could honestly say that Mi was my client. Since Sugar's agency was representing her, and I was working for Sugar, Sugar would be crazy not to give me responsibility for her. After all, I was the reason she was staying here. According to Mrs. Vine, she was one of the hottest new-look fashion-forward models out there—and there was loads of work for her in all the best magazines. I was her agent, I was her man; I saw myself accompanying her to all her appointments, all her photo shoots. I'd go with her everywhere.

By nine thirty I was dressed and ready to go. I put on a shirt of black shiny cotton with the buttons running diagonally down the front. The thin tab collar was white. Because it was made by Comme des Garçons, a Japanese label, I thought Mi would notice it. It felt a little strange on me—I wasn't used to wearing clothes this edgy—but I figured what the hell. Mi would like it.

Mi and Yuko were already at the table when I arrived at Tropical Deco. The place was designed to look like Miami Beach in the twenties and thirties. Very old-time, lots of fancy gold-framed paintings of starry nights and sunsets on the walls, cane tables and cane chairs, light fixtures that looked like something your old aunt might have in her house. I guess you could say it was retro trendy. The crowd was super-trendy, no one over thirty-five. The men looked rich, the women looked beautiful, and Mi looked more beautiful than all of them. As I approached her, she broke into a broad smile. I bent down and kissed her on the cheek. I wasn't sure whether this was done in Japan or not. Maybe I should have bowed, but I couldn't help myself. I had to kiss her. Just to cover my bases, I kissed Yuko as well. She was a little surprised. Compared to the other women at Tropical Deco, Mi and Yuko were understated. Yuko was dressed in deep black and Mi in pure white.

"Y'all look like a matching set," I said to Yuko, who translated my words for Mi. Mi laughed and said something back.

"She says," said Yuko, "we are salt and pepper."

"And what does that make me?" I asked.

Through Yuko, Mi's answer was, "You are sweet as sugar."

"There's only one Sugar," said the man himself, who arrived in another Akoo outfit, this one a flaming red fleece hoodie and baggy black jeans. "And this Sugar is ready to party."

He gave me a hug before kissing both Yuko and Mi on the lips. They were a little taken aback—I knew Sugar was being too forward with them—but Sugar was the boss and the boss was in a good mood. The boss was buying Dom Perignon champagne; the boss was buying steak and lobster; the boss was telling us nonstop stories about all the editors and art directors he'd met in New York, all the new models he'd seen, and how the Renato Ruiz Agency was the talk of the industry.

The talk went on all during dinner—Sugar's talk, because no one else could or even wanted to get a word in. Sugar was talking about his plans to make his agency the biggest in the world. He was talking about opening offices in New York and L.A. and then Europe—first

Paris, then Milan. Yuko struggled to keep up with his talk as she hurriedly translated for Mi, but I could tell she was always about two sentences behind. Mi tried to look interested, but it was obvious that she wasn't. A little Latin band was playing music with a Caribbean groove, and, taking a chance, I asked Mi if she'd like to dance. Yuko relayed my request to her friend and Mi said yes.

I could see that she felt the music. We didn't dance close. I knew to keep my distance. There was some touching—I touched her hand, I touched her waist, I gently grazed her arm. But mainly we were moving to the groove, reading each other's rhythms like we did when we were walking. Without talking, without thinking, we were in sync. The groove was beautiful, the groove was easy, the groove was bringing us closer together. Without saying it, without knowing a word of her language, the words were loud and clear. I could read the words in her eyes: "Tonight's the night."

When the band hit a slow jam, we stayed on the floor and I brought her close to me. I held her tight. The song was in Spanish. The song had to be about love. It had to be about desire. My desire was hard. I pressed her into me so she could feel how much I wanted her. She didn't back off. She moved even closer. Mi was mine, I was hers, it was happening. I closed my eyes as the music had us dancing on a cloud. I thought of Beauty; I thought of Mi; I thought of Beauty; I thought of Mi. It didn't matter. Beauty was far away, living in a world I knew nothing about. Mi was here. Mi was in my arms.

We went back to the table, where Yuko and Sugar were sipping champagne and laughing out loud. It was a great night all around. Lots of people came up to greet Sugar, to compliment him about this or that. He seemed to know everyone in South Beach. He had good manners. He never forgot to introduce us to his friends. I didn't care that he called me his assistant. I was happy to hear him describe Mi as his hottest signing.

The band was on break, and we'd been sitting around the table for several minutes when a brown-skinned young dude with a pencil-thin mustache and flipped-around Florida Marlins baseball cap came over to say hi. He was wearing baggy jeans and a blood-red silk shirt unbuttoned halfway down to show off his pecs. Given the powerful look of his upper body, I figured he lived in the gym. I guessed he was my age, nineteen or maybe twenty.

By then Sugar was a little tipsy. He glanced up at this dude, who said something to him in Spanish, and, just like that, Sugar's eyes turned from friendly to frantic. Something clicked in Sugar's brain. As the dude reached into his pocket, Sugar leaped up and violently turned over the table—dishes and ice and forks and knives and bottles flying everywhere—hitting the dude in the hand that was now holding a .45 pointed at Sugar's head. Next thing I knew, gunshots were ringing past my ear, I'd been thrown on the floor by the overturned table, I was under the table, and so was Yuko, and people were screaming, more shots were fired, someone stepped on my hand, pain shot up my arm, but all I was thinking was, *Where's Mi? Where's Mi?,* when I turned my head to see Sugar on the floor, his arm bleeding, while the dude with the gun was running out the door. Trying to get up from under the table, I was desperately looking around for Mi. I couldn't see her. I called for her and got no answer, but with people crying and yelling and running in every direction, I couldn't be sure that she wasn't up and running too until I myself managed to get up. That's when I saw her. She was slumped over in the chair where she had been seated between me and Sugar when one of the bullets meant for Sugar had hit her in the chest, had ripped through her heart, her white dress covered in blood, her eyes closed, her body limp, no breath, no life left inside her, nothing . . . nothing . . . nothing . . .

Get Back Up, Got Your Back

The songs kept playing in my mind. I heard the songs in all the clubs. One was called "Get Back Up," the other "Got Your Back." I kept going to the clubs when Sugar kept saying, "Get back up, I got your back." I pretended to be okay, but I wasn't. The last few weeks had been a blur. The last weeks brought back all the pain of losing my mother—and losing Beauty as well. This time I lost someone I had just met, someone I barely knew, and yet the pain was so strong that sometimes I woke up at night unable to breathe. I felt myself choking on pain.

I kept playing and replaying the night of Mi's murder. Sugar was the target, and Sugar's reaction—overturning the table—had thrown the assassin off balance so that his shots were scattered, and for no reason except pure fuckin' fate, Mi caught the worst bullet. After that, it was chaos. Cops and medics, stretchers and ambulances, hospital hallways, doctors and nurses and phone calls to Japan by Yuko, who controlled her hysteria long enough to call Mi's parents in Tokyo.

"I don't care what it costs," said Sugar, whose arm had suffered a flesh wound but nothing more. "Make sure she gets back to Tokyo first-class. I want to send her back in style."

I wanted to say to Sugar, *Motherfucker—she's dead. What the fuck does first-class matter to someone who's dead?* But I didn't because I knew

Sugar was shook up by the attempt on his life. Sugar had escaped death in the blink of an eye. And by "first-class" he meant make sure that her body got home as quickly as possible with flowers all over the portable casket. With Yuko's help, I made those arrangements. I was there when the transport company came to the hospital and packed up her corpse. They asked me to identify her. I didn't want to, but I also didn't want the wrong body to arrive in Tokyo. I saw her face for the last time. Her face looked peaceful and calm. I felt anything *but* peaceful and calm.

I drove Yuko to the airport. She was going on the same flight to Tokyo that was carrying Mi. After having helped me with all the arrangements, she was now free to fall apart. She did. She cried her eyes out, cried and sobbed and wept like a little child.

"My heart . . ." she said through tears, "my heart is sick."

"My heart is broken," I said.

"Broken," she repeated. "Very broken."

I parked and accompanied her inside, carrying her bags. I waited as she checked in, then walked her to the security line.

"I'm sorry" was all I could say.

Her eyes were still filled with tears as she reached in her purse and found a small piece of notepad paper shaded in light purple and smelling of lavender. On it was a Japanese letter.

"I want you to have it," she said.

"What does it mean?"

"It just says 'Mi.' It is her name."

I took the small piece of paper into my hand and examined it for a long while. The letter looked like a piece of sculpture.

"'Mi' has special meaning in Japanese. Do you know what that is?"

"No," I said.

"'Beauty,'" Yuko explained. "'Mi' is 'beauty.'"

. . . .

When I got back from the airport, I called Wanda to make sure Beauty was okay.

"Why wouldn't she be?" Wanda asked.

I couldn't go into it. "I just need to know that she's all right."

"If it makes you feel better, I'll call. But I'm not giving you the number. I told her I wouldn't."

Five minutes later Wanda called back to say that nothing was wrong.

"Is something wrong with *you*?" Wanda asked. "Boy, you sound like you done lost your best friend."

"It's all good," I lied.

Weeks had passed since that happened. Weeks when my mind was fucked up. Weeks when Sugar explained why the dude with the Marlins cap was looking to off him.

The dude called himself Gigante. Turns out that Sugar had caught the dude's brother—Pretty Boy Pablo—trying to leave Miami with fifty kilos of Sugar's primo inventory. According to Sugar, Pretty Boy was the scum of the earth, a fellow Cuban who pretended to be his best friend while all the time plotting to steal from under his nose. Pablo had set up a secret organization with the sole purpose of bringing down Sugar and taking over his property and possessions. Sugar hadn't seen it coming until a girl—a chick whose specialty was balling gangstas—whispered the truth in Sugar's ear. Sugar personally took out Pretty Boy Pablo with a baseball bat.

"Why you'd use a baseball bat?" I asked Sugar.

" 'Cause he rooted for the Marlins. I like Tampa Bay."

"And Gigante? What are you going to do about him?"

"I figure there's more in it for you than me."

"How do you figure that?"

"He only got a little piece of my arm," said Sugar. "But he got all of your girl, didn't he?"

I hesitated to answer. I didn't know what to say. To be honest, I wasn't sure how I felt about it. Part of me wanted to see Gigante dead.

He had killed a beautiful young woman with her whole life in front of her. The killing, though, was an accident. He had meant to kill Sugar. So shouldn't Sugar be the one to get him? Gigante and his brother, Pretty Boy Pablo, were part of Sugar's story, Sugar's world—not mine.

"I know what you're thinking," said Sugar, "that this here shit, homes, is my bizness, not yours. But your bizness and my bizness are the same bizness. We in this together, ain't we? Besides, it's time to pop your cherry. Maybe that's why Slim sent your young ass down this way. Slim knows this is cherry-poppin' territory."

Sugar had called Slim right after the shooting to assure him I was all right. When Slim called me, he didn't sound too worried.

"You livin' the life, boy, ain't you?" asked Slim.

I didn't say nothing about Mi. What would be the point?

"I'm lucky to be alive," I said.

"You a blessed man," said Slim. "You hanging tough, baby. You ain't backing off and you building a rep strong as steel."

I didn't see it that way. Truth is, I didn't do shit that night. It was Sugar who turned over the table and saved his own ass. Maybe I would have chased after Gigante if I hadn't been pinned down—or maybe I wouldn't have. No way of telling. But now I was suddenly faced with that decision all over again. Was I gonna chase after Gigante and bring him down?

"I gotta go to Atlanta this weekend and catch up with Slim for a hot minute," I told Sugar. "We can work it out when I get back."

"When will that be?"

"Day after tomorrow."

"No problem, hombre," said Sugar. "No fuckin' problem at all."

I figured Sugar knew that I was going home to ask Slim's approval. He knew it was something I couldn't discuss on the phone—and he also knew that since Slim had been his mentor as well as mine, it wasn't a bad idea.

. . . .

I was back in Slim's house in Cascade Heights with the ice-white walls and mermaid fountain. I had arrived at eight P.M. Now it was ten P.M. and Slim was just pulling up. He'd bought himself a new lotus-green Maybach 57, the kind of sedan that sells for $350,000.

"What do you think?" he said, leaping out of the car and giving me a hug. Dre was behind the wheel.

"Beautiful," I said. "Business has got to be good."

"Business is beautiful," said Slim.

"P-P-P-P-P-P-P-Power," said Dre, dressed elegantly, as always, in a custom-tailored pinstripe suit. "M-m-m-m-m-man, it's good to see you. Y-y-y-y-you okay?"

"He's alive, ain't he?" said Slim. "He's out there dodging them bullets. This boy is damn near bullet*proof.*"

"Th-th-th-th-th-th-that's g-g-g-g-g-good," said Dre.

"You wanna drive this thing?" Slim asked me. "Motherfucker drives likes a dream, don't it, Dre?"

"It sure d-d-d-d-d-do," Dre agreed.

I didn't feel like driving a car. The plane ride had been turbulent from takeoff to landing. My stomach was queasy and my head, filled with questions about how or if I should deal with Gigante, was aching.

"I'd rather be driven than drive," I said, "if that's okay."

"M-m-m-m-m-m-my p-p-p-p-p-p-pleasure," said Dre. "You ge-ge-ge-ge-ge-gentlemen hop in the back. I'm glad you're back h-h-h-h-ho—"

"Shut the fuck up, Dre," Slim snapped. "We don't got time for you to spit out those words. We got biz to discuss."

I felt bad for Dre and wanted to say something but figured now wasn't the time. I had more pressing things on my mind than trying to get Slim to stop humiliating Dre.

"This here leather is the finest money can buy," said Slim, sliding in the backseat. I nearly choked on the smell of leather. Slim hit a button to electronically close the curtains that separated us from Dre. He hit another button that turned on the video screen showing soft-core porn. "See shorty with the crazy red wig and that booty from outer space? She was over two nights ago. She something, ain't she, Power?"

I nodded. I wasn't really in the mood to watch fake fucking on the Maybach's DVD player. I turned away from the screen. Sensing my seriousness, Slim turned it off and said, "You do understand that Sugar's out of the modeling biz, don't you, Power?"

"He hasn't really discussed it with me."

"Nothing to discuss. One of his models murdered right at his table. What the fuck are the other models gonna do? They gonna ditch him. They leaving like rats running off a sinking ship. He got to go back to his core biz. And no doubt he will. Sugar's a practical man. He knows he's got to do what he does best."

"The dude who shot him . . ."

"The brother of Pretty Boy Pablo . . ."

"You know about him?"

"I know about everything I needs to know about."

"He's called Gigante. And he's still out there."

"Not for long, baby. Sugar will see to that."

"He wants me to see to that."

My last statement stopped Slim cold. He took off his dark Gucci sunglasses and looked me deep in the eye. I think he was trying to see whether I was scared or not.

"I see," he said. "Now I see what's happening."

"What do you think?"

Slim put back on his shades and, without missing a beat, said, "I think you've been given a job, boy."

"And that's it?"

"That's the life. You done had all the foreplay you need. Now it's time to stick it in. That what you came home to hear me say?"

"I guess so."

"Well, sir, you done heard me say it." And with that, Slim turned back on the DVD to watch the lady with the red wig and big butt.

The dreams were crazy. They started on the plane back to Miami when I drifted off. In one dream I took a butcher's knife and slit the throat of a pig. In another I blasted a lion with a shotgun and the lion turned into a little boy. There was another dream where I was strangling an old man whose face was covered with pimples and wet blood. As I strangled him, blood oozed from his pimples.

"We've located him," said Sugar on my first day back in the office. It was early August, only days from my twentieth birthday. "We know where he is."

I didn't say anything.

"What did Slim say?" asked Sugar.

"He said the modeling agency was in trouble."

"Hey, man, fuck the modeling agency. What did he say about Gigante?"

"Same thing as you're saying."

Sugar smiled. "I got you an address. So get going."

"Just like that? No plan. No prep. No word on his posse."

"I figure you're the Lone Ranger. You're Slim's star student. You don't need no help. Far as machinery goes, ask and you will receive. Whatever you want. But the main thing I got for you is an address. Boca Raton. Ever been to Boca?"

"Never."

"You'll dig it. Nice class of people."

Sugar opened the drawer to his desk and pulled out a sheet of paper and a small envelope. He handed me the paper, which had the words "1236 Marble Street" on it. Then he emptied out the contents of the envelope on a mirror.

"I'm taking one little hit that'll last me for the next few days. You down?"

"I'll pass. I got to stay clear."

"This'll help," said Sugar.

"Like you said, I don't need no help."

Sugar half laughed before snorting up all the blow, including the line he had left for me.

I thought about that statement: *I don't need no help.* I guess I made it as a declaration to Sugar and, though he wasn't there, to Slim. I also made it a statement to myself. I didn't see any other way. If Slim had said, *No, I don't want my boy involved in any payback shit,* I'd have had an out. In truth, I would have welcomed the out. The idea of flat-out murder didn't thrill me. On the other hand, if Sugar had given me a couple of guys and a game plan, I might have felt differently. But I was given nothing. I was told nothing except this one lousy address. It was all up to me.

I recognized this is as part test, part initiation rite. In Chicago, I had seen some stuff go down, but I wasn't the guy who brought it down. Now I *was* the guy. Now my only choice was to leave this life or do what the life required. If I left this life, where would I go? I didn't see any future outside of it. Besides, I was being groomed as a leader. This life—the life given to me by Slim after the death of my mom—had rewarded me handsomely. Beginning with my move to Slim's place, look where I'd been living—in mansions, hip lofts, fancy apartments. Look who I'd been meeting—super-powerful men and superfine women. Look what I'd been learning—how to deal with real life, real problems; how to make real money. Now I had a real challenge: figure out how to kill the motherfucker who killed Mi and tried to kill Sugar.

My mind was made up, but my motivation needed to be stronger. I thought how this scumbag Gigante had robbed Mi of a long and good life. That got me mad, but mad enough to murder him? I wasn't sure. I thought of how Gigante had tried to take out my friend Sugar. But was Sugar really my friend? Maybe yes, maybe no. It didn't matter. Sugar was one of the teachers Slim had assigned to me. Sugar was testing me. I'd either pass or flunk. And I wasn't about to flunk.

Back in Atlanta, Andre Gee had schooled me in the use of handguns. He'd given me long lessons on how to handle small arms. I liked Dre because, even though people were often impatient with his stutter, he showed patience with others. He said, "Power, y-y-y-y-y-you a youngblood with g-g-g-g-good aim and g-g-g-g-good eye-hand c-c-c-c-coordination. You ain't afraid of n-n-n-n-n-n-no guns."

I wasn't. Dre took me into the woods, where I shot squirrels with a shotgun. I was quick and steady and liked the kickback and release that came with shooting. Squirrels were one thing, though. Gigante was another.

Gigante stayed on my mind as I drove up to Boca Raton. Sugar had arranged for a car—a plain-looking Ford Taurus—that couldn't be traced. I was packing enough heat to take out Gigante and, if need be, his six closest friends. I drove carefully, obeying all the rules. The last thing I wanted was to be pulled over. I figured that, given Gigante's agenda the night of the shooting, he hadn't noticed me. I doubted if he could recognize me, but just to make sure I shaved my head and gave myself an entirely different look. Being bald helped give me a new attitude. I thought of Dre and his shaven head and how he must have handled many situations like the one facing me. Dre was tough, Dre was fearless; according to Slim, there was no one he trusted more than Dre to get the job done.

Getting the job done—that was my mantra, my focus, my only reason for being alive. That's how I had to think. That's how I had to be. I couldn't look back, couldn't be sentimental. I had to stuff all feelings except the one that said, *This motherfucker is history. This mother-fucker is dead meat.*

I checked into a Hilton Suites hotel. My room overlooked a park-ing lot. I unpacked my things and, first thing, went to the bathroom, where I shaved whatever stubble remained on my head. For some reason keeping my head shaved perfectly clean was important. I got a pair of cheap shades at Rite Aid and went to a sporting goods store to buy a Marlins baseball cap, just like the one Gigante had worn. Before locating the address that Sugar had given me, I decided to work out in the small hotel gym. I wanted that muscle burn that comes with lift-ing too much weight. I needed to feel pumped.

Just after the sun went down, I drove over to 1236 Marble Street. It was an apartment complex called the Floridian, not fancy, not slummy, just a plain two-story building. I walked into the lobby, where there was a wall of mailboxes and a painting of pink flamingos drinking out of a pool of blue-green water. Of course his name wasn't on any of the mailboxes. I'd just have to stake out the place until he showed up. When I got back to the Taurus, the sky broke open and rain came down in sheets. The rain broke up the torrid August heat and felt good. But the heavy rain prevented me from seeing who was coming in and out of the building. The rain got worse. It wouldn't let up. Two hours later, I knew that tonight wasn't the night.

Back at the Hilton Suites, I couldn't sleep. I didn't want to sleep because I knew the dreams would come. Every night the dreams grew more violent. It was crazy—I felt more afraid of my dreams than the job I had to do. When I finally did drift off, I didn't dream at all. Thank God.

I didn't wake up till ten A.M. The sound of rain was even louder against the window. I got up and looked outside. The downpour was something to see. Felt like the whole world was being washed away. I went back to bed and felt this tremendous urge to call Beauty. I wanted to discuss the situation with her. I wanted to tell her what was going through my mind. But I didn't have her number, and Wanda wouldn't give it to me, and even if I asked Wanda to call her and ask her to call me, I knew that Beauty wouldn't. She wanted to be left alone.

I wanted to get this over with, but the rain wouldn't let me. It didn't make any sense to try something while the storm was still raging. I could sit outside the Floridian, but even if he came out, the rain would get in my way. I took a shower and shaved my face and my head. I got dressed, grabbed an umbrella, walked to the car, and went looking for a place to have lunch. I stopped at a deli called Uncle Lou's. When Irv took me to delis in Chicago, he told me the best things to order. At Uncle Lou's, many of the customers looked like Irv—retired Jewish guys with tired eyes. I ordered a pastrami on rye. When it arrived I covered it with hot mustard. I hadn't realized that I was famished. I wolfed it down. It tasted as good as anything I've ever eaten in my life. I had cherry cheesecake for dessert. My mouth was thanking my mind for ordering such great food. I looked outside to see if the rain had let up. It hadn't.

Next to the deli was a video store. I stopped in. There was a porn section in the back, but porn was the last thing on my mind. I knew I needed something to kill time. I needed something to help me wait out this rain. I bought *Scarface*. I love *Scarface*, every single scene. I stopped at a Radio Shack and got a cheap DVD player so I could watch the movie. I loved it more than ever. I realized that I needed it more than ever. It showed me what I needed to see. I needed to hear Tony Montana tell Manny, "This is paradise . . . this town like a great big pussy jus' waitin' to get fucked." I needed to hear Tony tell Mel, just before Mel is shot dead in cold blood, "Maybe you can hondle yourself one of them first-class tickets to the resurrection." I needed to see him getting drunk in the fancy restaurant and screaming at the high-class people, "What you lookin' at? You all a bunch of fuckin' assholes. You know why? You don't have the guts to be what you wanna be. You need people like me. You need people like me so you can point your fuckin' fingers and say, 'That's the bad guy.'" And in the best scene of all, I needed to see him with his grenade launcher telling his attackers, "Say 'ello to my little friend!"

I watched the movie twice. It made me feel a lot stronger. It made me feel like I was living a movie. I was an actor, like Pacino, in the role of a lifetime. I could fuckin' well do it.

Sometime during the night the rain finally stopped. By morning the sky had cleared and it looked like the most beautiful day in the history of the world. The world was sparkling. The world smelled fresh and new. I put on a new pair of black Air Jordan Fadeway basketball shorts, a black Billionaire Boys Club T-shirt with no lettering, fresh Adidas Heat Checks, the Marlins cap, and the Rite Aid shades. I drove by Uncle Lou's and thought about stopping in for breakfast but decided against it. Fuck the delays. I had to get over to 1236 Marble Avenue.

I parked down the street from the Floridian where I could see the front door of the building. I waited for an hour, then drove around for a while and, when I came back, parked in another place. I got out of the car and walked up and down the street, never losing sight of the door. This became my routine. I did it all day. Lots of people came in and out, but no one who resembled Gigante. I figured he'd probably changed up his appearance in some way, but I'd recognize him by his built-up chest. He wasn't going to get by me. Not now. Not ever.

Come seven o'clock I was starved. I drove to a nearby McDonald's for a Big Mac and fries. I wanted to get a vanilla shake but sometimes too much milk and sugar make me sleepy. I had to be alert. I went back and this time parked two blocks away from the Floridian. A pair of small binoculars let me see what I needed to see.

At nine o'clock I saw him come out. It had to be him. It was his chest, his bulky size. He was wearing a stingy-brim hipster's hat and a Miami Heat jersey. I got ready to follow him as he climbed into a black Audi sports car parked in front of the building and peeled off in a hurry. I stayed far enough behind so he wouldn't know I was on his tail. My heart was racing like crazy. I started to sweat. He pulled into a strip mall and parked in front of a beauty salon. This place was called Boca Beauty Shoppe. I thought about Judy and her Hair Is Where It's At. Gigante got out of his car and walked in. I parked the Taurus nearby and stayed behind the wheel, waiting. A few minutes later he walked out with a woman who was several inches taller than him. She was Asian—either Japanese or Chinese or maybe Vietnamese, maybe Korean, I couldn't say for sure, but definitely Asian, definitely gorgeous, definitely the same tall elegant thin body shape as Mi and Beauty. As they walked to his car, they held hands.

As they took off, I stayed discreetly behind. My mind was reeling, my mind was a mess, my mind said, *Follow him, don't get too close, don't lose him, just follow him.* My mind also said, *Come back when he's not with a woman, wait till later, wait till tomorrow, forget this whole crazy fuckin' thing.* My eyes were on his Audi as he drove all the way to West Palm Beach, where he pulled up to the valet parking area of a nightclub called Attitude. The parking lot was filled with fancy cars, and the people going in were dressed in diamonds and denim. There were a lot of Hispanics, but whites and blacks as well. The crowd was young. As Gigante and the Asian chick walked through the door, I saw they had to pass a metal detector. I realized that if I were going in, I'd have to go without heat. It was another good excuse to turn around. But I couldn't. I wouldn't. I had to see this goddamn thing through to the end.

I left the heat behind. I made a survey of the grounds outside the club and put a plan in place before going in. I paid a fifty-dollar cover charge. I looked around. Neon palm trees in white and gold. A long bar made of bamboo. A dance floor made of distressed white wood. Two chick DJs spinning Drake and Trey Songz. Lots of flash and cash, champagne popping, couples bumping to the jams, the jams getting louder in my ear, my eyes searching for Gigante and the girl. I lost them for a minute but caught a glimpse of them as they slipped into the VIP room on the back side of the club. I could have probably talked myself into VIP, but that didn't seem like the move. The move was to be cool and wait. And watch. And catch my breath. And repeat the mantra—*It's a job, it's gotta get done, it will get done, nothing and no one can stop me from doing it.*

I went to the bar and ordered a Sprite. I sipped on it and surveyed the scene. One black shorty came my way, said a few nice things, and asked me to dance. I was about to politely refuse when I heard my jam—"Get Back Up." It seemed like the cue to hit the floor. It seemed like a good idea to mingle with the crowd and not look like some gawking dude surveying the scene. I danced with shorty. She had nice moves, an easy smile, a willing way. I looked over and saw Gigante and his girl. He couldn't dance worth a shit. His girl moved like a cat. Her eyes told me she was stoned. Gigante was probably fucked up too. Maybe it was champagne, or weed, or blow, or X. Maybe all that shit. Good. The more wasted he got, the better for me. I escorted shorty back to the bar. She wanted to talk. I made it clear that I didn't. She got a little pissed. I apologized and said, "Sorry, baby, I'm just passing through."

I took my time. Kept throwing back Sprites. Kept moving around the dance floor. Kept my eye on the VIP. Gigante and his babe would come out every four or five jams for a spin. Each time he hit the floor, I could tell he was more wasted. Adrenaline had taken over my body, my head, my heart, my arms, my legs. I felt more pumped than at any time in my life. More scared. More determined. More fuckin' crazy. The club got more crowded, I could hardly move across the floor, the strobe lights putting everyone's moves in slow motion, bodies on bodies, sweat on sweat, music sweat, sex sweat, danger sweat, Gigante sweating so hard, his eyes so fucked up that I knew he had hit his high. At one point, he fell on the dance floor. His girlfriend had to help him up. They both laughed. They both disappeared back into VIP.

A few minutes later I saw him stumbling across the club looking for the men's room.

It was time.

I followed him in. The bathroom was crowded. He had to wait and then stood at a urinal taking a piss. Seemed like the piss lasted for an hour. He almost nodded off. When he was through, he didn't wash his hands. He walked out the door. I was right behind. As we passed by an exit door, I put my full body weight into him and shoved him outside. We were in the alley behind the club. I knew where we were because I had cased out the geography earlier in the evening.

"What the fuck you want, asshole?" he asked, still staggering.

"You," I said.

"You a fuckin' faggot?"

I didn't bother to answer. I reached into a garbage can where I had earlier taped a Golden Eagle German stiletto. Before I could dislodge it, though, Gigante lunged at me with his right fist. Even in his fucked-up condition, he got lucky and the blow landed on my right eye. My face radiated red-hot pain. I was furious. I reacted. By then I had the stiletto in my right hand and plunged it in his throat. He spit out blood. I pulled out the knife and plunged it in his throat a second and third time. Then I plunged it through his heart. He went down and out without a sound. I wiped off the bloody knife, put it in my pocket, and walked around the shadows of the parking lot until I found the Taurus. I was shaking, but I was steady enough to drive.

I'd done the job.

Whatever You Like

When I got back from Boca Raton the day after I put down Gigante, I showed up at Sugar's Shack wearing a black patch over my right eye. Sugar was up in the penthouse partying. He had a posse of pussy, one bitch finer than the next.

"Holy shit!" he said when he saw me. "We got ourselves a motherfuckin' pirate! What the hell happened?"

"A little skirmish" was all I said. "My eye's messed up."

"And what about the other guy, homes?"

"Not to worry."

"So it's like that," said Sugar.

"Just like that."

"You sure?"

I didn't bother to answer. I just nodded.

"Cool," said Sugar. "I see you got your swag on. That's what success will do to a man. Make him wanna rock a whole room of women. You ready, Power?"

I just nodded.

"Well, if what you say is true, you deserve all can you handle. Pick any two, baby. Pick any three."

I walked around. Some girls were dancing alone. Some were reclining on the couch. Some were out on the balcony enjoying the view. I didn't look at them the way I usually looked at women. Usually I wanted to know who they were, where they came from, what they did for a living. Usually I saw women as people. But that night I looked at them as bodies. I saw their faces, but I didn't see their eyes. I didn't want to see their eyes. I didn't want to look deeply. I didn't want to understand who they were and why they were there. I knew why they were. They were there for me. Sugar said so. Sugar confirmed a feeling that had been coming over me ever since I'd left Boca. I was returning a conquering hero. A fuckin' conquering hero. And these beautiful luscious willing women were my rewards.

Nothing to think about. Nothing to worry about. Nothing to analyze. All pleasure. All good. All night long.

That night I had two. The next night I had two different ones. The night after that Sugar moved me out of the little apartment I'd been living in to a high floor with a view of the beach. That night I had a bitch from Brazil who was like three bitches in one. I'd never seen anything like her before. The more I had, the more I wanted, the more it made me feel like I could do anything, be anyone, get anywhere. And yet, if I were to tell anyone the truth, I'd have to admit that the longer I fucked, the harder it was for me to cum. I wanted to, but I didn't want to think about Beauty, and yet, in spite of these amazing bodies on these amazing South Beach models and dancers and would-be actresses, I couldn't cum without imagining being inside Beauty, Beauty beneath me, Beauty above me, Beauty all over me.

Slim was right. Because of what happened to Mi at Tropical Deco, the modeling agency suffered major losses. The girls didn't want to be associated with Sugar—at least not professionally. Sensing the business was going down fast, Pat Vine quit. Without Pat Vine, Sugar was lost.

So he quickly closed up the Renato Ruiz Agency to concentrate on his core business—drugs. His drug operation was divided down the middle. There were street drugs that he distributed through a network of dealers headed up by an old-school cat named Jordash Jackson. They called him Dash and he handled the down-and-dirty corner-by-corner, block-by-block dealings. Then there was what Sugar called his premium trade. Those were high-end customers who bought drugs like they bought Piaget watches. They didn't give a shit what they cost, as long as they got the best. These were customers who Sugar catered to; he handled them personally, and because of my work with Gigante, I was awarded several of these customers myself.

Premium buyers didn't only buy for themselves. They also bought for their friends. Sugar didn't know whether the high-end buyer marked up the drugs when he or she sold them to a friend—and Sugar didn't care. The profit on the initial sale was so huge it made no difference.

"Homes," said Sugar, "these fuckin' people are so filthy rich no one cares what anything costs—as long as they get off. And I make goddamn sure I got the shit that gets them off."

I spent a lot of time with Sugar and could see why, at least in the world of drugs, he was so effective. He gave Dash B-quality product and left him alone to do his thing on the streets. He and I handled the good shit. Every night before we made our rounds—going to a customer's party or a customer's mansion—he'd tap out a line for himself. "Just to test it," he said. "One line and that's it." He always offered me a quick toot, and now and then, I took Sugar's lead. I took a small taste. A long line was too much for me. I'd just knock off a little, and a little was enough.

A little lifted me higher. For me, it was a high period in all respects. I often made deliveries to Jose Rojas, a dude who had moved to Miami from Panama, where he had inherited his father's fleet of supertankers. Jose was a super-fan of Sugar's high-priced shit. He was part of Sugar's young-men-on-the-move millionaire's club. He had a thing for French chicks. He'd fly to Paris and bring 'em back in his Gulf-stream, three or four at a time. His parties usually didn't start till three in the morning. When night turned to day, he pushed a button that automatically activated blackout curtains that darkened every window. That way night could go on until three in the afternoon. Jose presented me with a woman named Adrienne who came from Nice and had a thing for American black guys with Southern accents. Whatever accent I had naturally, I thickened up. Jose also invited me to a weekend trip to Vegas. But Sugar didn't think it was a good idea for me to go. Sugar didn't like the idea of me getting that cozy with a customer.

I couldn't imagine anyone getting cozier with his customers than Sugar. There was a real estate mogul from Montreal who owned half of Miami Beach. He and Sugar went to Antigua for a weekend and wound up staying for nearly a month. I liked that because it left me on my own. Sugar trusted me with his best clients. I knew every single one, and I never failed to deliver the quantities and quality they demanded.

My favorite was Jason Riley, the Internet king who invented computer software that made him richer than the Pope. Jason was thirty-something, a fast-talking speed demon who actually raced at NASCAR. He became a professional driver. He had blond hair that he wore to his waist, wild blue eyes, and a funny-shaped ski-jump nose. He lived in a loft. Compared to Jason's loft, my loft in Chicago was a closet. This Miami Beach loft was actually a converted power plant with a TV screen that wrapped around the four corners of a room the size of a city block. Jason was also a chess player who liked a challenge. We had ferocious matches, and against Sugar's advice, I never let him win if I could prevent it. Jason respected that. One night, after he was really loaded, he came on to me. I was surprised. Jason always surrounded himself with luscious ladies. I never suspected that he liked guys.

"I don't," he said. "I just like you."

I made it real clear that nothing physical could ever happen between us. I left no room for doubt.

Jason respected my honesty. He accepted my statement at face value. He withdrew and then asked, "Well, will you at least go out with me for a pastrami sandwich? I have a thing for pastrami. And I got a place where they have the absolute best."

"At this time of night?" I asked, looking at the clock, which said four A.M.

"They never close."

It was the least I could do.

Eisenstock's Deli was up on Collins Avenue. It smelled of pickles. It looked like it had been there for decades. The wooden tables and chairs were rickety. The plastic booths were torn and the stuffing was coming out. The menu was a mess of torn plastic. The place was empty except for a guy behind the deli counter. He didn't look happy to be there.

Jason went up and ordered us pastrami sandwiches. The meat was delicious, spicy and lean. He started to tell me about his life. His father was a math genius who taught college in California. His mom was a shrink. He went to Stanford, where he drove his Harley off the road and broke both arms. It was in the hospital where he came up with this software for product distribution. It worked for practically all products, including Sugar's. He told me, off the record, that he had developed a shadow software system for Sugar under another name in another country that could only be accessed by a complicated code. Only he and Sugar had the code. Who knew that Jason was actually a partner of Sugar's and the main reason his product distribution ran so smoothly?

"I'm telling you this because I trust you, Power," said Jason, talking in his bang-bang mile-a-minute manner. "I've trusted you from the first day we met. You got charisma. You know that, don't you?"

"Thanks," I said in a low-key kind of way. I didn't want to do anything to encourage his interest in me.

"And you're kicked-back and cool," he added. "Nothing bothers you."

"There's definitely stuff that bothers me," I admitted.

"Like what?"

I didn't want to get personal. I wanted to keep this guy at a distance.

"Look, I understand that you're straight, and I respect that. I'm straight myself. I've always had all the women I wanted."

"That's good," I said.

"It was—for a while. And then I ran into this problem. It's a problem I've never told anyone. But I'm telling you because, like I say, Power, I can trust you. This is a deep problem."

Jason paused for a bite of pastrami.

"They call what I have premature ejaculation syndrome. Have you ever heard of it?" he asked me.

"I have. I have a . . . a good friend with the same problem."

"So you know it's devastating."

"He doesn't really talk about it. But I can imagine . . ."

Jason continued. "It's hard to imagine how it fucks you up. You can't perform. You just can't. You close your eyes and try to imagine something that has nothing to do with sex, something like your aunt's funeral, anything to keep you from getting too excited too quickly. You have foreplay for a half hour, an hour. You give her head forever. You work on your mind, you tell yourself, *Take it easy, go slow, give it time.* And then the second you go in, you explode. You cum before she can feel a thing.

"Do you have any idea what that does to a man, Power? It's the most fuckin' humiliating thing in the world. You beg the girl not to say anything to anyone. You pray to God she won't because you don't want your friends to know. You live in fear that this thing's gonna haunt you your entire life. I'm telling you, man, there's nothing good about it.

"I've read dozens of case studies on men with this syndrome. There have been instances when they're so enraged with themselves they wind up beating women. Even killing them. Don't get the wrong idea, Power. That's not me. I've never done as much as screamed at a lady, much less hit one. But I can understand it. I can understand why men—men who can't satisfy women—go crazy."

"Does doing lines help or hurt?"

"I've tried it both ways. I started in tooting because, after years of struggling with this thing while I was dead sober, someone said toot helped. They said if you snort it or even put it on your cock you'll last longer. Well, it didn't work—not one fuckin' bit. But the blow did do something—it washed away my bad feelings. Made me feel great. It became a substitute for sex. Maybe it's even better than sex. Less complicated. But then I started to get a thing for you and started thinking, *Hell, maybe I'm not straight after all.* Maybe I cum quick because I don't want a woman. Maybe I want a guy like you."

Here we go again, I thought.

"How do you know you're not gay, Power, if you haven't tried?"

"Jason," I said firmly, "back the fuck off."

"Oh, well, you can't blame me for wanting to experiment, can you?"

I didn't answer.

While Jason got lost in his sandwich, I kept thinking of Slim and the medical report I'd found in the garbage. Slim and Jason had the same problem. Jason was saying how cumming too soon could drive a man crazy, twist his mind into knots, and turn him violent. I didn't know what to think about the problem. But I did know one thing—I needed to keep making it clear to Jason that, no matter how confused he might be about his sexuality, I wasn't confused at all. I liked women.

While Jason went up to the deli counter to order another pastrami sandwich, I realized that I was about to fall out. I'd been up for nearly twenty straight hours. I needed to sleep. I needed Jason to finish his food so he could drive me back to his loft, where I'd left my car. Fact is, I was so exhausted that for a moment I closed my eyes and actually nodded out. When I opened my eyes I looked at a man who was walking through the front door of Eisenstock's. I had to be dreaming. I squeezed my eyes closed and opened them again. I wasn't dreaming. It was Irv, and he was walking right to me.

By then Jason had returned to the table, and I had gotten up to greet Irv. I was so shocked I could hardly speak. Had Irv been transferred to a hospital in Miami Beach? Had he wandered out of his room? Was he sleepwalking? Would he even recognize me?

"Power," he said, "introduce me to your friend."

I stumbled before I calmed enough to say, "Jason, this is Irv Wasserman."

"Nice to meet you, sir," said Jason. "Care to join us?"

"Oh, no," said Irv. "I couldn't sleep so I came for a little tea and maybe a piece of cheesecake. I don't want to bother you boys. I'll give you my number, Power. Call if you get a chance. No hurry. No worries."

As Irv walked to the counter to order, Jason asked me, "Who's that?"

"Just a guy," I said.

Next day I slept past noon. My dreams—about tornados and earthquakes, fires and floods—were intense, though I couldn't remember the details. It just felt like the world was coming to an end. When I opened my eyes, I forgot where I was. Atlanta? Chicago? No, I was in Miami Beach, in my apartment in Sugar's Shack. I was working for Sugar. I was his most trusted customers' man. He let me service his best clients. When he went to the celebrity parties where movie stars and athletes hung out, he took me along. He introduced me to the finest ladies on the planet. He gave me a crazy salary, he leased me a Jaguar, and he had me living in a luxury apartment rent-free. Even if he did call me his assistant, I couldn't complain about the way he treated me any more than I could complain about the way Slim treated me or, for that matter, the way Irv treated me. I was a blessed man. But on this particular morning, after a long sleep filled with end-of-the-world dreams, I was a confused man. I didn't know why in hell Irv had turned up. I didn't know if he knew I was going to be at Eisenstock's Deli or whether it was pure coincidence. I didn't know if he was in his right mind—he had, after all, recognized me and sounded normal—or whether he had escaped from a nuthouse. I didn't know anything except that he had given me his number, and before I did anything, I found myself reaching out to him. I had to know what was happening.

He answered on the first ring.

"Irv, it's Power."

"Glad you called."

"You okay?"

"As okay as an old man can be. Better that I see you in person. The phone's no good. Can you come over?"

"Sure. Just tell me where."

"Palm Beach. You know where Worth Avenue ends at Ocean Boulevard?"

"I can find it."

"There's an apartment building. The Kirkwood. Ask for Milton Eisenstock."

"That was the name of the deli from last night."

"Owned by my late uncle Milton, may he rest in peace. Don't come too late. I go to sleep early."

"How about in a couple of hours?"

"A couple of hours is good. By then I'm up from my nap."

. . . .

The huge apartment overlooked the ocean. Irv looked tired. He wore a navy sports shirt and black pants. He walked slower than I remembered. Lumbering, he led me to the living room furnished with overstuffed chairs and an L-shaped couch the color of golden wheat. The sliding glass door was open to let the ocean breeze blow through. In the middle of the floor was an easel that held a painting of an old man with a gray beard who sat alone in a boat in the middle of the sea. The figure of the man was small in comparison to the size of the sea.

"You like art, Power?" was the first thing Irv asked as he sat on the couch. I sat on a chair across from him. We both stared at the painting.

"Don't know anything about art," I said.

"Me either. But today I bought a painting. I bought this painting. I can't tell you why except that when I saw it I knew I had to have it. I saw it at an art gallery down the street. I'd walked by that gallery a hundred times before, but never once did I think about stopping in to buy or even look. But today this picture was in the window. Today I stopped in and looked, and today I had them deliver this painting into my living room, complete with an easel. I bought it for one simple reason."

"I guess that's because you liked it."

"No, Power, it's not that I like it. Of course I don't dislike it. But I bought it because I have to look at it. It's saying something to me that I have to hear. And do you know what it's saying?"

I didn't know what to say. I still wasn't sure about Irv's mental condition. I figured it was best to let him do the talking.

"What's it saying, Irv?" I asked.

"It's saying that I'm alone, Power, that's what it's saying. It's also saying I better get used to it. There's no way around it. You want a cup of coffee, Power? A cup of tea?"

"Coffee would be great."

"Cream and sugar?"

"Please."

Irv raised his voice and called, "Maria . . . bring us a tea and coffee . . . both light and sweet."

Irv kept staring at the painting. "So now you understand why I had to buy this thing," he said. "You're seeing what I'm seeing, aren't you?"

I looked at the painting and then I looked at Irv. "You're seeing yourself," I said.

"I'm seeing myself," Irv confirmed. "I'm out there sitting in a sea of nothing."

"But you have a lot. You have your health back."

"My health never went away."

"The last time I saw you in Chicago, though, you were acting like—"

Irv stopped me and said, "*Acting* is the right word."

"But why?"

"Well, Power, if you act one way, sometimes people act another."

"I see," I said as the tea and coffee arrived on a silver tray with an assortment of chocolate cookies.

"I saw plenty," said Irv. "I saw things I didn't want to see but things I needed to see. There were things that made me sick, the same things that put me in the boat and blew me out to sea. So that's where I am now, drifting. Just drifting."

"And what about the others?" I asked.

"Which others?"

"The ones who didn't understand you were acting."

"Gone."

"John Mackey?" I asked, remembering the pale-skinned consigliere who smoked those skinny cigars.

"Terrible accident. A truck ran him off the road. His car went up in flames. Nothing left of anything . . . or anyone."

"And Judy?"

"Gone."

"Where?" I asked.

"Last I heard, Dubai, but I don't ask. What's a Jewish girl doing in Dubai? Pretending she's not Jewish—that's what she's doing. I don't care. I cut her off. My own blood, but I'm through. Not another cent."

"And your business?"

"Sold."

"Everything?"

"Everything."

"Why?"

"Ask the man in the boat why he's alone. If the painting could talk, he'd tell you that's because there's no one left to trust. That is the great fact, Power. That is the reason God woke me up in the middle of the night to get a piece of cheesecake at my late uncle's deli, may he rest in peace. God wanted that I should bump into you. He wanted that I should tell you the Great Fact. Your uncle Slim wanted me to teach you, but I couldn't teach you until I learned it myself. And what I learned was the people—the very person—I trusted most fucked me the worst. Three words, Power, three little words that took me a lifetime to learn. Don't trust anyone."

"But aren't you trusting me by telling me all this?" I asked.

"I don't need to trust you. I don't need to trust anyone anymore. There's no more operation. No more merchandise. No more Candy Girl and no more interest in the music business. Nothing to buy, nothing to sell, nothing to steal. No businesses, no budgets, no P&L statements. Only a little account in a bank in Switzerland."

I wanted to ask how "little" that account really was, but of course I didn't. I could only imagine. I didn't say anything while Irv nibbled on a chocolate cookie and took a sip of tea, all the while staring at the painting. "Judy was in on it," he finally said.

I kept silent. I knew I didn't have to say anything. Irv needed to tell someone—and I just happened to be that someone.

"Judy and her mother both. Judy, her mother, and her mother's fuckin' husband, Harvey, the guy with the car dealership. They were in on it with John Mackey. The whole thing had been in the works for months."

"What made you suspect?"

"I saw a couple of e-mails from Judy to Mackey. Because I never had a computer in the office, and because I never told Mackey I can use a computer, he thought I didn't know how to use one. But when everyone started using them, I got a teacher who came to my home. I learned how to use a computer. I started smelling shit on Mackey's computer. That's when I knew if I wanted to find the truth I had to lose my mind."

"Or make it seem that way," I added.

"Sometimes it felt like I wasn't acting. Like I really was going crazy. To have a daughter do this to you. To have your most trusted man stab you in the back and try to rob you blind. This is something no man can endure. But I endured it. I looked at the situation and said, 'This is happening to you. This is real. You are not as smart as you thought you were. People fooled you. People used you. People cannot be trusted. So just get in your boat and sit. Get used to being alone.'"

"Did you say anything to Judy or her mother?"

"What could I say? It was enough that Harvey, the Cadillac dealer, suffered a great misfortune. A disgruntled employee went crazy, put a gun in Harvey's ear, and shot him dead. They never caught the employee. But the whole thing scared Judy and her mother. Her mother moved to Bermuda and Judy went off to live with the Arabs."

I finished my coffee. I didn't know what to say.

"I've called you out here on this beautiful day," said Irv, "to tell you a sad story. I'd like to sweeten the story. I'd like to make it prettier than it is. But I owe you the truth. Now come, let's look at the sunset. Looking at the sunset is the highlight of my day."

I followed him out to the balcony. As the sun slipped behind the horizon, the sky turned purple-pink. "It's worth living in Florida," said Irv, "just to see these sunsets."

After a few minutes we went inside and took our seats. "I haven't asked you what you're doing in Miami, Power. I haven't asked you any questions because I don't need any answers. I figure you're here because Slim sent you to keep learning. I figure you're still following Slim's lead."

"And shouldn't I be?"

Irv offered a half smile. He didn't answer my question but instead said, "I have a present for you. The painting. I want you to take the painting."

"But I thought you loved it."

"I didn't say I loved it. I didn't even say I liked it. I said I had to look at it. Now I've looked at it enough. I want you to have it. Hang it on your wall. It's not ugly. It's well done. The man in the boat looks real. The sea around him looks like a real sea. It tells you a story you can't forget. It's my story, Power. It's my gift to you."

Irv stood up, signaling that this encounter was over. I thanked him for the coffee, the cookies, and the painting. I lifted it off the easel and carried it out. When I got back to my apartment at Sugar's Shack, I hung it on the wall across from my bed. Before I fell asleep that night I looked at it for a very long time. It got into my dreams. I got into that boat. The boat started shaking. I looked down to see a killer shark was after me, like in that movie *Jaws,* a killer shark going for my throat. I woke up in a sweat.

Ride Wit Me

My encounter with Irv took place toward the beginning of winter. I'd been in Miami for slightly over a year. Two weeks after Irv had given me the painting, I called him, just to see how he was. The number was out of service. I waited awhile but decided to visit him again. But when I went to the Kirkwood in Palm Beach, the building manager said that no one was living in the apartment of Milton Eisenstock. It had been sold and was presently being renovated for its new owners, a family from Melbourne, Australia. When I asked if he had forwarding information for the man who had been living there, I was told that the gentleman specifically did *not* leave a new address or phone number.

"Did he say whether he was staying in Florida?" I asked.

"He didn't say anything. One day he was here, the next day he wasn't." I wanted to talk to Irv because our last meeting left me unsatisfied. I understood how being betrayed turns your world upside down. I understood how it can make you do things that you wouldn't normally do. You wanna strike back the way you were struck. You wanna get even. You get crazy and violent and you'll stop at nothing to see that justice is done—whatever it is you consider justice to be. I understood all that.

What I didn't understand, though—and what I desperately wanted to know—were the details of the betrayals. I wanted to know more about the relationship between Irv and John Mackey. How long had Mackey worked for him? As I remembered, it was decades. During those years when things were going well, didn't Irv have at least some suspicion that Mackey might be plotting against him? I kept hearing those three words he had left me with—"Don't trust anyone." But there had to be exceptions.

Okay, his ex-wife and his daughter and his consigliere had been out to get him, but when he was a kid he trusted his mother, just like I had trusted my mother. Or did he? Was that a mistake? "Don't trust anyone" sounded smart, but was it practical in the real world? You have to trust the elevator repairman at Sugar's Shack to fix the thing so the cables don't snap. Driving down I-95, you have to trust that the drivers going in the opposite direction aren't going to switch sides and hit you head-on. Without some trust, you lose your mind. Without some trust, you never leave your apartment. You become a recluse.

Maybe Irv had become a recluse. If so, I wanted to find him and learn more about him and this latest change in his life. I felt like he had more to teach me than "Don't trust anyone." I guess I was feeling that, strange as it seems, I trusted Irv to teach me about trust. But most important of all, I wanted to ask why, when I asked him if I could trust Slim, he didn't answer me. He just gave me this half smile. Maybe I was making it up, but I thought there was something behind that half smile—and I had to know what it was.

My last weeks in Miami went by with the speed of high-powered blow. I could see that the drug, even though I thought I wasn't overdoing it, was creeping up on me. It sure as hell was creeping up on Sugar.

I had learned to like cocaine. If I had the cheap stuff, maybe I'd have had negative associations, but I didn't. I had the best. I liked the way the best stuff lightly burned my nose; I liked the drip that came after the first few snorts; I liked the rush to my heart and the heady excitement to my brain. With just a single line, all the red lights turned green. I'd take off from that first line and run through an evening of good vibes with clients and good sex with one of a half-dozen women waiting for me to call. I got into threesomes. I got into X. I went way to the other side of wildness. I drew the line when it came to men though. If it was a scene of more than two players, I'd have to be the only man. I got no complaints. Fact is, I got rave reviews.

"You're a fuckin' star," said Sugar, who was able to work with his high-end clients less because I was working with them more. "You're so good at this shit," he added, "I'm giving you a raise."

The raise was minimal, but I didn't care. I knew it made Sugar feel secure to keep me on a short leash. I never hit his suppliers. Within an hour of getting paid by a customer, I'd have the money in Sugar's hand. That's how he wanted it. And I was happy to accommodate. I was happy to ignore the remark of the wife of one of our best clients when she saw me leaving their palatial Coral Gables estate.

"That crap he's selling separates you from your soul!" she screamed to her husband, president of the local yacht club. "Keep sniffing it up your nose and you won't remember what it's like to have a soul."

I ignored the remark at the time but remembered it the night Sugar told me he was buying a state-of-the-art greyhound racetrack complex that included a club with a bar, a dance floor, and a dozen poker rooms. He snorted up a line and began describing the place. "Man," he said, "you've never seen anything like it. It's all silk and steel. I mean, the place is laid out cold. You wanna see it?"

"Sure," I said.

He laid out another line and, before offering me a hit, had it all up his nose. His old adage of "one line is enough" had flown out the window.

"Two lines means I ain't driving," he said, throwing me the keys to his Benz.

On the way over, I saw him opening up a small vial and doing even more coke. This time he asked me if I wanted some. I'm not sure why I said no—something told me it was a good idea to stay sober—and I politely turned him down. He didn't think twice about it. "More for me," he said, smiling and snorting up the vial.

When we got to the track, he was flying. The greyhounds were flying as well, and it was exciting to see the animals in action. They were graceful and beautiful to watch. He placed a bet. He lost. He went into the men's room and came out even more loaded. Another bet, another loss.

"Doesn't make a shit, Power," he told me. "I'm buying this whole thing, lock, stock, and barrel."

In the club, he introduced me to the manager, a man named Horatio, who took me and Sugar to a booth in the back of the dance floor. Several ladies came our way. Sugar felt compelled to tell every single one that he was buying the place—and doing it soon. We took a tour of the poker rooms. He sat down at one of the tables and within twenty minutes lost $30,000.

"What difference does it make?" he asked me as we walked outside so he could dip into another vial. "All that money's coming back to me anyway."

Back inside we bumped into a gorgeous young woman who had been signed to Sugar's modeling agency before it fell apart. She asked me to dance. Speaking for me, Sugar said, "No, he doesn't dance. Besides, you're my date tonight. He's my driver."

The three of us left together. They got into the backseat while I drove. He demanded that she give him head. She was hesitant. He started forcing her. I started to say something. "Shut the fuck up!" he screamed. "Your fuckin' job is to drive."

After she did him, he said, "That's the worst fuckin' blow job I've ever had. Who taught you how to suck dick, your mother? Get the fuck outta my car." In the rearview mirror, I saw him opening the door and trying to push her out. I stopped the car.

"Can't do that, Sugar," I said.

"Fuck you!" he screamed in my face.

We were on a busy street. The girl was scared. I got out of the car, reached in my pocket, and handed her a wad of twenties. "Take a cab home," I told her. "He's not himself tonight."

By then Sugar was out of the car standing next to us. He went for the girl's face with his fist. I blocked his arm before he reached her. He knew he was in no shape to fight me. He backed off. Back in the car, he reached in his pocket for another vial. The shit was up his nose before I pulled away. I was relieved when I saw the girl get into a cab.

All the way back to the Shack, Sugar didn't say a word. When we arrived, I figured I'd leave him on his own. He didn't want that though.

"Come on up," he said. "I wanna show you how business is done in this town."

Once in the penthouse he went to his safe, dialed the combination, opened the door, and pulled out a fresh quantity of coke. There was no stopping him now.

"I'm calling my broker," he said. "This scumbag owes me fuckin' everything. He built his business on me. If I say, 'Jump,' he's gonna say, 'How high?'"

Sugar put his desk phone on speaker and punched out the number. A man answered. He had obviously been asleep.

"Is this Craig, my scumbag real estate broker?" asked Sugar.

"Hey, Sug, everything okay?" asked the man in a daze.

"You sleeping?"

"I was."

"Well, get the fuck up. I want that deal for the dog track done by ten tomorrow morning."

"Let me remember the details," said the broker.

"It's your fuckin' job to know the details."

"I'm thinking, Sugar, I'm thinking. I'm remembering now . . . you guys were some three million dollars apart."

"Bridge the gap. Make it happen. I'll up it by a mil."

"That might not work."

"I pay you to make it work, scumbag. Make the fuckin' deal or I'll find someone who will."

Sugar slammed down the phone. "That's how you deal with pricks like Craig. You put the fear of God in him. How 'bout a toot?"

"No, thanks," I said. "I'm tired. I'll see you tomorrow."

"Where the fuck you going?"

"To sleep."

"The hell you are. This party is just getting started. Get the bitches up here."

"Which ones?"

"The crazy ones. The ones hanging in VIP. Just bring bitches, the wilder the better. You and me are gonna be the only swinging dicks up here."

"Hey, man, I'm really exhausted . . ."

"I don't give two shits if you're about to fall out. Take a hit and get started, boy."

Against my better judgment, I took a short hit. A wave of energy surged through me. I went down to the club and, a half hour later, came back up with a half-dozen ladies, wild and willing to get wilder.

I did a little bit more blow that night—just enough to stay awake. I just watched. The party was all about Sugar degrading these women. It wasn't a turn-on for me. It was disgusting. At one point, I tried to stop it, but neither Sugar nor the women wanted to stop. They had consumed enormous amounts of cocaine. The cocaine had separated them from their souls. I wondered what the hell was happening to my soul. At that moment, I realized that I didn't simply dislike the drug,

I fuckin' hated it. I wanted my brain to stop spinning. I wanted Sugar to stop howling with delight as the women violated themselves and each other with oversized sex toys.

Dawn arrived. Light began streaming into the penthouse. The girls had passed out while Sugar, more than half-crazed, was telling me how he was going to redo the greyhound complex. His eyes were beet red, and his talk was a nonstop stream of ego-inflated bullshit. I didn't see how he could keep it up much longer, but he did. He called Craig, the broker, and by midmorning the deal seemed to be going down. Then it hit a snag. To secure the loan, the banker wanted more collateral than Sugar was willing to provide. That's when Sugar lost it. On a conference call with the broker and banker, he called them both dick-sucking scumbags and threw the phone across the room. It struck one of the girls, asleep on the couch, in the forehead. She began bleeding profusely. I ran over to her. She was crying hysterically; the wound was deep. I got my phone and called 911.

"What the fuck you doing?" Sugar shouted.

"Getting help."

"Let the bitch bleed!"

"I'll carry her downstairs to my place."

"I said let her bleed!"

"Are you crazy? She'll die."

"Who gives a shit?"

I ignored Sugar. I picked up the girl and began carrying her out. Sugar came after me. It didn't take much to stop him, just a quick kick to his nuts. He went down.

Two days later I was back in Atlanta, sitting across from Slim at Junior's Barbershop, where he got his weekly trim. Christmas was around the corner.

"And the girl?" Slim asked me when I told him about the incident.

"Wasn't hurt as bad as I thought. She's okay."

"And you paid the hospital?"

"In cash," I said.

"No police report. Nothing to trace it back to Sugar."

"Nothing."

"And the bitch is cool? She's not going to the law?"

"I took care of her. Ten G's."

"So you did good. You protected your man."

"I don't ever want to see that asshole again."

"I understand."

"I'm not sure what you had in mind when you sent me over there," I said.

"Are you kidding, boy? You learned a lot."

"I learned what *not* to do."

"Son," said Slim, "that's more important than learning what *to* do. You see what happens when you start dipping into your own stuff. The fools get fucked up on the primo goods. They can't keep their hands off it. The smart ones, like me, stay straight as an arrow. You learn that lesson, Power, and you good for life."

"I ain't going near no blow," I said. "That shit is evil."

"Does my heart good to hear you talking that way. Makes me feel like I'm raising you right."

By hooking me up with a guy like Sugar? By leaving me in Miami for over a year? These were silent thoughts. But I didn't say anything about that. Instead I told him about the high school equivalency program that I had completed through the mail.

"And here I thought you were getting nearly as much pussy as me," said Slim, "and meanwhile you got your head stuck in books."

"It kept me sane," I said. "All that partying was turning my brain into scrambled eggs."

I spoke the truth. I had never completely turned away from everything that Sugar offered, but those last months were getting to me. The night at the dog track was the last straw. Before that I'd been studying during the days and actually enjoying reading books on history and psychology. I was always good at math. The truth was that this correspondence school was almost too easy. It made me want to go to college. I wanted to study business and economics. I had the urge to hang out with people who were interested in something other than sex. Wasn't that I didn't like sex or even getting a little high now and then. But, man, for someone still not twenty-one, I'd had more than my fair share.

Slim was obsessed with this idea of being a champion athlete in bed. I wasn't. I had proven myself. More than likely, he hadn't. I didn't need to keep talking about it. He did. I was bored with the discussion. When he asked for details about the hottest women in South Beach, I told him that they blurred together in my mind. What I couldn't tell him, though, was that I wanted a woman like Beauty—a woman with brains and class, charm and wit.

I steered the conversation to education. When I mentioned college, though, Slim wasn't happy.

"What the hell you gonna learn there?" he asked.

"Business. Economics."

"Street business is different than straight business. Street economics is different than Wall Street economics. You need to stay in the streets."

"I've been in the streets now for years. I think it's time I got some serious book learning. I'm ready for that."

"Well," he said, jangling his matching diamond wristbands, "it's hard to fault a cat who says he wants college. I know you a deep thinker, Power, even if I do continue to whip your pathetic ass at chess. Yes, sir, only a fool would bad-mouth a college education, and I ain't no fool. So I'll give you a choice. You go on to college. You stay here and pick any college in Atlanta you want. You hit those books, boy. You study up and work that brain. And I'll get someone else to fill that slot in New York."

"New York?" I asked. "You were sending me to New York?"

"Yeah, I was. New York was going to be the last course in my educational plan for you. But it's another street hustle, and now I know you prefer college."

I didn't say anything for a few seconds. I didn't have to. He knew he had me. The last thing I had heard from Wanda about Beauty was that she was still living in New York. Slim leaned back in the big barber chair and smiled the smile of a winner.

The man was still full of surprises. He still knew how to get to me.

The Holly Windsor Agency

Before I left for New York, Andre Gee said he wanted to take me to dinner. He also said that it'd be better if Slim didn't know. I loved Dre and assured him that it would be strictly between us. I was curious to hear what he had to say—and why in secret?

Because he did a lot of Slim's dirty work, Dre stuck to himself. Because of his stutter, he didn't say more than he had to. So he wasn't all that social. But he was a sweet cat who always had my best interests at heart. And he was also a cat who took such abuse from Slim that you couldn't help but feel for him.

We met at a Buckhead steakhouse called Bones. We went to a private room and sat at a table in the back.

"H-h-h-h-h-have whatever you l-l-l-l-l-like," he said.

Like me, Dre wasn't much of a drinker. We ordered a couple of Cokes and two big steaks.

"T-t-t-t-tell me about M-M-M-Miami, Power. How w-w-w-was it?"

To get the words out, Dre squinted his eyes or hit the table with a fist. I'd known other people with stutters. Most of them had managed to get around their blocks, but Dre was different. His stutter stopped him at practically every other word. But his stutter made me like him more; it made him more lovable. His eyes were filled with sincerity. The brotha had soul.

I thought of Irv's advice—and even mentioned it to Dre. I said it was hard to trust anyone. Dre nodded in agreement.

"You d–d–d–d–don't g–g–g–g–gotta say n–n–n–n–n–nothing," he struggled to say.

But I spoke anyway. Dre could be trusted. So I told him the long story about my adventures in South Beach. When I was through, he gave out a long sigh. By then the steaks had arrived. We ate in silence.

After dinner Dre said, "And n–n–n–n–n–now it's New York."

"Leaving next week," I said.

"B–b–b–b–b–b–beautiful, baby. That's a g–g–g–g–g–good thing."

"We'll see. At this stage in my life, man, I'm not really sure of anything, Dre."

"I kn–kn–kn–kn–kn–know what you mean, b–b–b–b–bro. But I am sure of one th–th–th–th–thing. R–r–r–r–r–real fuckin' su–su–su–su–sure."

"What's that?"

"D–d–d–d–d–don't c–c–c–c–come b–b–b–b–b–back."

"You're kidding, aren't you?"

"I'm d–d–d–d–d–dead s–s–s–s–s–s–serious. D–d–d–d–d–don't c–c–c–c–c–come b–b–b–b–b–back."

I could see how hard it was for Dre to say the words. But I could also see how deeply he meant them.

"Why are you saying all this?" I asked.

He wouldn't say. He just looked at me with pleading eyes.

"Is that why you asked me to dinner?" I asked. "To tell me this one thing?"

He just nodded.

"And I don't get to know why?" I asked. "I don't get to hear any of your reasons?"

He shook his head no, paid the check, and left.

I left for New York with enthusiasm. That was because of Beauty. I saw fate bringing us closer together. I realized that the chances of bumping into her in a city of eight million wouldn't be great, but I also knew that just walking the streets that she walked would give me hope and maybe even keep me happy. I was happy that I was able to get into a community college not far from the apartment I found on lower Broadway in Soho. The apartment and college were all within walking distance of the offices of the Holly Windsor Agency.

Holly was the one who had lost her modeling agency to Sugar, when rather than bail her out, Slim had let her sink. I presumed that was the end of the story—but it wasn't. When Sugar started slipping in Miami, Holly started rising in New York. Somehow Slim got back in her good graces, taking credit for saving her from a disastrous situation in Miami real estate and encouraging her to start a new business in New York. According to Slim, that business also involved the fashion world. Again, I got excited because I knew that was a world that Beauty had already entered. When I asked for details, Slim couldn't give me any—only that Holly Windsor was one of the smartest women he'd ever met, and he was absolutely sure she had lessons I needed to learn.

I arrived in the city in January. Moms had been gone four and a half years. It felt like twenty. Between Chicago and Miami, I'd walked through heaven and hell. Despite my ties to Slim, I felt adrift. I had proven to myself that I could adapt and survive. I'd negotiated my way through a number of situations. I had learned to kick back and observe. I had learned that most often things are not what they seem. I had learned to trust no one, and I had learned not to sample whatever merchandise I was selling. I had seen that business was cruel, people were cruel, and, more often than not, people were out for themselves. I had concluded that if I talked less and listened more, people presumed I liked them. Everyone wants to tell his story. Everyone thinks his story is the most important in the world. And everyone, because I try to be patient, assumes I think his story is the most interesting one I've ever heard.

This much I had learned for sure: Just sitting across from someone and listening gives you power. It gives you information about them. It's like you're in the audience watching a play. You can relax, watch the action, and enjoy the plot. You don't have to do anything. You just show up, take your seat, and settle back. That's the approach I took when I went to meet Holly Windsor for the first time.

It was a mild winter for New York City. The air was crisp and clean, and the rhythms of the city got under my skin—the stream of yellow cabs, the people on the street, the anxious hurry-up attitude that makes New York New York. I felt energized. After the sticky humidity of Florida and Georgia, the cold felt good against my skin. I liked wearing an overcoat. I liked seeing women fashionably dressed in long woolen skirts and sweaters. I'd seen enough South Beach bikinis to last me a lifetime. To me, New York had class.

The Holly Windsor Agency lobby had plenty of class. It was in a converted hat factory turned high-tech office building. The brick walls were exposed and the lighting subdued. The furniture was curvy and sleek, like pieces of modern sculpture. The receptionist looked like Lady Gaga. I wondered what Holly Windsor looked like.

I didn't expect her to have purple hair and be as tall as me. Her hair wasn't entirely purple—it was basically black—but it was accented with purple highlights. She wore a black pantsuit and silver jewelry except for purple earrings that matched the highlights in her hair. She wasn't pretty, but I wouldn't call her ugly. She knew how to work with what she had. She had height. She had a thin body. Her neck was long and her mouth small. I noticed that her fingernails were painted black. I also noticed her shoes—purple Adidas sneakers. She looked at me straight in the eye. Her own eyes were misty gray. She spoke in a low, excited voice, something like an actress.

"Oh, Power," she said, extending her hand, "since the first I heard your name I have been dying—darling, I mean *dying*—to meet you. What kind of man carries the name of Power? I had to know. I had to see for myself. Now that I see, I understand. Follow me into my den. There's much to discuss."

Her den had no desk, only two matching black suede couches and a silver love seat. On the wall were paintings of exotic birds and sexy flowers. Purple drapes were drawn and fell all the way to the floor. Outside I could hear the traffic on Broadway. Her iPod was on low volume, but I could hear a love song by Prince.

As Holly leaned back in the love seat, I tried to guess her age. Forty? Fifty? Somewhere in there.

"You come highly recommended," she said. "You must tell me all about yourself."

"Not much to tell."

"Oh, please, darling. Even at your ridiculously young age, I know you've lived a life of adventure. Tell me about the people you've been working with."

"I've just been training here and there. Looking to learn."

"And have you learned?"

"I think so."

"Charles Simmons tells me your best quality is discretion," she said. "And I can see that your reluctance to discuss your former employers is an indication of that discretion. But of course I know Mr. Irv Wasserman, and naturally I know Mr. Renato Ruiz, and I am certain you would not be here had you not served them both with absolute loyalty and discretion. As a matter of fact, my agency is all about discretion. So feel free to say whatever you like about your former employers. I assure you, love, that it will go no further than this room. I hope you don't mind if I smoke."

"It's your office."

"It's a den, darling, not an office." She placed a cigarette in a slim black holder and lit it with a silver lighter. "Tell me what you've been through, Power. Open your heart."

"I've just been trying to mind my own business."

"While helping others with theirs. But what was their business like? What was it like to be working with a man like Wasserman? And what is your take on our mutual friend Mr. Ruiz?"

"They're interesting men."

"Discretion! You are the quintessence of discretion! A quality to be admired, but now you are in New York, far away from your former bosses, and I must know what you think and how you feel about everything. If I am to trust you, darling Power, I must know you."

Holly took a long drag of her cigarette and blew out a perfectly formed ring of smoke. I watched it float up to the ceiling.

"Once we start working together, you'll get to know me soon enough," I said.

"Why do you think that Ruiz's attempt to take over my agency met with such catastrophic results? Can you tell me that?"

"Not really."

She laughed out loud. I liked her laugh. It was almost musical. Her laugh made me smile.

"He failed because he's a fucking idiot, isn't he? He failed because, when it comes to women, he knows nothing—absolutely positively nothing. He failed because he's a lowlife drug dealer. He failed because he's a sleazeball looking to operate in a world of class. Wouldn't you agree with me, dear Power? Wouldn't you say that I've hit the nail on the head?"

"I'm not sure."

"Please, dear, spare me your loyalty. Admit this man is trash."

I stayed silent.

"You're perfect, Power, you really are. Given the chance to bad-mouth people you must really want to bad-mouth, you still say nothing. Most impressive, darling. Most impressive indeed. That makes me feel like when our time together is over, you'll also be discreet in discussing me. And, importantly, in discussing my clients."

"Who are your clients?"

"Brilliant question. You don't know?"

"If I did, I wouldn't ask."

"Women. My clients are women, beautiful women. That's why you're here, isn't it? Aren't you here because you love beautiful women and beautiful women love you?"

"Not really. I'm here because Slim sent me here."

"Charles told me that, like him, you are a great connoisseur of beautiful women. He told me that you are an old-fashioned man who likes to protect beautiful women. Am I wrong?"

I just shrugged. I didn't know where this was going.

"Do you understand what a modeling agency does?" she asked.

"Find work for models," I answered.

"And what sort of work?"

I didn't know why I was being questioned like this, but I guessed that was Holly's style. "Magazine work," I said. "Work on TV commercials. The usual."

Holly smiled. "A reasonable answer from a reasonable man. You are a reasonable man, aren't you?"

"I think so."

She put out her cigarette in a silver ashtray and stood up. She had good posture. She walked over to the window, pulled back the drapes, and pointed to the street below.

"Most men aren't reasonable. Most men think with their dicks. Wouldn't you agree with me, dear?"

"I've never taken a survey," I said.

"Are you a man who thinks with your dick?"

I laughed. "I like to think that I think with my brain, Miss Windsor."

"Holly," she said, correcting me. "I am Holly and you are Power. And your power in sitting in my den and having this dialogue with me, darling, this *extraordinary* dialogue, is quite evident. This is a screen test, Power. This is your moment. And I must say you're doing wonderfully well. Are you proud of yourself? Are you feeling good?"

"I'm feeling fine," I said, thinking that the lady was more than half nuts.

"Good, because what I'm feeling is that you're right for this job. I say that because I'm a woman who lives life instinctually, not scientifically. Science is overrated, wouldn't you say?"

"Don't know."

"Well, I do, sweetheart. I know that most men think through their dicks. I have experience in that area. Tremendous experience. Experience is our greatest teacher. Books are fine. You're studying certain books, aren't you?"

"At the community college, yes."

"And what books are those?"

"Business books. And a history one."

"You're ambitious, Power, which is another reason you're sitting in my den subjecting yourself to my scrutiny. Only ambitious people interest me. Without ambition life is a boring train ride from the crib to the grave. That sounds philosophical, doesn't it? Are you taking philosophy at that junior college?"

"No."

"Good. Philosophy is a waste of time. I don't like it. But I do like psychology. Are you taking a psychology course?"

"No."

"You should, darling. See if it's not too late to register for Psychology 101. I think of myself as a psychologist. And recently I've been tested. Intensely tested. And I must say that I've passed with flying colors. Would you like me to explain?"

"Yes, I would."

"You have a generous spirit, Power, and a spirit that does not judge. That's important in this work. Most people love to judge. They judge others so they don't have to judge themselves. I have had to learn not to judge. Of course there are certain people—and I do confess that I have your former employer Mr. Renato Ruiz in mind—who don't require judgment because their fatal flaws of character will conspire in ways to bring them down. They will fall, as Mr. Ruiz has fallen, and their humiliation will be absolute. Other people—take your Charles Simmons, for example—elude judgment because their brilliance keeps them three or four steps ahead of us mere mortals. Are you following me, darling?"

"I think so."

"Now I will speak of myself. I will speak of myself in the third person—as Holly Windsor. I will look at myself like a character in a play, a girl from Tulare, a small city in the very fertile agricultural belt of central California, a city that was neither here nor there. This girl, this Holly Windsor, grew up on fashion magazines because her mother loved fashion. Her mother, June, was a failed model who, having missed the mark in New York City, found herself back in her hometown of Los Angeles modeling at a car show, where she met a wealthy farmer named Jack Windsor. Jack grew tomatoes, asparagus, and apricots. Jack appreciated beautiful women and June was certainly beautiful. Her first and only child—Holly Windsor—was not. You might say that she was homely. But June couldn't accept that fact and, with the magic of makeup, worked on Holly for years and years. Do you know why I'm telling you all this, darling?" she asked.

"No."

"Because it's absolutely essential that you know Holly Windsor. You must know who she is. She must reveal herself to you with complete candor. She must tell you that she has suffered at the hands of a mother who could not accept a simple reality—that her daughter had the face of her father, not her mother. Am I boring you, darling?"

"Not at all."

"Good, because there is more to tell about Holly Windsor. She tried to see herself through her mother's distorted lens. Her mother trained her in poise, taught her posture and charm. Her mother gave her all the skills that, as a young lady, her mother had lacked. But because Holly lacked beauty, she, like her mother before her, failed as a model. So she left New York and flew south to Miami. Before I go any further, there is an essential detail in this story that explains why Holly Windsor and June Windsor no longer speak. Can you guess what that detail might be?"

"I wouldn't want to try."

"Holly Windsor loves women. She loves them passionately. Does that shock you, darling Power?"

"No."

"Does that surprise you?"

"Not really."

"So you had come to that conclusion on your own?"

"I hadn't really thought about it."

"Discretion! You are the soul of discretion! How I love this man! How I thank the sweet fates of good fortune for sending him my way! Do you think of yourself as a Southern gentleman?"

"My mother taught me good manners."

"They show. They really do, darling. They make a woman feel at ease. Holly Windsor thought that by moving to Miami *she* would feel at ease. The pace would ease up. The pressures of New York would be lifted. She found work at a swimsuit modeling agency answering the phone. Five years later she was second in charge. And five years after that, she ran the place. Let me ask you a question, my love. Have you seen *Scarface*?"

"Sure."

"Well, Holly Windsor became the Scarface of Miami modeling. She took over the city. She scooped up every salable model in sight— and she got top dollar. She taught herself Spanish. *Habla español,* Power?"

"No."

"Well, Holly does. Holly went to Brazil and Colombia, to Venezuela and Chile, where she sold her models to the top magazines. Holly went to France, Holly went to Italy. Holly became rich, richer than her rich farmer father, who, along with her mother, vowed never to speak to her again because she loved women. Let me be clear, though. And let me be honest. Holly did love many of the models she represented, but Holly did not touch one—not a single one—because Holly learned what the jackass sleazeball Mr. Renato Ruiz never learned. You don't sample your own merchandise. Ever. Are you in agreement with me, Power?"

"I am."

"Good. But just because Holly understood that one lesson didn't mean she understood other lessons. Cocaine isn't the only seductive drug that can bring you down. Real estate is just as lethal. Especially in South Florida. The lust for property—beachfront property—can overwhelm a woman from Tulare, California, looking to conquer the world and prove to her parents, who have scorned her for loving women, that she is, above all, a genius. Have you ever met a genius?"

"I'm not sure."

"Holly Windsor thought she was a genius. She was absolutely convinced of the fact. Holly Windsor was also in love. Her lover was a real estate agent, a former beauty queen from Palm Beach named Maribel Joyspring. Can you imagine such a name, Power? Maribel was convinced that she too was a genius. So we have two self-proclaimed geniuses, Holly and Maribel, sharing a bed and a vision of buying up South Beach, one block at a time. What Holly the genius didn't know was that Maribel the genius was also crooked to the core.

"Lust is one thing. Lust in and of itself is not confusing. Lust is what it is. But love—love, my darling, is the most confusing emotion on God's green planet. And when you have lust and love all wrapped up in parcels of pricey real estate—well, you can see what happened. The modeling agent followed the crooked real estate agent down the primrose path to financial ruin. So what did Holly Windsor do? She begged and borrowed and kept it all together until it all fell apart. And she fell apart. Did Mr. Charles Simmons tell you this story, Power? Am I boring you?"

"Yes . . . I mean, no, you're not boring me, and yes, Slim told me something about the story, but not much."

"Well, I'm telling you *too* much, but I have to, darling. I can't leave anything out of the story since you're now part of the story. A vital part. Because even though Humpty Dumpty Holly Windsor fell off the wall and had a great fall, all the king's horses and all the king's men *did* put her put back together again. She put herself back together again. She always has and she always will. That's because she's a woman who, having made a mistake once, will not make the same mistake twice. Other mistakes, perhaps. Other mistakes, certainly. But not that mistake—not the mistake of mistaking lust for love. Because if we confuse lust for love we lose reason. And reason is all that's separating us from the sleazeballs looking to steal our gold. I'm speaking of Mr. Renato Ruiz and I'm speaking of Miss Maribel Joyspring, that cunt.

"But all that is past tense. It's time to live in the present. We're told if we live in the past or worry about the future we'll miss the present. And we don't want to do that. So here's how I see the present: Presently the modeling business is a pounding headache. A nightmare. The girls are tiresome, ambitious, and bitchy. The buyers—the fashion editors, art directors, and such—are prejudiced for this type or that. The competition is fierce. In my view, the market is limited. So I've moved on. No more models."

"But I thought you ran a modeling agency."

"You thought wrong, my dear. I run an escort agency. And believe me, it's an upgrade from what I'd been doing. The market is far wider, the buyers more diverse, more generous, and, of course, infinitely more numerous. You will meet many of those buyers, as you will meet many of the women they are buying."

A whorehouse, I thought. *Slim has sent me to work in a fuckin' whorehouse.*

"Oh, darling," said Holly, "I'm afraid you don't look happy. You don't look happy at all. Does this come as a shock?"

I shrugged it off. I didn't know what to say.

Holly continued. "Well, I can assure you that you will meet a far more cultivated set of women than if you were working in a modeling agency. And you may even fall in love . . ."

"I wouldn't worry about that."

"You sound bitter, my dear. Did Mr. Renato Ruiz's excessive womanizing turn you off?"

I didn't say anything.

"This is a new world you're entering, Power, so I'd advise you to forget everything you thought you knew about women. You're about to be educated, young man, in an entirely different area of human behavior. I know you like to learn, and, believe me, you will study subjects that your community college does not offer."

"What exactly will I be doing?"

"A precise question deserves a precise answer. You will not be pimping, if that's your concern. You will be assisting me, but on the highest executive level. You will be the only man in this office. You will wear a suit and tie every day. I will personally take you shopping to make sure you have the right look. Not too formal, not too casual; elegant, European, custom-tailored jackets and suits that will make you feel like a prince. You are a prince. Prince Power. Prince Power will be seated at Queen Holly's right hand. You will meet the girls who I hire. You will give me your candid evaluation because, in truth, they are far closer to your age than mine. You will enjoy meeting them. They will enjoy meeting you. The ambience of this office, darling, is one of extreme professional dignity. We will do our work in an atmosphere of cordiality. From time to time, you will meet our clients. They too require scrutiny. Your male perspective will be invaluable. You will be forthright with me, you will be candid, you will tell me which clients you feel are suitable and which are not. In both areas—the girls and their clients—I have made some mistakes. That's why I realize I need a man's point of view. I am placing great trust in you, my dear—a trust that, according to Mr. Charles Simmons, is more than warranted. Just being with you, even for this short amount of time, assures me that Mr. Simmons is right. My inner voice says that Power is a prince, Power is here to help, Power is a great addition to what is becoming the classiest escort agency in America's classiest city. Prince Power, welcome to New York."

New York City has its own groove—fast, nervous, and impatient. You just go with it or you get swallowed up. Holly Windsor had that kind of groove. You couldn't shut her up. It was almost like you had to go with her. At least that's how I felt. If someone had said, "That woman's full of shit," I wouldn't have argued. She was an actress in some play. At the same time, I couldn't stop watching her act. I liked the play. And, in spite of myself, I even liked her. Maybe the reason I liked her is because she never stopped saying how much she liked me. I went for the flattery. And I was impressed by how honest she was about herself. People don't usually go on and on about their own mistakes. I'd never met anyone like Holly Windsor. Nothing in my life had prepared me for her way of talking or her outlook on business.

My initial thought—that I'd be working at a whorehouse—was in some ways right, but in most ways wrong. First of all, there was no house. The girls always worked on the outside. They met their dates in hotel rooms, apartments, homes, private jets, and even yachts. The big surprise, though, was the way they looked. They looked like they worked as bank managers, or lawyers, or ad executives. They looked like young ladies on their way up in the world of high finance. They wore dark pinstriped suits where the skirts were never too short. The suits were tailored to fit their perfect shapes, but the tailoring always left a lot to the imagination. Of course when they first came up to the office to be interviewed they didn't always look that way. The experienced ones did—the ones who knew that the more expensive the service, the more conservative the look. But the new ones, who had learned about Holly through mutual friends, often made the mistake of wearing way-too-sexy clothes that showed off too much cleavage or booty. For the first months, I was fascinated just watching Holly interview these women.

"Darling," she would say—she called everyone "darling"—"tell me about your mother."

That first question would throw them. They wouldn't know what to say. Some thought it was a joke, but it wasn't. Holly was dead serious. If the girl answered, "Oh, she's real nice," Holly would say, "You must tell me more than that, sweetheart." If she replied, "I can't stand her," Holly would keep the questions coming until she got the whole picture. It came down to this: If a woman had a lousy relationship with her mother Holly wouldn't hire her. If it was good, the girl had a chance. When I asked Holly about this, she said, "Darling, I told you to take psychology, didn't I? Well, you don't really have to take it because I'm teaching it. I'm teaching you that a girl's most important relationship is her first. That's with Mom. If that didn't work, chances are most of her relationships after that won't work either."

"Didn't you say that you have a terrible relationship with your mom?" I asked. "Didn't you say she doesn't even talk to you?"

"That's why I could never be an escort. Too emotionally unstable.

I look for girls with emotional stability. With stability, they have a chance to become a star in this business. Without it, they're lost."

Another stock question came early in the interview. Holly would take a cigarette, stick it in the black holder, light up, turn to the prospect, and say, "When did you lose your virginity?" When the question was answered, she'd ask, "Was it good?"

Later Holly told me, "If the first time was bad, that's not a good sign, darling, not at all. My ears are eager to hear a girl talk about how the first time was wonderful. I need girls who learned to love sex early on. I need girls who have positive attitudes about this most primal of acts. That's why my other questions involve religion. Too much religion often leads to lousy sex. My girls need to be unencumbered by guilt or a god interested in punishment of any kind. If a client wants to be punished, that's one thing. But it's the girl who will be doing the punishing, not God almighty."

I have to say that this interviewing process was interesting as hell—so interesting that I actually did sign up for a psychology course at the community college. I saw right away that studying human nature was something I'd been doing very seriously ever since my mother died. Maybe that's the real education Slim was trying to show me.

Slim never had anything good to say about college, so I didn't bother telling him that I had enrolled. My night classes didn't get in the way of my work at the Holly Windsor Agency. In addition to psych and history I was going to take a business course, but I figured it'd be better to stay general. I was learning enough business just by virtue of my work. My history teacher was a little boring, but my psych teacher was great. She came from Rome and spoke English with an accent. Professor Anna Severina was in her seventies and sharp as a tack. She talked about personality development and ego defense mechanisms and had me thinking about my own personality and defenses and whether I was suppressing the fact that I killed a man in cold blood. How did my personality develop to the point where I was able to do that? Professor Severina talked about denial and suppression and all kinds of ideas that had me wondering whether I was denying my true character by brushing off that murder as part of the education Slim was giving me. Sure, I killed. But soldiers kill every day. I was a soldier who Slim had hired out to Sugar. I did my duty—that was all. But having done it once, could I—and would I—do it again?

I gotta be honest: Part of me felt proud that I had been able to go through with it. Part of me was proud that I hadn't panicked. But another part of me was ashamed of being proud. Pride and shame lived together in the same compartment inside my head. I tried to close the door to that compartment, but it was hard. Taking psych, I began to see how the mind can play with itself—how you can keep certain doors closed. After class, I talked to Professor Severina and asked her lots of questions about human behavior.

"That book you gave us about family," I said, "is always talking about the huge influence of the mother and father. But it doesn't talk about what happens when the father dies young, when there is no father."

"The dynamic changes," she said. "It changes radically. Many times the young boy will seek out a substitute father."

"And will the substitute dad have as much influence as the dad?"

"Most definitely," said Professor Severina. "Often even more influence. The fatherless boy is so eager for a strong male figure that, in embracing a role model, his vulnerability is extreme. He's looking for strength, pure and simple. That strength can have a positive character, or in the case of young boys attracted to gangs, the strength is brutally negative."

The phrase "brutally negative" stuck with me. I couldn't get it out of my mind. During these talks with Professor Severina I was beginning to see my own mind from the outside. That made me understand myself more. Maybe the act of killing wasn't the real me. Maybe it was something I did in response to this role model. Or because of "peer pressure." "Peer pressure" was another term Mrs. Severina used in describing why certain kids become violent. Their nature isn't violent, but the cool kids are violent, and they want to be cool. I knew enough gangbangers back in the ATL to realize that this was true. It was a way to conform.

In contrast, I was seeing how the pros working for Holly were anything but conformists. They were conforming in their dress—they looked like lady bankers. They were conforming in their talk—they spoke like lady lawyers. They were dignified, they were polite, they looked like they obeyed all the rules of society, but when I got to know them, I saw that they were really rebels. They hated normal society. Take Lisa.

Lisa wasn't her real name. Most of the girls changed their names. They changed their whole histories. They reinvented themselves. If they had really grown up in Iowa, they'd say they grew up in Connecticut. Lisa said she grew up in England, but she really grew up in Brooklyn. A vocal coach taught her an English accent. I was there the first day Lisa came in the office applying for an escort job.

Holly had me in on all the interviews. She was training me to see who was real and who wasn't. The training was fascinating because usually the girl who was *not* real—the one who could act and look the part of a classy career woman, not a hooker—got the job.

Lisa wanted the job real bad. She was honest. She began by saying that as a girl in Brooklyn she dreamed of being an actress. She thought that was possible because she was beautiful. Her dad was Puerto Rican and her mom Irish. She had reddish hair and blue eyes and skin the color of dark gold. Right after high school, when she was eighteen, both her parents died—her dad got killed in a freak accident in his construction job and her mom got cancer. She was all alone and needed money. She worked as a waitress. She moved to Manhattan, where she found roommates in an ad. She secured an acting teacher, looked for agents, and tried out for parts. Nothing happened.

She talked about dating. The goal of every guy was to fuck her. She had seen that ever since she was fifteen or sixteen. That was nothing new. But when she got older, she expected more. Instead of getting more, though, she got less. She saw that if a guy took her out for a nice meal, he expected return payment in the form of pussy. That made her mad. The whole system set up by society made her mad. If she didn't give up the pussy, the guy flew into a rage. It was crazy, it was frustrating, and she wanted nothing to do with it.

She thought about modeling. She met a photographer who took a bunch of pictures of her. He praised her to the sky, but then he made a move. He'd get her work only if she gave him pussy. It was the same thing. For a while she thought her beauty would get her somewhere in the theater. No such luck. The apartment she shared was turning into a condo and she needed another place to live. The restaurant where she worked had lost its lease. With no job, she was down to her last dollar and had nowhere to live. By chance, a director who had auditioned her kept her cell number and called. He didn't want her in a play, but he did want her in bed. She went out with him to a cool restaurant in Tribeca. Afterward he asked her over to his brownstone. The guy owned the whole building. She slept with him that night and in the morning told him the truth—that she needed a place to stay. Could she stay for a day or two until she found a job? He said no. That's when she decided that if she was going to get fucked, she was going to get paid.

I liked Lisa and so did Holly. We liked her because she didn't hold back anything. "She understands herself," Holly said after Lisa had left. "She sees into her own mind."

When Holly wasn't sure about the credibility of a client, she had me talk to him on the phone or meet him in person. This was interesting as hell. I'd dress up in a suit, a vest, and a $150 silk tie. I felt like I was running a corporation. I'd meet a guy in the bar, say, of the Four Seasons Hotel, on Fifty-Seventh Street just off Park Avenue, where the cheapest room goes for $1,100 a night. One time there was a guy in his fifties, an overweight, balding, happy-go-lucky guy. His name was Harper. He said that he wanted a complete evening—dinner and a show followed by jazz at the Blue Note downtown. He wanted to make sure his date liked the theater and appreciated jazz. He wanted to talk about jazz. I told him that I didn't know the musical tastes of all of our escorts, but I assured him that they were charming and cultured. He liked hearing that. There was a gleam in his eye. He was willing to pay the going rate—fifteen thousand—for an all-nighter. I was ready to close the deal when I saw the waitress walk by with a tray of drinks. He tried to do it subtly, but I saw him stick out his foot so she tripped over it. The drinks went flying. I saw that same gleam in his eye; he tried to hide a smile, but he couldn't. In spite of his apologies, he enjoyed the whole thing. I figured the guy got off on humiliating women. I told Holly to forget about him. When I explained why, she agreed and said I was catching on.

I caught on so quickly that Holly turned the New York office over to me while she opened up escort services in Chicago, San Francisco, Los Angeles, and, yes, Miami. The woman was a whiz. She didn't believe in advertising of any kind. Not even on the Internet. She called the Internet too public. "Darling," she said, "any two-bit hooker can set up an escort service on the web. But that's so crass, so terribly available. The truly exclusive services must be just that—exclusive. That means word-of-mouth only."

Holly's primary job was generating word-of-mouth. She developed a national network by cultivating the powerful. A captain of industry, a U.S. senator, a world-famous athlete—she knew how to connect to these people. Part of her pitch was the fact that her agency had no presence on the Internet. Absolute discretion was the key. She'd show up at exclusive parties. She met these men at a time when, more than ever, they were worried about being caught. She didn't use e-mail or texts. She talked to you face-to-face. In New York, she had me talk to the customers the same way. We went old-school—in-person meetings, no electronic traces, and of course cash only.

One client was a brotha in his forties who'd gone to the Wharton School of Business. He owned his own ad agency and had heard about us through a client of his. We met for drinks at the Carlyle Hotel on Madison Avenue. That same night George Clooney was at the bar with friends. The brotha started telling me about his wife. After their second child, the sex stopped. He tried convincing her it was her marital duty. She wasn't buying. He got into porn but porn didn't satisfy him. He snuck out to titty bars but they made him feel cheap. He started secret dating but that got complicated. He got caught lying about being single. Talking chicks into pussy was hard work. He wanted to relax. He was willing to pay big bucks for a nooner—that meant a blow job and quick fuck. He turned out to be one of our steadiest customers. And no trouble. The guy had great manners.

I was getting good at psych and liking it. I was feeling strong. I was feeling confident. I was feeling really good about myself. Holly Windsor never held back the compliments. "Sweetheart," she said, "you understand subtlety. You yourself have a subtle mind for this, the most subtle of businesses. A successful month is one during which no complaints are registered and no news is made. We aim for a drama-free business. In fact, during these past six months or so that your subtle presence has been part of the agency, we have experienced no drama. I salute your subtlety, darling, and look forward to seeing it grow as the days fly by."

On a day that should have been a red-letter celebration—my twenty-first birthday—I took a subtle approach. I didn't tell anyone. Slim called from Atlanta, but that was it. I knew, of course, that Beauty knew, because her birthday was only a week away, but I didn't expect to hear from her—and didn't. The pressure of school and work had taken up most of the space in my head. There was always a special place for Beauty, though. I couldn't deny that because she still appeared in my dreams two or three times a week. We met in my dreams. When Professor Severina said that dreams represented suppressed desires, I thought of Beauty.

The more I got into the job at the Holly Windsor Agency, the more I got into my psych course. The two went together. I was doing psychology day and night. In fact, I decided to major in psychology. I loved looking at people's minds from different angles. Now I could see why, without a dad, I had clung so closely to my mom. I could see why, without a father figure, Slim made such a deep impression on me. When Professor Severina talked about posttraumatic periods in people's lives, I thought about that period after Moms had died. I wondered how long that period had gone on—if it was still going on. When I interviewed the ladies wanting to be escorts—and man, you can't believe how many women out there wanted the job—I heard plenty about their traumas. A couple of them had been raped. One had been beaten by a boyfriend. Another had run away from home at eighteen because her stepfather had tried to mess with her. This one woman from California who was prettier than Halle Berry and couldn't have been older than twenty-five said she had been married three times. Her first marriage, to a preacher, happened when she was sixteen—and with her mother's approval. The preacher was rich.

I got good at understanding who could handle the job and who couldn't. Not that I didn't make mistakes. I thought Betty Langston would be perfect at the job. Great shape, sunny personality, no interest in romantic entanglements. She just needed money to complete law school and this was the easiest way. But after spending two nights with the head of a big Wall Street brokerage firm, she called to say she'd fallen in love with the guy.

"How does he feel?" I asked.

"The same, Power. He's ready to leave his wife."

"Stand by," I said. "I need to discuss this with Holly."

Holly was in Seattle, setting up her newest office.

"Disaster," she said. "Disaster with a capital D. And I don't have to tell you why, do I, darling?"

"Confusion of love and lust."

"Exactly. This poor dame is cruising for a bruising. And if she gets hurt, she'll pass the pain on to us."

"So what do I do?"

"Fire her. Tell her she's through. Do it now."

"And what about him? He's one of our better clients."

"Call him and tell him that the little lady has become emotionally involved and, as responsible and discreet agents, we must ask her to withdraw from our organization. We do this to protect our clients. He'll appreciate it. And he'll also have the option to pursue her on his own or drop her."

He dropped her. A week later, Betty was crying to me about how he had disappeared. She wanted her job back. In saying no, I was gentle but firm. The parade of women who came through our office—at any time, the Holly Windsor Agency handled twenty active escorts in New York alone—never failed to fascinate me. I had learned from Sugar not to sample the merchandise, and, oddly enough, I wasn't tempted, not even by the more gorgeous women, maybe because none of them was Beauty. Even the smartest wasn't as smart as Beauty. Even the prettiest wasn't as pretty. I looked on these ladies with interest but not desire. Desire would mess me up. I also got to see what desire had done to many of the clients I met. They were addicted to escorts like junkies addicted to smack. Some guys had to have four different escorts in the same week. Others were risking financial ruin just to pay our crazy prices. These guys were out of control. I didn't want to be out of control. I wanted to learn more about the human mind. I thought about Irv's mind, Sugar's mind, Slim's mind, and the amazing mind of Holly Windsor.

A Quiet Place in the City

The months flew by. Life fell into a routine. And then it happened. It happened in the one place where it never should have happened. It happened over the one weekend when I felt happy about getting off the grid. Professor Severina was going to a four-day conference in Boston and asked me if I could house-sit. Her regular house sitter had the flu and my teacher's two dogs and cat needed care. I was happy to help. I was also happy when my cell phone went on the blink. I'd get it fixed, but I'd wait till Monday. That meant no one could reach me. It felt good to be unreachable, especially as I sat in the place that I called my refuge.

It was where I went practically every night and every morning, in between work and before and after classes. It was where I put my mind at ease, sat and drank a glass of wine or a caffe latte, or just kicked back and listened to a gifted brotha play gentle jazz on his acoustic guitar. It was a combination café/bar/coffee shop nestled in between an office building and an art gallery. I went in the first time because of its name—A Quiet Place in the City. I was looking for quiet. I loved how the walls were covered with cushiony fabrics and the floors covered with thick carpets. The noise of New York was never to my liking. New York restaurants and bars stuck with a policy of "the louder the better." The racket of people talking was supposed to indicate that this was a hot spot for business deals and romantic hookups. After work, that was exactly what I wanted to get away from. So I loved A Quiet Place. I felt safe there. I felt centered. Fact is, two months before I had kept my twenty-first birthday quiet and spent it there alone. Never in a million years would I have guessed that A Quiet Place was where my life would change forever.

Funny how life deceives you. Life looks like it's giving you a rhythm, a reason and a rhyme. Life seems to be making sense. Things seem to be settling down. I had a new sense of self-assurance and self-knowledge.

After a long day at the Holly Windsor Agency, I settled down at A Quiet Place in the City. It was beautiful sitting there by the window and looking out on lower Broadway. People rushing by. Traffic fierce. Cool fall weather. After living in the city nine months I was beginning to understand what Slim was wanting for me. Slim wanted me to see how Irv Wasserman operated. He operated subtly; in the end, he didn't trust anyone. Slim wanted to see what I'd become under the influence of Sugar—a guy consumed by ego and deadly drugs. And finally Slim wanted me to see how a brilliant woman like Holly Windsor brought balance to business—by cutting out the emotions.

I thought I had cut out the emotions. I thought I was ready, after this time in New York, to go back to Atlanta and work with Slim. When I arrived in the city, I thought fate was bringing me closer to Beauty, but I soon realized that no one really knows what the fuck fate has in store. Then here comes Holly Windsor with her view on life. I knew that Holly Windsor was, in her own way, a psychologist herself. She read people right. She especially read women right. And she read me right. She knew I could be taught. She saw that I listened. She picked up on the fact that the girls could trust me—and so could the clients. She ran around the country setting up operations while I held down the fort in the most important city in the world. That made me feel important. It was a quiet feeling, though. I didn't have to talk about it. Didn't have to tell anyone. The escorts respected me because I didn't hit on them and made sure that their clients were cool. The clients respected me because I made sure their escorts were cool. Holly was happy because the office was running smoothly. My life was running smoothly. I got A's on my psych tests and wrote a paper on ego defenses that Professor Severina called "insightful." The spelling and grammar could have been better, but she said that my ideas made sense. Everything was starting to make sense, especially sitting there in A Quiet Place in the City.

A Quiet Place had the right atmosphere to let me look back a little. I thought about Irv and Evelyn Meadows, the woman who shot him; I thought about Irv's crazy daughter, Judy, and her boyfriend, Dwayne, who got murdered; I thought about John Mackey, the consigliere killed in a car wreck; I thought of Sugar and Yuko and Mi and how Mi got shot by Gigante and how I stabbed Gigante to death. All those thoughts were noise in my head. Here, though, the thoughts drifted away while the brotha played his soft jazz guitar. Several students in A Quiet Place were working on their laptops in easy chairs. Two women, sitting at the wine bar, spoke in a quiet whisper. I think they were Chinese. A tall Dominican dude who I recognized from my psych class sat across from me, took out his iPad, and disappeared into cyberspace. I was gonna check my e-mail but decided instead to lose myself in the chords of the quiet guitar. The world was at peace.

And then I felt my phone vibrate against my thigh. At first I was pissed that the thing was working again. There went my escape. I didn't bother to answer the phone, but it kept buzzing until I got fed up, fished it out of my pocket, and glanced at the caller ID to see who was calling. It was a New York City exchange. I didn't recognize the number. Something told me to ignore the call, but something else told me to answer. I remember feeling that something was really wrong. So I answered the call. That's when I heard a voice I hadn't heard in five years. My heart started hammering. My throat went dry.

"Power," said Beauty, "Slim's gone crazy. Last week he had Dre murdered. Today Wanda Washington is missing, and I think he's killed her. He's killing anyone close to him, just like he killed Moms."

At first I couldn't speak. I couldn't process the information. It took me a while to say, "I don't believe it. That's not right. That can't be right. Are you sure? How can you be sure?"

"Call anyone you know in Atlanta and they'll tell you. Dre's gone. Wanda's gone, and you're next, Power. You gotta start running."

"To where?"

"I don't know."

"Where are you?" I asked.

"I'm here in New York."

"I gotta see you, Beauty."

"I'm afraid, Power. I'm really afraid."

HER

Anita Ward

Two weeks after her sixteenth birthday, Beauty was seated in the last row of the coach section of a Delta flight from Atlanta to New York's LaGuardia Airport. She was leafing through *Vogue* magazine when the plane flew into an unexpected thunderstorm. The turbulence was so severe that the elderly white woman next to Beauty grabbed her hand.

"It's going to be all right," Beauty assured her.

"How do you know that?" asked the woman. "Have you flown a lot?"

"Actually this is my first flight."

"Well, it's not mine, and I've never been through anything like this. Something's wrong. The plane shouldn't be shaking this much. It's gonna crash . . . I feel like it's gonna crash."

"It can't crash," Beauty stated calmly.

"What makes you say that?" asked the woman, her eyes closed as she squeezed Beauty's hand even harder.

"Because I won't let it crash," said Beauty.

"I want to believe you."

"Believe me, it's going to take a lot more than a little lightning and thunder to get in my way. My future's in New York, and nothing can stop my future."

Just then the plane took a sudden drop. The older woman let out a scream.

"It's just like a roller coaster," said Beauty. "It can be scary, but it always comes to a stop and lets you off safe and sound."

"Roller coasters petrify me," the woman confessed.

"Roller coasters are fun."

"I think you're a very nervy girl, but I hope you believe in a god that answers prayers, because only God is going to get us through this storm."

At that moment a bolt of lightning struck the plane. The jolt was intense. Sparks flew. A flight attendant, going up the aisle to make certain seat belts were fastened, was thrown to the floor. The woman seated next to Beauty began to cry. But Beauty stayed centered. She closed her eyes and pictured the streets of New York that she had read about; she imagined herself walking through Barneys on Madison Avenue and Lord and Taylor on Thirty-Ninth Street; she thought about the fabulous hat collection at Henri Bendel on Fifth Avenue and the fashion district on Seventh Avenue, where so many of the designers and manufacturers had offices; she saw herself riding the crosstown bus and the uptown subway, exploring Greenwich Village and Central Park and the bright lights of Broadway. When Beauty opened her eyes, the flight attendant had picked herself up off the floor and the plane had flown out of the storm. An hour later it landed without incident.

In the baggage area Beauty noticed a handsome, distinctly Jewish-looking man in his twenties with dark hair, wide shoulders, a broad nose, brown eyes, and a serious look on his face. He held a sign that simply said BEAUTY.

She approached him and said, "I'm Beauty."

"You sure are. Miss Ward sent me. She asked me to help you with your bags and take you to her place."

"Thank you."

"My privilege."

"Do you work with Miss Ward?"

"Yes, I work in her department at Bloom's department store. I run errands and do some modeling. By the way, my name is Solomon."

"Like the king," quipped Beauty, impressed with the man's powerful physique.

"Actually more like a queen," said Solomon, who gave her a little wink.

Even though Beauty knew that many gay men worked in the fashion world, Solomon was a surprise. He looked like an athlete.

On the way into the city, while Solomon drove the black Lincoln Town Car and Beauty sat in the back, they began chatting.

"Have you ever been here before?" he asked.

"No."

"You've come to model?"

"Oh, no, I'm just a student."

"College?"

"High school."

"I don't believe you."

"Why would I lie?"

"To impress me with your youth."

"I wish I were older."

"How old are you?" he asked.

"Sixteen."

"You look nineteen."

"Thank you—I guess."

"How do you know Miss Ward?"

"Long story."

"That you'd rather not tell."

"Actually, I'm so excited seeing that skyline, it's hard for me to concentrate on talking."

"So it's okay if I do the talking?"

"Sure."

"I was born in Israel. I'm guessing you were born in Japan."

"I was born in Atlanta, Georgia."

"But to a Japanese mother," said Solomon.

"My mom was black."

"*Was?* She's gone?"

"You were going to do the talking."

"Just trying to be polite and not dominate the conversation."

"I think you're nosy," said Beauty.

"I think you're right. But my nosiness is harmless. Though to be honest, I wasn't at all harmless when I fought in the Israeli army."

"You were a soldier?"

"Highly decorated."

"How come you have no accent?" Beauty said.

"I have American-born parents."

"And when did you come here?"

"A year ago."

"Why?"

"For the same reason you're coming to New York," said Solomon. "Fortune and fame in fashion."

"And how's that working out for you?"

"Well, I'm driving you to the apartment of one of the shrewdest buyers in America. I aspire to be her protégé. Now it appears that you have that job sewed up. So if I can befriend you, I'll still be on track to get closer to Miss Anita Ward."

"She's that good?" asked Beauty.

"Better than good. 'Amazing' is the word."

As Solomon went on about Anita Ward's genius, Beauty stopped listening. She had to savor the moment—they were driving over the Queensboro Bridge into Manhattan. Last night's rainstorm had washed away the smog and left the city sparkling. The energy was high, Beauty was high; Beauty stretched her neck to look up and out and around, Beauty rolled down the window to breathe it all in, to hear the honking cabs, the roar of the traffic, the sounds of a city more alive, more wonderful, more exciting than she had ever imagined.

"Miss Ward lives off Gramercy Park," said Solomon. "Would you mind if we stopped by my apartment first? I need to make sure Amir is up. He has an appointment he can't miss."

"It's nearly noon. Why wouldn't he be up?"

"He's a musician. Musicians work nights and sleep days."

"This is your boyfriend?"

"My significant other."

"Also an Israeli?"

"Actually a Jordanian."

"An Israeli and an Arab living together?"

"In peace and love. Trying to set an example for the world to follow."

"If you want to wake him up, why not just call him?"

"Because I want him to meet you. If he meets you, he will be crazy for you and you will be crazy for him and that will tighten the bond between the three of us. That way I will be in an even better position to become a part of Anita Ward's inner circle."

"How do you know he'll be crazy for me?" Beauty asked.

"He loves beautiful women."

"And Israeli soldiers."

"I didn't tell him I was a soldier until after our first date."

"And how did he react?"

"He ran. But then I ran even faster—and caught him. Here's our place. Come in for a sec. We'll serve you coffee and sweets on a silver platter."

Their apartment was in the basement of a Murray Hill town house. It was narrow and dark but filled with white lilies that gave off a delicious scent.

"Amir has a part-time job at a florist. He brings these home for free."

Amir was still in bed. Beauty waited in their tiny living room/kitchen area while Solomon went to wake him up. The walls were covered with dozens of Polaroid photos of family members of every description. There was also a large calendar displaying the great mosques and synagogues of the world.

After a few minutes, Solomon walked out of the bedroom followed by Amir, who was dressed in a white terry-cloth robe with the words "Holiday Inn Amman Jordan" sewn across the front pocket. He had small sleepy eyes, dark olive skin, and long wavy jet-black hair. If Solomon was five-ten, Amir was five-eight. Solomon was stocky and muscular, Amir was wire-thin and graceful. He seemed to glide across the room.

"Is this Beauty or is this not Beauty?" Solomon asked Amir.

"I am happy to meet you," said Amir, soft-spoken and a bit shy. "What can we offer you to eat?"

"Oh, I'm fine."

"Do you like sweets?" asked Amir.

"Say yes," said Solomon, urging her. "Amir takes offense if anyone doesn't like his sweets."

"Well, I do like sweets," said Beauty.

"Last night I made *kunafa*. It is a kind of cheese pastry with honey on top. Please try it," Amir beseeched in his softly accented English.

"It sounds delicious," Beauty said.

"It is good with tea," said Amir. "I will make you tea."

A few minutes later, the three of them sat close together on wicker chairs surrounding a small kitchen table. They nibbled on *kunafa* and sipped sweet tea. Beauty loved the taste of the honey-covered cheese dessert. She asked Amir about his music.

"Difficult to explain well," he said. "It is hip-hop but also jazz, and then we have a rapper who was born in Iran."

"The jazz musicians are Israeli friends of mine," said Solomon. "They are how I met Amir."

"Are you the hip-hopper or the jazz guy?" Beauty asked.

"I do both from a synthesizer. As a boy, I learned classical piano and then fell in love with electronic music. That's how I happened to come to America. And when I was here, well, I heard so many other sounds that fascinated me. I began trying a little bit of everything. I still don't do it very well, but I am trying."

"Amir is modest," said Solomon. "He is a musical visionary. He put together this current group."

"What's it called?" asked Beauty.

"All," said Amir. "That's all I could think of."

"You must hear them," said Solomon. "You must come to the club where they play. All will blow your mind."

"Please, Sol," said Amir, "leave this Beauty alone. She is just arriving here and her heart must be filled with desires to go to lovely places and see lovely things that have nothing to do with my music."

"Guess her age," Solomon told Amir.

"It is not polite to guess the age of a lady."

"She doesn't mind," said Solomon.

"If you are twenty-six and I am twenty-five, she must be twenty."

"She's sixteen!" Solomon exclaimed.

"My word," said Amir to Beauty, "you are wonderfully mature for your age. You will have a brilliant life here in this brilliant city."

"I told you that you'd like this guy," Solomon said to Beauty, who was all smiles.

"Have another piece of *kunafa*," Amir told Beauty.

"I've got to get her over to her godmother's," said Solomon.

"Anita Ward is not my godmother," Beauty said, correcting him.

"I mean her mentor," Solomon said.

"She's not my mentor."

"She will be."

"How do you know?" asked Beauty.

"I just know about these things," stated Solomon.

"My friend can be a little brusque," said Amir about Solomon, "but he does have a certain feeling for the future."

In the short drive from Murray Hill to Gramercy Park, Solomon asked Beauty, "When was the last time you saw Miss Ward?"

"I never have seen her."

"But you do know about—" Solomon stopped himself.

"Know about what?" asked Beauty.

"You'll see for yourself. It's okay. Just forget I said anything."

"Now that's impossible."

"You can handle it. You're the girl who can handle anything."

"You talk like you've known me for years."

"I have. Here we are at the park. What do you think?"

Gramercy Park reminded Beauty of an illustration out of a children's book. It was small and clean. The grass was cut and the shrubbery was pruned. Nannies pushed infants in their strollers. An older man wearing a blue blazer and red bow tie sat on a bench, where he smoked a pipe and read the *New York Times*. Kids played hide-and-seek. Solomon parked in front of an old four-story brownstone that overlooked the park.

"Miss Ward has the top floor," said Solomon. "They installed an elevator just for her."

The entryway was small, but the elevator itself was tiny. Beauty had never seen anything like it. The cabin, big enough to hold a single person—and a small person at that—was constructed of wrought iron. Figures of twin peacocks were sculpted on the doors.

"You ride on up," said Solomon. "I'll carry your bags up the stairs. Just press number four."

The elevator rose slowly, rattling as it went. As a little girl, Beauty had read *Alice's Adventures in Wonderland*. Now she felt like she was in that book. She had never met a character like Solomon or Amir. She had never seen a brownstone before, never ridden on a one-person lift decorated with wrought-iron peacocks. When the elevator reached the fourth floor and the doors slowly opened, Solomon was waiting.

"She has the whole fourth floor," he said. "You'll like it—if you like peacocks."

Peacocks were everywhere—pencil-drawn sketches of peacocks, oil paintings of peacocks, color posters of peacocks. The living room faced the park, and on the long wall between two windows was an enormous Plexiglas frame that housed an elaborate display of peacock feathers. Past the kitchen was a narrow hallway with three doorways. The first was to a bathroom, the second to a neatly furnished small bedroom with a view of an air shaft, and the third to a large master bedroom with a bathroom of its own. The master bedroom overlooked the park and its several windows were covered with elaborate gold-and-blue satin drapes. The bedspread carried the same design as the drapes. An antique vanity table holding an antique mirror sat in the corner.

"I'm guessing this is your room," said Solomon, placing Beauty's bag in the small second bedroom.

"Good guess," said Beauty, looking around and loving what she saw. The walls were covered with framed fashion sketches of female models from the nineteenth century, the drapes were a beautiful shade of grayish green, and the bedspread was dark green chenille.

"So you're all set," said Solomon. "All I need is your cell number and I'm on my way."

"And what are you going to do with my cell number?"

"Invite you to dinner at our place. Then once you're in Miss Ward's good graces—which will be soon—I'll get you to invite me to dinner over here."

"And if I refuse?"

"You'll lose your only friend in New York City."

"I can't afford to do that," Beauty said with a smile.

"You certainly can't."

Beauty read off her number while Solomon entered it in his phone. Before he left he kissed her on both cheeks. "Stay focused," he said.

"On what?" Beauty asked.

"Fashion. It's all about fashion."

Beauty spent the rest of the afternoon unpacking, neatly folding her things and placing them in the chest of drawers that stood across from the single bed. She carefully hung her clothes in the closet and then decided to sit in the living room and look through the magazines and books on the coffee table. Everything was about fashion—a history of Coco Chanel, the legendary French designer; a biography of Valentino, the famous Italian couturier; and an elaborate photography collection devoted to the work of Japanese-American artist Isamu Noguchi. Beauty got lost in the Noguchi book, her imagination enflamed by the boldness of his graceful lamp shades and landscapes. She was on the last page when she heard the door open.

Beauty's first thought was that Anita Ward looked like a little bird—an injured bird. She was severely bent over and walked with the aid of a cane. The extravagant handle of the cane was polished gold and gave her a queenly demeanor. She peered over at Beauty—it was impossible for her to stand up straight and look her directly in the eye—and gave a nod and a small smile.

"Wanda was right," said Anita. "You are stunning."

Beauty rose. "Oh, thank you. Thank you for inviting me, thank you for having me, thank you for putting up with—"

"You mustn't go on, my dear. You are most welcome here. I am lonely in the evenings and have longed for company. Moreover, Wanda tells me you are a girl of wonderful manners and great kindness."

"I love your place, Miss Ward."

"You must call me Anita."

As the lady slowly walked to the armchair that faced the couch and carefully sat down, Beauty could see her face more clearly. Her skin color was medium brown, the same shade as her smallish eyes. Everything about Anita Ward was small. Her hands were delicate, her legs thin. She wore a knitted suit of black-and-white checks that Beauty considered extremely chic. She also wore a beautiful black hat that tilted to one side.

"So have you eaten, my dear?" Anita asked.

"Solomon and Amir gave me this Jordanian dessert."

"Solomon and Amir?"

"The man you sent to pick me up."

"Oh, yes, Solomon Getz. A lovely man, even if somewhat pushy. In the world of fashion, though, who isn't pushy? Wasn't I? And won't you be?"

Beauty didn't answer. She didn't know what to say.

"Of course you will be pushy," said Anita. "I'm afraid it's either push or get pushed. Well, for today I've pushed enough. I'm going to clean up and then take you downstairs for a nice Italian meal. You do like Italian food, don't you, my dear?"

"I love it."

"That settles it. I'll change into something more comfortable and we'll leave in just a few minutes."

Anita Ward had her own booth at Da Tato, a restaurant on the ground floor of the building adjacent to the brownstone. The booth was in front and gave an obstructed view of the park.

"I have been eating here for over twenty years," said Anita. "It is among the many indulgences that I have awarded myself since coming to New York. Life here is hard, my dear, and indulgences are in order.

Without them, this concrete city is a ceaseless grind. Good food is essential. And good wine, I might add, even more essential. Of course you are underage and too young for wine, but a small taste will do you no harm. I consider the relationship between wine and food something like the relationship between the sexes. If well coordinated, it is a pleasure. If off-balance, a catastrophe."

Anita had changed into a wheat-colored pantsuit. She wore a brilliant scarf of golden silk across her shoulders. Seated in the booth, she appeared normal. At the table, it was possible to forget about her painfully stooped-over posture.

"Did Wanda tell you about my kyphosis?" asked Anita.

"I'm afraid not."

"I didn't think so. That girl is too kind. She likes to think of me the way I was before I left Atlanta—not the way I am now. In any event, I am who I am—there's no way around it. I can still walk a block or two. I can still get in and out of cabs by myself. I can still manage to step down the hallway at work to the ladies' room. Yes, I have much to be thankful for. Kyphosis, however, does not exactly elicit gratitude. It is, you see, a form of advanced osteoporosis. My spinal vertebrae are shot through with holes. Those poor vertebrae are weak beyond repair. But I can assure you that while my body shows signs of dramatic deterioration, my spirit is not in decay. Not at all, my dear. My spirit is enlivened and excited by your arrival. You are a fresh breeze."

"Any way I can be of help . . ." Beauty began to say.

"Just looking at you helps. Just seeing youth in its blossom. Seeing eyes that are clear, a heart that is hungry, a mind that yearns for nourishment."

When the red wine arrived, the waiter, who knew Anita by name, poured a glass for both her and Beauty.

"You see, my dear," Anita said, "you have everyone in this city believing that you are of age. Now sip slowly. That half of a glass must

last you the evening. Far as I'm concerned, though, I intend to celebrate your arrival. These days I readily welcome any cause for celebration, and you are good cause indeed. Tell me about Wanda, Beauty.
How is she doing? I don't know how she manages to work for Snake
Simmons."

"You mean Slim?"

"I call him Snake because he is a snake. For years I've tried to get
Wanda to come up here. She'd find work. She's a gifted woman with
a keen instinct for retail. She'd do well selling at Bloom's. I've told her
that countless times."

"Then why doesn't she come?"

"You tell me, my dear. My thought is that she's a Georgia girl
through and through. New York is alien territory. Not everyone can
adjust. And then again, as I'm sure you've seen, Wanda is a caretaker.
Some see that as a beautiful quality in a woman. I, for one, do not.
Our first job as women is to care for ourselves, not some hapless man.
Most men are looking for their mothers. Snake Simmons is no different. Wanda has become his mother. You know that, I know that, the
world knows that. I am not a believer in the traditional sense, not
since the preacher back home put the make on my sweet mother when
I was a child, but I do pray for Wanda. She is a good soul."

"I love her."

"And she loved your adoptive mom. I didn't know the lady, but
from all reports she was a doll."

"She cared for me when she didn't have to."

"And she has a son as well, your half brother, is that right?"

"Really not my half brother. His mom is the woman who adopted
me. My father is Japanese."

"A beautiful pairing, the Asian and African-American genes. You
are a remarkable example of cross-cultural breeding."

"You make it sound like I'm a plant!" said Beauty.

Anita laughed. "Oh, child, forgive me, I get carried away with silly metaphors. When I began at Bloom's many years ago, they put me in the advertising department and had me writing copy because my boss—a white man, of course—said I had the gift of gab. He told me to apply my power of description to Bloom's merchandise. When I did so, and did so well, he took the credit for all my brilliant head-lines and ad ideas. I watched him elevate himself to the executive floor and a vice presidency, all on the strength of my work. I didn't know what to do. I lacked the courage to go over his head and tell his bosses the truth. So I toiled away in anonymity. I finally got fed up and played the only hand available to me. I quit. He panicked. He raised my salary to a livable wage and gave me a title, copy chief, but continued stealing my thunder.

"After a year as copy chief, I marched into the office of the great Harold Lawrence Bloom, the grandson of the founder and chairman of the board. He didn't know me from Adam. I think the only reason he did not kick me out immediately was because of his lifelong posi-tion as an NAACP board member.

"I shocked him by saying, 'Mr. Bloom, I have toiled in the fields of your advertising plantation now for too long. It is time to bring me into the big house.' He laughed nervously and asked me what I had in mind. 'I know everything there is to know about this store's advertising,' I said, 'and can be of no further help in that area. The sales lag we are experi-encing this year has nothing to do with the advertising. The problem is the merchandise. Your buyers lack vision. They are too cautious and two bars behind the beat of every major trend.' 'Then what do you propose?' he asked. 'Make me a buyer. Give me a department. Within a quarter you will see results. If, sir, those results are not forthcoming, fire me on the spot. No severance, no pity, simply give me the boot.' He laughed again but did as I asked. He gave me the least-glamorous department, bed and bath products—towels, linens, pillows, shower curtains. But there was no stopping me. I contacted Silvio Nunzio, the Italian designer famous for dressing our first ladies, and asked him how he felt about sheets. Well, my dear, he didn't simply like sheets, he *adored* them. The man couldn't wait to design patterns for sheets, pillowcases, and bedspreads. In fact, at my initiation, he became the first of the major designers to go into bed and bath products. The move turned the industry on its ear, and Bloom's had Nunzio's line on an exclusive basis. Profits soared and Wanda Washington's best friend from the projects of Atlanta, Georgia, was on her way."

"Nice," said Beauty, feeling a little tipsy after her first few sips of wine. As Anita spoke, Beauty was with her all the way, marveling at this small woman's courage.

"Of course in those days my back was straight as a board," Anita added, finishing her second glass of wine and starting in on her third. "I didn't have the distraction of poor health. That was a beautiful blessing. And another thing I didn't have in my private life was the burden of bad men. My long-suffering mother had a special skill for attracting bad men. She had supported a virtual army of bad men. Firsthand I had come to know their disloyalty, hypocrisy, and violence. No, sir, whatever physical pleasure I might have denied myself— and I am speaking candidly, my dear . . . this superb Bordeaux has me speaking with perfect candor—yes, no deprivation could overwhelm the joy of being an independent woman free of romantic ties that would have surely bound and restricted me in ways that I can only imagine. To be free is a magnificent thing, dear child. To be free is the only thing. That is not to say that I was—or am now—free of interacting with men.

"When I entered the business I was a pioneer. No one had told me that here, in this most urbane and sophisticated of cities, I would be dealing with gunslingers and cattle thieves. No one said that the New York retail business was the Wild West where men ruled through fear and psychological warfare. Do you know what helped me, Beauty? My smallness and lack of beauty. Men are not threatened by petite women. Men hardly notice women who are not overtly sexual. Of course I know how to dress and I like to think—hell, I *know*—I have style, but it is a style not geared to attract men. It is a style geared to please myself. Homosexual men appreciate me. The gentleman who picked you up at the airport, Solomon Getz, is one such admirer. He seeks to learn from me. That is flattering, but the men I had to win over to get where I am were not homosexual. Mr. Bloom and his brother and his sons and nephews have wives and mistresses. I could not win them over with flattery or sexual favors. I had no desire to do so. I had to win them over with the one element they could not ignore: the bottom line. But I am boring you, dear child, with all this talk about my distant past."

"No, not at all," said Beauty. "I love hearing about this."

"If I finish off this bottle of wine and find myself unable to walk, you might have to carry me to the elevator. I can assure you, though, that I am quite light. Not to mention light-headed. This wine is divine. But let me pause this monologue long enough to ask you a pertinent question. Are you a virgin?"

Beauty was taken aback. She paused before answering.

"You don't have to reply if you'd rather not," said Anita.

"It's okay. Well, yes, no . . . I mean, I am not a virgin."

"Good."

"Why is that good?"

"Because I don't have to hold your hand as you go through the deflowering ordeal. You've already been through it. And I presume it was not love. He was not the man of your dreams."

"Not at all."

"I could have predicted. And am I correct in presuming that it did not lead you into a period of promiscuity?"

"I'm not sure what you mean, Anita."

"I mean you don't go around sleeping with every man who looks good to you."

"Oh, no."

"A young woman as stunning and shapely as you must have a vast choice of men. You must be assaulted constantly."

"Not exactly."

"New York will assault you. You will see that soon enough."

"Should I be afraid?"

"You should be cautious. You should be suspicious. You should be scrutinizing. But, no, you need not be afraid. You should be fearless. The plain fact is that in the battle of the sexes, women clearly have the upper hand. We have what they want—and they want it so badly that they will risk their money, power, and position to get it."

"It sounds like you just don't like men."

"You are blunt, my dear, and I appreciate that quality in a young girl. Bluntness will serve you well. Especially with a blunt woman like me. Why beat around the bush? Why not say what's on your mind? Well, what's on my mind now is another little glass of wine before our fettuccine arrives."

Anita's speech, absolutely correct to this point, began to slur. Beauty also noticed that the more Anita drank, the blacker she sounded.

"The brothers are an interesting crew," said Anita. "They run in packs. They even call themselves dogs. 'He's my dog.' 'Yo, dog, what up?' Well, here's what's up, dear sista—intimidation is what's up. Swag is what's up. Attitude is what's up. But, look here, my lovely, under the swag and attitude is a whole lot of fear. The boyz in the hood are afraid. And you know what? So are the boyz on the board. See, I learned that early on. The educational background is different. Skin color is different. But all that posturing, whether it's the dude on the street corner or the pinstriped CEO in the corner office, is a mask. Rip off the mask, my dear, and you'll see a frightened little boy looking to be led. Now where in hell is our goddamn food?"

Anita had polished off the first bottle of wine, and with the pasta came a second. Meanwhile, Beauty had stopped drinking after the first few sips. She didn't like the taste of wine, and besides, Anita didn't want her to have any more.

"I'm a do-what-I-say kind of woman," Anita explained. "I don't want you to start doing what I do."

Beauty couldn't remember food tasting this good. She could concentrate on eating because, in between bites of pasta and swallows of wine, Anita kept up her monologue.

"I have given a great deal of thought to your arrival, Miss Beauty. That's why tomorrow Solomon will spend the day showing you how the subway works. The subway here works beautifully. You need to learn the system like the back of your hand. I rode those dirty trains the first twenty years in the city. I got my ass pinched. You'll get your ass pinched. A pinched ass is the price a woman pays for life in New York. No big deal. Don't bother to turn and protest or slap the man because the man might have a knife or a gun, so you're better off just moving on. Always move on, Beauty. Move away from the crazies. Goddamn city is filled with crazies. Then next week it's school in the Village, only a few stops away. This school is not for fools. You'll excel. You'll fly. I hear you can sew."

"I can," said Beauty.

"That's why I put you in alterations. Bloom's has a big alterations department. Boring as all hell, but a perfect Saturday-afternoon and summer job. I'll give you a few months to adjust to school and then, after New Year's, I'll take you to Bloom's. I want you in that store where I can make sure you're learning what you need to learn. You need to learn the store. The store needs to learn you. There's a method to my madness. I want more wine. I always want more wine but perhaps it's time to stop. Then again, it's only a few steps home and we are celebrating the birth of a star. Do you see yourself as a star, my dear?"

"No, not really."

"Well, you are. Wanda said so. Wanda has never asked me to look after anyone before. That's because Wanda knows that my standards are high. I have no interest in mediocrity. You have no interest in mediocrity. This food is not mediocre. This wine is not mediocre. I'd rather slit my throat—forgive my drama—but yes, I'd rather slit my throat than lead a mediocre life. Excellence is everything. Help me up, my dear. The night is young but I am old. This old lady has lost her balance. They will charge all this to my account. I can't be bothered with checks."

Beauty helped Anita out of the booth. She held her arm as they walked the few steps to the brownstone. Beauty realized that, without her help, the old woman, more stooped over than ever, would collapse. Anita was smashed. Tiny Anita and thin Beauty were small enough to both fit into the elevator. By the time they reached Anita's front door, Anita was out cold. Beauty had to open Anita's purse and fish out the key. Once inside, she had to carry Anita and place her in bed.

That night, excited and confused by all that had happened during this first day in New York City, Beauty had a tough time falling asleep. When she did, she drifted off into a dream. Only when she awoke did she realize the dream had involved Power. It was a deeply erotic dream that left Beauty in a state of longing.

"Your breakfast is ready," she heard Anita announce from the kitchen.

Beauty put on a robe and went to the dining room. Anita was wearing a white apron over an off-pink pantsuit. Although stooped over, she looked fashionable and fresh as a daisy. The apartment smelled of fresh coffee. The sunny-side-up eggs were cooked to perfection and the toasted bagel was covered with cream cheese.

"I'm not doing this every day, my dear," said Anita. "But on this, your first full day in the city of dreams, I want to make sure you start off right."

Nina Golding

The differences between living in New York City and Atlanta were so great that Beauty found that she could go through an entire day without thinking about Power more than three or four times. At night, though, he appeared in practically every dream. In one, he rescued her from a burning building; in another, she cheered for him as he scored the winning shot in a championship basketball game; and in the most frequently recurring dream of all, they lived together on a faraway island where they ate fruit off the trees, walked the moonlit beach at night, and slept in a grass hut to the sounds of chirping birds and gentle waves washing ashore.

Beauty wondered why she would be dreaming about a remote island in the middle of nowhere when the island she was really living on—Manhattan—thrilled her entirely. Her mind was completely stimulated, her sense of adventure completely satisfied. She couldn't have been happier. And yet . . .

The first day at Greenwich Village High School of the Arts had her comparing each boy she saw to Power. This one had Power's skin shade; that one had Power's height; the other one had Power's way of walking; another had a suggestion of Power's smile. At the same time, none of them was anything like Power. That was one of the reasons—at least this was what Beauty told herself—that she was so happy. The school was attended by kids who were artists and the children of artists. From behind, it was often tough to tell the boys from the girls. Some boys wore their hair down to their waist. Some girls shaved their heads completely. Other girls dyed their hair emerald green or electric blue. Tattoos and piercings were commonplace.

Her first friend at school, Nina Golding, whose white dad was a sculptor and whose black mom traveled in a modern dance troupe, had a tattoo on her left arm that read DISCIPLINE and another on her right arm that read CHAOS. Because they were both biracial and interested in fashion, they bonded quickly. Nina had wildly curly black hair, a quick smile, crazy energy, and a love of style that excited Beauty. Nina was obsessed with Erykah Badu and Janelle Monáe. On some days she wore her father's vintage tux to school; on other days she wore overalls several sizes too big for her slight frame, which she bought at an army-navy store on Canal Street.

Beauty met Nina in sewing class, where the other girls tended to be conservative. They were interested in sewing conventional dresses and blouses. When asked what she wanted to make, Nina said, "Combat uniforms for female marines." Under her breath but loud enough to be heard, a classmate whispered, "What a dyke!" Nina, who was not a lesbian, turned to her accuser and told her to fuck herself. The teacher called for order. That same day, when Nina saw Beauty eating alone in the lunchroom, she joined her.

After quickly running down their racial backgrounds, Nina had lots of questions.

"Are you an only child?" she asked.

"Well, kinda."

"What do you mean 'kinda'?"

"I have an adoptive brother."

"How old?"

"Our age."

"Cute?"

Beauty didn't answer. Nina asked again. "Is he cute?"

"Most people think he's nice looking."

"And you don't?"

"I don't think about it," Beauty lied.

"You're lying," said Nina.

Beauty laughed.

"I think I should meet him," said Nina. "If he's cute, I need to meet him. When's he coming to visit you?"

"I'm not sure he is."

"Don't you want him to?"

"Not really."

"Something happen between you two?"

"We have different mothers and different fathers. His birth mother happened to adopt me—that's all."

"You sound so detached about him. What gives, girl?"

"He's no big deal."

"What's his name?"

"Power."

"Wow! Quite a name."

"His real name is Paul."

"But you call him Power?"

"Everyone calls him Power."

"Is he an athlete?"

"You have sisters and brothers?" asked Beauty, changing the subject.

"Only child. Can't you tell?"

"How can you tell an only child?" asked Beauty.

"Extreme self-involvement."

"I don't think you're so self-involved. You're asking me all these questions, aren't you?"

"You can be nosy and self-involved at the same time. That's me." Beauty laughed again.

"You a virgin?" asked Nina.

The question took Beauty aback. Anita had asked her the same thing. Why was everyone in New York asking about her sexual experience? She paused before answering.

"You don't have to tell me," said Nina. "But I'll tell you. I'll shock you. I am a virgin. You shocked?"

"A little."

"Because I look so artsy?"

"Maybe," said Beauty.

"Well, you can look artsy and be artsy and still be afraid of what it feels like to have some guy shoving his thing in you. What does it feel like?"

"Depends on the guy."

"So you've had more than one," said Nina.

Beauty looked down at her lunch tray. The conversation with Nina had been so fast and furious that she hadn't even taken a bite of the vegetable quiche.

"If the guy is nice, he'll be gentle," Beauty said.

"How many nice guys have you had?" asked Nina.

"Just a few."

"Was it heaven?"

"It was okay," said Beauty.

"Just okay?" asked Nina. "No pain?"

"A little pain at first."

"Then all pleasure?"

"I liked it," Beauty admitted, thinking of Power.

"Think I'd like it with him?" asked Nina, indicating a dark-skinned black guy with long dreadlocks eating alone at the table next to them.

"Who is he?"

"Raymond. Calls himself Ray Ray. Think he's cute?"

"Very cute."

"He's a deaf-mute," said Nina. "But he's a rapper."

"How does that work?"

"He raps with his hands. Raps in sign language. So I'm learning sign language. I've decided he's gonna be the one to de-virginize me. It's gonna happen in exactly a month, on my seventeenth birthday. What do you think of that?"

"Have you let him know?"

"No, but I will. I'll tell him in sign language next week."

As the weeks flew by, Beauty went to Nina's Tribeca apartment many times, where she met Nina's father, Arthur, a burly, gregarious man whose delicate sculptures filled every room, and her mother, Cynthia, a tall, thin woman who spoke in a whisper-quiet voice. They welcomed Beauty with great kindness. Nina's dad loved jazz and her mom, a well-known dancer, prepared dishes she had learned to cook in Italy and France. Nina also became friends with Solomon and Amir. And, in fact, after Nina fulfilled her promise and lost her virginity to Ray Ray the silent rapper, she introduced Ray Ray to Amir, who, in turn, included Ray Ray in his group All. Using dramatic hand and arm gestures, Ray Ray not only rapped in sign language but wrote out parts of his raps on large chalkboards.

Beauty felt secure in this small but tight community of friends. In a certain way, they were a group of loners who had come together. And yet, because she herself was a guest of Anita's, she had not invited any of them to the fourth story of the brownstone on Gramercy Park. Finally, though, in mid-December she thought it would be cool to ask Nina over. Nina went directly from school to Anita's apartment, where she was fascinated by the peacocks.

"They're a hoot," she said. "Does this woman wanna be a peacock?"

Beauty took Nina on a tour of the place and, in doing so, felt a certain pride, as if she herself was the owner.

"I can't believe this lady is such a square," Nina gushed. "Does she drive you crazy?"

"Oh, no, she's great. She leaves me alone. She encourages me."

"To design dresses that look like peacocks?"

"No," said Beauty. "Anita's taste in interior decoration is one thing, but her taste in clothes is another. She's really trendy. She has to be. She's the chief buyer at Bloom's."

"Doesn't Bloom's carry predictable shit?" asked Nina.

"Not really. They have far-out stuff."

"But stuff calculated to sell to rich East Side ladies with money to burn."

"Fashion is all about selling," said Beauty.

"'Put art first,' says my dad, 'and sales will follow.'"

"Anita loves art. She's taken me to all the museums here."

"My father won't exhibit at the establishment museums or galleries. He says the art establishment is corrupt. Plus, he won't allow his sculptures to be used as interior decoration."

And so went the discussion. Beauty saw how Anita's notion of beauty clashed with Nina's approach. And the minute Anita arrived, Beauty also saw that Anita immediately sensed Nina's disapproval. They tolerated each other, but barely.

When Anita walked in the door she was a wearing a gray cashmere cape over a chic black woolen dress. Nina was dressed in one of her crazier outfits—a thrift-shop 1940s lime-green pleated skirt with Minnie Mouse leggings and a yellow sweatshirt with the words HIGHLY CREATIVE NEUROTIC scrawled across the front in glitter letters. Anita looked over Nina's ensemble and forced a smile. She told the girls she was a little tired and asked if they would mind if she ordered in Thai food. The girls said that would be fine, and Anita went to her bedroom to change.

When Anita returned, she was wearing a Jil Sander leisure suit in navy silk. Watching Anita slowly walk across the room with her cane, her back so painfully bent, Nina decided that she looked like some aging duchess out of a history book. Anita opened a bottle of white wine, poured herself a full glass, and then poured a half glass each for Beauty and Nina.

"Welcome to our home, Nina," she said. "Here's to your health, my dear."

Beauty was struck by the fact that Anita said "our" home. That made her feel good. Maybe the evening would go well after all. The good manners and polite exchange between Anita and Nina, though, didn't last for long.

"Beauty tells me your parents are artists," said Anita.

"Dedicated artists," Nina said.

"That's wonderful. Beauty also says you want to go into fashion."

"Well, I think I'm already in fashion. My own fashion."

"I see."

"I see fashion as something different than most people," said Nina.

"In what way?"

"I see fashion as pure expression."

"And what is it that you want to express, my dear?" asked Anita, finishing off her first glass of wine.

"The truth is that changes every day. I really don't know."

"I'd respectfully suggest that you find out before graduation."

"Why the rush?" asked Nina.

"I suppose there is no rush if making a living is not essential."

"If making a living means kissing the ass of a corrupt industry, I'd rather starve."

"I doubt very much if your folks would let you starve."

"My father spent the first ten years of his career starving."

"And then what happened? Did his work begin to sell?" Anita asked.

"No, he met my mother."

"And she has worked steadily?"

"She's a much in-demand dancer."

"Well, my dear, I think it's wonderful that she supports the family. Unfortunately, I've never been in that enviable position. I've had to deal with commerce."

As the conversation went silent, Beauty felt the tension build. Sipping an always fresh glass of wine, Anita continued. "To be truthful, I've never seen a contradiction between commerce and art. To my mind, true creative genius is expressed in the marriage of the two. It's rather easy to be crassly commercial without regard to art or, conversely, self-indulgently arty with no concern for commerce. But if you can incorporate design into a piece of clothing—or for that matter, any product—that is both aesthetically pleasing and appealing to the public, then you have something."

"I'm not interested in products," Nina said plainly.

"I see," Anita replied. "But you would agree that any object you put out there in the market can be considered a product."

"The word sounds cheap to me. It cheapens your work. Do you think Picasso thought of his paintings as products?"

"I've never met the man, but I have met Rei Kawakubo."

"Sure," said Nina. "She owns Comme des Garçons. She designs all their dope clothes. I love her."

"She has no problem calling her artistic creations products. She's a realist. If you're going into fashion, you must be realistic. And no matter how far afield you go, reality takes you back to commerce."

More silence. More wine for Anita.

"The food is delicious," Nina said, changing subjects. "Thank you for having me over."

"My pleasure, my dear. I've heard so much about you from Beauty."

"Hey, Beauty," Nina said, turning to her friend. "You ever heard of Candy Girl?"

"No."

"She's new," Nina explained. "She's out-there. She's kind of a combination dancer/rapper/singer. She wears evening gowns and tears 'em down the middle halfway through her act."

"Delightful," said Anita.

"She's raw," said Nina.

"And raw is good, sweetheart?" asked Anita.

"Raw is real," said Nina.

"Well done is also real."

"She does raw real good," said Nina. "You'll love her, Beauty. She's performing this weekend."

"Beauty's coming to help do inventory at the store this weekend," Anita announced.

"I am?" asked Beauty.

"Yes, they need some extra help. If you're available, Nina, and you don't mind minimum wage, I'm sure you can work as well."

"Not if it gets in the way of Candy Girl," said Nina.

"Heaven forbid," Anita replied.

"Can't it wait for another week?" asked Nina. "I want Beauty to go with me. It'll be an experience."

"I'm sure it will, my dear, but retail is a cruel mistress. Unfortunately—or fortunately—Beauty has work to do. She has been entrusted to me to learn the hard lessons of commerce and, Miss Candy Girl's extravagantly creative show aside, those lessons will most definitely be learned."

"You don't like rap, do you?" Nina asked Anita.

"I don't know rap. And rap doesn't know me."

"Do you like jazz?"

"I adore jazz. I adore Ella Fitzgerald and Billie Holiday. I adore Dinah Washington and Nancy Wilson. You will see their LPs on my shelf."

"What's an LP?" asked Nina.

"An LP is a long-playing record, an antiquated form, a product of a bygone day."

"Well, if you like jazz, you should like hip-hop. It comes from the same thing."

"My dear child," said Anita, "it most certainly does not. Jazz is among the most sophisticated musical forms. It is about the tension between freedom and form. Hip-hop is vulgar, pornographic, misogynistic, and hypermaterialistic."

"So you hate it."

"I ignore it."

"But you have all those pronouncements about it," Nina said.

"Nina, when you get to my age you are entitled to pronouncements. And at your age, sweet one, you are entitled to ignore them."

"I will."

"I am not surprised."

From there the conversation grew even more heated. Beauty stayed silent as Anita and Nina went at it. In politics, Anita was a right-to-center moderate. Nina was a left-wing radical. In sports, Nina loved roller derby and women's soccer. Anita had no interest in sports. Nina liked horror films; Anita loathed them. The more wine Anita consumed, the more sarcastic she became. The more sarcasm Anita showed, the less respect Nina offered. Beauty was deeply uncomfortable and greatly relieved when, after dinner, Anita excused herself and went to her bedroom, where she watched TV before falling asleep at ten P.M.

"Oh, my God," said Nina as soon as Anita was out of earshot. "She's such a bitch. How can you stand to live with her?"

"I like her," said Beauty. "She's good to me."

"She's going to turn you into a robot. You're going to wind up designing clothes with peacocks all over them."

"She knows the business inside and out."

"What business?" asked Nina. "The business of selling out and turning out shit?"

"Have you ever been to Bloom's, Nina? Bloom's does not sell shit."

"Bloom's sucks. Hillary Clinton shops at Bloom's. Martha Stewart shops at Bloom's. I wouldn't be caught dead in Bloom's. You can't work at Bloom's. Bloom's will corrupt your soul. This woman will corrupt your soul. You gotta get outta here, Beauty."

"And go where?"

"You can live with us. My folks won't mind. They'll like it. You don't take up much room, and you don't eat much. They'll be thrilled that I have a sister. I've always wanted a sister, haven't you?"

"Well, sure, but—"

"No buts about it. Pack up right now. Let's go."

"Nina, I can't—"

"Are you scared?"

"No, it isn't that. But this woman took me in. She's getting me a job. She has things to teach me."

"Bad things. She's a bad influence," said Nina.

"I don't see it that way."

"You're getting brainwashed."

"I'm getting a beautiful apartment to live in," said Beauty. "She didn't have to take me in."

"She took you in to brainwash you. You gotta get out. You're an artist like me. This woman is a whore. She'll turn you into a whore."

"Wow . . . Nina . . . do you really believe that?"

"I feel it, I know it."

"Well, I don't know anything except she's not charging me any rent."

"Don't you see—you're whoring yourself out to her. Besides, she's an obvious drunk. She drank a whole bottle of wine by herself tonight. The woman's a lush. She probably has to drown her guilt for all that ugly merchandise she buys for people with no taste."

"Whatever . . ."

"Look, Beauty. This place is creepy. The peacocks are creeping me out. I'm outta here. You coming?" asked Nina.

"No."

And with that, Nina was gone.

That night, nagging thoughts kept Beauty awake. She kept hearing Nina's words, and while she was not inclined to pack up and leave Anita, she couldn't help but think of Power's relationship with Slim. Slim had given Power a place to live. Slim had made Power comfortable and secure. He had taken Power under his wing and was leading him down the path that Slim had traveled. Slim's money and success were too much for Power to resist. Well, wasn't this also true of her and Anita? Hadn't Anita given her a place to live, made her comfortable and secure? Wasn't Anita taking her under her wing? Wasn't Anita's money and success too much for her to resist? All true, thought Beauty, except that Anita was a good person and Slim was an asshole. And besides, Beauty wasn't turned off by the crass commercial world of fashion the way Nina was. She understood what Nina was saying. She got the fact that designing clothes was like painting or music. She knew it was an art form. But what was wrong with an art form that pleased people? What was wrong with an art form that made lots of money? Beauty wanted to make lots of money.

She also wanted to keep Nina as her friend. Nina had befriended her when the other girls at school had not. Some were jealous of Beauty's striking looks. Some made fun of her Georgia accent. Beauty was definitely an outsider at a school that bred cliques. Nina was an insider and leader of the clique of the coolest kids. She brought Beauty into that circle of coolness. Beauty appreciated that. She liked Nina, liked hanging out at Nina's apartment, like Nina's gutsy way of looking at the world. Nina had shown Beauty the ins and outs of lower Broadway. She had shown her the trippiest boutiques in Soho, the piercing and tattoo parlors, the galleries, the dance clubs. Nina was a teenage hipster who, at least from Beauty's point of view, had New York City dialed up. It was okay that Nina didn't like Anita and vice versa. That was understandable. Two different worlds.

Beauty, though, related to both worlds. She didn't want to give up either. And, as far as she was concerned, she didn't have to. She finally fell asleep with a calm feeling that all was well and that, despite the differences, she could enjoy the comfort of having Anita as her guardian and Nina as her best friend.

Cold reality, though, hit her hard the next day at school. Nina snubbed her in sewing class. She acted like she didn't exist. In the cafeteria, when Beauty sat down at Nina's table, Nina got up and left. Everyone saw what was happening. Beauty was humiliated. She felt like crying. During the week, it got worse. Nina managed to turn all the cool kids against Beauty. She told stories about the crazy peacock lady whom Beauty lived with. She told everyone that Beauty wanted to be a super-square fashion plate and design dresses for rich old ladies with no taste. Before long, Beauty became an outcast. The hipsters wanted nothing to do with her—and neither did the conservative kids, who had never liked her to begin with. She was alone.

She had Solomon and Amir, but not for long. Anita fired Solomon because she thought his sense of fashion was too edgy for Bloom's.

"I tried to train the man," she told Beauty, "but he just didn't realize the basic conservative nature of the New York consumer. Europeans and Middle Easterners often view New York through an avant-garde lens that may be accurate when it comes to painting and music, but not fashion. New York wants to be in style—but not that far out in front. This is a cautious town, my dear, where money, not art, rules the streets. You must remember that."

When Beauty called Solomon the next day, his first words were, "The bitch is brilliant, but the bitch is ruthless. Be careful, Beauty. Anita Ward has ice running through her veins."

Solomon found a job selling in the men's department at Neiman Marcus on Michigan Avenue in Chicago. Amir went with him, and

Beauty found herself alone. Amir's group All stayed together, but when Beauty went to see them at the Cornelia Street Café in the Village, even Ray Ray, doing his fantastic silent raps, gave her the cold shoulder. Seemed like Nina had poisoned the world against her.

"All of us are alone," Anita told her one night when, once again, they were dining at Da Tato. "At the end of the day, we have no one to count on but ourselves. That's the hard lesson we must face. I wish someone had told me that when I was sixteen. It sure as hell would have saved me a lot of grief."

After trying to keep the story to herself, Beauty finally told Anita about her falling-out with Nina.

"It's the best thing that could happen to you," said Anita. "She's a pretentious little twerp. Do you know how many artsy-fartsy know-it-all girls like Nina are running around this city? And do you know how many of them will find success as artists? Practically none. Most of them wind up behind the cosmetics counter at Macy's. When their parents stop paying the bills and force them to deal with the real world, they can't. Their ambitions go up in smoke. They think they're going to become Grace Jones or Yoko Ono or Madonna or Lady Gaga. They want to be stars but they have no insight, no talent, no tenacity. They are in love with art for art's sake. They are in love with rebellion. It's all such fun, it's all so easy, it's all so glamorous, my dear, until you have to pay the rent. That's where the rubber meets the road, a road made of unyielding, unfeeling, uncompromising, cold concrete."

"But I liked Nina," said Beauty. "She was my friend . . ."

"'Was' is the right word. She is past tense. She has proven her worthlessness. She is a flighty girl, this one, and undoubtedly will fall into hard drugs and loose sex. You mark my words. These are dark days for the promiscuous. Sexually transmitted diseases will kill you quicker than cancer. These hallucinogens and stimulants going around will kill your clarity, destroy your sanity, and have you acting the fool.

If you find that school unpleasant, Beauty, if you continue to feel out of place, we will find another. I don't want you mixing with the wrong crowd. I want you down at the store on Saturday. You're to work in alterations. Belinda Sanchez will supervise you. Belinda can sew rings around any teacher in that school of yours. Belinda is a whiz."

Noah Sanchez

After working at Bloom's for five months—on Saturdays and during the summer—Beauty had sex with Noah Sanchez, the son of her sewing mentor, Belinda Sanchez. It happened at the end of her junior year a few months before her seventeenth birthday. Noah was her first intimate physical encounter since the night that she and Power found themselves in bed after the death of Moms.

Noah reminded her of Power. He was Power's height, skin color, and weight. His mother was from the Dominican Republic and his father managed a post office in Harlem. The Sanchez family lived in Inwood, the Dominican section of upper Manhattan, across the street from a park that overlooked the Hudson River. Unlike Gramercy, though, Inwood Hill Park was two hundred acres of hidden paths and woodsy trails. To walk in Inwood Hill Park was to leave Manhattan and enter a forest. It was there, in a secluded alcove on a warm summer night under a full moon, where Noah and Beauty made love. It was there where, in a silent scream, she called out Power's name. It was there where Noah said that he loved her. It was there where Beauty started crying.

"Did I do something wrong?" asked Noah. "Did I hurt you?"

Beauty couldn't tell Noah that she hadn't been with him. In mind, body, and soul, she had been with Power.

"No," she said, "it's just a lot of stuff I've been going through."

They got dressed, picked up the blankets they had used to cover the ground, and began walking through the park. Through the trees, the light of the moon danced on the surface of the river. To the south were the lights of the George Washington Bridge. In the distance was the roar of an ambulance speeding down 207th Street. When the sirens stopped, the sound of crickets filled the sweet, fresh-smelling air. For a long while they walked in silence. Noah wanted to ask Beauty whether she had enjoyed the sex. He had felt her climax, but he also had not felt her presence. He wondered what was going on in her mind. On top of the highest hill of the park, they sat on a bench that looked across the river to the New Jersey Palisades.

Beauty sensed that Noah had questions for her but still said nothing. Finally, he broke the silence.

"My mom said something about an election. I hope you're not taking that too seriously, Beauty. I thought I'd be elected captain of the basketball team this year and my best friend got it instead."

"I didn't even want to run to be a representative on the school fashion board," said Beauty, "except that some of the girls nominated me. I didn't know they nominated me to humiliate me. But that's what happened. Someone made a copy of the actual voting results and stuck it in my locker. It was probably Nina Golding. Anyway, I got two votes. The girl who won got a hundred and sixty votes. The next day at school I heard everyone laughing at me behind my back."

"Anita never laughs at you. And neither does my mother. They love you. We all love you."

"I'm never going back to that school."

"You don't have to."

"It was a mistake to go there in the first place."

"My mother says that as a seamstress she's never seen you make a mistake."

"Sewing's one thing, designing is another."

Noah turned to Beauty and said, "I'm ready to design my life around you."

Beauty didn't know how to respond. Noah, like his mother, was a good-hearted and sincere human being. It was his mother who introduced him to Beauty and encouraged the relationship. Anita discouraged it. She didn't think Noah was good enough for Beauty. She had respect for Belinda as a craftswoman. She knew Belinda's husband and had met Noah. They were a lovely family but not for Beauty. Beauty was going places and couldn't be held back by a teenage infatuation—if, in fact, she was infatuated with Noah Sanchez.

"I'm just getting started here in New York," Beauty told Noah that night in Inwood Hill Park.

"I know you're super-talented," said Noah. "I know you're going to be a superstar, and I can tell you I'll never get in your way. I got into Columbia for next year. I'll be living at home and studying my head off. I'll be prelaw. I have dreams of my own, but I want our dreams to flow together. You're my dream and I want to be yours."

"You're so serious, Noah."

"About you . . . yes, I'm serious about you. When you meet your soul mate, you can't let her go—not for anyone or anything."

Noah's words warmed Beauty's heart. Noah was a gentle guy. He loved to read about art, hike in the woods, help out his parents with errands. He worked part-time at the Cloisters, the nearby museum in Fort Tryon Park, where he tried to make the story of medieval tapestry come alive for underprivileged kids.

"He's not just a jock," Beauty told Anita the next day when Anita questioned her about being out so late. "He's a really well-rounded guy. There are so many parts to him."

"I'm sure, my dear, but I'm also sure that the part about you he likes most involves sex."

Beauty took offense at the remark but didn't feel inclined to argue with Anita. She wanted to defend Noah more vigorously, but she also had to admit that, other than his resemblance to Power, she wasn't nearly as attracted to Noah as he was to her. He was a good guy, but maybe almost too good. There was no adventure in him, no edge, not even the slightest hint of risk. He was a safe choice, and Beauty was hardly interested in safety.

Despite all this, Beauty continued to date Noah. There was nothing threatening or unpleasant about Noah. They had sex occasionally, but only when Beauty wanted to fantasize about Power. They went to movies and art exhibits and baseball games at Yankee Stadium. He provided a companionship that Beauty needed. And even though she continued to tell him that she could not commit to a long-term relationship, Noah harbored hope that she'd change her mind, refusing to give her up.

Meanwhile, worried that Noah might prevail, Anita decided to ship Beauty out of the city. She sent her to Los Angeles, where she could complete high school and work for Soo Kim, a former protégée of Anita's who had become one of the most successful designers in the country. Naturally Beauty was excited at the prospect—she had never been to California—and Anita was gratified that her plan was falling into place. In August, though, Noah announced that, through some last-minute maneuvers, he had been awarded a full scholarship to UCLA. He'd be living in the same city as Beauty.

"I know you like this boy," said Anita, "and I know he's absolutely crazy about you, but for God's sake do not get tied down and do not get pregnant."

. . . .

Come September, Beauty would be living in the guest room of the four-thousand-square-foot penthouse apartment in the Ritz–Carlton Residences next to the Staples Center in downtown Los Angeles, which Soo Kim shared with her husband, Primo Dalla Torre. Meanwhile, across town, Noah would be staying in a dorm room in Westwood that he'd share, by sheer coincidence, with Lee Kim, Soo's younger brother, who, like Noah, was a UCLA freshman.

Calm and Cool Clothing

On the flight from New York to L.A., Beauty wondered about her new home. What awaited her? Her anticipation was especially great because of the background Anita had provided about Soo Kim. As the jet winged its way westward, Beauty remembered the fascinating details of that story. Over several evenings and several bottles of good wine, Anita had narrated the adventure with great relish.

Ten years ago, Soo Kim had come to New York to work at Bloom's as a trainee under Anita Ward. She was a Korean American born in L.A. to fundamentalist Christians. Her parents owned a small dry-cleaning establishment on Olympic Boulevard near Western Avenue. Behind the dry cleaner was an apartment where the Kim family lived in three small rooms. Her parents were born in Seoul and never learned English. They read the *Korea Times,* watched Korean television, listened to Korean radio, shopped at Korean stores, and never left the all-encompassing world of Korean L.A. They took their children to church every Sunday and strictly supervised their every move. They wanted their daughter, Soo, who was seventeen years older than their son, Lee, to become a dentist or a doctor. Instead, in a quiet way, Soo reacted against her rigid upbringing and, after college at USC, went to New York to fulfill her dream as a designer. Her parents were aghast. But Soo assured them that she would come home in a few years, make a fortune, and buy the building that housed their dry cleaner. That way they'd no longer have to pay the exorbitant rent that hung over their heads every month. In the month that Beauty arrived, Soo celebrated her parents' fortieth wedding anniversary by handing them the deed to the building. At thirty-five, she had made good on her promise, but not without the help of Primo Dalla Torre, a man whom her father and mother could barely tolerate.

When Soo had returned to California from New York, having learned all she could about retail fashion, she opened her own store in a midcity Sixth Street strip mall in a largely Korean neighborhood. Since she was bilingual and understood the tastes of Korean women, her idea was to travel to Seoul twice a year, buy the merchandise there at a good price, and cater to the local L.A. clientele. She borrowed a few thousand dollars from her parents, went into business, and, within a year, went broke. She thought her goods were conservative, but apparently they were not conservative enough. Soo had to admit that, try as she might, she couldn't sell to her own people. Her tastes were simply too fashion-forward. She wanted to be a good girl and please her parents, but she was a rebel, and her rebellious nature prevailed, even when she tried to run a small dress shop. She was telling her customers what she thought they should wear, not what they themselves wanted to wear. It just didn't work.

She decided instead to embrace her true self and begin a line of casual clothes aimed at an inner-city demographic that, though not quite ready to go the distance with post-punk fashion, was looking to separate themselves stylistically from an earlier generation. She thought of them, like herself, as half rebels, one foot in the present, one foot in the future. She tapped into the young artists' communities all across Southern California and found inspiration from Chinese-American painters, Latin-American graffiti painters, black portrait painters, and even a Hungarian woman who designed wallpaper patterns to help her visualize a concept that was at once cool but calm. Thus Calm and Cool Clothing. Her first success was a silk-and-cotton sweatshirt featuring a golden leaf torn in half. She made retro T-shirts from organic cotton, recycled polyester, and rayon that featured Asian comic book characters. She designed oversized sweatshirts and sweatpants for young men that, though hinting of hip-hop, were rendered in patterns of plaids and argyles that gave the clothing a preppy flavor. In forging this new kind of cautiously edgy line, Soo consulted with Anita on a regular basis. Recognizing her desire to synthesize rather than revolutionize, Anita encouraged Soo and became her closest advocate. When it became apparent that Soo was ready to go national but needed a serious infusion of cash, it was Anita who put her in touch with Primo Dalla Torre.

Primo had homes in New York, Paris, Rome, and Milan. He was a venture capitalist with an interest in fashion. He had bought and sold two major luxury brands—a clothing retail chain and a leather goods manufacturer—at exactly the right time. He had modernized his father's furniture plant, the foundation of his family's fortune, reconfiguring the merchandise to sell to Target and Walmart. At fifty, his skin was darkly tanned from his frequent Caribbean getaways. He was a stocky man of medium height who was especially vain. He wore an expensive wig of dark curly hair. Because Anita had known Primo for years, she recognized the toupee the first time she saw it, but others presumed it was his natural hair.

Born in Venice but educated in England, he had only the slightest trace of an Italian accent. He had a short attention span, a love of sailing and water-skiing, and a strange attitude about women. Other than his immediate family, he interacted with European and American women only in a business context. He recognized the fact that many had keen business acumen and Primo was, above all, a businessman. Sexually, however, only Asian women interested him. Twice a year he made sure to schedule trips to the Pacific Rim. He told his colleagues that the trips involved important meetings, but they were really rendezvous with Asian women. He met them through high-level friends—often government officials—and the encounters were always discreet. He disclosed this fact to few people. Anita was one of the first.

"Your personal life is a mystery to me, Primo," she said one afternoon over lunch at the Four Seasons on Park Avenue. "All I know is that you are not a cautious man."

"I wouldn't say that," he said.

"Well, at least in business you are hardly cautious. It has been my observation that in business you are daring."

"Is that why for years you've been daring me to buy Bloom's?"

"That, and because if you do buy Bloom's you'll surely make me a first-tier executive."

"As it stands, Anita, you are a first-tier buyer."

"Not the same as someone who runs the place. And, as you well know, Bloom's continues to be run poorly."

"And yet their selling price is outrageous."

"But not out of your price range."

"The time isn't right. Perhaps when I come back from Asia."

"You're always running off to Asia."

"So I can conduct my private life in private."

"Then it must involve Asian women."

"Who are the most discreet, most understanding, most old-fashioned yet strangely modern of all women."

"Are we discussing professional women?" Anita asked.

"And by professional you mean what?"

"Those who charge for their services."

"Strange, Anita, but here in New York, for example, you can date a woman—what you would call a nonprofessional woman. You can spend five hundred dollars on dinner. You can take the lovely lady to a show where house seats cost a thousand dollars. At the end of the night, she may or may not submit to your advances. If not, another date is required. This time you gift her a bracelet, a necklace, a simple ring. This time you spend two thousand dollars. And with that, and the promise of more to come, she yields. In reality, aren't you paying for her services just as surely as you pay for the woman who, from the beginning, lets you know that she is for sale?"

"You're only talking about one particular kind of woman."

"Well, I'm only one particular kind of man. I admit I want submission, but please, no games."

"And your Asian women meet this criteria."

"Indeed. They meet it with style. They shun endless conflicts and pointless discussions. They are able to separate the heart from the mind. They realize that the body controls the mind. And they are wonderfully skillful in giving and receiving bodily pleasure without the confusion of an emotional overlay."

"It sounds so clinical. Like going to the doctor."

Primo laughed. "A lady doctor perhaps."

"And so," said Anita, "your infamous private life excludes all women who have demonstrated talent in your world—the world of commerce—and includes only those women whose talents are demonstrated in the bedroom."

"Essentially, yes."

"And what if you find a woman whose talents are equally extravagant in both areas?"

"I'm not looking for such a woman but if, in fact, you know of one, please let me know. And, of course, it would help your case enormously if she were Asian."

A few months later Soo came to New York looking for investors. Calm and Cool Clothing was selling nicely, but due to extremely slow payment from retailers, there was a decidedly negative cash flow. The venture had been undercapitalized from the start and now the situation was critical. Without a few hundred thousand to sustain her, Soo couldn't continue.

"You need more than that, my dear," said Anita, who understood virtually every aspect of the business. "To give yourself a fighting chance to make a mark, you need a cool million."

"I don't have those kinds of resources," said Soo. "Where am I going to get that kind of money?"

Anita Ward took a long hard look at Soo Kim. She was certainly beautiful. She had long, luxuriant black hair that fell to her shoulders. Her small mouth and petite nose were placed perfectly on her thin, elegant face. She dressed with flair and individuality. She was a determined woman, but her determination was not apparent. Her drive was well hidden by her gentle approach. Her manners were exquisite. When she was Anita's assistant there was no job, no matter how small, that she wouldn't embrace. She liked to help people. She liked to serve. She kept her personal life private, but from a couple of things Soo had said in the past, Anita knew that she favored mature men.

"I have someone for you to meet, Soo," said Anita. "But I think such a meeting would work better over a quiet dinner."

"Whom do you have in mind?"

"Primo Dalla Torre."

"*The* Primo Dalla Torre?"

"He's a friend. He happens to be in the city this week. Shall I arrange it?"

Soo didn't hesitate. "Please," she said. "I'd be grateful."

It worked. Primo was dazzled. Soo showed up in a red tunic worn over black silk pants, clothes of her own design. In conversation, she allowed him to take the lead. She answered his questions honestly and easily, and she asked him smart questions of her own. She spoke openly of her background and underplayed her independence. Having spent the day before reading about Primo on the Internet, she showed great familiarity with his many business dealings. He was flattered. He was smitten. He was aroused. He wanted her badly.

The cat-and-mouse game was on. The sole proprietor of Calm and Cool Clothing was calm and cool. She did not submit easily. When after dinner he suggested they have a drink in his suite at the Carlyle, she talked about the many meetings she had scheduled for the morning and her need to get a good night's sleep. When he asked about her plans for the rest of the week in New York, she referred to her BlackBerry and said her schedule was crowded but, if he were interested in her business plan, she would certainly make meeting him again a priority. He said he was.

Their second meeting took place at the bar of the Mandarin Oriental Hotel thirty-five stories above Columbus Circle. They sat by an enormous window overlooking a cityscape cast in the romantic light of a rainy afternoon. Soo was prepared. She had a five-year plan carefully detailing the expansion of her business. She had a market analysis and profit projections. She put all this in a leather-bound presentation folder titled "A Calm and Cool Approach to Realizing the Potential of Calm and Cool Clothing."

Primo was charmed and also convinced that she was among the sharpest businesswomen—not to mention the most talented designers—he had ever encountered. Rather than agree on the spot, though, he suggested that he come to Los Angeles for a closer look. She was most agreeable. She was flying back to California in a few days. He suggested that they make the coast-to-coast trip together in his Gulfstream G650 jet. Soo had no reason not to accept his generous offer.

Before boarding the sleek plane at Teterboro Airport in New Jersey, Soo considered her situation. She understood what Primo wanted. And of course she knew what she wanted. He was twenty years older than her but hardly an old man. He was vital and assertive and brilliant. He had a sexual energy that she did not find repellent. In her dealings with men, she had always been highly selective and extremely cautious. She had found her previous two boyfriends—both Korean Americans—perfectly adequate but not terribly exciting. Primo was exciting. It was exciting to travel with a billionaire in a private jet. It was exciting to be in the company of a man of powerful instincts and seemingly no fears. There was an animal magnetism about Primo Dalla Torre that Soo could not deny.

And yet she could continue to deny him, during the cross-country flight and even after their first evening in L.A., what he so desperately desired. She could do so not only because she was a woman of high standards and sturdy ethics, but also because she knew that it strengthened her position. The more he wanted her, the longer she made him wait, the more interested he became in Calm and Cool Clothing.

In the middle of the week of Primo's stay in Los Angeles, Anita called from New York.

"How's it going, my dear?" she asked Soo.

"He seems to like my plans. We toured a warehouse today that's twice the size of the one I've been leasing. Primo is thinking of buying it. He's interested in a real L.A. presence."

"He's interested in you," said Anita.

Soo didn't reply.

"Make certain this is a business-only trip," Anita said insistently. "It's important that you do that."

"I agree," said Soo. "That has always been my intention."

Anita smiled. Soo was the perfect protégée.

Primo left Los Angeles without as much as an embrace from Soo. But she was careful to shake his hand warmly. He understood how she wanted to play it, and he went along. Back in Europe, he thought of her obsessively. He decided to back her plan and put in a million. They would become partners. Lawyers got involved. Papers were drawn. Negotiations were prolonged and hard-nosed. E-mails went flying back and forth. The principals—Soo and Primo—allowed their attorneys to do battle. They did not speak during this two-month period. Finally, the issues were resolved. Primo Dalla Torre became the majority owner of Cool and Calm Clothing. Soo Kim was managing partner and creative chief. He flew to Los Angeles to sign the papers and celebrate the collaboration. But it took another month and another trip for him to coax her into bed. As far as Primo was concerned, though, it was worth the wait. Soo was also well satisfied.

By the time the plane landed, Beauty had gone over this story again and again. She was dying to meet Soo in person. When she did, she was convinced that Miss Kim was the most composed woman in the world. Like her line of clothing, Soo was calm and cool.

At the Ritz-Carlton apartment, she greeted Beauty with measured warmth. The expansive living room had a breathtaking view of the glittering skyscrapers of downtown Los Angeles, just blocks away.

"Primo is in China for the week," she said, "but he told me to let you know that he welcomes you to our home. We both adore Anita and are thrilled that she has turned you over to our care. She says you are an extremely talented young lady."

"She thinks you're wonderful. She's really proud of you, Miss Kim."

Soo smiled and said, "Please call me Soo. Let me show you your room."

The room, in the far rear of the apartment, had been built for a maid, but the view, looking down on L.A. Live, a complex comprised of the Staples Center, the Nokia Theatre, the Grammy Museum, and a slew of restaurants and nightclubs, gave off a luminous neon glow. There was an enormous color screen in the center of the action that alternately advertised a Prince concert and the Lakers-Knicks game.

"Some say it reminds them of Times Square," said Soo as she

looked below. "But to me it's more like a slice of Tokyo or Seoul. In fact, they built L.A. Live at the eastern edge of Koreatown. If you look farther east you'll see the fashion district, where we have our warehouse and office. I'll take you there tomorrow."

"I can't wait."

"They say that L.A. is a city without a center, but situated where we are, I think you'll feel extremely centered."

That feeling never came to pass.

Beauty spent her senior year in a magnet high school feeling especially uncentered. Her part-time work at Calm and Cool Clothing was instructive, and she learned a great deal, but after sensing Primo's attraction to Beauty, Soo turned guarded and distant. She saw Beauty as competition. Not only was the teenager a fine seamstress, but she also showed promise as a designer. When Beauty presented Soo with some initial sketches, though, Soo rejected them as frivolous and immature. Beauty was hurt. The criticism was not at all instructive. What had begun as a warm relationship between the two women soon turned cold.

Complicating matters even more was the romantic tension involving Beauty, Noah Sanchez, and Lee Kim, Soo's brother. Noah continued to pursue Beauty, who, although she would see him on occasion, did not want to be reminded of his resemblance to Power. She had had enough of those incessant dreams about Power and wanted to avoid anyone or anything remotely connected to that emotional and sexual energy. Ultimately, she made it plain to Noah that while they could remain friends, romance was out. Seeing the opening, Lee Kim who, like Noah, played freshman basketball for UCLA, tried to step in. Soo encouraged the move. She felt that if her brother won over Beauty, body and soul, her husband might lose interest in the teenager. She wanted to see Beauty attached to a man who was age appropriate. To that end, Soo invited her brother to dinner at the penthouse at least once a week. Afterward, she never failed to leave the couple alone in the apartment. If Primo was in L.A.—which wasn't more often than one week out of seven or eight—Soo made sure that they had after-dinner plans. As they walked out the door, leaving the young people behind, Soo noticed Primo looking at Beauty with an unmistakable longing in his eyes.

Lee had that same longing. He was good-looking—tall, engaging dark eyes, a well-groomed crew cut that gave him the appearance of an earlier era, the fifties. He was pleasant. He liked science fiction novels and loved the movies. Like Soo, he was devoted to his parents and, after undergraduate school, had plans to become an engineer. There was no reason in the world for Beauty not to like Lee, and she did. But it stopped there. She lacked even the slightest sense of romantic love for him. And beyond that, although she'd told Noah that she did not want to be a girlfriend, she also did not want to hurt Noah by dating his roommate. At the same time, she did not want to hurt Soo's feelings by rejecting her brother. After all, it was Soo who was allowing her to live in L.A. rent-free and apprentice in her company. In short, at every turn Beauty was navigating tricky and even treacherous waters.

Every day there were text messages from either Lee or Noah. Mostly she ignored them, hoping they'd get the message. But neither guy gave up. Lee and Noah's relationship suffered and one day during basketball practice they went after each other. The coach didn't know they were, in fact, fighting over a woman. That happened in June. Then in July, two months after graduating from high school, Beauty learned that Soo was flying to Seoul the next day on business. The day after Soo's departure, Primo turned up at the apartment. This had never happened before. Beauty was somewhat alarmed, but Primo was reassuring. He told her that he was leaving for China in a few hours and asked if she would like to join him for dinner at the Palm, directly across from L.A. Live. She agreed. She had never before been alone with Primo and was curious to see what that was like. She also felt safe knowing that he would not be spending the night in the apartment.

At the restaurant, Beauty ordered pasta and Primo ordered steak. He began talking about his business exploits. He said it was unfortunate that his interests kept him from being in L.A. more often, but his international dealings kept him on the move.

"I haven't told Soo that we're having dinner," he said. "In fact, she doesn't know I'm in L.A. This has all happened quite suddenly. You see, I'm on the verge of buying Bloom's. As you know, they have stores in San Francisco, Chicago, and Dallas as well as the flagship store in New York. You've been living out here how long? Seven months?"

"Ten months."

"And you're seventeen?"

"About to turn eighteen."

"I see," said Primo as his phone buzzed. He reached into his Oxford three-piece blue pinstriped suit for his Vertu Signature M Design eighteen-karat-gold cell phone, which he'd purchased the week before in Berlin for $35,000. "Yes," he told his caller, "I arrive in Beijing tomorrow, and then I'm off to a private meeting with the Chinese minister of finance. Immediately afterward, he's honoring me at a state dinner. So this will have to wait till Saturday when I arrive at the Mandarin Oriental in Tokyo. I'll call you when I get to Japan." Primo clicked off and apologized to Beauty. "This schedule of mine gets crazier every day."

"It sounds exciting."

"It's exhausting. A treadmill without an 'off' button. But we were talking about you, not me."

"You said you wanted to buy Bloom's."

"I *am* buying Bloom's. The deal should be done by month's end."

"And I'm not sure what all this has to do with me."

"I think you're incredibly talented, Beauty. Anita has said so. And looking over Soo's shoulder, I've seen some of your designs. Fabulous. Daring. I think you have the potential to be a star in this industry. But I also think that Soo—a perfectly wonderful woman—is like so many other women when it comes to other talented females. She's competitive. Of course that's good. Without the competitive spirit, she wouldn't be where she is. But that can be bad when it comes to supporting younger talent. When it comes to you, I'm afraid that she feels threatened. To be candid, I see her holding you back. And in that regard, I think you'd be better off in New York. Once the deal goes through, my plan is to make Anita executive vice president and merchandise manager of the entire chain. You'll be working directly under her. My plan is to eventually have you develop your own line of casual wear. I recently bought a large apartment in the Plaza Hotel where you'll be quite comfortable. And of course you'll have a generous monthly check for your living expenditures. You'll have absolutely nothing to worry about."

Beauty was astounded. She felt repelled, excited, afraid, eager, cautious, and confused by this offer. Clearly, the man was setting her up to be his mistress.

"What would I possibly tell Soo?"

"I have all that worked out. You see, Soo hasn't been all that comfortable with you living with us, and she too has suggested that you might be better off back in New York with Anita."

"But I won't be with Anita. I'll be in your apartment in the Plaza."

"A detail that's of no concern to Soo."

"And what about Anita?"

"Anita and I are coarchitects of the plan."

"The plan to buy Bloom's or the plan to move me to New York?"

"Both."

"I'm not sure," said Beauty.

"I am," said Primo. "I am quite positive that there is no downside to this arrangement—for you or me. I can change your life. You will require a couple of years of training, and to that end Anita and I will put you with the most brilliant designers in New York. The future is all yours, Beauty, and nothing can stand in the way."

"I need time to think . . ."

"Of course. You'll want to call Anita."

"I will."

"And you'll want to keep this between yourself and Anita—no one else."

"I understand."

The next evening, when Beauty reached Anita at home, she realized that Anita had been drinking. That wasn't unusual, of course. On most nights by ten P.M. Anita had polished off a bottle of expensive wine. When she drank, she spoke in great torrents of words. She gushed.

"Oh, Beauty," she said, "I'm so glad you called, my dear. I'd been expecting to hear from you. Primo called me. He's something, isn't he?"

"He told me that you know the plan."

"I've been working on the plan for ten years. That man is exceedingly more cautious than he appears. Dear God, how I have worked on that plan!"

"He's talking about buying Bloom's."

"Of course. It's the perfect marriage. Finally he sees that. Finally! For a shrewd man, he can be a slow man."

"He doesn't seem slow to me at all."

"You mustn't look at it that way, my dear. You see, he's a European, and European men have a different outlook on women."

"I feel like he wants to buy me."

"No, no, no . . . you misunderstand, Beauty. He wants to help you. He wants to nurture you, train you, prepare you—the same as I do."

"He wants me to be his mistress."

"An old-fashioned term," said Anita.

"What would you call it?"

"He wants you to be his friend."

"Please, Anita . . ."

"You told me you have been with several boys. Well, now it's time for you to be with a man."

"A married man three times my age?"

"An unconventional man for whom marriage might have been an impulsive mistake. But a good man nonetheless. And the perfect man to get you what you want. A perfect opportunity. I see no downside."

"That's just what he said."

"We think the same."

"I don't think of myself as a prostitute, Anita."

"Let me be blunt, Beauty. Primo Dalla Torre is a man not unaccustomed to patronizing prostitutes. He has had the most expensive and discreet prostitutes the world over. Prostitutes who charge tens of thousands of dollars. Prostitutes who make Halle Berry look ordinary. Prostitutes who have been with sheikhs, princes, and kings. If he wanted a prostitute, he would flip open his phone, hit a button, and buy a prostitute. But this man, my dear, this extraordinary man does not see you as a prostitute. He sees you as a talent, as a flower he wishes to grow. He wishes to place you in a garden where you are protected, cultivated, and cared for. He sees deep into your soul. He has endless appreciation for your talent. Don't you see that?"

"I see he wants to sleep with me," said Beauty. "I've seen that ever since I met him."

Beauty heard Anita slurping a large quantity of wine. "Who you sleep with, my dear," said the older woman, "is strictly your own affair. In that regard, I have seen you make mistakes. Your judgment is not infallible. You chose to sleep with the seamstress's son, and you yourself have told me that it led nowhere. When he followed you to California, all that did was cause you further agitation. Am I right? Speak your mind, dear Beauty, am I describing the situation accurately?"

"One thing doesn't have to do with the other. What does Noah have to do with Primo?"

"Both men desire you. Both men seek to impact your life. The contrast is telling. The choices we make are critical. You are at a critical juncture."

"And if I tell both to go away?" asked Beauty.

"Then that too is a choice. In my estimation, it would be a catastrophic choice. But one that is entirely up to you. Excuse me while I look for that other bottle of wine. It was around here somewhere."

"I don't know what else to say," said Beauty.

"You don't have to say a thing. You'll either come back here with Primo or you won't. I trust you to make the right decision, my dear. You're too clever a girl to undermine your life over some notion of conventional morality."

Anita's last comment stung. Beauty took it to mean: *Don't be stupid; let this man buy you if he wants to buy you; it's the shortest way to success.* Beauty put down the phone and looked out the window of her bedroom in Soo's Ritz-Carlton apartment. The lights from L.A. Live were blazing. Lady Gaga was giving a sold-out concert at the Staples Center that very night. Lee Kim had bought tickets and invited Beauty. Beauty liked Lady Gaga. She admired her originality and style. She considered her audacious and cunning. She admired how Lady Gaga had made an impact on the crowded field of pop music and pop fashion. Beauty liked how the entertainer had the courage of her ambition. She liked her drive. Beauty considered her own drive. She thought about the crowded field of design. She thought about a phrase that Wanda Washington had used in justifying her working for Slim Simmons. "Opportunity," she had said, "only knocks once."

When Lee arrived to pick up Beauty, she thought he was dressed all wrong. He was preppy in every detail. You don't dress preppy for a Lady Gaga concert. Beauty was dressed vintage. Her flowered dress was from the forties and her hat, an enormous violet affair adorned with white feathers, looked like it came out of an MGM musical of an earlier era. Lee was stunned and delighted by her look. He loved

Beauty and wanted to please her in every way possible. He indulged her with flattery as they walked across the plaza to the Staples Center. She accepted the flattery and also the fact that this perfectly nice guy bored her to tears. Lady Gaga did not bore her for a second. The show was a marvel of invention and imagination. Lady Gaga came out as Marie Antoinette, then an Aztec princess, then a creature from outer space. Her outfits were brilliant. Beams of red light exploded from her breasts. Fireworks shot off the top of her cotton-candy-shaped pink wig. She sang her heart out. She danced on stilts. She flew over the audience, harnessed by invisible ropes. She did it all.

Beauty thought that she too wanted to do it all. What did it take to do it all? Her birth mother, Isabel Long, was a hardworking woman with whom the world had dealt cruelly. The man she loved had left her. Breaking all his promises, he had gone back to Tokyo to his wife and family. Isabel's dreams were dashed. She died of ovarian cancer a week after turning thirty-one. Beauty's guardian, Power's mother, Charlotte Clay, was another hardworking, good-hearted woman. But look what happened to her. Life was cruel. Life was unpredictable. Life was cold. And in the light of this knowledge, what was a young lady to do?

Lady Gaga knew what to do. *Go for it!* Sitting next to Lee Kim, Beauty could see that he was not overwhelmed by the show. He liked the spectacle but didn't get the audaciousness of this performer. Beauty wanted to be audacious. Beauty wanted to be bold. If Lee had made a sexual move that night, she might have respected him more. But she could feel that he had been intimidated by the sexual spell that Lady Gaga had cast over the evening. Afterward they went for drinks at an L.A. Live bar, jam-packed with an after-show crowd. Everyone was talking about Lady Gaga.

"She's great," said Lee, trying to convince Beauty that he was on her wavelength.

"Why do you think she's great?" she asked, challenging him.

"She doesn't care what people think."

"I believe she does care," said Beauty. "I believe she thinks about what people might think—and then she does whatever it takes to scandalize them."

"Well, isn't that the same thing?"

"No. If you don't care what people think, you aren't calculating. She is calculating. She's calculating what it will take to make a scandal onstage."

"I'm sure you're right," said Lee. "You know more about these things than I do."

When they walked back to the Ritz-Carlton, the entry was filled with paparazzi and fans waiting for Lady Gaga. It was a mob scene.

"Let's hang around for a while," said Beauty, "and see if she shows up. I want to see what she looks like up close."

"I better get going, Beauty," said Lee. "Big exam tomorrow. I still have studying."

"Thanks for taking me," said Beauty.

"No problem," said Lee as he leaned over and kissed her on the cheek. "I'll call you soon."

When he did call the next day, all he got was voice mail. A week later, Soo told Lee—who in turn told Noah—that Beauty had packed up and moved back to New York.

The Plaza

When Beauty arrived in New York in August, she was greatly relieved that Primo was not there. Traveling in Australia, he would not be arriving for another three weeks. His absence meant that Beauty did not have to worry—at least for now—about what were or were not her obligations to him.

Directly across from Central Park, the Plaza was filled with restaurants and banquet halls decorated in the style of Louis XV. If L.A. Live was something like a dream of the future, the Plaza felt like a dream of the past. Compared to the Los Angeles apartment at the Ritz-Carlton, Primo's residence at the Plaza Hotel was Old World. Soo had done up her place with tubular steel furniture sculpted in a modern mode. Primo had furnished his New York digs with antiques and tapestries, European still-life paintings of fruits, portraits of duchesses, and landscapes of softly lit cities built on the side of Italian hills. Beauty couldn't help but be charmed. It was like living in a small museum. She liked the formality. It made her feel safe. There were two bedrooms—a large master suite and a smaller room that held a single bed. She chose the smaller room.

When she left Los Angeles, she did so in a hurry. Soo seemed relieved and asked few questions, presuming that Beauty was going back to live and work with Anita. Few words were spoken between Soo and Beauty. Beauty sensed that Soo just wanted her out of there. She also knew that Soo did not have the slightest idea that Beauty was living in Primo's apartment. The intrigue of it all bothered Beauty, but not enough to keep her from going ahead with the plan. Meanwhile, Anita encouraged her every step of the way. She came to the Plaza the very night Beauty arrived, and over a great deal of wine at the hotel's famous Oak Room, she kept saying how proud she was of her protégée.

"At first I wasn't sure, my dear," Anita was quick to say, "that you understood the uniqueness of this opportunity. I was afraid that your conventional background might hold you back."

"I don't think my background is at all conventional," Beauty replied.

"Well, by 'conventional' I mean the provincial attitude that one acquires by growing up in the South. You were raised, after all, by two women who were products of the South."

"I don't think that's bad," said Beauty.

"Not bad, my dear, just restrictive. In life we must learn to go beyond the province in which we were born. We must expand. Your mother and adopted mother never left the borders of Georgia. You have. You understand what it means to explore and fulfill potential. You have courage."

Beauty listened as Anita went on with her words of praise. The words felt good, but what had happened to Anita's attitude of independence? Wasn't she the woman who spoke proudly of using her brain—and not sex—to advance in the world of fashion?

"You *will* use your brain," said Anita when Beauty questioned her. "No doubt about it. If Primo didn't see you as a brilliant and talented woman, he'd have no interest."

"But he's interested in more than my intelligence."

"That's only natural."

"I don't say this to hurt you, Anita, but you also have interests here."

"You don't hurt me in the least, my dear. Of course I have interests of my own. We all do. We're all practical people. And that's nothing to be ashamed of."

"It feels so messy."

"On the contrary," said Anita. "Primo is a man of discretion whose ability to compartmentalize his life is absolutely flawless. He will care for you; he will guide you; he will treat you like the precious jewel that you are."

It was difficult for Beauty to challenge Anita, especially when her mentor was tipsy.

After dinner, when Beauty showed Anita the lavish apartment bought and furnished by Primo, the older woman exclaimed, "It's the work of Dietrich Strom."

"Who's he?"

"A German interior decorator who lives in Milan. The greatest decorator of the day. He recently redid the Pope's summer home. How's that for a plum client? He does everyone who's anyone."

"It's a bit much, isn't it?" asked Beauty.

"It's exquisite. If you note, you'll see each piece—the bureaus, the end tables, the love seats—is from the eighteenth century. This place is a marvel of elegant opulence. You see how much Primo values you, my dear, by the attention he has spent on this apartment."

"I thought you said Dietrich Strom spent the time doing this, not Primo."

"But don't you see, Primo spent the time making sure that Dietrich would take this assignment. If you're working for the Pope, Prince Charles, and Queen Sofia of Spain, you're not easy to get. Last year, for example, I was told that Dietrich personally told Sophie, the Countess of Wessex, that he couldn't possibly redo her summer castle for another five years. You can imagine then the importance he gives to a man like Primo Dalla Torre."

As they wandered through the apartment, Anita saw that Beauty had put her things in the small bedroom. Anita began to comment but instead stayed silent. In the white-and-black-tiled kitchen she saw there was a double-door forty-eight-bottle wine cooler stocked from top to bottom.

"Let's see what sort of refreshment the good signor has provided for us," said Anita. She opened the cooler and brought out a bottle of red. "By God, a 1985 Barolo. We simply must have a taste." Expertly opening the wine, she poured herself a glass. Beauty declined. "Well, my dear, I drink alone but I do not drink in sadness. I drink to you, sweet Beauty, and all the good fortune that life has in store for you. Merely to witness that good fortune is, for me, both an honor and pleasure."

An hour later, after her third glass, Anita fell asleep on the antique armchair in the living room. Beauty had to pick her up and help her out. She couldn't let her go home alone, so she rode in the car with her. Inside the taxi, Anita passed out again. When they arrived at the Gramercy Park brownstone, Beauty carried Anita out of the cab, into the elevator, into the apartment, and placed her in her bed. For reasons she didn't quite understand, Beauty went to her old bedroom and spent the night there. The next morning, Anita woke up early and, discovering Beauty asleep, made her breakfast, just as she had done on that first morning, two years earlier, when the young girl had arrived from Atlanta.

It was as though Beauty was waiting for Primo to claim her. At least that's how she felt. It was September in the city and the days were long and warm. Her initial reaction to the apartment—that it made her feel safe—began to change as time went by. She saw herself as a bird trapped in a gilded cage. She stayed away from the place as much as possible. That was easy because Anita had arranged for her to work in the Seventh Avenue design studio of Lena Pearl, whose women's-wear line had been a strong seller last season. Unlike Soo, Lena had no conservative instincts. Raised in an artists' colony by her folk musician grandparents—her own parents were victims of the sixties' drug abuse—Lena encouraged Beauty to go through books on Abstract Expressionism and Pop Art to get ideas for dresses, blouses, and trousers. She also told her it was important to see foreign films and read good novels. Lena herself had gone to college and majored not in design but in English literature.

"Where will you be going to college?" asked Lena.

"I'm not," said Beauty. "I guess the plan is for me to work and learn in the real world."

"The imaginary world feeds the real world," said Lena, who dressed in all black to make her short chubby body look smaller than it was. She had prematurely white hair—she was only forty—wore lots of rouge, and radiated a warm smile. "Were it not for poetry and music, literature and art, the real world would be drab and gray. The best fashion designers are well-rounded people who look outside their field for inspiration. I really think you should go to college."

"Not a good idea," said Anita when Beauty mentioned it to her.

"Why not?"

"I didn't go to college. I had the chance. I even took a course or two. But I realized—and rightly so—that my youthful energy was better applied in the world of reality, not theory. Besides, the things I wanted to learn—the same things, I presume, that you want to learn, my dear—I learned on my own. And so can you. You can learn the history of fashion by reading books. You can learn about the major figures in the industry today by reading magazines. You can learn by going to runway shows, by going to the library, by digging out whatever information you feel is necessary to your growth as a designer.

College will set you back years. You can't afford to get behind. In our field, the competition is ferocious. I've given you a head start. Now Primo is placing you in the very front of the pack. You've got an edge, dear Beauty. Get distracted by the world of academia and you'll lose that edge."

"But Lena Pearl says a great designer must be well-rounded. She talks about novels and art films. Her best friends are painters and sculptors and musicians."

"Lena Pearl was hot last year and maybe, if I decide to buy her line again for next season, she'll stay hot for another year. But I don't see her going beyond that. What you have to learn from Lena is to read the moment. She understands what a certain kind of woman is looking for today. That woman thinks of herself as being trendy, and Lena has caught the trend. But the trendy woman is a fickle woman. Oh, yes, she is, my dear. And Lena has yet to prove if she's good for more than one or two seasons. At the most, I'll give her three. So when she starts to lose touch and her line languishes, what good will her intimate familiarity with the arts do her? Right now it's easy for her to pontificate because she's making money. But come back when she's not and see if she's still singing the same song."

Beauty considered Anita's point of view. She didn't reject it out of hand, but she also knew that Lena had struck a chord within her. Beauty loved fashion and harbored all sorts of ambition. No doubt about it; she wanted to make it at all costs. At the same time, she was curious about the wider world. She wanted to learn more. She wanted to be around college kids, college teachers. She yearned to take college courses. And when Lena Pearl mentioned that her best friend taught at Pratt Institute in Brooklyn, a noted institution of higher learning specializing in art, design, architecture, and the liberal arts and sciences, Beauty took the subway to Brooklyn to look over the school for herself. She decided to apply and, if accepted, would enroll next semester. She thought it best to mention none of this to Anita.

Meanwhile, the days went by as she waited for Primo's arrival. He postponed his New York trip three different times because of pressing business somewhere else in the world. These postponements both relieved and agitated Beauty. Part of her never wanted Primo to arrive; another part of her just wanted to get it over with. She imagined what would happen. He'd show up at the apartment, see that she had chosen to sleep in the small bedroom, and immediately insist that she join him in his king-sized bed. She would refuse. He would insist. He would say, "Why in hell do you think I put you in this apartment?" She would say, "Because you want to help me." He would say, "I am help-ing you. But this help comes with a price." She would say, "I'm not willing to pay the price." And he would say, "Then get the fuck out. And forget any ideas you might have about a design line of your own."

Beauty would also imagine other scenarios: Before he arrived, she would move her things into his bedroom. The very first night, she would willingly submit to his advances. He would be gentle, kind, and tender. The lovemaking would be wonderful and satisfying. But then the scenario would turn sour when she thought of his age. He was old enough to be her father, even her grandfather. Sexually, older men had absolutely no appeal. In appearance and manner, they could not be any further from Power, the living symbol of her sexual desires.

After five weeks in New York, the phone call finally came on a Friday. Primo was in London.

"I'm finally getting there," he said. "This has been such a hectic period, but I've cleared my schedule and will spend at least three weeks in New York. Monday I'm set to sign the papers that will give me ownership of Bloom's. Monday afternoon I'll hold a press confer-ence and announce my new plans. Anita will be by my side. I haven't wanted to come to New York until I knew that the deal was done. Now it is. So I can relax. I'm terribly eager to see you, Beauty. Anita tells me you're doing great. Are you getting used to the apartment?"

"Oh, yes, the apartment is lovely."

"Dietrich Strom did a marvelous job, didn't he?"

"He did."

"I hope it's not too fussy for you."

"Not at all."

"I land tomorrow about seven in the evening and should be at the Plaza by eight thirty. We won't go out, Beauty. For our first night together, I think it would be better if we dined in. I've asked Daniel Boulud, the best chef in the city, to prepare one of his five-course tasting menus. He and his waiter may get there a little before me, but go ahead and let them set up. I want this to be an evening you'll never forget."

When she put down the phone, Beauty's heart was heavy. She wasn't ready to sell her body for a fancy apartment and a five-course tasting menu. But she had to face facts: That's what she was doing. Until this call, her life had been on an even keel. She had been meeting Anita once a week for dinner at Da Tato. Afterward, she'd help the old lady, more stooped over than ever, upstairs and then put her to bed. She wondered how someone could drink as much as Anita and still be able to work. Beauty's own work, though, was being supervised by Lena, who had encouraged her to audit a night course at Pratt on nineteenth-century art. Beauty had a found a good rhythm to her work and study. She felt grounded—until this call. This call from Primo had her feeling afraid.

When she awoke Saturday morning, she felt like fleeing, leaving this emotional mess behind her. But to where? And with what money? She had no funds except her monthly allowance from Primo. He was her sole support. She had agreed to this. She had made the decision. She had made her bed and now it was time . . .

She was due to meet Anita for lunch but decided to cancel. She didn't want to face the old lady, not today. She called her and said, "I've got a lot to do today. Primo arrives tonight."

"Oh, don't you worry your pretty head about me," said Anita. "I completely understand. This is a big day for you. And Monday will be a big day for us all. You will be at the press conference, won't you?"

"I haven't thought about it."

"It will be something to see. The international business press will be in attendance. The coverage will be extensive. I'm certain we'll make page one of the *New York Times*. After all, Bloom's is a national institution. I can't tell you how excited I am to see ownership shift from the Bloom family—those bastards have underappreciated me for decades—to a man of vision and guts. My life is changing, my dear, and so is yours."

"Well, I must run," said Beauty. "I have all these errands."

That was a lie. She had no errands. She had nothing to do except think about what she would wear tonight. And even that problem was solved when, at two P.M., there was a knock on her door. A package was hand-delivered from Francoise Coteau, the most exclusive designer in Paris. It had been flown in from France. Inside were two articles of clothing. The first came with a card that said, "For dinner." It was a long black evening dress, elegant and simple. The second came with a card that said, "For after dinner." It was white silk lingerie, revealing and elaborate. Beauty examined them carefully. She waited an hour before she tried them on. The evening dress made her feel like a movie star. It fit perfectly. It was an extraordinary garment. The lingerie, which also fit perfectly, made her feel like a prostitute. She wanted to rip it to shreds, but she didn't.

At four P.M., another delivery, this one from Tiffany. She opened the small blue box and found a pendant of petite round diamonds set in eighteen-karat white gold. There was no note.

At five P.M., the house phone rang. She was told that her hairdresser had arrived. A few minutes later Beauty opened the door and met Sheila.

"I'm from Elizabeth Arden," she said. "I've come to do your makeup and hair."

"You have?"

"Yes, weren't you told?"

"No."

"Well, you're a lucky woman. Now where shall we work?"

Beauty wanted to send her away. She wanted to tell her that she wasn't needed, but Beauty understood that she was needed. The woman had come to remake Beauty in whatever image Primo required.

They went into the master bathroom, where Beauty sat at a vanity table set in front of a large antique mirror. The woman trimmed her hair somewhat radically. "He wants a pixie look," said Sheila. "And your makeup is not to be heavy. He doesn't like heavy makeup. He also specified a certain rose-petal-pink shade of lipstick."

Beauty was relieved that the haircut was becoming and the makeup light. She herself disliked heavy makeup and could derive some satisfaction from the fact that Primo did not want to paint her face to look like a whore. At the same time, he had not asked her whether she wanted this special treatment. But then again, the treatment was not for Beauty's satisfaction—it was for Primo's.

By six thirty, the woman was gone and Beauty decided to draw a bath. She did so in the master bathroom. The marble tub was enormous. She was careful not to disturb her makeup. She stayed in the warm bubbly water for a long while, her eyes closed, her mind heavy with thoughts of what the evening would bring. She tried to convince herself that she was the luckiest woman in the world. She had everything she could possibly want. Comfort. Luxury. A promising future. What was there to complain about? Why did she need to fill her head with doubts and regret, fear and self-condemnation? Forget those thoughts. Just enjoy the feeling of the warm water. Just enjoy the bath.

At seven thirty Daniel Boulud and a waiter, both dressed in white, arrived. They went directly to the kitchen to start preparations. Candles were lit in the dining room, where the place settings—antique sterling silver and Rosenthal bone china and crystal—were meticulously arranged. Meanwhile, Beauty put on the black evening dress and the diamond necklace. Inspecting herself in the mirror, she felt more glamorous than at any moment in her life—and more apprehensive. She felt both very expensive and very cheap.

At seven forty-five, Claude Browning, a violinist from the New York Philharmonic, arrived in a black tux. He explained that he would be providing the evening's music. Beauty showed him to the living room, where he began to play classical selections. He played beautifully.

At eight, the phone rang. It was Primo. "I'm in the car and should be there within a half hour. Has Daniel arrived?"

"Yes."

"Ask him to serve the pâté de foie gras. You must be starved."

"I'm fine."

"Did the clothes arrive from France?"

"Oh, yes, thank you."

"And you like them?"

"I do."

"And the necklace?"

"It's beautiful. Thank you."

"And did Elizabeth Arden send someone over?"

"Yes."

"And the violinist?"

"He's in the living room."

"Good, so we're all set."

"Yes."

"Just relax. Have a glass of Dom Perignon. See you in a few minutes."

She sat in the living room while the waiter served champagne. The fragrance of the food cooking in the kitchen was enchanting. The pâté de foie gras was heavenly. Ten minutes passed. Then fifteen. Then thirty. Any second now she would hear a knock at the door.

Any second now Primo would be arriving. Forty minutes passed. He must have gotten stuck in traffic. She had another glass of champagne. It was good to drink champagne. Good to get tipsy. Good to feel light-headed and lose her inhibitions. Tonight would be okay. Maybe even fun. And, if she could only wrap her mind around the fact that she was consorting with an older married man, maybe even romantic. The champagne would help. But now an hour had passed since he had called and she sensed something was wrong. She waited another fifteen minutes and decided to call him on his cell number. It went directly to voice mail. What could have happened?

Daniel Boulud, a most charming man, came out of the kitchen and began to worry with her. "I've known Signor Dalla Torre for many years and have never known him to be late. I am hoping that nothing is wrong."

Beauty felt foolish—sipping champagne, nibbling on pâté de foie gras, dressed in a fabulous evening dress, waiting for a man whom she barely knew. Maybe there had been an accident. Maybe he had changed his mind and remembered another kept woman whom he preferred. Maybe he had been kidnapped and was being held for ransom. Whatever it was, by ten o'clock, Monsieur Boulud, a world-renowned chef who had only agreed to cook this meal himself because of his close friendship with Primo, began making calls. Beauty had stopped drinking champagne. The violinist had stopped playing Schubert. The mood, sublimely romantic, had turned stone-cold. Fear was in the air.

Boulud was in the kitchen, speaking in a hushed voice. When he came to the living room, he was pale. He looked at her and spoke plainly. "I've just spoken to Primo's assistant. In the car over here, he had a massive heart attack and was rushed to the hospital."

"Is he all right?" Beauty asked.

"He's dead."

Her eyes went wide. She had no idea what to say or feel. She went numb. All she could think of was Anita. She would call Anita and Anita would know what to do. But no one responded at Anita's apartment. She called Da Tato and asked if Anita was there, but she wasn't.

By ten forty-five, Daniel Boulud, along with the waiter and violinist, had left. Beauty was alone in the apartment. She had never felt more alone in her life. She tried watching TV, listening to the radio, reading the newspaper, but nothing worked. Nothing could remove the confusion from her mind. After the falling-out with Nina, she had made no friends in New York. Solomon and Amir were in Chicago. She thought of calling them, but it was the middle of the night. She thought of calling Wanda Washington in Atlanta, but Wanda didn't even know that Primo was supporting her. She felt frantic. She felt helpless. She realized that she was still wearing the black evening gown. She went to the small bedroom where she had kept the white lingerie in its box. She opened the box and touched the silky garment. Then she put on a pair of plain cotton pajamas and tossed and turned until sheer exhaustion pulled her into sleep.

It wasn't until late the next evening when she learned that, the day after Primo's heart attack, Anita Ward had suffered a stroke in her Gramercy Park apartment and died instantly.

Emmanuel Baptist Church

Beauty couldn't remember another day like this. There was no weather. It was early October, and it was neither hot nor cold. The sky was a grayish blue. There was no breeze, no clouds. As she and Wanda Washington walked into the Gothic-revival-style church, built in 1882 in the Clinton Hill section of Brooklyn, Beauty felt empty inside. Her heart was heavy and her mind dark with confusion and uncertainty. They had arrived for the funeral of Anita Ward.

Wanda had flown up from Atlanta the day before and made the arrangements. Aside from a few distant aunts and uncles, Anita had no family. Her only tie to her past was Wanda—and it was Wanda who decided that there should be a church service.

"Don't care if she hadn't been to church in thirty years. Through my preacher back home, I found this real nice church up here. She gonna be sent off from church. Ain't gonna have it no other way. Me and Anita, we went to church together as kids and no one's gonna tell me she didn't believe in Jesus. I remember her praying to Jesus."

Beauty remembered Anita saying that she had no use for organized religion and was not a believer, but Beauty wasn't about to argue with Wanda. She was glad to see Wanda and glad that Wanda was in charge.

The day after Primo died, Beauty had moved out of the Plaza, taking all her belongings while leaving behind the black evening gown, the diamond pendant, and the white silk lingerie. She asked Lena Pearl if she could move in with her for a day or two. Late that evening, Lena, having just learned the news about Anita, informed Beauty that her mentor had died. Lena knew nothing about Beauty's connection with Primo. In fact, aside from those who came to set up the Saturday evening dinner, Anita was the only one who had known. Beauty prayed that Soo would never find out, although there was nothing to discover other than the fact that Primo had allowed her to live in his apartment.

The ornate church was filled with many people from the fashion world. Members of the Bloom family were in attendance. Several spoke about Anita with admiration. Her taste, tenacity, and keen business sense were lauded. Wanda went last. She was the only one who spoke with real love. "I came up to testify and say good-bye to someone who, as y'all know, was a highly unusual individual. I knew that way back when me and Anita were nappy-headed little girls running 'round Fair Street and Ashby in Atlanta. She was the only one in our class who could draw. She learned to read and spell and write correctly before any of us. While we were out there playing hopscotch, she was sewing up a storm on her mama's broken-down Singer. After high school, when none of us had ever been outside the city limits, she said, 'Wanda, I'm taking that Trailways bus to New York City and get me a job.' 'Anita,' I said, 'you stone crazy. What you gonna do up there in New York City? How you gonna get a job? You don't know nobody up there.' 'You watch me, Wanda,' she says. 'You just watch.' Well, I sure enough did watch. Watched this girl go from nothing to something. Watched her make something of herself. She was alone— no husband, no brothers or sisters to help her, no welfare, no charity. Even her health problems—and she had plenty—didn't stop her. Nothing could stop Miss Anita Ward from Atlanta, Georgia, because the good Lord had given her the will to succeed and the courage to go all out against the odds. God gave her talent and God gave her a good life. I say thank you, Jesus, for the good life of Anita Ward. A hard life, yes. But a good life. A good woman. A good friend. A good soul who's gone on to glory, where she's resting in the bosom of the Lord who loves us with a love we can't even understand but can sure feel. I feel you, Anita. I feel you inspiring us to keep on keeping on, and I say, 'Girl, we gonna miss you, but you in a better place.' Praise the Lord!"

After the funeral, Wanda remained in New York for several days. She closed down Anita's apartment and located Anita's will. The money she had accumulated was substantial. She gave it all to a foundation that supported research for osteoporosis.

"She had a generous soul," Wanda told Beauty. "She wanted to help people who were stooped over like her. The poor lady suffered, but you never heard her complain about it, did you? You never heard her play the victim."

"Never," Beauty agreed.

"While it's true that she liked her wine, my personal belief is that the wine relieved her pain. If drinking wine helped her cope, I got no arguments with the wine. Besides, the wine never got in the way of her work, did it?"

"Not that I saw."

"She didn't have no men. She didn't have no family. So she was entitled to a li'l ol' wine. And now we see she gave all her money away to charity, just like she was charitable with you, wasn't she?"

"She was," said Beauty, who remained silent about Anita's role in encouraging her to move into Primo's apartment in the Plaza. When Wanda asked Beauty about her current living arrangements, Beauty was evasive. She didn't want to go into it. She didn't want to explain the fact that, following Anita's advice, she was being kept by an older man who had been on the verge of buying Bloom's.

Meanwhile, the newspaper was filled with stories about the death of Primo Dalla Torre. Soo Kim had flown to New York to claim his body, but so had a twenty-six-year-old woman from Beijing who declared that she had five-year-old twin sons by him. The lady furthermore claimed that, in accordance with Chinese statutes, she was his common-law wife. She hired a battery of lawyers. So did Soo Kim. And complicating matters further, another group of top-flight lawyers, working for Primo's family back in Italy—his two brothers and a sister—fought Soo's claim and pointed to a prenuptial contract that left her only his interest in Calm and Cool Clothing. Meanwhile, there was nothing calm or cool about the state of Primo's buyout of Bloom's. Given the contentious claims against his estate and holdings, chaos prevailed and the deal fell through. Moreover, the man who replaced Anita as chief merchandise buyer had no interest in Beauty or Beauty's new mentor, Lena Pearl. In rejecting Lena's new line, he virtually closed the door on her operation. In short, Beauty was out in the cold.

"Come back to Atlanta," said Wanda. "Come back home. I'll find something for you to do."

"I can't work in the wig shop."

"Wasn't thinking of the wig shop. There are designers setting up shop back home."

"I can't go back home, Wanda."

"Power's not there. He hasn't been there for a while."

Beauty wanted to ask Wanda where he was, but she stopped herself.

"He keeps asking for your number," said Wanda, "but I won't give it to him. I figured you don't want him to have it."

"Thank you. You're right. I just need to be left alone for a little while."

"And what will you do? Where will you go?"

"I'm not sure."

"You know that Slim will always help you."

"I don't want to hear about Slim," said Beauty.

"He's helped Power. He's helped him a lot. All you got to do, baby, is give me the word and—"

"I'm fine. I'm strong."

"I know you're strong, Beauty, but even strong people need help. I think you need help right now. What are you going to do?"

"I'll figure it out. I love you, Wanda. You're a wonderful woman and you've done nothing but help me. I appreciate everything you've done. I truly do. Now, though, I need time to decide what to do."

"When you figure it out, let me know?"

"Of course."

"And you're sure you don't wanna come home with me, sweetheart?"

"I'm sure, Wanda."

"And will you be staying in New York?"

"I don't know. That's what I've got to figure out."

Claire's

Solomon Getz couldn't attend Anita Ward's funeral because it came on the day of an important storewide sale. As head of the men's department at the big Neiman Marcus store on Michigan Avenue along Chicago's Magnificent Mile, he couldn't get away. But the day after the service he did manage to reach Beauty by phone.

"I know you're reeling," he said. "I know it's hard for you."

"I'm glad to hear your voice, Solomon."

"When did you get in from L.A.?"

"I've actually been here for a while," she said. "I moved back some weeks ago."

"I had no idea. What happened in California?"

"Well, it turned out differently than I thought."

"How do you mean?"

"It's too complicated to explain on the phone."

"With Anita gone, though, are you all right? Do you have a job?"

"Not really."

"Any money?"

"Very little," said Beauty.

"I think you should get out of New York."

"Why do you say that?"

"I just think it would be good for you. It sounds like you've had it with New York for a while."

"Maybe . . ."

"Besides, if you're really interested in making money in fashion you need to spend some time away from either coast. Come to the Midwest and you'll get a real down-to-earth sense of what Americans buy. Come to Chicago and your whole sense of what sells and doesn't sell will change. You'll get a good taste of reality. Besides, it's a wonderful city. You'll love it."

"What am I going to do there?"

"Work. Get a job. I'm telling you, it's just what you need. New city. New job."

New city. New job. The words made sense to Beauty. The more she read about the lawsuits flying back and forth between Soo Kim in L.A., the Chinese woman, and Primo Dalla Torre's estate lawyers in New York, the more she wanted to get away from both cities. Chicago started to sound like a reasonable escape. Solomon made it even easier by telling her that she could sleep on his couch until she found work and a place to live. Amir got on the phone and told her that she was sorely missed and would be a most welcome guest.

"You've been through a lot," said Amir. "I don't know any of the details, but I can hear it in your voice. Now is a good time for you to be with friends."

Some two months after her nineteenth birthday, Beauty arrived in late October when Chicago was experiencing a pleasant fall. Under ample sunshine, the lake glistened. Beauty stood by the river that ran through the center of downtown and studied the reflection of the

Wrigley Building. She had never been here before, never imagined this many bold and innovative buildings, this much bustle, this much urban charm. She walked the streets of the Loop, excited by the roar of the elevated train. She perused the fancy shops on the Magnificent Mile, the malls and boutiques, the great hotels like the Drake and the Palmer House. The sensation of being in a powerful new city allowed her to chase away the confusion of the past months. Part of her still felt shame that she'd sold herself to Primo in exchange for career advancement; yet another part of her regretted his death because it canceled that advancement. The fact that Anita was gone—Anita with all her encouragement and plans for Beauty's future—added to the emotional funk in which she found herself.

Solomon's spirit helped her out of the funk. From the moment he had picked her up from the airport, he couldn't stop talking job ideas. "There are a couple of openings at Neiman's in sales. One is in shoes and the other costume jewelry. They're busy departments and the time will fly. What do you say?"

"I appreciate your help," said Beauty. "I'm happy to get any work I can."

On one level, that was true. But on another level, she wasn't happy at all. She knew it was a step down. After all, she had been training not only to become a designer but to also fashion her own line. That was her heart's desire. But that desire would have to be put on hold. The shock of two sudden deaths changed everything. She would have to adjust to this new reality. She would have to follow the lead of a friend, a practical man himself, who had her best interests at heart. She would sell shoes or costume jewelry at Neiman Marcus—whichever opening came first.

As it turned out, both openings had been filled by the time Beauty applied. Solomon was surprised. Days earlier he had listed her as an applicant and was assured she'd get an interview. He complained to Richard Waterford, the head of human resources.

"You've saved me a phone call," said Waterford, an officious Englishman. "I was about to ring you up and ask you to come in."

"Good," said Solomon, "then you realize my friend has been overlooked."

"I'm afraid it's not about your friend. It's about you, Solomon. As of the end of the week, we're terminating you. We're not at all pleased with your performance."

"My performance has been flawless," said Solomon.

"That's subject to interpretation. Our interpretation is quite negative. You're entitled to two weeks' severance. Good-bye and good luck."

When Solomon arrived home that night to report the bad news, Amir was in the midst of teaching Beauty to make a Middle Eastern lamb stew. The apartment was practically floating on the fragrance of a spicy sauce. When Solomon told them what happened—that not only had Beauty's job prospects fallen through but that he had been fired—they stopped what they were doing and came over to console him.

"I'll get a job that pays," said Amir, whose current band had been playing free concerts in Millennium Park. "Maybe I can work in a record store."

"There are no more record stores," said Solomon.

"Or a bookstore," said Amir.

"They're closing down as quickly as record stores," said Solomon.

"Look," Amir added, "we're all young, healthy, and smart. We'll find jobs. We'll just have to take whatever we can get."

A week later, Amir was working at the Apple Store. He had been an Apple whiz for years. Solomon found a buyer's job at Macy's in Water Place Tower, an upscale mall on Michigan Avenue, not far from Neiman Marcus. Meanwhile, Beauty began pounding the pavement.

She read the want ads, scrutinized Craigslist and other online postings, and started in on a long series of interviews all over Chicago.

Probably because Solomon and Amir had maintained such a positive spirit and found jobs themselves, she was not discouraged, at least not for the first two weeks. She got to know the city. But she also learned that, in a down economy, jobs weren't easy to come by. She applied at all the major department stores. She went to dozens of clothing shops. She made a good appearance and spoke of her work at Bloom's and her internship at Calm and Cool Clothing.

Some employers were impressed, but most pointed out her absence of sales experience. It was hard not to be discouraged. She appreciated Solomon's and Amir's warm hospitality, but their couch sagged and her back ached. After several long weeks of searching, her head ached.

"Someone said that Claire's has an opening for a salesclerk," Solomon announced at the beginning of her second unemployed month in Chicago.

"What's Claire's?"

"Weren't you once a preteen?" he asked.

"Of course."

"Then you know Claire's. All preteen girls know Claire's. That's where preteen girls go to get their ears pierced and buy Justin Bieber lunch boxes."

"Somehow I missed out on Claire's," said Beauty.

"Well, time to catch up. Actually Claire's is a great training ground for you. The truly hip people in our industry study preteens more than any other group. Preteens are indicators of the new direction in fashion. If you get this job at Claire's, you'll find yourself facing a fascinating learning curve."

Beauty got the job. She learned to pierce ears. She learned the tastes of preteen girls. They liked earrings designed in the shape of tiny zippers, earrings made to look like cups of hot chocolate, earrings with peace signs, and earrings in the form of sparkly half-moons. They liked headbands made of gingham flowers and hair clips of polka-dotted daisies. There were also matching BFF necklaces and fuchsia studded-bow satchel purses.

The mall was busy and Claire's was always crowded. Beauty was not unhappy. She liked the energy of preteen girls. They were interested in fashion as fun, a concept she had forgotten about while working for Anita Ward, Soo Kim, and Lena Pearl. The preteens could be frenetic, but they also seemed carefree. They were far more sophisticated than Beauty had been at their age. Beauty had always worked, sewing with her mom and adopted mom after school and on weekends. She had never run around the malls of Atlanta looking to buy butterfly rings and scarves of fake leopard skin. At the same time, she wasn't envious of these young girls who had the freedom to shop at will. She enjoyed their spirit. It was a welcome relief from the seriousness of Anita, Soo, and Lena.

When an eleven-year-old African-American girl named Joyce bought a $9 gold-painted peacock pin, Beauty thought of Anita. She remembered the peacocks in Anita's apartment. She remembered the kindness that Anita had shown her when she'd first arrived in New York. She also remembered how difficult it was to mourn for Anita. Not that she didn't appreciate and admire the woman. But the way it happened—the dual deaths of Primo and Anita—made it difficult for Beauty to process. She still resented that it was Anita who had encouraged her to sell herself to Primo. Anita was an instigator and a manipulator. So, of course, was Primo. And so was Soo. The unholy and secret alliance between Primo, Anita, and Beauty had taken its toll. Their deaths removed the pressure and offered Beauty an emotional reprieve.

After her third month, she moved into a studio apartment on Wabash Avenue close to Columbia College Chicago, where she began to audit a course on fashion/retail management. She liked the location of her place because she could walk to the school and hear concerts and lectures on everything from the art of Japanese flower design to contemporary film. She was starting to feel settled and relatively calm. She had survived a storm.

But when winter arrived and the freezing wind blowing off the lake turned the city bitter cold, Beauty fell into something of a funk. To some degree she could share her recent experiences in L.A. and New York with Solomon and Amir, yet she couldn't share everything. She couldn't tell them how much time she spent wondering about and dreaming of Power. This was especially true when she moved into her own apartment. She'd wanted to be alone. She preferred not to lean on Solomon and Amir for help. She was, after all, despite—or because of—everything she had gone through, an independent soul. She was eager to reclaim her independence. In doing so, though, she found herself fantasizing more and more about Power. For the thousandth time, she relived their night in bed after the explosion. For the millionth time, she thought of picking up the phone and asking Wanda to put her in touch with Power. He had reentered her dreams on a nightly basis. He even had her believing, at least on one Thursday afternoon, that he was following her through the mall.

She had come to work that day and, for reasons she couldn't understand, felt his spirit close behind her. She wanted to turn around and look but she didn't. She went to the store, punched the clock, and started greeting customers. At one point, though, she thought she caught a glimpse of Power walking past the shop. She almost stopped what she was doing and ran out of the store. She wanted to see if it was really him. She wanted it to be him, but she also did not want it to be him. The last thing in the world she needed was the complication that his presence in her life would bring. She needed quietude. She needed steadiness. She had a decent job, a decent apartment, and close proximity to a college she found stimulating.

Then why, night after night, did she torture herself with thoughts of the man? Why didn't she—why couldn't she—simply forget him? The prospects for her future had dimmed but not disappeared. Her manager at Claire's, a pleasant woman named Sue, had praised her highly and said if her good work continued, she might recommend her as assistant manager. At least two or three times a day she would be approached for a date by a male shopper in the mall. Her invitations were countless and her refusals absolute. She did not want to bother with men—not now. After what had happened in New York, she felt vulnerable. She did not want to be taken care of, not even for a night. She did not want to be offered a free dinner, a free movie, a free concert, or a free anything. When she remembered how she had felt being bought, she recoiled.

Solomon and Amir had a close circle of other gay men friends, and she enjoyed their company. One named Thomas worked in public relations. His partner, Randy, taught art history at Columbia College Chicago, the same school that Beauty frequented. Solomon, Amir, and their friends were stimulating. They spoke of movies and books, politics and fashion. Together, they went to photography shows at the Art Institute of Chicago and blues jams at Buddy Guy's Legends club. Thomas and Randy invited Beauty to her first opera, *Aida,* at the Chicago Lyric Opera. When the weather broke and spring arrived, she, Solomon, and Amir saw Kanye West give a spectacular outdoor performance in Millennium Park.

She liked this group of guys, not only because of the absence of sexual tension but also because of their ambition. After his setback at Neiman's, Solomon quickly worked his way up at Macy's to become the chief buyer of men's clothes. Amir got a grant from an arts foundation to write original music. Thomas's public relations firm promoted him to work on the Chicago Better Business Bureau account. At twenty-seven, Randy became the youngest professor at Columbia College to be given tenure.

The men were older than Beauty, and yet they treated her as an equal. They had empathy for her difficult past and recognized her need for support. They praised and encouraged her. They took her to a fancy dinner when she was named assistant manager of Claire's. They were always talking about setting her up with straight men who they knew, but she wasn't interested. They sensed her need to avoid romantic entanglements and, after a while, avoided discussions about her love life. She became their little sister, a woman they loved, respected, and protected.

It was a cold day in November, at the start of her second winter in Chicago, and Beauty arrived at Claire's at noon. She was working the late shift.

"Let's take a few minutes and go over to Starbucks," said Sue, the store manager. "There's something I need to tell you."

Beauty's first thought was that she was being fired. Sue had dismissed three different salesclerks in the last two months. Business had been down, and although Beauty often relieved Sue and, as assistant manager, had been given the responsibility of closing the store and dealing with the cash and sales receipts, she knew that she was not irreplaceable. No one is.

A blond woman from Wisconsin with a brusque manner of speaking, Sue got them both caffe lattes and found a table in the back.

"Let me get right to the point," Sue said. "Claire's doesn't want you working in Chicago anymore."

Beauty's throat went dry. She *was* being fired.

"They want you in Atlanta," said Sue. "They want to you to assist managing their store in the Cumberland Mall."

Beauty expressed relief and surprise.

"I'm from Atlanta," she said.

"I know. That's why I recommended you. I thought you'd be glad."

"Well, I appreciate the recommendation, but, well . . . can't I continue working in the store here?"

"I'm afraid not. I'm being transferred to Milwaukee and they're bringing in a new crew. Besides, they're giving you a substantial raise and the promise that, as soon as you turn twenty-one next August, you'll manage a store of your own. They have you pegged to be the youngest manager in the history of Claire's. They want to do a lot of publicity around that. And that's only nine months from now."

"Can I think about it?" asked Beauty.

"Of course. But I thought you'd jump at the chance."

"I just need a little time."

"It's a career move," said Solomon that night, "a good career move."

"I don't want to be stuck at Claire's my whole life," Beauty argued.

"You won't be. But Claire's is teaching you things—you've seen that for yourself—and the idea of being the youngest manager in the history of a major chain is a coup. It's a stepping-stone. It'll lead to bigger and better things."

"We'd hate for you to move," said Amir, "but I think Sol's right. They're advancing you because they recognize your talent. That's a beautiful thing."

"What is it?" asked Solomon. "Is the idea of going back home bothering you?"

Beauty had not gone into details, but she had mentioned Slim Simmons to Solomon and Amir. She had told them how repulsive she found the man.

"Atlanta is a big city," said Amir. "You'll have nothing to do with him. He doesn't have to know you're there."

"He wouldn't," said Beauty. "He couldn't."

Buckhead

It had been nearly four years since Beauty had been back in Atlanta. She was not at all thrilled at being home, but she was determined to make the best of it. She was determined not to let her fears deter her future. Her future was her career, and at least for now, her career was with Claire's. Solomon was right: Claire's had much to teach her. It was a streamlined retail operation with expertise in proper pricing and careful merchandising. Their products moved, their customer base was loyal, and the stores had a steady stream of eager young shoppers. Beauty liked waiting on the preteen girls who sought out bracelets and backpacks. She remembered the time in her life when she herself had gone from Hello Kitty stickers to *Tiger Beat* magazine. Most important, Claire's afforded her stability.

It was one thing to climb the corporate ladder at Claire's but another to reenter the city that had caused her so much pain. Yet Atlanta was merely a stopover to bigger things. She was told by her new manager, Dorothy Blairsworth, that come Beauty's twenty-first birthday, she would have her own Claire's to manage. In all likelihood that would be a new Claire's due to open in Marin County in the north San Francisco Bay area, one of the most beautiful sections of the country. The location was perfect. It would transport Beauty to a new realm. For these coming months then she could tolerate being home, but only by living in Buckhead, an upscale uptown neighborhood called the Beverly Hills of Atlanta. She found a small studio apartment on Peachtree Road, leased a Corolla for $170 a month, and settled in quickly.

She liked driving through the residential streets of Buckhead. They were lined with mansions of virtually every architectural style. In the shopping area, fall and winter fashions were on display in the stores of Lenox Square and Phipps Plaza. Those shops—Giorgio Armani, Kate Spade, Fendi, Salvatore Ferragamo, Valentino, Bulgari—all gave Beauty a sense of well-being. The Claire's location at Cumberland was less tony. The mall was anchored by Sears, Costco, and Macy's. It was a twenty-five-minute drive through traffic in her Corolla, but she didn't mind. The neighborhoods where she lived and worked were not the neighborhoods of her childhood.

And yet she often felt anxious about running into someone she knew from her past. But why? She hadn't broken any laws. She hadn't done anything wrong. She'd gone to New York and worked, then to L.A., then back to New York, and then on to Chicago. She had never *not* worked except in Chicago when she was busy looking for work. She had nothing to be ashamed of. There was, of course, the episode with Primo Dalla Torre, but in truth he had never touched her. He had merely sponsored her.

A few days after arriving in Atlanta, Beauty met Wanda for lunch at Bistro Niko, a busy French eatery near Beauty's apartment on Peachtree. Wanda showed up in a black polka-dot hat with a high crown, a wide white bow, and a sweeping brim of silver glitter. Her black dress, snug for her ample body, also carried the polka-dot theme. The lustrous jet-black hair of her expensive wig fell to her shoulders. After ordering iced tea and salads, the two women began to talk.

"I was shocked when you called, baby," said Wanda, "but I was happy. Happy to see you back home. Got tired of that Chicago weather, did you? Well, this Georgia sunshine gonna warm you up in no time. Glad to see you, Beauty, I really am. To tell you the truth, I was a little hurt that you didn't want to come back to Wanda's Wigs to work, but Lord knows I understand. You're way beyond that. Claire's is a big national operation and they got their eye on you, don't they?"

"I think so. I hope so."

"I know so, honey. They ain't stupid. They know when they got a winner in their organization. And they carry cute things. I know. I've taken my niece to Claire's. Took her to get her ears pierced when she turned seven. She been wearing crazy earrings ever since. She loves Claire's. All the girls love Claire's. I'm proud of you, Beauty. I really am. After what happened to Anita, you picked yourself up, dusted yourself off, moved out there to Chicago, found you a job, and did what you had to do. You made of strong stuff, girl. You know where you're going."

"Well, I'm here and I want to make the best of it, Wanda. I wanted to see you, but, like I said on the phone, I'm not calling everyone I know."

"I understand. You don't have to worry about Wanda Washington. Wanda knows how to keep a secret. But I just don't understand why it has to be a secret."

"Well, it's not a complete secret. I called Tanisha, my friend from high school. She's married to a lawyer and they don't live far from here. She has a little baby boy. I'm going to see her next week."

"That's wonderful. So you are reconnecting."

"I just don't want to reconnect with Slim. Or Power."

"Power hasn't lived in Atlanta for a while."

Beauty had to stop herself from asking Wanda where Power was living.

"And Slim," said Wanda, "well, he's not the same man he used to be. I don't see him that much."

"He still owns your store, doesn't he?" asked Beauty. "Isn't he still your boss?"

"He's the boss all right, but I avoid him. He's changed. And not for the better. I do believe the man has mental problems."

Beauty wanted more details about those problems—she wanted to hear that her own instincts about Slim's murderous nature were absolutely right—but she also didn't want to discuss the man. His very name made her cringe.

"But you're all right, aren't you?" Beauty asked Wanda.

"I'm fine, baby," said Wanda. "I've been dealing with that man so long I know him better than he knows himself. He don't scare me none. He never has. It's just that I've always been able to bring out his better nature. But recently that better nature is getting worser."

"Is there a way you can get away from him entirely?"

"You mean retire? Why should I? I love the store and the customers love me. The customers depend on me. Half of the women in this city are wearing my wigs. It's a going concern. Has been for over thirty years. Besides, it affords me a good living. Reverend at church looks to me to tithe, and I never fail. I'm proud to tithe. Proud to hold my head high and praise the Lord every Sunday for giving me what I need. There are times when I need a man, and I got my choice there. You'd be surprised, Beauty, you really would, but I got me a whole army of men at my command. Got four or five on speed dial that will drop everything the minute I give the word. And I'll tell you something else, Beauty, that I don't tell most people. I'm telling you, though, 'cause it's a good lesson for a young woman to learn. These men I'm talking about—and none of them are married, because I do not believe in fooling with married men—these men are sweet and kind and eager to please, but I do not trust them entirely. Truth is, before we get into anything heavy, I demand a health certificate. I make them go to a doctor for serious testing. I got to see for myself that none are carrying any of those awful diseases running through this city. You see, I understand human nature. I understand men. They are not built for one woman. They may tell you you're the only one, but you ain't. That's why I never married. I'm a realist, baby. And what's real is that men wander and will keep wandering as long as they can. So if they wanna wander over my house, that's fine. Like any woman, I get in the mood. I want me a wandering man, but I understand that after we have our fun he'll be wandering off. And as long as he don't leave me with no disease, let him go wandering. That's why you're looking at a woman who is a hundred percent healthy. My doctor says I need to lose thirty pounds, but my doctor is a white man who don't understand black women are big-boned and made different. I'm feeling fine, Beauty. Never felt no better."

"Well, you look great."

"There's only one favor I'd like to ask of you, baby."

"What's that?" asked Beauty.

"Come to church with me this Sunday. It's something both your mamas would want you to do."

"I've never really been much of a churchgoer," said Beauty.

"That don't matter. God is patient. But he's waiting for you. He's been waiting for you. Just a matter of you accepting his gift."

Beauty didn't want to argue with Wanda about religion. She liked her too much. She also recognized Wanda's genuine love for God. She wished she could share it, but she also didn't want to be hypocritical.

"Maybe sometime," Beauty said, "but right now I'm just getting used to being back."

"God will never lose patience with you," Wanda said assuredly. "God *is* patience."

Beauty patiently pursued her new life. She stayed focused on her goal—do well as assistant manager at the Cumberland Mall and move on to manage the store in Marin County. One night she dreamed that she was living in a house that sat across the Golden Gate Bridge with a view of San Francisco. The house was all wood and glass and filled with fragrant flowers. Upstairs the master bedroom overlooked a blooming garden. Downstairs the living room and den were furnished with rustic chairs and overstuffed couches of butter-soft leather. Jaheim, her favorite R&B artist, was singing soothing songs on the radio. She went to the kitchen and began preparing a breaded macaroni and cheese dish that her adopted mother, Charlotte, had taught her. A plump tabby cat named Snuckles sat by her feet and purred. When the dish was ready, she carried it to the kitchen, highlighted by sunshine-yellow tiles, and set the table for two. "It's ready, darling," she called upstairs. She waited for a moment or two, and then, wearing only his pajama bottoms—his broad chest bare—Power appeared. He was smiling.

When she awoke, she did not dismiss the dream. She wanted to keep it, relish it, allow it to linger. It felt good. There was no one in the world she would ever tell about this dream. She didn't have to tell. She could simply keep the images in her mind for five or ten minutes while she remained in bed. But then came the guilt and shame followed by the return of her resolution that she would not, under any circumstances, renew that relationship. It was too complicated, too emotionally entangled. She didn't want to reexamine or reapproach it.

Nine months went by quickly as Beauty fell into a life that met her criteria for what was sane and productive. Although Tanisha and her husband, Grant, wanted to set her up, she still refused to date. Their family, and especially their baby boy, Isaac, brought her comfort and joy. They asked her over often, and she liked spending time with people who were stable and drama free. Once or twice she went to church with Wanda, where she found the music inspiring and the preacher long-winded. Three times a week she audited courses at Georgia State University, one on sociology, another on world history, and a third on techniques of modern marketing. She was determined to be a well-rounded person. She avoided the singles bars and dating websites. For her twenty-first birthday in August, Tanisha took her to dinner at Jalisco Mexican Restaurant, Beauty's choice. She didn't want anything fancy. She didn't want to draw attention to herself.

Not drawing attention to herself had been her game plan in Atlanta. She only wanted to do the work necessary to manage her own Claire's store in California. When summer turned to fall, she began asking her supervisors when that would happen. They were evasive, claiming that there was a change in plans for the Marin County store and a more senior manager would have to be brought in. Beauty was crushed. She had been counting on this promotion. She wanted to get away from Atlanta and move up the corporate ladder.

Her ambition had not diminished. She was growing impatient with Claire's. The job, once exciting, had grown routine. How many ears can you pierce? How many turquoise bangles can you sell to eight-year-old girls wanting to look eighteen?

At night, when she returned from her courses at Georgia State, she looked through the sketchbooks she had been keeping for years. Working for Anita and Soo and Lena, she had begun accumulating ideas for what she had always envisioned as her own line of clothing. Recently she had added jewelry designs. She had watched the best and was convinced that she was just as good. Primo Dalla Torre had recognized her talent, just like his wife, Soo, and Soo's mentor, Anita. Lena Pearl had told Beauty that her stylings showed originality. She had done particularly well at Claire's because of her ability to accessorize the preteen customers with flair. She felt not only that she was ready to manage a Claire's store but that she was perfectly capable of being a Claire's buyer, even a Claire's designer. In that regard, she wrote a letter to the president of Claire's, arguing that her talent was being overlooked. With three thousand stores in the United States, two hundred in Japan, and another four hundred throughout the world, Claire's could make better use of her. She reminded the president that she was tagged to be the youngest manager in the history of the chain and that the promotion, a golden publicity opportunity that could be used to attract Claire's young customer base, was being squandered. Two weeks later, the president responded, saying that he appreciated her letter, her diligent work, and her can-do attitude. He was passing on her letter to a vice president who would be in touch with Beauty's supervisors. Attention would be brought to the matter. Beauty waited a month, then another month, and finally gave up.

She fell into something of a depression. Atlanta was weighing on her. Her self-inflicted isolation was weighing on her. She was growing lonely and restless. She accepted a date from a man she had met at Wanda's church, a successful real estate agent and former football star. He was handsome. His face and build were reminiscent of Power. But he could do nothing but talk about himself—his achievements, his money, his status as the head of the church's building fund. At the end of the evening when he took her home, she did not ask him up. When he called the next day for another date, she invented an excuse.

The days were long and the nights even longer. Beauty was bored and wanted to leave her job and this city behind her. But where would she go?

Kato Yamamoto

Fine's Department Store sat around the corner from the Ellis Hotel in downtown Atlanta. It was the store where Beauty's mother, Isabel Long, had met and befriended Power's mother, Charlotte Clay. Both women had been bookkeepers, both had young children the same age. They had helped each other through troubled times. When Isabel's Japanese lover, who sold goods to the Yamamoto family, the owner of Fine's, abandoned her and her infant daughter, Charlotte was there for Isabel. It was Charlotte who took a leave of absence for more than a month to stay with Isabel during her losing battle with cancer. As a young girl, Beauty often went to Fine's. When Isabel—and later Charlotte—had extra work to do on weekends, they would bring Beauty along, sit her at a desk, and let her color or read. Sometimes she'd wander off into the store and marvel at the clothes in the women's and children's sections. Fine's was her first taste of fashion and glamour. Yet those happy memories of Fine's were also mixed with the memories of loss. When Beauty was eleven, she lost Isabel. At sixteen, she lost Charlotte. For those reasons she had not been back to Fine's for many years, and certainly not since this recent return to Atlanta.

Yet on this Saturday morning, she felt like driving downtown to the store. She was working the late shift at Claire's and didn't need to be at Cumberland Mall till one P.M. At ten, she found herself walking through those familiar doors through which she had walked so many times before. She knew this old elegant store well. It was one of the first luxury clothing establishments to be built in Atlanta and had a feeling of history. Beauty's personal history with the store filled her imagination. She remembered all the times that both her mothers, who were able to buy there at deep discounts, allowed her to pick out her own clothes. She remembered how happy she had been walking up and down the aisles. The enchanting fragrances in the perfume department, the great chandeliers and fixtures from the 1920s, the old-fashioned elevators with their polished silver doors—everything about Fine's was magical. Beauty was excited to be back.

She wandered around, relishing good memories at every turn. Rather than lament the loss of both her mothers, her heart recalled the kind and good things they did for her. So many of those things happened in this store. On the third floor, she walked to the back of the lingerie department to the hallway that led to the executive offices. This was where the bookkeepers—including Isabel and Charlotte—had toiled for so many years. The accounting department was right next to the suite housing the men and women who ran the store. Beauty stood in the hallway for several long seconds, feeling gratitude that two such wonderful women had loved her so deeply. Tears streaked down her cheeks.

Just as she was about to turn away, a man walked down the hallway and approached her. At first she didn't recognize him, but he immediately recognized her.

"You're Beauty, Miss Charlotte Clay's daughter," he said.

Then she realized who he was: Kato Yamamoto, the son of the Japanese couple that had bought the store many years ago.

"Yes," she said. "You and your family were kind enough to make a condolence call."

"It was the least we could do. I'm so glad to see you. Are you still living in Atlanta?"

"Yes, but only recently. I've been living in New York, Los Angeles, and Chicago."

"That sounds exciting. I'd love to hear about it. Would you like to have a cup of tea with me at Rebecca's?"

"I would. That sounds lovely."

Rebecca's, named for the wife of Sid Fine, the original owner of the store, was a beautiful dining room set in the refined style of a former era. The walls were dark wood engraved with figures of birds and flowers. The tablecloths and linens were the same shade of pink as the waitresses' uniforms. Rebecca's was where the ladies of high society liked to lunch. It was where Isabel, and then Charlotte, had always taken Beauty for her birthday.

"Nothing changes here," said Beauty as they sat at a corner table and ordered Earl Grey tea for two from the attractive blond waitress in pink.

"That's the charm of Rebecca's, isn't it?" asked Kato.

"Exactly," Beauty agreed as she felt Kato's strong gaze. He was an attractive twenty-three-year-old Japanese man who stood at five eleven, far taller than his diminutive parents. Unlike them, he spoke accent-less English. Born in Kyoto, he moved to America as an infant and had been brought up in Atlanta's best private schools. He was thin. His eyes were a liquid brown and his hair, thick and slicked back, was brownish black. His blue Versace cashmere blazer fit tight at the waist; his gray woolen trousers broke perfectly at the top of his Prada leather loafers. He sat with a relaxed air, yet his interest in Beauty was obvious and intense.

"I remember my mother saying that you had another tragedy earlier in your life," he said, "when your first mother died. I believe she also worked here."

"Yes," said Beauty. "I have a strong connection to this store."

"Forgive me for bringing up such painful memories."

"That's all right. When you came down the hallway, I was thinking about both women. They were wonderful."

"And so I've heard. But please, tell me about yourself. Where are you working in Atlanta?"

"At Claire's in the Cumberland Mall."

"That's a good operation."

"I'm assistant manager."

"At so young an age. I'm impressed. And what work were you doing in New York?"

"I worked at Bloom's."

"You're kidding."

"No, I'm serious."

"We're on the verge of buying Bloom's. Did you know that?"

"I had no idea."

"What was your job there?"

"Assistant to Anita Ward."

"Anita Ward was instrumental in recruiting Primo Dalla Torre to buy the chain, wasn't she?" he asked.

"Yes," Beauty answered.

"And you knew about all that?"

"I did. You see, Anita sent me to Los Angeles to work under Mr. Dalla Torre's wife, Soo Kim."

"Of Calm and Cool Clothing?"

"The same."

"This is so strange. I don't have to tell you, Beauty, but when Miss Ward and Mr. Dalla Torre died, his deal fell apart and Bloom's really hasn't recovered from the blow. Miss Kim tried to honor her husband's offer, but apparently she and the estate are at odds. She has no access to his assets. There are also enormous tax problems being litigated in Italy and here. The court fights will go on for years. Meanwhile, Bloom's has been in a tailspin. Are you still in touch with Miss Kim?"

"No, I decided it was time to leave. That's when I moved to Chicago. It was a struggle at first, but I finally found this job at Claire's. It was Claire's who transferred me from Chicago to Atlanta."

"But tell me about the work you did with Anita Ward and Soo Kim."

"I also worked with Lena Pearl. Do you know her line?"

"Of course. She does great work. And a couple of her lines have done extremely well. Bloom's used to carry her. You've had great experience. So you're a designer."

"Yes, I've always wanted a line of my own. That's what the training with Anita, Soo, and Lena was all about."

"And it all stopped with those two unfortunate deaths?"

"I'm afraid so."

The tea arrived. It was served on a sterling silver tray along with English butter cookies.

"But you're happy at Claire's?" asked Kato.

"I'm coping at Claire's."

"Am I right to assume that's because Claire's isn't exactly the career trajectory you had in mind?"

"It isn't. It's a corporation. I was told I'd be the youngest manager in their history when I turned twenty-one. But I'm still waiting."

"The corporate culture can be maddening," Kato said. "It can make you feel so powerless. Your fate is in the hands of people whom you don't know and, even worse, people who don't know you."

"You're right. But we've been talking about me. What about you, Kato?"

"It's an interesting time in my life. I graduated from the Wharton School of Business almost a year ago and came back here to help my folks. After a long struggle, I've convinced them that we have to expand, and Bloom's is our first step. I'm set to fly to New York next week to hammer out the details with the firm we've hired to facilitate the acquisition. But getting back to you, Beauty, I'm astounded to know all the common ground between us. That's absolutely fascinating. I'm afraid I have to get back to the office for a meeting, but I'm wondering if it's possible to see you before I leave on Thursday. Are you free for dinner Tuesday evening?"

His words flowed freely, and so did Beauty's response. "I am," she said.

"Great. Then please give me your number and I'll call. I'm so glad I ran into you and can't wait to learn more about you."

As Kato got up, he gave the blond waitress, who was on the other side of Rebecca's, the thumbs-up sign. Beauty wasn't sure what that meant. Was he telling the waitress to forget about the check, or send it to the executive office? Or was he telling her that he had scored?

In the days that followed, Beauty could not deny the excitement she felt about seeing Kato again. She even called her friend Tanisha to discuss it.

"Oh, my God," said Tanisha. "He sounds perfect for you."

"It's not like that," said Beauty.

"Then what *is* it like?"

"Well, he's cute. He's very good-looking, but I'm not feeling a strong attraction in that way."

"But *he* obviously is."

"Why do you say that?"

"Because he asked you out immediately," said Tanisha. "And you immediately said yes."

"Maybe it's just a business connection," said Beauty.

"That would be cool. Any way you look at it, it's cool."

Beauty looked at it every way possible. She spoke the truth to Tanisha. Sexually, he did not stir her. What did stir her, though, was the fact that he was a power player. She couldn't deny that. She kept thinking about that. Not only was Kato a player, but he was an owner—or the son of the owners, a guy with international connections and international ambition. She tried not to think about everything he could do for her, but the fantasies kept coming. He could take her off the going-nowhere-fast track at Claire's and put her back on the track to somewhere. It would be a giant leap.

After Primo, though, hadn't she sworn off this kind of life? Hadn't she made up her mind that she would not sell herself at any cost? But *was* she selling herself? Had Kato even made an offer? No. He had simply asked her to dinner. He liked her. She liked him. That's all there was to it. All this analysis was getting her nowhere, keeping her up late as she waited for the night of her date. Would he call that morning or would the whole thing slip his mind?

He called that morning. He picked out Matsuda, an elegant sushi restaurant close to her apartment in Buckhead. He was already there when she arrived. He was dressed casually, turtleneck and jeans. She wore her favorite blouse by Miyake. The first thing he said was, "Miyake, I love it. I've been trying to get Fine's to carry the line here but it's a little far-out for this provincial market. You wear it beautifully"

The conversation went smoothly. He told her about the difficulties of convincing his parents to move into a new world of a retailing. They didn't understand expansion. They were conservative people who, to a large degree, did not understand the future. At the same time, they recognized that, as the first brilliant student of business the family ever had produced, Kato's formal training gave him distinct advantages. He understood the way in which the world was changing. Unlike themselves, he understood youth. He was youth.

"I tell them that youth is impatient," Kato said to Beauty. "Don't you agree?"

"Well, I know I'm impatient."

"For what?" he asked.

"Well, I guess my career to be where I want it to be."

"I feel the same."

"But you're in control of your career, Kato."

"The struggle is ongoing. My parents are always saying I'm moving too fast and I'm saying they move too slow. This buyout of Bloom's has taken a long, long time, and even though we're in the final stages, they're still threatening to pull out if we don't get certain considerations. Those considerations, by the way, aren't even logical. I think my parents simply want to queer the deal. They're afraid I'm taking on more than I can handle."

"And are you afraid?" asked Beauty.

"Sure," he said, "who wouldn't be? But that's part of the fun. No risk, no reward. I don't mind risks and I don't mind being scared. I think people who say they aren't scared are either lying or living a life that's so boring it's not worth living. How about you, Beauty? Are you scared? The way you've been running around the country on your own doesn't lead me to believe that you're at all scared."

"I have my fears. I mean, I suppose that's why I'm still at Claire's. After having gone through some years of pretty heavy turmoil, I'm in my cautious phase."

"And that attitude also applies to men?" asked Kato.

"I suppose it does."

"What was the turmoil like?" he asked.

"In the world of fashion, I was riding pretty high early on. Or at least I was close to people who were riding high. It was exciting, but in the end I found myself alone and unemployed."

"And with men?"

"A personal question," said Beauty, taking a bite of yellowtail sushi.

"Too personal?" asked Kato.

"Well, the best way to answer the question is to say that I'm not involved. I'm more interested in finding the right path to a satisfying career than the right path to romance."

"And if both paths happen to merge?"

"That's a long shot."

Kato took a sip of sake and relished the taste in his mouth. "Maybe not such a long shot," he said.

Beauty was surprised, relieved, and also disappointed when he dropped the subject and began talking about the difference between the retail business in Asia and in America. The subject fascinated her, but she wondered why he didn't pursue the topic of career and romance. She thought he was more than hinting that he was interested in both courting her romantically and helping her professionally. Of course it was easier this way. She didn't have to worry about the conflict she had experienced with Primo. If it was a romance-only relationship he desired, she could evaluate that on its own merits. Or if it was a business-only relationship he wanted, she could do the same. But now he was talking about neither. He was asking her about the classes she had taken at Columbia College Chicago and the ones she was auditing at Georgia State. Sociology, world history, and marketing were subjects that fascinated him, and he had a lot to say. He asked her questions and offered comments of his own. His mind was quick and his curiosity keen. The evening went by quickly. He paid the bill, she thanked him, and they got up to leave. They had arrived in separate cars.

"There's a nice bar next door," he said. "How about a nightcap?"

"Sure."

Over cognac, the conversation got a little deeper. Kato asked Beauty about Isabel, her birth mother. Beauty disclosed the fact that her dad was a Japanese businessman from Tokyo who had worked with Kato's parents. Kato did not know him but was curious how Beauty had navigated her way through the Atlanta schools as a biracial girl. The question provoked some stories that Beauty had long forgotten—instances when she had been called names. Kato had stories of his own about growing up Japanese in Georgia. He had gone to a private school where he always felt out of place.

"When most people look at you, Beauty," he asked, "do they see a Japanese or an African American?"

"Most people don't say," she said. "But what do you say?"

"I say I see Japanese. But I'm prejudiced. I think Japanese women are the most beautiful in the world."

"Thank you . . . I guess I should thank you."

"Or thank your dad."

"I don't know much about him."

"Are you curious?"

"There was a time when I was. But when he left my mom pregnant with me, she never got over that pain. And anytime I'd mention him, she'd tell me to hush. So I stopped asking."

"If you're still curious, I could ask my parents about him."

"Now isn't a good time. Maybe someday."

"And you've never been to Japan?"

"Never."

"But you'd like to go."

"I would," Beauty said.

"You'll love it. I would like to . . ." Kato paused. Beauty thought he was about to say, *I would like to take you there,* but those words were not spoken. Instead an awkward silence lasted several seconds.

"Well, it's late," Kato finally said. "Tomorrow's a heavy day. I have to prepare for my trip."

"And I need to be at work early for inventory."

Kato walked Beauty to her Corolla. They stood there for a while, enduring another silence. He leaned over and kissed her on the cheek. "I really love spending time with you," he said, "and I hope we'll get to do this together again."

"I do too."

. . . .

The date lingered in Beauty's mind for the next several days. She was disappointed that he had not suggested going back to his place. Not that she would have agreed—but, in fact, she would have liked to have been asked. She was also a little disappointed that he had not said that he wanted to show her Japan, or even take her to New York. She felt certain—at least for now—that she would have declined all such invitations. But to have not received them was something of a letdown. She knew he was attracted to her. And she felt that the attraction was strong. He knew that she was unattached. She had said so in plain terms. So given all that, why didn't he act more assertively? She had expected more than a kiss on the cheek. And yet maybe that was his method. Certainly a kiss on the cheek had her wanting a bit more. But then again, could he be gay? She didn't think so—he seemed straight—but maybe she misread the sexual signals. She hadn't sent out strong signals of her own. She hadn't taken his hand or even offered him a small hug when they left. Her own actions could be seen as standoffish. Could it be a case of both parties playing hard-to-get? Beauty laughed at herself and her analysis. Maybe it was simply a single date that would lead nowhere. She'd forget about it.

But she didn't. She looked at the *Wall Street Journal* and other websites every day for news about Fine's buying Bloom's. That week there wasn't any, but the following there was. The deal had gone through. Kato Yamamoto was mentioned prominently in the article. He was called a "whiz kid who had graduated at the top of his class at Wharton and was now poised to take over the family's retail operation." And the article noted, "All eyes will be on Mr. Kato Yamamoto."

That same week Beauty kept her eye on her cell phone, looking for a call or text from Kato. She wondered when he'd be returning to Atlanta. After ten days passed and she still hadn't heard from him, she considered calling his office. Why not? A woman can call a man. She would merely congratulate him on consummating the deal. She wouldn't be asking him out or inviting him to bed. On the other hand, what purpose would be served by such a call? If he were truly interested in her, he'd phone. His silence spoke volumes. Her initial assessment—that it was a one-time date and a one-time date only—was probably accurate.

Closing time at the mall; nearly nine P.M. on a Thursday night. A long busy day. Dozens of pairs of earrings had been sold. Dozens of brace-lets, dozens of headbands, dozens upon dozens of giggling preteen girls looking over merchandise designed to tickle their fancy. Beauty was exhausted. She was glad to be walking to the door to let out the last customer and turn the key in the lock. That's when she looked up and saw Kato.

"I'm too late?" he asked.

She smiled. "No, not at all. You're right on time."

"I wanted to catch you before closing. I wanted to see if we could grab a late dinner."

"You could have called."

"I thought it might be more exciting just to show up and take my chances. I'm trying to live life a little more adventurously these days."

"From what I read about your trip to New York, you're doing a good job."

"Before you close up, take me around the store and show me your bestselling items."

"I didn't know you were interested in this sort of merchandise," said Beauty.

"I am. But I also have a hidden agenda."

Beauty pointed out the most popular items in the store. Kato looked and listened carefully. Afterward he said, "Let's discuss all this over a drink. I presume you drove to work."

"I did."

"Well, then, let's meet at the bar in the Ritz–Carlton on Peachtree.

I'm actually living there temporarily while my place is being redecorated. The bar is usually quiet on weeknights."

"Fine," said Beauty. "See you there in a little while."

Driving over, she wondered what was in store. What was his hidden agenda? She was excited but wary. She didn't understand this man. He waited ten days after returning to Atlanta to contact her. She had counted him out. And then, just like that, he showed up in person. She drove slowly; she wanted him to arrive before her.

He was waiting at a table in the back. The bar was practically deserted. He ordered Courvoisier. She ordered Chardonnay. He began the conversation.

"I want to be blunt," he said.

"Good," Beauty replied.

He paused for a sip of his drink. She wondered if his blunt remarks would involve work or romance. She guessed romance. She was wrong.

"I want you to work for Bloom's."

She didn't reply. She didn't know what to say. Her first emotion, though, was positive. If she had to choose between work and romance, she'd certainly choose work. But would the two paths—as Kato had suggested last time—merge?

"I want to set up within Bloom's an extensive preteen department modeled on Claire's but upgraded considerably. I think there's an untapped market for higher-priced merchandise for this demographic. Would you agree?"

"I've thought so for a long time. I've been petitioning our buyers to do exactly that. I think young girls are expecting and wanting higher quality."

"Great. So we're on the same page. I realize this is not giving you the design line that you're dreaming of. But don't give up on that dream. One day it will come true. Right now, though, I want you to prove to the new management I've put in place that you can run this department profitably. We'll start with the flagship store. If it works, we'll take it to Chicago, San Francisco, and Dallas. I've told Marge Schraft, my new merchandising vice president, all about you and she's eager to meet you."

"Where is she?"

"New York. You'd be working in New York."

"She wants to interview me?"

"Yes, but I've made it clear to Marge that you have the job. You're on board—that is, if you want to be on board. Whatever you're making at Claire's, we'll double it and give you a little more as a living allowance. I don't have to tell you that life in New York costs a fortune. There's a Marriott hotel within walking distance of the store. We'll put you up there until you have time to find a place of your own. How does all this sound?"

"It's sudden."

"Sudden good or sudden bad?" he asked.

"I don't think there's anything bad about it. I think it's great, Kato, I really do. I'd love to take the job and I'm really grateful to you for thinking of me."

"I think of you more than I like to admit."

Those last words just hung out there—untouched. Beauty didn't reply. Those words changed the equation. Until then it had been all business. Now here comes romance. What would be his next move?

"And I guess I'm hoping," said Kato, "that the feeling is mutual. Am I right?"

Beauty took her time in responding. She thought about her feelings before expressing them. Kato was a very correct young man. He was well-mannered, well-spoken, and extremely intelligent. His mind was organized and his plans were now clear. It was also clear that he was not gay. There was also a nerdy aspect to him. He was studious and very precise to a fault. He was definitely a square—an ambitious square—who had thought long and hard about how to approach Beauty. His plan was evident. He was offering her a job that made eminent sense. The job had a tremendous upside and a bright future. But there was also a distinct indication that he wanted more than a professional relationship. How to respond?

"I feel strongly that I can handle this job, Kato. I'm extremely confident. The work I've done at Claire's is the perfect preparation."

"No doubt, but you've avoided my question."

"Well, I'm not all that good at expressing my personal feelings. It takes me time to get to know a person. I'm cautious by nature. I hope you understand."

"I understand that you're saying 'maybe,'" said Kato with a smile. "'Maybe' is certainly better than 'no.' 'Maybe' means I will have to be patient—and my parents are always saying that the more patient I am, the more successful I will be. So I thank you for forcing a little more patience on my part. 'Maybe' also means that it would be far too forward for me to invite you up to my suite for another drink."

"You're understanding and tactful, Kato, and I appreciate that. I really do."

"Just understand, Beauty, that we are about to travel down two paths—yet one does not depend on the other. The professional path is clear. You are uniquely qualified for the job. You can stay on that path, succeed, and keep on that path until you reach your goal. The other path—the one where the heart, rather than the career, is the guide—is still in doubt. That's the 'maybe' path."

"I understand."

"Then you'll tender your resignation and come to New York."

"I will."

"And do so quickly."

"I'll tell them tomorrow."

"I'm happy."

"I am too. I couldn't be happier."

. . . .

Beauty drove home happy. Her new job was great. She was getting out of Atlanta and moving back to New York. And while Kato made his romantic intentions known, those intentions were not a condition. He accepted her "maybe." He made no demands. He was a gentle-man, and she was grateful. She couldn't wait to pack up and leave. She'd give Claire's two weeks' notice and no more.

Back in her apartment, she readied herself for bed. She took off her makeup; brushed her hair; applied hydrating eye cream, hand cream, and face cream; and changed into a nightgown. Then the phone rang. It was nearly one A.M. Who would be calling on a Thursday night at one A.M.?

"Beauty, it's Wanda."

"Something wrong?"

"No, well, not yet anyway."

"Tell me," said Beauty.

"I don't want to alarm you."

"Wanda, it's one A.M. I'm already alarmed."

"You don't have to be, sugar. Everything's gonna be all right. The Lord has our back. He's in charge. But sometimes we gotta be a little proactive. Sometimes we got to pick up those hints that help us get out the way of the coming shit storm."

"What shit storm?" asked Beauty. "What's coming?"

"Slim's been acting strange and, well, I think it's best you be mov-ing out of Atlanta."

"He knows I'm here?"

"No, but I don't want to take the chance of him finding out."

"You've never talked this way before, Wanda."

"Never seen him like this before."

"Seen him how?"

"Agitated. Paranoid as a mother. A little off his rocker."

"Are you in danger?"

"Me? Heavens, no."

"Is Power?" asked Beauty. She was suddenly overwhelmed by concern for his safety.

"Power is his boy. You know that. Power's fine."

"Are you're sure you're all right?"

"Honey, I'm the last person in the world that he's likely to harm. We been hooked up too long. We too tight. Besides, me and him, we got no issues. He knows everything about me and I know everything about him."

"Maybe you know too much," said Beauty.

"No, darling, it ain't about me. Wanda Washington can take good care of herself. I just don't want to agitate him in any way."

"What way?"

"By accidentally running into you."

"Why would that agitate him?"

"You're one of the only people who ever told him to go fly a kite. He didn't like that none. I think it's just better for you not to be in Atlanta."

"Well, maybe your God is protecting me, Wanda, because I just got a job offer today to go back to New York."

"Thank you, Jesus! That's the kind of God we serve! He's getting you out of Dodge at exactly the right time. You are blessed. What's the job?"

"Bloom's."

"The same Bloom's where Anita worked? The same Bloom's that was just bought by Fine's?"

"The same."

"How'd you hook it up, baby?"

"I didn't. Your God did. By accident, I ran into Kato Yamamoto, the son of the owners. We started talking and the next thing I knew I had a job."

"Y'all bumping?"

"Wanda, please."

"Didn't mean to offend, sugar. I was just wondering. That boy is a hell of a catch—at least money-wise. Is he cute?"

"Extremely nice."

"I couldn't be happier for you. When you leaving?"

"I'm giving Claire's two weeks' notice."

"Make it one. I want you out of here, I really do."

"Okay, Wanda, if you say so. I've got no reason to hang around Atlanta."

"And you got another reason to move to New York."

"What's that?"

"Power's up there."

New York

It was a cold rainy Sunday in early November when Beauty arrived at the Marriott. Her room overlooked Lexington Avenue. The traffic was loud and the afternoon was dreary. Something was wrong with the hotel heat and she was freezing. She was looking forward to tomorrow, when she'd be going to Bloom's for her first meeting with Marge Schraft. She was also relieved to be out of Atlanta. She made the move in just about ten days. Nearly every day Wanda had called, encouraging her to hurry. That worried her, but that also motivated her to get going. Now that she was here, though, she felt somewhat let down. Maybe that's because she knew that Power was also here. She wanted to call him, but she wouldn't. She knew what that would lead to. Her life was back on course. Kato had set her on that course. The last thing she needed was drama with Power.

But, as her mother Isabel once put it, "the heart has a mind of its own." She had overheard Isabel say this to Charlotte Clay when Isabel was explaining why she had carried on with a man she knew was married and attached to his family in Japan. Her mother had been foolish, and yet that foolishness had resulted in Beauty's very life. Beauty was determined that her own life, though, would not be defined by foolishness.

Power's life was entangled with Slim Simmons, and Slim Simmons meant nothing but trouble. She needed to avoid Power. She would avoid Power. She turned her mind away from him and turned on the TV, where MTV was running a documentary on pop star Candy Girl, who'd found herself in and out of four different drug rehabs in the past year. At least Beauty had never had the slightest interest in drugs. Drugs were dangerous. New York City was dangerous. Life was dangerous.

She turned off the TV and went downstairs for a late lunch in the Shelton Grille off the hotel lobby. She'd fight this ominous feeling that danger was around the corner. It wasn't anything—just the rain, the gloomy day, the transition back to a city filled with fresh memories. She thought of Anita, thought of that town house on Gramercy Park, thought of Primo, thought of the apartment in the Plaza, thought of their deaths, thought of the fear and emptiness that followed. But the future didn't look fearful or empty. The future was filled with promise. She ate a Cobb salad and tried to focus on the future.

Wandering through the hotel she stopped and noticed some historical markers in the hallways. Before becoming a Marriott, the hotel was built as the Shelton House in 1924. At the time, with its thirty-four stories, it was the tallest hotel in the world. The great painter Georgia O'Keeffe had lived in and actually painted the building. There was a replica of an O'Keeffe painting called *The Shelton with Sunspots*. Beauty recognized it because she'd often seen the original on her visits to the Art Institute of Chicago. She had also heard the painting discussed in a course she had audited at Columbia College. It was a rendering of the hotel itself with a burst of sunlight exploding off the top of the building. She had loved the painting when she first saw it in Chicago, and she loved seeing it again now. It spoke to her. It said, "It may be raining today, but the sun will be shining tomorrow—on this very hotel."

Come Monday, though, the sun was not shining. The rain kept coming. Beauty got dressed, put on a raincoat and rain hat, grabbed her umbrella, and walked over to Bloom's, a store she knew so well.

Uncannily, Marge Schraft had set up shop in Anita's old office. That was a shock to Beauty, who nonetheless kept her composure in front of her new boss, an overweight white woman with piercing angry eyes. Rather than look at Beauty, Marge seemed to glare at her. She had a large fold of chins under a very pretty face punctuated by a thin nose and small ears. Her short black hair was accented with streaks of gray. She wore a tent of olive-green corduroy. In her own way, she was fashionable. She spoke with a thick Chicago accent. To break the ice, Beauty made mention of her time in Chicago, but Marge had no interest in small talk.

"When I left Chicago," she said, "I never looked back. Now, as always, it's time to look ahead. Kato Yamamoto has set you up in quite a situation here. You and he must be extremely close."

Beauty felt immediate tension. Marge was insinuating that she and Kato were lovers.

"I've known him a very short time."

"He said that he's known you quite a long time. It seems that you had relatives who worked at Fine's down there in Atlanta."

"Well, he might have known about me," said Beauty, struggling to find the right words, "but we really never knew each other until recently."

"I can assure you that your personal relationship with Kato is of no interest to me. That's between the two of you. He has, however, put you in a precarious situation. In my judgment, he has given you responsibility far beyond your qualifications."

"But I have experience—"

"Limited experience. Certainly not enough experience to justify setting up an entire department of your own. Mr. Yamamoto has made it clear that you are to copy me on everything you do, but that ultimately you will be in charge of the merchandise and the look of the boutique. He's also given you the power to hire your sales staff. I tell you this so that we can have a good understanding from the get-go. I do not approve of his decision, but there is nothing, short of resigning, that I can do about it. Since I have no intention of resigning, all I can do is sit back and watch. I think you are being set up to fail, and my hope is—for your sake and the store's—that happens as quickly as possible with minimum damage for all concerned."

"Well, that's encouraging," said Beauty with unrestrained sarcasm.

"I'm not a hypocrite. I'm a straight shooter, and I can't pretend to be happy about a department over which I have no control. You're on your own."

"So that's it?" asked Beauty. "That's your attitude?"

"That is my attitude."

"So you're sending me out there without even a 'good luck.'"

"Your good luck came in your involvement with Mr. Yamamoto. Now you'll need business acumen to get through this ordeal, not luck."

Beauty got up and left. She was despondent. She was even outraged. How the hell could a boss treat a new employee this way? Marge Schraft, that bitch, was doing everything in her power to erode her confidence. What was wrong with that woman? What was her problem? In essence Marge had told Beauty that she was rooting for—and even expecting—her failure. She hadn't even bothered to show Beauty her new office. Marge's assistant was assigned that task.

The windowless office was tiny. The desktop computer was in need of repair. The old metal desk was stuffed with files from another department. No one had bothered to empty it out. There was no telephone, only a note saying one should be installed by the end of the week. Until then, what was she supposed to do? How was she supposed to get started? She had wanted to discuss her plans with Marge, but obviously Marge wanted nothing to do with her. Marge had stuck her in the corner with the hope that, rather than build a profitable preteens division, she'd have a nervous breakdown instead.

Well, Beauty was not about to have a nervous breakdown. She was not about to take this shit much longer. Not only was it outrageously impolite, it was lousy business. She was due to have dinner with Kato that very evening. She had every intention of telling him what had happened. How else could she deal with the situation?

Del Posto, a sophisticated Italian restaurant in Chelsea, was bustling. Kato was already there, seated at a prominent table near the front. He was drinking champagne. He rose to greet Beauty with a kiss on both cheeks. This was their first meeting in Manhattan.

"Welcome to New York," he said.

"I don't feel very welcomed." He helped her remove her raincoat. Her dress, a simple green satin affair, hung on her perfectly proportioned frame as though it were custom-tailored.

"Why don't you feel welcomed?" Kato asked.

"Marge Schraft."

"Marge Schraft is considered one of the great merchandising minds in the business. It was a coup to get her on my management team. What did you think of her?"

"I hated her. She was an absolute bitch. She practically bit my head off. She attacked me as though I was after her job."

"Well, aren't you?" asked Kato.

"No!"

"Not now you're not, but perhaps in time. Maybe that's what she sensed. Maybe this kind of head-on conflict is what you need to sharpen your fangs."

"I am not interested in having fangs. I'm not interested in killing the people I'm supposed to be working with. I just don't know how I can work under someone like her. She's just waiting for me to fall on my face."

"I'm telling you, Beauty, that attitude will keep you on your toes."

"I'm already on my toes, Kato. I don't need to work for someone who is actively seeking to destroy me."

"You won't be working *for* her, you'll be working *with* her. Shall we order? I'm starved."

"I'm hardly hungry," said Beauty. "I'm really upset."

"Have a little champagne."

"I'd rather have hot soup."

"Then hot soup it is."

After they ordered, Beauty still hadn't cooled down. "What I don't understand, Kato, is why you would create this kind of situation. You had to know that I'd be walking into a lion's den."

"I knew Marge Schraft was unhappy with my decision to hire you, but I didn't know the degree of her distress."

"She didn't tell you that she thought I was unqualified?"

"She did, Beauty, but when I explained that my mind was set, she seemed agreeable."

"Agreeable as a rattlesnake. She thinks the only reason I got the job is because we're having an affair."

"If only she were right."

"I don't know how to take that, Kato."

"As confirmation of my confidence in your ability. Our nonexistent affair is not her business."

"But how do you think I feel starting off a job with her telling everyone that I've slept my way into the position?"

"I'll talk to her about that."

"I've sure she's already told everyone."

"It's all gossip, Beauty, it means nothing. People will always talk. I'm sure women have always been jealous of your looks and brains. This can't be new."

"It's poisonous. The atmosphere really is toxic. I'm not sure I can work there."

"That's her intention. She obviously wants to run you off before you not only prove yourself, but prove that you can outthink her."

"But who wants to be involved in that kind of vicious competition?"

"Is the world of fashion you love so dearly anything but vicious and competitive?"

"I know that, Kato, but this is extreme."

"Yes, I've given you an extremely rewarding opportunity."

Beauty sighed. She tasted her cream of asparagus soup. It was hot and flavorful. She thought before she spoke. "Look," she said, "I want this job. I appreciate this job. And I'll do what I have to do. But someone's gonna have to get me a computer that works. I don't even have a phone on my desk, and my office is the size of a small closet."

"She wants to make you feel insignificant," said Kato.

"And I want you to insist that, at the very least, I am treated with the same respect she would afford any new employee."

Beauty thought about that last statement. She thought about the conflicts she'd suffered about being kept by Primo. Yet here she was manipulating a romantic situation to get her way. Or was she? Wasn't she merely expressing genuine anger? Wasn't she just battling back against a woman—this nasty piece of work called Marge Schraft—who was doing everything she could to cause her downfall?

"You're right. I'll call her first thing in the morning."

"Another meeting like the one we had today and I'll tear her eyes out. I swear I will."

"I'm sorry it was stressful for you today, Beauty, but I do admit that I like seeing this fiery side of you. It's a side I haven't seen before."

"I have a lot of sides you haven't seen."

"And, believe me, I want to see them all."

Beauty was surprised to hear herself talk this way—surprised and also a little thrilled. She no longer felt reluctant to employ her physical charms to advance her agenda. Besides, she hadn't made the first advance. Kato had. Now she was merely going along with a program that had, in fact, been his creation.

They ordered dinner. Kato asked for a seared duck breast; Beauty had whole wheat spaghetti with Dungeness crab. The chef and owner

Mario Batali came by the table to greet Kato and ask if all was well.

"It's all great, Mario," said Kato. "As usual."

Kato introduced him to Beauty, who had seen pictures of the famous chef in the newspapers.

"How do you know him?" Beauty asked Kato when Batali had moved on.

"He was seated next to me on a flight to Tokyo last month. We got to talking. You know how that goes. Flying first-class has its advantages."

"I agree."

"I'm still feeling that you should fly first-class to Tokyo. Tokyo is filled with creative ideas in the field of preteen merchandising."

"I'm sure I'd learn a lot."

"Well, then when do we leave?"

"*We?*"

"I have business there myself."

"I just got to New York."

"Now that you've made your presence known here, maybe it's time to let Marge Schraft cool her heels while you explore the preteen scene in Asia."

"I have deadlines," said Beauty. "This division has to be set up and ready to go. I can't afford to take off any time now."

"Those deadlines can be pushed back."

"I'd want to at least establish my office here and set certain procedures in motion. And I also have to start looking for a place to live."

"I've just bought a place in Chelsea. In fact, it's around the corner. There's lots of room."

"Oh, Kato," said Beauty with a sigh.

"What is that sigh about?" he asked.

"On one hand you arrange for a hotel room until I can get myself a place. And then on the other you suggest I move in with you."

"I have a spare bedroom."

"That's ridiculous."

"Why?"

"Well, because it's ridiculous for a female employee to be sleeping in the spare bedroom of her male employer's apartment while the male employer is sleeping in the next room."

"I agree. Far better to sleep in the same room. A far more sensible option."

"Then Marge Schraft will be right. I'll be your live-in protégée. The girlfriend with a leg up on everyone else."

"By the time we get back from Tokyo, Marge Schraft will be gone."

"Now you're firing her?"

"After what you've told me, I think I have no choice. I think you're right. I can't subject you to that kind of emotional abuse. It's irresponsible and unprofessional of her. She was especially unwise to do it days before her employment contract was signed. It will be difficult finding a replacement, but our headhunters are superb."

"And you'd do this for me?"

"I have to protect you. I have to protect you not only because of my strong belief in your professional abilities—you are one of the keys to our company's future—but because I can't stand to see you hurt."

He took her hand, leaned toward her, and kissed her on the cheek.

That same night, in Kato's apartment on the twenty-fifth floor overlooking the Hudson River, an apartment done in a motif of bold, flowing black Japanese silk drapes and black-and-white prints of ancient Japanese places, Beauty and Kato slept together. In the art of lovemaking, he required instruction. He was inexperienced but eager to learn, awkward but motivated. He allowed her to lead. She had to explain timing to him. He kept apologizing, but he also kept obliging. Finally, they fell into a position that suited them both. She found satisfaction but only by reverting to her usual device of envisioning the man she had sworn to forget.

Tokyo

It was a blaze of neon, a crazy electrical maze of giant screens and high-def billboards that lit the sky with images of magenta, green, yellow, and high-pitched red. The signs screamed from one side of the sprawling city to the other. The wattage was wild. Tokyo was on overload.

Tokyo excited Beauty like no other city she had ever seen. It was also strange. Though she spoke not a word of Japanese, she was greeted in that language. Her Japanese facial characteristics had everyone assuming that she was a native. Because Kato was with her virtually all the time, he was happy to translate. In fact, he was happy and proud to have Beauty by his side.

They stayed in the presidential suite of the Imperial Hotel. The living room overlooked the Imperial Palace gardens and from the master bedroom she could see the lights of the Ginza. From the day they arrived, it was a whirlwind of tourism and business activities. "After this," said Kato, "New York will seem like a small city."

From the rocking nightclubs of Roppongi to the high-fashion boutiques of Aoyama, from the glittering skyscrapers of Shinjuku to the ginkgo-tree-lined temple of the ancient Yasukuni shrine, Beauty was thrilled by all she saw. Kato took her to the Kabuki-za Theater and Tsukiji Fish Market. Together they walked through the wonders of the electronic district called Akihabara.

In the giant department stores like Mitsukoshi and Wako, she studied their preteen departments and immediately saw that Kato was right to bring her here. The Japanese understood merchandising and point-of-purchase display on an advanced level. They were bold and innovative retailers. Beauty was inspired.

The evenings were fun—the sushi bars, the jazz clubs, the distinctly Asian discos. Kato introduced her to his many friends and business associates. He showed her off. He called her his girlfriend and his colleague. There was no doubt that he was putting her on display, and for much of the time Beauty did not mind.

As a lover he made modest progress, but still she required the mental vision of Power to bring her to climax. He tried his best but found it difficult to relax. Insecure and too eager to please, his techniques were lacking. Beauty simply put up with it.

At the beginning of their second and final week in Tokyo, Kato had gone to a meeting and Beauty was seated in the dining room of their suite. She had been served an American-style breakfast by a private butler who had also brought a copy of Tokyo's English-language newspaper. A front-page article caught her eye. The headline read, YAKUZA REPORTEDLY DEEP INTO FOREIGN FINANCING.

The story concerned attempts by the Yakuza, the Japanese crime syndicate, to widen their influence by investing in non-Japanese capital ventures. Apparently they had become silent partners in the acquisitions of European banks and Latin-American security firms. In the final paragraph, it was this sentence that stunned Beauty: "According to one source, the Yakuza has helped finance the acquisition of an established retail store chain headquartered in New York City with stores in Chicago, Dallas, and San Francisco."

Beauty's heart started to race. They had to be referring to Bloom's.

But was there any way in the world that Kato could be involved with a Mafia-style outfit like the Yakuza? She noted the reporter's name and toyed with the idea of calling him but decided against it. When Kato returned later that day, though, she presented him with the article. She watched his eyes as he read. They seemed to widen. She saw a bit of panic in his expression.

"They're talking about Bloom's, aren't they?" she asked.

"They might be, but they might also be confusing my investors with Yakuza members."

Beauty was alarmed by the word "might." She was expecting a full denial.

"I didn't know you had investors."

"I do."

"And they're financially strong?"

"They are."

"But not criminals."

"Look, Beauty, I can't tell you that I ran super-comprehensive background checks on every person who helped finance this endeavor. I can tell you, though, they are powerful business partners—which is exactly what I needed."

Beauty was shocked. In essence, he was telling her that the article was true. He was involved with the Yakuza. She was troubled and wanted to question him further when a question of his own stopped her dead in her tracks.

"Would you like to meet your father?" he asked.

"What are you talking about?"

"Your biological father. I spoke with him today."

"Why?"

"To tell him that you were here—and that we were together. He'd love to see you."

Beauty was speechless. She didn't know how to feel or what to say.

"I didn't ask you to do that," she said.

"I know. But I thought you might like me to. It was easy. My parents had his name and number."

"You had no right to—"

"Look, Beauty," said Kato, "it's merely an option. You don't have to see him if you don't want to. Give me the word and the whole thing will go away, just like that. No pressure."

"How can you say 'no pressure'? Now of course there's pressure. You've created pressure."

"I haven't. I merely talked to the man."

"Why couldn't you have first asked me whether I wanted you to talk to him?"

"I didn't think I needed your permission. Besides, I was curious myself. If I had found him not worthy of meeting you, I'd never have mentioned it. But he seems okay. He's still in the fashion business. He owns this clothing store for teens in Harajuku. How's that for a coincidence?"

"I'm not interested in coincidences, and I'm not interested in him. And I really don't appreciate the way you took this matter into your own hands, Kato. I find it overbearing. No one put you in charge of my personal history—least of all me."

"Wow. I had no idea you felt that way."

"Well, now you do."

"Okay, Beauty, I get it. I understand. Just forget the whole thing. Forget about your father."

Beauty couldn't. How could she? How could anyone forget about a long-lost absentee father who suddenly pops up out of nowhere? Of course she was curious to see him and meet him and tell the no-good son of a bitch that he had deceived and deserted her mother. When Beauty got old enough, the scenario became clear: Her dad had been carrying on with her mother during his trips to Atlanta with the idea that one day he would divorce his wife in Japan, move to America, and marry Isabel Long. At least that was Beauty's understanding.

What she didn't understand, though, was why Kato had gone to the trouble to find a man whose name she didn't even know.

"If you're interested," said Kato, "his name is Akira Matsui."

"I already said I'm not interested."

"I understand, Beauty, and I'll leave you alone about this, but eventually I believe you'll want to meet your father."

"Why?"

"Because he's your father. You're his blood."

"Maybe, but not now. Not this trip."

"There will be other trips. Tokyo will definitely be a big part of our lifestyle."

Our *lifestyle?* Beauty thought. He was talking like they were a permanent couple. Too confused about the Yakuza article in the paper and the news that Kato had located her father, she said nothing else. Suddenly what had been a sunny trip turned dark.

On the night before their departure, almost in defiance of Kato, she invoked the image of Power while Kato made love to her. She allowed herself the pleasure of pretending that another man—a more passionate man, a more sensual man—was deep inside her.

"That was amazing," Kato said afterward, noting the power of Beauty's orgasm. "I think I'm getting good at this, don't you agree?"

Beauty forced a smile but said nothing.

Young Beauty

The idea came to Beauty while she and Kato were staying at the Kahala Hotel in Honolulu, a stopover on their way back from Japan.

"After all the electricity of Tokyo, the beaches of Hawaii are just what we need," Kato had suggested. "Have you ever been on those beaches?"

"Never," said Beauty.

"Well then, let me introduce you to them. They'll relax you."

Kato was right. Japan was far more intense than Beauty had anticipated, and she welcomed a respite. Hawaii sounded great.

Hawaii looked great as she walked the secluded beach just beyond the hotel. Kato was back in the room, lost in a long business call. Beauty had the beach to herself. As the sun set, the sky turned orangey pink. The sand felt good under her toes. The trade wind felt good against her skin. She walked to the water's edge, where soft waves washed her feet. The world was at peace. During the flight from Tokyo, she was haunted by thoughts of her father and Kato's ties to organized crime. Here in the middle of the Pacific, staring out into the endless ocean, the thoughts vanished. The slate was clean. She closed her eyes, took a deep breath, and when she exhaled, the idea was there:

Young Beauty.

That's what she would call the boutique within Bloom's, the pre-teen boutique that would carry her stamp. It was the perfect handle, the perfect catch-all phrase that expressed what girls aspired to be. It was sophisticated without being pretentious, pretty without being corny. It was perfect. It was her. And because she was not entirely satisfied with the various lines of clothing available to preteens, she wanted develop a Young Beauty line of her own. Young Beauty, exclusively at Bloom's.

That evening she and Kato dined on their private patio. They ate fresh pineapple and succulent pork. While sipping on a glass of island wine, she explained the Young Beauty concept to Kato.

"I love it," he said. "It's brilliant."

"And I have the freedom to design a custom line for the boutique?"

"Of course. I want you to be happy."

"That's not the point, Kato. The point is, does the idea make business sense?"

"I think it does," he said. "I know it does. And with Marge Schraft gone, you'll have no more bad vibes."

"Who's taking her place?"

"A man I believe you know."

"Who?"

"His name is Solomon Getz."

"Solomon Getz! You're kidding."

"I thought you'd be happy. I've been tracking his career."

"How do you know about his career?"

"You had mentioned him to me when we first met. You said he was a super-sharp merchandise guy who got mangled in the Bloom's corporate culture and wound up in Chicago. I've looked up his record and seen that you were right. He was running the entire men's division at Macy's. They were about to promote him, but we grabbed him in time. I had a colleague go out there and recruit him. We're bringing him back to New York and putting him in charge of merchandising."

"Does he know about our connection?" asked Beauty.

"Not unless you told him."

"I haven't spoken with Solomon in a while. Kato, this is wonderful. This is so perfect."

"I thought it'd make you happy."

"It does. I know he'll support me in this effort. He really believes in me."

"And so do I, Beauty. I'm supporting anyone who's supporting you. I want you to realize that there's nothing I wouldn't do to ensure your success and happiness. To be honest, I can't picture living the rest of my life without you."

Beauty didn't respond. She was afraid he was going to propose, and that would require a rejection. It was one thing to become this man's lover. That was all well and good. But to be his wife was something else entirely. She wasn't ready for that. And she didn't think she ever would be. The feelings she had for him—friendship and gratitude—did not extend to love.

He sensed the meaning of her silence and said, "Look, it's still early in our relationship. I don't want to push you, Beauty, I really don't. But I also want you to see my goal. You know me well enough to understand that when I create a goal, I always achieve it. You're my goal. You're the best goal I've ever had. And, well . . . I love you."

Beauty's heart sank. She looked out over the water, a mirror reflecting a crescent moon. The sky was lit by a million stars. She looked back at Kato, took his hand, kissed it gently, and said nothing.

"I've been calling you every night, and all I get is your voice mail." Wanda's voice sounded frightened. She was on the phone from Atlanta. Beauty was back in Kato's penthouse apartment in Chelsea.

"Sorry," she said. "I've been overseas."

"I've been scared to death. Thank God you're okay."

"Scared of what, Wanda?"

"Slim. He's off the deep end, baby. I'm glad you're safe up in New York. Wish you had stayed overseas, though. You'd be better off overseas."

"You really think I'm in danger?"

"I think he's forgotten all about you, baby. I pray to Lord Jesus every night that he's forgotten about you. I don't want you crossing his mind, because when anyone crosses his mind he's convinced they're going to do him in. He's gone psycho paranoid."

"How bad is he?"

"Three weeks ago he kicked out the woman he's been living with. Beautiful gal no older than thirty. He thought she was working for the FBI. Threw her clothes out the house and told her to scram. Well, next thing you know she's at the beauty shop talkin' 'bout how Slim Simmons can't last in bed with no woman more than ten seconds. She says he's done cum before you got your drawers off. Everyone's talking and laughing about it.

"Now I've known Slim's got problems, but you know Wanda. Wanda can keep a secret. Wanda ain't spreading trash about no one, especially no one with the wherewithal of Slim Simmons. But this sista is steamin' mad and she's bad-mouthing Slim to anyone and everyone who'll listen. She's telling the world, and a week after she does all this telling she up and disappears. No one can find her. Not her brothers. Not her mama. No one. The girl is gone. Her people go to see Slim to ask about her, but of course Slim says he has no idea and he'll help them find her. Slim's acting real concerned, but when I see Slim, he's laughing about it. He's letting me know that I better not be spreading no rumors about him or I'll be disappearing too. I've been knowing this man for fifty years and he's never talked to me this way. *Never.*"

"Maybe you should get out of Atlanta."

"And go where?"

"You could come up and stay with us."

"Who's us?"

"Me and Kato."

"You mean you've moved in with the man?"

"I have."

"Oh, sugar, that is wonderful. Has he proposed?"

"In a manner of speaking."

"And you said yes?"

"I didn't say anything."

"But you will say yes," said Wanda.

"I don't think so. I don't really love him."

"Then learn to love him, baby, because this is a match made in heaven. It's got nothing but good written all over it."

"Look, Wanda, I'm worried about you and I want you up here with me."

"And leave Wanda's Wigs?"

"Yes."

"Wanda hardly ever leaves Wanda's Wigs."

"Make an exception."

"That would only make Slim furious. After all, he owns this place. If I up and leave, he'll get even more nuts. He'll figure that, like everyone else, I've turned on him. No, baby, it's better for me to stay here and calm his crazy ass down. You just lay low in New York."

"And what about Power?"

"I already told you. Power's his boy. He looks at him like a son. Power's been going along with his program from day one. Slim's still guilty by how he messed up Charlotte."

"What you mean 'messed up Charlotte'?"

Wanda hesitated. "I mean . . . well, you know . . ."

"I really don't know," Beauty said sternly. "But in my heart, I felt he had her murdered."

Silence. Long silence. Dead silence on the other end of the line. Wanda said nothing. Beauty felt that Wanda wanted to confess something she'd known all along but had been unwilling to confess. In that silence, both women felt a world of worry, fear, regret, and guilt. Beauty wanted to press Wanda further, but the silence said it all.

"I wish I could say something," said Wanda.

"You don't have to," said Beauty. "I know. I've always known."

The Young Beauty concept took off, and its creator was thrilled. The enterprise exceeded Beauty's wildest dreams. It took time to get the in-store look to where she was pleased. It also took time to develop her own line of preteen shirts, skirts, and dresses. At the same time, she ordered merchandise from preexisting lines and hired a staff of salespeople. Solomon helped her every step of the way. He could not have been more supportive. He realized that it was only through Beauty's connection with Kato that he had secured the kind of position he'd been dreaming of. His salary was large enough to support both himself and Amir, who was delighted to be back in New York and reunite All, his original band. That tight triangle of friendship—between Beauty, Solomon, and Amir—was reinforced. There were times when Kato joined them on social occasions. Beauty was pleased to see that he harbored no prejudices against gay men and was comfortable in their presence.

By concentrating on the spring opening of the Young Beauty boutique inside Bloom's, Beauty was able to forget about Power. She called Wanda from time to time to make sure she was okay.

"I'm laying low," Wanda said. "I'm keeping my distance. I'm doing my business and making the man money. So far he's cool with me. So far."

Meanwhile, Young Beauty opened with a splash. Kato, Beauty, Solomon, and the head of publicity put their heads together, developed a major advertising and PR campaign, and threw a preview press party that was splashed all over Page Six in the *New York Post*. The clothes got rave reviews and initial sales were brisk. To celebrate, Kato, Beauty, Solomon, and Amir went to dinner at Jean Georges, the elegant restaurant inside the Trump International Hotel at Columbus Circle.

Because Kato knew how much Beauty adored Solomon and Amir, he was especially warm and cordial with both men. Tonight was no exception. And because Solomon, like Beauty, had proven to be so productive at his job at Bloom's, Kato could praise him with a genuineness that he knew made Beauty happy. Making Beauty happy had become one of Kato's great skills.

"I want to toast Solomon," said Beauty, raising her glass. "If he wasn't with me all the way, I'd never have had the confidence to do what I did."

"And I want to toast Kato," said Solomon, nodding toward Beauty's Japanese boyfriend. "Without his risk-taking courage, none of us would be here."

"I must toast Beauty," said Kato. "She is the reason we are all here. She is the amazing creative spirit that brings us together and points us to a bright future."

"And I have to toast the four of us," added Amir. "May we all prosper in our creative endeavors. May our friendship last and grow."

They drank, they ate, and then, sometime around ten P.M., Beauty suddenly felt dizzy, excused herself from the table, and as she headed for the ladies' room, fell to the floor in a dead faint.

When she awoke, she was in a room at Lenox Hill Hospital, where doctors were running tests. Kato, Solomon, and Amir were by her side. As they told her what had happened—that they had rushed over here to the emergency room—their words sounded fuzzy to Beauty and their faces appeared out of focus. She closed her eyes and once again fell into a state of semiconsciousness.

What followed was a long period of feverish and painful regurgitation. She suffered extreme chills. Her body shook uncontrollably. The doctors ruled out food poisoning. She had contracted some sort of virulent bug that could not be identified. She was ordered to remain at the hospital overnight. That proved to be one of the worst nights of her life.

She descended into a kind of mental hell. Images attacked her without relief. And every image concerned Power. He was being chased over rooftops. He was pushed off the side of a building. He was thrown in front of a speeding car. He was blindfolded, placed in front of a firing squad, and riddled with bullets. He was hanged by the neck, knifed in the heart, suffocated, drowned, poisoned. The images never stopped, and with each one Beauty jumped out of bed, convinced that what she had seen was not fantasy but cold reality. Her screams alarmed the nurses, who came to reassure her that all was well. But the second Beauty closed her eyes and drifted off again, fresh images of Power appeared, one more horrible than the next. Still trembling, still unable to control the chills that had her arms and legs shaking, she was convulsed with a kind of fear that she had never experienced before. A powerful sedative quieted her screams but did not stop the images of Power, a bloody ax separating Power's head from his torso, a crazed wolf ripping Power's heart from his chest.

When she finally came to in the morning, Kato was by her side. He took her hand and said, "The doctors say that your fever has passed. They don't see anything wrong now. I can take you home."

"I need to make a call first."

"Of course. Use my phone."

She called Wanda, who was sobbing.

"What is it?" asked Beauty. "Is it Power?"

"No, baby, it's Dre."

"What happened to Dre?"

"They say he killed himself."

"How?"

"Hanged himself in his garage."

"Do you believe that?" asked Beauty.

"No, baby," Wanda said through her tears. "I talked to Dre just the other day. He was saying what we all knew. He was saying how Slim was believing everyone had turned against him. Slim was believing that Power was conspiring to take over all his businesses."

"Dre said that?"

"Child, those were his very words."

"But why would Slim hurt Dre? Dre was his most trusted man."

"I told you, Beauty, the closer you get to Slim, the more dangerous he thinks you are."

"You gotta get out of there," said Beauty. "I want you to book the first flight out."

"I'm different than the others," Wanda explained. "I go back longer. He got no reason—"

"He needs no reason. If you don't come up here, Wanda, I'm coming home to get you."

"Better that you stay up there and look after Power. You best find Power and tell him to go undercover."

"Have you called him?"

"I tried, but his number don't work. I can't find him."

"I will."

"You have to."

"I love you, Wanda."

"You take care, Beauty. You and Power—you gotta take care of each other."

Beauty hung up.

"Who's Wanda?" asked Kato.

"A friend," said Beauty. "A wonderful friend."

"Who's Dre? Who's Slim?"

"Dre's dead. Slim's his killer."

"Killer? You're talking about killers?"

"I need you to help Power."

"Who's Power?" asked Kato.

"My brother," said Beauty. "I've got to save my brother."

Charles "Slim" Simmons

As the days passed by, Beauty couldn't sleep or concentrate on work. She could think of nothing but Power. She had to find him. She had to elicit Kato's help, even if it meant revealing that Charlotte Clay had been murdered. When she finally told him the story, Kato listened carefully before asking, "Are you sure this man's a killer?"

"Positive."

"You've been associated with a killer?"

"I cut off all association with him. I ran from him. I had nothing to do with him."

"And your brother?"

"He stayed. He got seduced by his money. He got sucked into his world."

"Then why not leave him in that world?"

"Because he's my brother."

"But not your blood brother."

"What difference does that make?"

"All the difference in the world. You don't have the same father or mother."

"We were raised together," Beauty explained.

"And then he made a bad choice and a wrong turn. He went down a dangerous path. You don't have to chase him down that path."

"I'm not chasing him, Kato, but I have to warn him."

"Well, first you have to find him, Beauty."

"Will you help me?" she asked.

"I'm leaving for Europe day after tomorrow."

"That still gives you a little time."

"This is not the kind of business we want to get involved with."

"Kato, I need your help. I need to find Power."

Sensing that his life would be less complicated if he avoided the entire situation, Kato was tempted to tell Beauty no. But denying Beauty anything was virtually impossible. He agreed to help.

The chief of security at Bloom's identified a service that specialized in locating people. They went to work immediately. Meanwhile, Beauty called everyone she knew in Atlanta to see if they had any idea of where Power might be in New York. As she frantically worked the phones, the chills returned to her. Her arms and legs trembled. Fear attacked her heart. All that week she couldn't go to work. When Solomon and Amir called to see how she was doing, she said she didn't have time to explain.

She had to find Power.

She had to find him now.

When Kato left for Europe, she barely acknowledged his departure. He expressed concern for her emotional well-being, he told her to give up this obsession, but she didn't hear him. She couldn't hear anything but Power's cry for help.

The weekend was hell. The service had still not located Power. Come Monday morning, she went into overdrive. She kept calling people in Atlanta. She located a high school friend who knew Power well. As she was speaking to him, Power's basketball coach called her back on the other line. She juggled both calls and, while doing so, another line rang.

"Hear you been making calls." The voice was deep and cold as ice.

Her heart stopped. It was Slim.

"What do you want?" she asked.

"You don't sound too friendly."

"I'm not. What do you want?" she repeated.

"I'm looking for Power. He there?"

"No."

"You know where he is?"

"No."

Beauty saw that her hands were shaking. She steeled herself. She didn't want her voice to quiver. She didn't want to show Slim her fear.

"You see him today?" he asked.

"No."

"Yesterday?"

"I haven't seen him in years."

"You lying bitch," snapped Slim.

"Fuck you," Beauty barked and hung up.

Her phone rang again. It was an unidentified caller. Assuming it was Slim, she didn't answer. Seconds later she saw a text flash on her phone that gave the exact address of the apartment where she was living with Kato. Slim wanted her to know that he had her location. She rushed to the window and pulled the drapes shut. Her hands were still shaking.

She thought of Kato, who was on a plane to Paris. She had to reach him. She had to reach someone. She thought of Solomon. He was at work.

But while she was making the call, another line lit up.

"Beauty, it's Tanisha."

"It's a bad morning, Tanisha," said Beauty. "I'm really frantic to reach—"

"I won't keep you, but I talked to Cheryl Green. She's my aunt. You remember her. She works at Wanda's Wigs. She's worked there for years."

"Is something wrong?" asked Beauty, her heart racing again.

"Well, Wanda has gone missing. She didn't show up for work this morning. That's never happened. No one answered at her house, and when they went over there no one was home. I know you and she are close and I was wondering whether she'd said anything to you about leaving town. The girls down at the wig store are really worried."

"Dear God," said Beauty.

"What are you saying?"

"I can't talk right now, Tanisha. Thanks for calling, but I have to hang up."

Her mind raced at a million miles an hour. *Panic. I can't panic. Panic does no good. Panic causes mistakes. I can't make a mistake. Power. I have to find Power. Slim has found me, so why can't he find Power? Why is Slim asking me about Power?*

She called the service.

"Any word?" she asked.

"We think we've got his number, but the phone seems out of service."

"Give me the number."

"We've been trying every half hour or so without luck."

"Just give me the number!"

Beauty got the number and called it every fifteen seconds, over and over again. She did so for two straight hours. The same recorded message—"This phone is out of service"—clicked on. She kept calling until her fingers ached. And then, miraculously, she did not hear the recorded message. She heard a ring. And then his voice.

"Power," said Beauty, "Slim's gone crazy. Last week he had Dre murdered. Today Wanda Washington is missing, and I think he's killed her. He's killing anyone close to him, just like he killed Moms."

"I don't believe it. That's not right. That can't be right. Are you sure? How can you be sure?"

"Call anyone you know in Atlanta and they'll tell you. Dre's gone. Wanda's gone. And you're next, Power. You gotta start running."

"To where?"

"I don't know."

"Where are you?" he asked.

"I'm here in New York."

"I gotta see you, Beauty."

"I'm afraid, Power. I'm really afraid."

165 Charles Street

When Power's psychology professor Anna Severina had invited him to her apartment with a group of her other students, he was surprised. He thought she probably lived modestly. He figured professors didn't make much money. But when he reached her address in the West Village, he saw a striking new building of all glass. It sat at 165 Charles Street like an elegant piece of sculpture. The apartment itself, on the top floor, was spacious. The view of the Hudson River was breathtaking. The floors were blond wood and the walls were covered with colorful modern art. Professor Severina explained that her father, a famous architect in Italy, had left her with a love for his profession and appreciation of beautiful forms. She also said that this apartment building was the work of the great modern architect Richard Meier. Power was deeply impressed and also flattered when, after the other students had gone, she asked him to stay for a short chat. She told him she thought he had special insight into psychology and encouraged him to major in the subject. He cherished the conversation and the many others that followed after class. No teacher had ever spoken to him like this before. Professor Severina saw something in Power that made him feel special.

But that was nothing compared to the feeling now coursing through Power as he headed over to the professor's apartment. He had given the address to Beauty, who said she was only ten minutes away. A Quiet Place in the City, the café where he'd been relaxing until her call came, was about the same ten minutes. But those ten minutes were the longest minutes he had ever experienced. He walked quickly—at one point he began to sprint—unable to contain his excitement. The thoughts in his head had him practically dizzy: She was talking crazy; or she was in danger; or they were both in danger; or Slim really had gone insane; or he was just acting insane to provoke Beauty. But whatever the thoughts, the one that motivated him most, the one that had him picking up the pace of his sprint, was the thought of seeing Beauty. Five years. It had been five long years.

When he got to 165 Charles Street, he looked around the lobby to see if Beauty had arrived. She hadn't. He decided to wait downstairs. He had to see her the second she came into view. He kept staring at the front door of the building. How would she be dressed? Would she look older? Or younger? Or the same? Minutes passed. He went outside to look down the street, first this way, then the other. His phone rang. It was probably Beauty. It wasn't. It was an old friend from high school named Smitty.

"Power," he said, "I just wondered whether you're coming to Atlanta or whether you're already here."

"No, man," said Power. "I'm in New York. Why would I be coming to Atlanta?"

"For your friend's funeral. I know how close you were to Andre Gee."

"Dre's funeral?"

"You knew, didn't you?"

"Someone said something but I didn't believe them. I thought it was just one of those rumors."

"Sorry, bro, I really am, but it's no rumor. It was all over the papers today. They found him dead in his own garage."

Power tried to say something but couldn't. At that moment he saw Beauty running down the street toward him.

When Beauty had finally gotten through to Power and learned where he wanted to meet, her hands were shaking so she could barely write down the address on Charles Street. She wasn't sure it would be safe to meet him there, but what else could she do? She wanted to get out of Kato's apartment—Slim knew her location—yet leaving meant she could be followed. She was confused and unsettled but, determined to get to Power before anyone else did, she got herself together and left. She rode the elevator downstairs and looked around the lobby. No one was there. Still apprehensive that she was being followed, she went out on the street and hailed a cab. One pulled over almost immediately. She looked at the cab driver. He was from Senegal. She wondered if he could possibly be working for Slim. Was he a henchman? If he was, it was too late. She got in the cab and told him the address. The short ride seemed interminable. The traffic was fierce, stop-and-go all the way. Beauty's mind reeled with fears, excitement, hope, dread. What would Power look like? Would he finally believe her? What would happen? She was petrified and she was thrilled. She prayed for the traffic to clear, but it didn't. What should have been a ten-minute ride was now turning into twenty. She had to get to Power. She had to get there now.

"What's the address again?" asked the driver.

"Charles Street. One hundred sixty-five Charles Street."

The cab turned onto Charles Street. Beauty didn't like the irony that the street where they were meeting had the same name as the man pursuing them. Charles Street was clogged with cars. A huge garbage truck had broken down. Nothing was moving.

"I'll just get out here," Beauty told the driver. "I'll walk the rest of the way."

She ran the rest of the way. She ran faster than she could ever remember running. She kept looking at the addresses as she flew down the street. She was getting closer and closer. She couldn't be more than a block or two away. She was almost there, very nearly there, when suddenly she saw him. It was Power! He looked wonderful! He looked even more handsome than she had remembered! It was him! It was Power! And just as she got close enough for him to recognize her, just as she caught a glance of his loving eyes and his warm smile, just as his arms began to open, two men grabbed him and violently threw him into the back of a coal-black Cadillac Escalade. By then traffic had cleared and the car sped off before Beauty could reach it. She turned around to see if she too would be captured, but no one was there. In their hurry to get Power, the kidnappers had not noticed Beauty. She stood there, in front of the elegant glass structure at 165 Charles Street, absolutely alone.

To be continued in . . .

Power & Beauty: Book Two
A Love Story of Life on the Streets